The Godling Saga

INFAMY

Mohamed Omar

Book 1

First published in United States by Icon Publishing LLC 2022
Paperback edition 2022

ISBN: 979-8-9856894-2-6

To my friends and family who put up with my late-night rambles of half-baked stories.

To all the teachers or librarians that I have met and will meet someday, I hope you get to instill passion into the students under your care just as I once was. To give them something to dive into whenever this world seems just a little duller than usual.

And lastly to the reader holding this book in your hands, I wish you the best and I can't wait to go along this journey with you.

CONTENTS

PROLOGUE

I was born in a world submerged in darkness, and my existence ended in the darkness. Monsters are born from one moment in time when we no longer fight our demons but embrace them, baring our teeth at the very things that chained us down. I was destined to be that monster from the moment I emerged from the dark. I was the law, destroyer of all beings, conqueror of life, and the master of death. As a child, I was forced away from my home in fear that my very touch would consume all. Leaving everyone that I loved broken and hollow. That was my mark, my curse in this life.

For centuries, I fought that very battle to inevitably give in, left with only a thirst for more. By denying my true nature, it had ultimately become my undoing.

Is there true free will if everything we do is already predetermined by men, monsters, and gods?

Free will means we get to choose what happens to us in this life; we get a choice on how we leave this world in the end. Then I choose to never leave. I refuse to leave this world without having accomplished what I was meant to do, for what is existence but the stage for your dreams to become reality. I refuse to be merely a shadow in the night, but a star that shines forever. Not even finding my true reflection could change me, all I saw were the scars inflicted upon me by the eaters of worlds. As they sank their tentacles of darkness into the deepest recesses of my soul, destroying a once bright, beautiful soul into a marred and ugly shade. Turning my very existence into an abomination.

Free will is just a dream for those who created it to make excuses for the things we do to one another. If only I had given in to my darker self sooner, maybe I wouldn't be dying at this very moment.

My friend, Ams, thinks that we make our way in life, that karma herself can't do anything to us if we believe she can't. I guess it all comes down to belief in the end; belief in ourselves, in humanity, and destiny.

I was a monster in sheep's clothing. Chained up by the dark gods, forced to do their bidding until I escaped. Wanting to burn the world down with me, to see it all fall into chaos. My friend made a way for me to come back and seek my vengeance on those who wronged me. Making me look like a saint compared to those dark gods. Hopefully, the reincarnation of me will be luckier in escaping from the gods' twisted vises. Trust and emotions were a chain to our kind, used to enslave and keep us in place.

As I lay dying on this cold hard stone, in this tomb of

memories, I've begun setting forth the biggest chain of events for my rebirth. To begin my reincarnation, I feel sorry for the harbinger that must be born from my dying breath. They shall know my pain and unleash justice on those that have wronged me.

CHAPTER 1

Hey Mom, you see my skateboard?" Malik Anomos Blackwood yelled down the stairs to his mom as he came zooming from his room. Their house couldn't be this big to lose one skateboard; he had just used the day previously. He looked frantically for his board anywhere he could think of, even behind his unopened boxes in his room he had left untouched for the last two months since moving to Portland, Oregon. It seemed hopeless as he moved around the boxes that sat in the hallway just outside his room.

"What'd you say, honey?" his mom yelled back, too preoccupied with making breakfast to hear him. Nina, his little sister, was playing loudly on her tablet at the kitchen table, adding to the noise in the kitchen.

Coming into view was his dad, as he roughly put on his tie at the steps of the stairs. He sighed in disbelief at what he was witnessing. "Malik, haven't I told you to stop putting your board next to the staircase? Someone's going to trip and break their necks."

Excitement filled Malik as he caught sight of his board

and quickly grinned, sidestepped his dad, and jumped for the board before it could be taken out of his reach. With it now in his hands, he tossed the board and himself onto the railing, sliding down to the kitchen area at a fast speed. The rush of the air and adrenaline carried him down the rail with rapidly accelerating speed. At the last minute, he jumped off with his board and landed semi-gracefully, almost slamming into the wall in front of him. He had slightly hurt his knee, groaning as he fully righted himself, rubbing it silently before his mom could bombard him with her disapproval. His sister had seen his mistake and laughed at him in amusement, which resulted in Malik giving her a mean look, causing her to laugh even more, completely ignoring her tablet in her lap.

"Anomos! If that's you on the railing again, I'm going to throw away that board!" Malik's mom scolded, as she came into view of the railing from the kitchen, shaking her head at her reckless son.

His dad boomed with laughter. "It's okay, Imani, let the kid have some fun. He's going to learn one day why we say no skating in the house."

His mom looked at both of them in disapproval. She shook her head at him, as he looked over to her; he saw that she had bags hanging under her eyes. Her hair was disheveled, looking as though she had just rolled out of bed. He wasn't sure if it was from staying up and working on her newest novel or something else.

"Mom, it's not a big deal, I'll stop if you want me to," Malik promised his mom, even as he crossed his fingers behind his back. Malik had to hide the grin he could feel coming at the corner of his mouth; he knew his mom didn't believe him whatsoever, but it was the thought that counted. Once he saw his mom somewhat believed him after a long inquiring look, he turned to the food at the table.

Reaching for a bagel, someone else go to it first–his little sister. She looked at him and threw a toothy grin at him as she took a bite out of it, she then proceeded to stick her tongue at him as if she had won. He felt there was nothing else he could do but pick her up and mess with her.

"This is the bagel monster; he wants all his bagels. Especially from little sisters who steal from their big brothers," Malik in a bad monster voice, reaching in and tickling his sister to hysteria.

"Put me down, Maylak," Nina begged even as she giggled all the way. She still called him the name she made for him when she couldn't enunciate her words. As she rolled in laughter from all the tickling, she forgot her bagel.

"Put her down Anomos, before she loses her breath." His mom laughed as her children played around, unable to hide her smile; they didn't usually have mornings to just the four of them.

Finally, he put his sister down, who just sat there,

gasping for breath, tears still evident in her eyes. He went to grab some milk from the fridge.

His mom addressed his dad. "Are you going to be home tonight, Virgil?"

Turning around, he saw his dad shake his head. "I have to talk to someone at the office about some priceless African Bantu artifacts found just last week. I'm trying to have them untouched before I can get there."

Virgil Blackwood was a collector of ancient and cultural history, mainly African history. His dad had traveled the world finding things such as artifacts and helping restore or bring knowledge about them. Malik had never understood who he worked for, but knew it paid good money and resulted in them moving around a lot.

His mom, Imani Blackwood, on the other hand; wrote African literature, mostly novels, but had published a few research books currently taught in college courses. Malik never understood how his mom and dad met, but he loved them both unconditionally, even though their work often meant their children were regularly babysat by other people.

"I have to talk to my editor tonight about my newest book release. We're having trouble releasing it overseas," his mom replied. She seemed to be very worried about it.

Malik groaned inwardly; he was used to this happening on the regular but was still disappointed that he wouldn't see his parents tonight together.

Just as he finished his last gulp of milk, he suddenly remembered his promise to see Jaden before class started. Quickly grabbing his skateboard and helmet, he rushed toward the door with the intent to race down to the school.

"It's cool, guys. I can watch Nina today after school, but I have to head out right now," he told his parents just before he walked through the door. He turned to them as he held onto the door to stay open.

His parents perked up, his mom curious as to why her son was in such a rush today,

"Why are you rushing to leave, Anomos?"

"I have to see Jaden before class starts." He quietly walked back inside, behind his sister, and grabbed the bagel before his sister could get another bite in.

Stuffing the bagel in his mouth, messing up Nina's little braids, and then opening the front door, he started to skate away. Halfway down the driveway, he heard his mom yell behind him, "Bring Jaden over sometime!"

As he waved back to his mom, he got to see the view of the Blackwood Manor, which was once owned by his grandfather and passed down the family for a few generations. It was supposed to be his next, once he was of age, but he wasn't sure if he even wanted it. It wasn't huge, but it was big enough to house four people, just on the outskirts of the town they lived in. A few miles behind them sat the Crimson Woods, leaving a very nature-like feel in the air, with the leaves now changing and falling to the ground at a rapid rate.

Rushing to school, the chilly late October weather was something he welcomed, as it was his favorite time of the year. It didn't hurt that it was almost his birthday as well; he was going to turn seventeen in just a few weeks. With his oversized hoodie on, he felt a cool breeze on his neck from the movement of the board, which felt freeing. The leaves had already started to turn that golden brown, just right before they would start falling and officially welcome November.

As he passed all the close-knit homes, he was reminded that they were so far away from their neighbors. He was still surprised by all of their eagerness to help his family settle into their new environment, which was why he always said his greetings whenever he could. Several of the neighbors had set up decorations for Halloween; some were very elaborate, with graveyards and giant skeletons. Some homes seemed to be commemorating the dead; Malik figured it was those families that celebrated Día de Los Muertos, or *Day of the Dead.*

Arriving at the high school in about fifteen minutes, he spotted his friend Jaden at the bicycle rack and quickly skated over to him. His friend was talking to a girl about their age; he recalled she was one of the Cabello sisters, though he did not know which one.

Jaden was just finishing his last sentence as Malik descended on them. He accidentally tripped over a rock he didn't see and went crashing toward the girl and Jaden, who had just raised his head in mild interest.

"Hey, watch out!" he yelled at the top of his lungs before he barreled into her.

Please don't be mad was the first thought in his head as he come fast at them with no stop. This was karma for this morning's antics.

The girl just stepped to the side and grabbed him before he could fall on his face. He watched in amazement as Jaden stopped the board with his foot.

"You, okay?" she asked in concern, looking him up and down to make sure everything was all right.

He was finally able to get up on his own. Having broken away from her, he took off his helmet and let his twists out from the stuffed protective gear. He had a better angle of the girl now, who he could tell was Hispanic. She was very pretty, to say the least, with her dark brown hair, big set of eyes, and full lips.

"Yeah, I'm good, how'd you grab me so fast?" Malik stared in wonder at the girl; he'd been a hundred percent certain that he'd hit her.

For her part, the girl just shrugged. "Fast reflexes," she replied in an unconvincing voice.

While he was still trying to process what happened, Jaden came up next to him with the board in his hands and grinned.

"If you have a thing for my ex, just say so, bro. I ain't

going to trip," Jaden grinned, looking amused at his friend.

He shook his head, denying everything. "No bro, nothing like that, I just fell on a rock, my bad."

"Well, next time be more careful, I'll be seeing you guys around," the girl cut in, and started to walk away from them toward the school. As she walked away, Malik's gaze followed her and saw a girl who looked just like her waiting at the top; he assumed it was her sister. The sister noticed him, grinning as if she knew what had happened and found it hilarious. Malik grinned back; he did not know why, but that sister of hers had a contagious smile. The sisters met up and walked inside the school.

Turning to his friend Jaden Williams, he reclaimed his board. Oddly enough, Jaden was his only friend. When they first met, he had thought Jaden would be very popular since he was built for sports. Even though Malik was personally into girls, he had to admit Jaden was an attractive dude, considering he was an African American kid who had a funny personality. Malik hadn't tried being friends with anyone, having gotten used to moving around a lot. He didn't see the point of it anymore. Jaden was the one that had reached out and offered friendship. Malik was grateful for it, and that he had someone to talk to, even if it was for a limited time.

"So, Jaden, why did you want me to come here so early?" Malik was intrigued by his request just the day before.

Jaden in turn just grinned at him; Malik knew he was in trouble from the moment the smile formed. Having only known Jaden for less than three months, he had come to know his reputation. Jaden somehow amassed information about everyone and everything.

That was partially why he didn't have many friends, either.

"They say that the football players are using steroids to get as big as they are, wanna find out with me?" Grinning from ear to ear, Jaden could barely contain his excitement.

Maliks shook his head; the last time he had gone with Jaden resulted in him getting a week out of school and regrowing one of his eyebrows.

"Nope, not even close. I do not feel like being jock meat, juice, or whatever they like, so count me out," he immediately protested.

Looking wounded, Jaden started to give him puppy eyes; he knew it was all a ploy to get him to join, but it wasn't going to work this time. His mom would kill him if he got injured again; she swore she'd disown him the next time he did it. Luckily, he hadn't told her it was Jaden who had caused him to lose his eyebrow, or she'd make him swear to stop hanging with Jaden.

"Come on man, just one look in their lockers, and we're out." Jaden tried to sound innocent, but it didn't come off right with the mad look in his eyes.

"Let's get to class man, I ain't missing more lectures for

you. You're on your own, Jaden," Malik told his friend firmly.

Shaking his head at Malik, Jaden muttered to himself, "No sense of adventure."

Instead of getting dragged into Jaden's crazy schemes again, he started walking toward Olympus High, with Jaden following beside him. He tried to change the subject.

"What were you talking about with that ex of yours?"

Looking up at him, Jaden had a guarded look for a moment before it disappeared to his usual conspiring expression. "Oh, Maya was asking about some family stuff; her dad left for a conference in New York and wondered if my mom knew when he'd be back."

He was concerned as to why Jaden had that look on his face if it was something as simple as that, but he gave up trying to figure out Jaden. It was a waste of time.

Malik decided to drop the subject. "Oh, that's cool, let's get to class."

Olympus High was a wasteland of stereotypes and boring classes. Malik groaned inwardly as he remembered the pile of assignments he had to complete as he had finally transferred to some college credit courses, even though he was technically only a junior. It was thanks to his mom always being on his ass about getting ahead of the curve, even with moving around more than actually staying in one location to settle in.

The only interesting part of the school was their big

statue of Atlas, the titan from Greek mythology, holding the world up, much like the myth said about him, located in the general entrance of the school. There was also the common hall, which was a wide-open space with pictures of god-like men battling monsters on the walls.

Even though he wasn't generally new to the school anymore, Malik still couldn't get used to this place. He looked around and laughed, telling Jaden, "You guys take your name seriously here?"

He looked over to where Malik was looking. "Yeah, I guess we do, but I never understood if the gods hate us for what we represent humanity's resilience in the face of unparalleled opposition."

Malik stared at Jaden as if he was starting to sound like his mom. "Okay, Jaden, I'll take your word for it."

Most of Malik's classes had been moved around thanks to the transfer from honors to dual credit and AP courses. That meant he saw Jaden more than ever before, as almost all of their classes were together.

Knowing what to expect of the usual ritual of the class by now, Jaden walked to the back of the room, ready to take a seat next to the window, and maybe take a nap as soon as he sat down. Even though he was always taking naps, he always knew the answer to any question and was one of the top students at the school. He guessed it just went to show that you didn't need to be overly perfect in school to get good grades; some people were just naturally gifted.

Malik's usual seat, however, was taken by a girl who he had seen around the school and just that morning. He recognized her with Jaden's ex, Maya, earlier; he had assumed it was her sister, but he wasn't so sure.

"Sorry, was this your seat?" She eyeballed him, smiling mischievously as if she knew the answer but just wanted to have fun with him.

He smiled, taking the seat next to her. "Well, I guess it's yours now, but what's your name? I haven't seen you in this class before."

For some reason, he couldn't get mad at the girl; there were no such things as assigned seats in Mrs. Taylor's History class. It was dumb anyway, plus he was talking to a cute girl.

"Well, I guess you do at least deserve to know my name–it's Bianca Cabello. I saw you with my sister earlier," she answered his question with a laugh. The laugh of hers was just as contagious as the smile he had seen previously that morning.

Nodding, he was starting to like her smile the more and more he saw it. He was so caught up in trying to ask her another question that he forgot class had started.

Clearing her throat, a couple of times, Mrs. Taylor had walked up to their table looking at Malik in disappointment. "I know that Miss Cabello just transferred to our class today, but could you refrain from disrupting my class and flirting until after my lesson is over, Malik?"

Blushing fiercely as they, both hadn't noticed the teacher come up to them until that moment, Malik and Bianca slumped in their chairs as they were embarrassed in front of the whole class. He tried to look nonchalant about it as Mrs. Taylor walked away from their table and focused on the class lesson once more. He could feel quite a few pairs of eyes still on them as the lesson continued; glancing at Bianca, he noticed she didn't look too embarrassed after the initial shock of everything. She even winked before going back to her work. That elevated his embarrassment somewhat, but it wasn't all bad as he got the chance to meet Bianca. Malik noticed that Bianca was more than just cute; she was stunning. He was surprised he wasn't drooling on the floor right now.

Bianca noticed him looking and giggled. She whispered, "You shouldn't be looking at girls like that unless you plan on taking them out."

Malik blushed; unaware she was paying attention. "I'm sorry, it just happened. But do you want me to?"

"It's cool, just don't let my sister see you doing that," laughed Bianca.

He couldn't tell if she was kidding until Bianca stated, "I'm serious, she's overprotective since she's older than me, but you're cute, so she'll give you a pass once."

Malik blushing fiercely, nodded, and looked away, trying to decide whether he was supposed to take it as a compliment or not. Malik went through the rest of class in silence, trying not to look at Bianca unless it was required.

The class ended finally, and Malik went through the rest of his classes. Jaden had left to carry out his scheme during his free period, while Malik went to the library to study for his Algebra course instead of causing more drama with Jaden. He found out later on that the football players weren't taking steroids, but simply doing a new workout regimen. He was laughing at the fact that Jaden sported a black eye by lunchtime.

As he grabbed lunch, he bumped into a trio of guys. They had a menacing presence wherever they walked. They were thugs that went to the school, Trayvon, Alex, and Michael. Everyone said they were part of a gang from the outer Portland area. Malik had been able to avoid them for a while now, but somehow today was not his lucky day, as they finally took notice of him.

Malik quickly looked away from them as they passed and almost apologized, but before he could, he heard one of them say, "We'll teach him a lesson for doing that."

He quickly got out of their way; having been born in Chicago, Malik was used to those types of people. He wasn't going to try to antagonize them into doing anything unpleasant; it was better if they forgot he even existed.

Sadly, he ran into another person on his way to sit with Jaden, Nico Gonzalez. Nico was also another thug, even though he didn't come in the same form as the last three. Nico was a jock, the Afro-Latino star baseball player who was also one of the most popular people at school. It didn't help that he seemed to be perfect in every way, everyone loved him. He was the definition of a perfection, with his tall frame of six-one with grey eyes and brown skin. He had light curly hair that seemed to naturally look good no matter what he did. Everyone seemed to follow his every word; no matter what he said, it was considered law. Malik had heard a rumor that both his parents had died in a gruesome death, and he was being raised by his uncles, but that didn't give him an excuse to be an asshole.

"Watch it Blackwood, some of us matter in life and don't need a nobody in our way like you," Nico told him in contempt.

"Chill out, oh great one, no one's trying to get in your way," snorted Malik, who was tired of being pushed around this week already.

It wasn't a smart move, as it caused Nico to stop, glaring daggers at Malik; Malik knew it wasn't a good idea to make enemies, especially with the star player, but he didn't care. It was better to assert his image now before others thought he was too weak and picked on him as well. Nico looked at him as if he was crazy. Malik grinned; he knew he had set the alpha male up in a way that was making him uneasy, to decide whether or not he was a threat.

Nico watched Malik for another minute before one of

his boys called him over to sit down. With one last look at him, Nico went to go eat with his friends. Malik just shrugged. He had just survived another dangerous high school encounter, and that caused him to be starving.

Finally, he made it to his table, where Jaden sat eating his carrots. The table was pretty much unoccupied. There used to be a kid named Lawrence Tomlinson, but he hadn't been at school for almost a month now. Now it was just Malik and Jaden's spot.

Malik got to savor his food in peace for only a moment.

"So, what was that about?" Jaden asked, cutting into the silence. He was shooting looks at everyone Malik had encountered.

"Just something stupid, the dude wanted to assert his dominance like he was the apex predator." He shrugged at Jaden, unsure what had just happened.

"I'd be careful. Tonight, is a full moon, you know it tends to make guys grow hair and sharp teeth." Jaden laughed

Snorting at Jaden, Malik raised his eyebrows in question. "Do you believe in the big bad wolf now?"

Raising his hands in mock surrender, Jaden answered, "You can't know everything that goes on. Who knows what truly lurks in the night?"

Malik had become used to Jaden saying random things and took it in stride. "Whatever you say, bro."

After that, they talked about everyday things like classes, the latest video games, and girls; there were no more mentions of crazy conspiracies. They had only two more classes before school ended, and it went by quickly. When the school day finally ended, Malik rushed home to take care of his sister, finding his parents arguing about something. His mom came out of his dad's office with tears in her eyes.

Malik rushed to his mom's aid. "Mom, is everything okay?"

She just smiled at Malik, shaking her head. "I'm all right, Anomos, I just got into an argument with your dad. One of his colleagues is coming here to talk about an artifact and I didn't want him here when I'm back, nothing big."

He smiled weakly at his mom. Why would a visit like that cause her to cry? There was more than what she was letting on, but he let it go. He knew it would just cause her to cry more, and he'd never get answers then.

"If you're sure, Mom, I'm going to watch Nina now," Malik told her, heading to his sister's room.

She stopped him before he could leave her presence. "Just know that I love you, Anomos. No matter what happens in your life, I'll always be there for you."

She then let him go, leaving him more concerned than ever why she would say something like that. For the next couple of hours, Malik played with his sister. They played make-believe with knights and princesses. When it was finally time to put Nina to bed, she fell asleep instantly. Malik still had some energy he needed to burn off, as well as questions from the impending visit from his dad's colleague. He decided to go outside after everyone had fallen asleep. When it was finally dark, he changed into sweats and a hoodie, headed to the woods behind their home.

He was mesmerized by the moon as it stood big and imposing up in the night sky. He sometimes wondered if it was also lonely, as no one was there to inhabit its craters. Malik pulled himself out of his doom and gloom as he got ready to head out and run off all his pent-up energy. Closing the door to his family's manor quietly, he breathed in the chilly night air; the wind just seemed to hug him, as if it knew he belonged with it.

He loved the feeling of being free, the feeling of the muscles effortlessly moving and pushing him forward as he ran with no destination in sight. Being able to run without anyone to bother him helped give him the feeling of purpose again. He hated the feeling of being lost without anything to push him forward to the next part of his life. His mom always said, "A person that has no purpose in life is going to disappear with no one to remember they were present."

As Malik ran, he came across Jaden sitting at the entrance to the Crimson Woods, which was weird given the late hour. Jaden was just relaxing there with a sandwich in his hands, as he seemed to be listening to some kind of music.

He glanced over to see Malik slowing down to talk to him. Getting up casually and brushing himself off, he waited until Malik was next to him to speak.

"What's up, Malik? Out for a night run?" Jaden asked casually as if he wasn't out past midnight on a school day.

He was stumped for a minute. Why was Jaden so casual about being out this late? "Oh yeah, I needed to clear my head right now… got so much on my mind."

"Wanna talk about it?" Jaden asked as he smiled at him.

Malik dodged the question. "Why are you out here anyway?"

Jaden looked into the woods as if searching for something. "Just need to clear my head, too. I come here some nights to watch the world pass by. I have trouble sleeping sometimes."

Malik shrugged; it was not his right to press Jaden for answers when he didn't want to answer why he was even outside.

"Well, I'm sure you'll figure it out eventually," Malik assured him with the most enthusiasm he could muster.

"It's not a big deal, we're still young. We can answer life's greatest mysteries another day," Jaden assured him.

He smiled at Jaden; he was different from most guys

he'd met. They both stood there for a moment before Jaden cleared his voice. "If you're going to run in the woods, I'd be careful. You might get hurt out there."

Malik looked at Jaden oddly and laughed. "Yeah, I'd probably be hurt by a branch or something."

"You never know, the big bad wolf could be out there." Jaden grinned at him.

"Oh, you're scared of the wolf Red Riding Hood?"

"Yeah, right, I'd be shitting bricks so much, the big bad wolf would run away in horror."

Jaden made a face of a scared kid at Malik when saying that. That response led to them roaring with laughter for a good minute. Once they had calmed down, Jaden started to collect his food and head out.

He looked at Malik for a moment before saying, "Just stick to the trail and don't go past it once it ends, you should be fine if you do that."

Malik nodded, thanking Jaden for his advice, though he didn't know why he needed to stay on the trail. Looking into the woods, he turned around to ask Jaden why he had told him to do that, but Jaden was already gone. He looked around for a minute, completely lost as to where his friend had disappeared to.

Once it looked like he was indeed gone, Malik turned toward the wood with the eerie sounds of nocturnal animals moving in the night; the only source of light was the moon and sparsely laid-out lanterns that seemed ready to flicker out at any moment. The branches of the trees brushed against each other as they created a howling noise deep within the woods. His body shivered as the cold crept on his neck more than ever, and he laughed a little nervously. "Why did he have to make me nervous now?"

Shaking off his nerves, he ran into the entrance of the woods, trying to stay on the trail, as this was his first time going in since moving to this town. As he ran, he played some music from his phone, getting lost in the music. Half an hour passed by, and he had forgotten Jaden's warning, having run well past the trail and into unknown ground.

As Malik ran into a clearing near a park bench, he slowed down to catch his breath, ready to head back home now that he released all his restless energy.

He was so caught up in his run that he didn't notice he wasn't alone until it was too late. He heard them first, the laughter that sounded more like an animal's than a human. Three guys were smoking and laughing as if they were back at home, not outside in the middle of the night.

The first guy saw Malik and pointed him out to his friends, who stopped smoking and got up to face him. Recognizing them from school, he was certain they were Trayvon, Alex, and Michael.

"Hey, whatcha doing out here, buddy?" Trayvon asked in a tone laced with malice.

"Maybe he wants to join us?" Alex laughed menacingly, dressed casually in jeans and a T-shirt.

"Well, he's gonna have to pay his way in to join," said Michael, who was big and looked the most menacing grinned viciously.

Malik decided it was best to not agitate these guys, and slowly backed up, but he wasn't fast enough, as they had decided to corner him. Malik felt things weren't going to go well, and he answered them with, "I'm just taking a run, I'll be out of your way now."

Alex shook his head and laughed. "Well, you gotta pay your way out of this."

He brandished a knife that Malik didn't see before. All three of them started to swarm Malik at once, as if they were hunting him.

CHAPTER 2

Keeping his voice calm, even though he was thoroughly scared, Malik said, "Look, I don't have any money and I won't bother you guys at all. I'm just going head out now."

Before he could get any further, Trayvon grabbed him by the shoulder and held him. Malik tried to get away, but his grip was too strong. He dug his fingers in like they were claws.

Crying out in pain, Malik wasn't sure what to do anymore, but he didn't want to get stabbed. His mom wouldn't want to find out her son had died like this.

As he dealt with the pain, Michael came up to him and did the oddest thing–he sniffed Malik, snarling at him with the most rage Malik had ever seen.

"Who are you? You should know this is our territory," Michael angrily demanded.

Terrified and lost, Malik didn't understand. Michael seemed to have lost his mind, with every intention of hurting Malik. He knew he had to get away before things escalated too quickly.

Unable to get out of the grip, he went for another tactic, even though he knew it would cause his assailants to become desperate. He lowered his body slightly, causing Trayvon to slightly loosen his grip. Malik knew he had only seconds before things got crazy. Working his body to be more at an angle, he quickly executed his move, grabbing Trayvon and wrenching his body to flip him over; Trayvon landed hard on his back, the wind completely knocked out of him.

"Damn, I should have stuck with those classes," Malik muttered under his breath, regretting quitting martial arts for the past four years. He was too rusty; he was going to get himself injured or worse.

Shifting into a fighting stance, he knew three against one wasn't a fair fight, but he wouldn't be able to run fast enough to get away from these guys; he was too worn out from his run already. Malik wasn't looking for a confrontation, but he knew it was inevitable. Looking around, there wasn't much to grab for a weapon; maybe he'd be lucky, and they'd get bored.

Trayvon groaned and slowly got to his feet, clearly very angry but not appearing hurt in the least. He snarled at Malik and for a moment, Malik thought he saw fangs in the guy's mouth. He shook his head, thinking he was seeing things in the heat of panic.

Knife still in his hand, Alex watched his friend get flipped and now gazed at Malik as if he wanted to murder him right there. "Well, I guess your payment is gonna be in blood tonight; no one's gonna miss you."

Then Alex attacked, quickly followed by his two friends. Trying to fend them off as well as he could, he wasn't so lucky, having to pay attention to three assailants. They quickly overpowered him and pinned him to the ground, Trayvon and Michael holding him down while Alex leered at him with his knife still in hand.

Grabbing his collar, Alex said in a voice that didn't sound even remotely human, "I don't know what you are, but we're outside the Sanctuary borders and there's no one to save you."

Gleefully, they started to beat on his body with so much force, Malik thought he would pass out from the pain. Seeing that he wasn't going to make it out of there, he thought of all the things that happened in his life. He didn't want this to be his last moment on Earth. He remembered his mom always saying, *why think separately from this life to the next, but that life is born from the last?*

Malik didn't want to leave period, but he didn't see how he could escape. Feeling so many emotions going on in his head, what he felt most was anger and fear. How could the world be so cruel as to make him leave? He still had his family to be there for, and to figure out his own life, as well as his place in it.

Malik felt a pressure build in his chest, a burning sensation that wouldn't stop. He felt like he would explode with every negative thought inside his head; his anger toward these guys intensified until he saw red. As they laughed, Malik knew he was truly going to lose it.

A voice called to him, sounding far away. *"If you want my power, then take it for yourself."*

Malik grasped at it as if it was the only thing tethering him to this world, and he gave in to that voice. Even if Malik was imagining things, he wasn't going to die without a fight, no matter what.

He reached for an invisible hand, some anchor to pull him through this moment, the faces of his family flashing before him. Slowly, he felt his body fill with energy, feeling like he was watching his body from a different point of view, looking down on himself, seeing his beaten body and what was about to happen to him.

Malik finally couldn't handle it anymore; that was when it happened. A red haze of energy that he didn't truly believe came out of him hitting the guys and everything around them. The world seemed to burn away, and everything around him was destroyed in its most carnal form. The trees burned at an unfathomable pace, the smell of burning grass and leaves hung in the air, giving off the heat of a midsummer afternoon. They were thrown so far, he was sure it had killed them.

Most importantly, he felt strong, but also weak at the same time. He could barely get up and was astounded at the surrounding wreckage. He felt powerful but was disgusted at the damage. Malik didn't truly believe what had happened, but in the back of his mind, he relished the power that he had.

He was suddenly sickened and slightly ashamed by that feeling. Malik didn't have time to think much about it because he saw them stirring and knew he had completely lost his mind. What stood in the place of the high school boys from before were now the vilest creatures he had ever seen; they seemed to come straight out of someone's nightmares.

One of them was now seven feet tall, with a face like a demonic-looking rat; it truly was hard to look at anything else. The other two were similar, but one resembled a bat-like monster and the other had an impish face but a huge body. They all had fangs and moved unnaturally; they snarled at him, and the drool coming off their mouths that touched the ground made a hissing sound as if it was acid. They all bound toward him with the intent to kill. Malik saw their eyes of pure crimson blood, and it was like looking at hell itself.

Just when they reached Malik, he knew he was going to die. He had no energy left and he didn't know how to do the thing he had just done again; it must have been a one-time deal because the voice had gone quiet. The first creature reached him and just when it came for his face with its big claws, a man with a sword came out of nowhere and blocked the attack.

The man turned to Malik and gave him the most cheerful smile Malik had ever seen, especially odd in a situation like this. His body could take no more surprises; he fell back onto the pavement and passed out.

Usually, falling unconscious didn't lead to seeing visions of monsters, battles, and epic love. But that's exactly what Malik saw. He saw his life, and at the same time a different life, a past life. Malik saw himself fighting monsters in armies and leading them. Memories of events that shouldn't have happened. It felt strange, but at the same time, oddly peaceful, like he was born to live this life, a life he never experienced before.

Finally, he was pulled from those vivid memories that weren't his own. Malik felt himself stepping toward an immense shadow that slowly spread and started to overwhelm all of his senses. The feeling of helplessness was in every part of his body; it felt as if the shadow was alive and searching for something worth devouring. He felt a chill come over him when he subconsciously stepped closer, and he was suddenly filled with fear for his life; the shadows seemed to notice his presence and grew excited to eat their meal. His instincts told him to run, but all he could do was stand there as they tried to swallow him whole without remorse. They grew until it filled everything and made him feel hollow. Just as they reached him, ready to enjoy their meal, they were forced to a stop, as if some barrier wasn't letting them closer; the shadows banged on it to reach him for a taste, but their relentless fight was a waste of time.

They finally stopped; the shadows now didn't completely acknowledge Malik's presence but said a word that sent him into complete terror. They seemed to whisper into his very soul. "*Anomos.*" As if they'd known him all his life.

Somehow, before he could completely lose it, light and warmth started coming back. The shadows and the weird dreams disappeared. Malik welcomed this greatly. He woke to see the strange man fending off the three creatures; they screeched in some broken language that was painful to the ears. Malik was able to pick up what the man said in English.

"I won't let you get near the boy anymore, demons, I felt your energy from miles away," the man declared.

The creatures, or demons, as the man called them, laughed in a disgusting assortment of sounds, and in gargled voices spoke in English. "We'll see about that, Guardian, you're a little far from home and no one's gonna know your death was our doing."

Even though he seemed to be a match for these demons, the man was tiring quickly. Malik looked around for something to help the man out and saw the knife the demons had dropped. He grabbed it; even though he knew that whatever he did wouldn't be a big help, at least he could distract one of the demons to help the man deal with the other two.

When he grabbed the knife, he felt a surge of power coming off the weapon. He looked at the knife and noticed weird symbols on it, mesmerized by them. The symbols seemed to speak to him. It took him some effort to ignore it and get out of the trance, but he got up and noticed his body wasn't as fatigued as he'd expected. Adrenaline coursing through him, Malik squared his body and readied himself to charge at the weakest-looking demon.

Springing forward faster than he ever thought he could, he reached the demon in three bounds and thrust the knife into the demon's back. The demon roared in unmistakable pain, and they turned to see Malik. The demon with the knife in its back swung with unbelievable speed at him, sending him flying into a tree trunk with a loud thud; the demon reached to its back and removed the knife.

The other demons seemed ready to end him, but the demon he'd wounded put out its arm and snarled in a low growl, "He's mine."

The man stood there, stunned at what just happened, but he was quickly tossed into the air by the two remaining demons, which brought him back to the present. The man seemed to shimmer in mid-air for a minute before coming back down as a nine-foot creature with claws and fur, the sword somehow still in his hand. The man-turned-beast howled at the moon, and Malik knew instantly that he was looking at his first werewolf. The werewolf charged at the demons with a speed Malik couldn't keep up with – all he saw was a blur of fur and claws, and the ringing of a sword.

Malik wasn't in as much pain as he expected, but the demon advanced at him. He had to quickly fend for his life and used every lesson his mother taught him to evade those claws and teeth.

The demon kept throwing him around. While he didn't feel the injuries, he knew the adrenaline rush would eventually go away, and he'd be in extreme pain. He was waiting for his moment to strike the demon, but until then, he'd just try to evade and take the abuse. The demon seemed to be tiring as well; it might have been from the fight with the man that was now a werewolf, but Malik could tell the demon was tired of this and wanted to end his little game.

The demon had a slight limp, and he left himself too open for someone his size. He figured it was because the demon thought he could take him without needing to be on his guard. Seeing the demon get too confident and start to destroy anything in his path, he knew he had it. He noticed the knife on the ground next to him and grabbed it once again.

Malik felt it calling to him for some reason but ignored it; he needed to focus to stay alive, so he tucked the knife away as the demon kept its onslaught of attack. The demon didn't seem to pay attention to it anymore, so Malik ran as fast as he could at the demon. The demon saw him coming, but it was what Malik counted on. Malik kept running, and when the demon brought down its arm, Malik plunged the knife into what he hoped was the demon's heart.

The demon seemed puzzled for a minute, then looked down and tried to wrench the knife out, but Malik held on with the last of his strength. The demon screeched an inhuman sound and stumbled backward. When it truly fell, Malik then let go, and the other demons watched their brethren fall and screeched a terrible sound in unison.

The demons seemed to forget the werewolf was still there. The werewolf used that opportunity to finish off both of them and when he was done, he quickly turned back into a man, still wearing the clothing he was previously in.

All the energy Malik had before disappeared as he crumbled to the ground. The man quickly rushed to Malik's side and looked him over.

The man said in a deep but warm voice, "You don't look like you've taken too much damage. Nice job, kid."

"I guess I wanted to survive." Malik smiled. Unsure how everything had happened, he was glad it was all over.

The man nodded like he understood exactly what Malik was going through. The man slowly helped Malik up and leaned him against a tree.

He noticed the man's strange tattoo on his shoulder, a

chest of some sort with swords and claws on it. As Malik looked at the man closely, he saw he was handsome, if you could call someone that had silver hair and a scar on his right cheek that connected to his chin "handsome." The man had a sword, but Malik didn't see a scabbard on him at all.

The man seemed to notice what he was doing and laughed. "The name's Andres, but everyone calls me Andy, and you are?"

He shook his head; he didn't have time to be looking at the man's wardrobe. "The name's Malik, but most people call me Malik."

It felt nice to smile, even though Malik didn't believe what had just happened.

"It's unusual that they attacked you," the man said. "I don't feel anything coming off you that would make them show their true selves."

No longer able to take everything that was happening, Malik started laughing uncontrollably; he couldn't believe this man was trying to rationalize what had just happened. The man seemed surprised but laughed along with him. The man could tell Malik wasn't believing anything that had just happened.

Movement caught Malik's eyes and he saw the demon that he put down earlier getting up, holding a giant burnt piece of wood with a sharp end.

He tried to scream out a warning, but it was too late;

Andy noticed the demon, and he seemed to make a decision. The demon plunged forward, and Andy shielded Malik with his own body. The wooden piece speared him viciously, and he started to cough up blood. Looking into the man's dying eyes, he could see he was at peace with what was happening. Malik looked on in horror, helpless to stop it.

The demon let out a roar of triumph. Andy looked at Malik and seemed to be saying, "It was worth it." The man suddenly burst into bright blue flames; the demon couldn't get away fast enough, and he too was engulfed in it. The flames licked at Malik but didn't truly touch him.

The demon let out a curse, screaming, "We'll get you next time Guardian, and you too, spawn!" As suddenly as it started, it ended, and the demon was gone like the others.

Malik reached out to Andy even though he was on his last breath of life, he looked at peace. Andy grabbed him urgently and pulled him in close to let him hear his last words.

"I'm glad I was able to help you in my last moments. Look for the wizard, he'll explain everything," Andy told him, his last wish.

Unsure why Andy had told him to do that, all Malik could do was honor the final wish. As scared as he was, he grabbed Andy's hand and begged him not to die. Malik had so many questions he wanted answered. All he could do was hold the body of the dying man, hoping to give him some sort of peace by being there for him.

Andres, or Andy, as his friends called him, died in Malik's arms under a beautiful white full moon in the charred and smoky clearing in the woods he should have never entered. Malik didn't know for sure but could feel that this was only the beginning of something bad.

Unrelenting tears streamed down his cheeks, and Malik let out a scream that felt empty and left a hollow feeling in his chest. His body finally gave out from the loss of adrenaline and sadness, he slowly started to lose consciousness.

Before truly blacking out, he heard several fast footsteps and multiple voices arguing.

"We were too late, we should kill him before it's too late, and we're all doomed."

He tried to force his body to wake up, but all he did was sink further into oblivion. He wasn't sure if he was going to come back … or if he would ever be the same.

CHAPTER 3

When Malik regained consciousness, he didn't expect to find himself back in his room, surrounded by the unpacked boxes he'd been neglecting to put away. He had somehow returned to the manor; the last thing he remembered was holding the body of the man who had just died, for him to live.

The thoughts of the man's death caused him to suddenly get up, but dizziness overcame him. Groaning in pain from the rush of blood to his brain, he sat back onto the bed; next to him was his little sister Nina, snuggled into his chest and breathing softly. He vaguely remembered some people found him right before he had passed out but didn't remember anything about the people.

He heard voices outside the door, down the stairs leading to his room. It sounded like his parents and an unfamiliar voice. They seemed to be arguing, and Malik could barely make out what they were saying.

"He's not ready, I won't let you tell him," Imani was declaring angrily to the other voices.

"Imani, when will he be ready?" his dad asked,

frustration evident in his voice. "He's almost reached the point where he could be a danger both to himself and others if he doesn't know."

Realizing that this was a lost battle, his mom replied, "Okay, then you'll wait for him to get used to his new home first, and then we'll tell him."

Before his dad could reply, another voice spoke; it was silky smooth, calming as a gentle wave of water from the beach. Malik felt like he had heard this voice before but couldn't tell from where.

The voice inquired, "That seems reasonable, doesn't it, Virgil?"

Silence followed and Malik assumed his dad had agreed to it, as nothing else was said back. Who was the stranger with the smooth voice? Too many questions ran around in his head; he hoped he'd find answers.

Then the voices spoke, quieter this time, so quiet that Malik couldn't make out what was being uttered, but he could tell something was happening. He got closer to the door to hear the last few words.

"He's not in any present danger," the stranger said. "The likelihood that someone would do something in the Sanctuary is simply an act of war."

Pushing himself too far to the door, Malik tumbled to the floor. He tried not to groan as he pulled himself back onto the bed so he wouldn't wake Nina. The voices stopped the minute he had made the noise – no matter what he did, he knew he was caught, and they weren't going to finish their conversation.

He heard their goodbyes with the mysterious man, his parents now coming up the stairs. He tried to act as casual as possible, like he just woke up.

His mom came in first, and immediately rushed to his side giving him a big hug, looking him up and down as if he was still injured. His dad also looked worriedly at him.

After looking him over, Malik's mom slapped his shoulder and he winced in pain, rubbing his shoulder as she demanded, "Don't you ever do that to us again! You hear me?"

He could only nod as the pain slowly subsided. He didn't see what the big deal was; things could have been worse.

"Malik, you had us worried, especially Nina. If something like this happens again, you will tell us immediately, do you get that?" his dad added.

"How did I get here? All I remember is passing out from my run," he said, understanding his parents' fear.

His parents gave each other a look before his mom spoke. "Your friends from school brought you here. They said some people tried to mug you, and you were able to fend them off long enough to call for help."

There wasn't any explanation of Andy or those so-called demons that he'd fought. Malik almost didn't believe it had happened. Somewhere in his mind, he knew it truly had happened, but he didn't understand who these 'friends' of his were–he only had one.

"What friends, Mom? I have quite a few of them," he asked, needing to know who she was referring to.

She looked at him strangely, as if he should already know, and shrugged before answering. "There were two girls and two guys. One of them was Jaden–who would have thought that handsome kid cared so much about you? Good friends are hard to come by. You still need to invite him over so I can formally thank him."

All he could do was nod; there were so many questions in his head, but nothing made sense. When he was finally able to talk, he regretted it the minute he asked, "Who was that man downstairs?"

The expressions on his parents' faces told him he had seriously made a wrong move.

"He's an old friend that came over to help me with my work and that's all I'm telling you, for now, so don't ask again," his dad sternly told him. There seemed to be nothing more he could say to make them answer his question.

In a softer voice, his mom comforted him, saying, "He's someone you have to find out about for yourself and on your own time. "

"Okay, enough of this talk, you've been sleeping for almost two straight days. You must be hungry; we'll leave you to get changed and come down to eat. After you've eaten, you can look around, then finish unpacking, it's a madhouse in here," his mom stated, as she rambled on trying to find anything else to talk about. She walked around, starting to move things around. He could tell her nerves were on the edge by the way she kept moving her eyes everywhere but at him.

"Luckily, your school was lenient about medical emergencies, so you'll go back Monday. That sounds good, Anomos?" she asked. He almost flinched at hearing his mother's pet name after remembering the dream from earlier.

Malik couldn't get a word out after his mom's mini speech. He thought about what he had just experienced, and that ruined his appetite. He needed to rest more; for some reason, two days of being in deep sleep just made him want to sleep a little more.

"Can I just stay in my room, Mom? I need to sleep and think about what happened. I can come down tomorrow, I'll probably need a buffet ready for me when I get down there, but I'm not feeling it right now."

Looking at his parents and their expressions showed that they understood and agreed with his idea. They moved to the door, saying their goodbyes.

His dad came back to get Nina, but Malik shook his head, signifying that Nina stayed at his side. His dad went back to the door, and on the way out said softly, "We're really glad you came around, Malik. I don't know what your mother would have done if you hadn't woken up today. We'll be waiting for you tomorrow."

He believed that his mom was the type to do anything for her kids, even if it meant going to hell and back. His dad left the room and left him alone with his thoughts, which kept leading back to the shadows in his dream. Even though the dream wasn't real, he felt like the shadows were watching him at that moment.

When Malik began to fall asleep, he wasn't as terrified of the shadows he'd seen in his dream. With his family here, he felt safe. He knew for sure something was happening, but he didn't understand what it was or why it was happening. That was the last thought Malik had as he snuggled with his sister and fell into a deep, peaceful sleep.

For the next two days, nothing eventful happened; he was spending a lot of time with his family, which he enjoyed. Both of his parents had postponed their job duties to take care of their kids. They did some of the things they had neglected for the last couple of months–spending time having Halloween movie marathons, game nights, and loud dinners together. They had all worked through setting up all the unopened boxes as much as they could, laughing, and just making each other happy. It was one of the best memories he had now with his family.

Monday came sooner rather than later, resulting in everyone going back to their old routines, but he felt closer to his family than ever before with his near-death experience. They didn't talk about the mysterious man, Jaden and his friends, or anything else that could bother their time with each other.

Malik woke to his mom coming upstairs. He quickly sat up and got ready to dress, realizing Nina wasn't there with him, as she had already gotten ready for school. His mom came to his room and looked around, seeing that every box was put away before addressing Malik. "Anomos, get up and get ready, you have an hour before you go to school."

"I'll be right there Mom, just let me get ready first."

His mom left Malik to get ready for the day. Malik sat there for a while processing it all, then got up to look through his boxes to find clothing for the day. He chose his usual graphic tee and blue jeans and decked out in his usual Vans, as well as a jean jacket over his hoodie. He had a feeling it was going to be a chilly November.

Malik went down the stairs to the kitchen, where his mom waited with a buffet of food. His stomach rumbled, as the smell of scrambled eggs and fresh bacon hit his nose. He tucked in before his mom could say anything. She just smiled at him while drinking her coffee.

Now that he was going back to school, everything that he tried to forget started to snake its way out from the recesses of his mind. Malik thought back to that night with the demons and wondered if things had happened differently, would Andy's death not have happened. He felt a twist in his stomach as he thought about the man that couldn't go back to his family because of him. He pushed his breakfast away, guilty for enjoying life while another one was gone.

Looking at his mom who was just enjoying her son's presence in the peace of their home, Malik asked her, "Why did we move here of all places, Mom?"

"For your dad's work Anomos, I've told you before," mom replied, putting down her dark-roasted coffee as its fragrance hit him more strongly.

He flinched, still scared of the shadows that he had dreamed about. "Why do you keep calling me that? My name's Malik!"

"It was your great-grandfather's name, and it's *your* name, and you should be happy to have a great and powerful name. It has a legacy like no other," his mom looked back at him angrily.

He had heard this many times before, but he still didn't know what the name meant. He tried to win his mom back by distracting her. "What was he like, my great-grandfather?"

Imani seemed to have a haze in her eyes; she started talking, and she wouldn't stop, "Anomos Syer Blackwood was a great man. I wish you could have met him. He fought in World War II, and he was great at it. Killing isn't something to be proud of, but he did his job for his country, and he did it well enough that he got honored by our president back then. He came back a changed man. I wasn't born yet, of course, but I was around before he died. He was there to see your birth, but he sadly passed away a day or two later. He talked about many of his war stories, as well as other things, like monsters."

Malik didn't know whether to believe all of it, especially the monsters part. Monsters didn't exist, except in books and your head, or at least that's what he had thought until he came face to face with four of them. Malik let his mom continue with her story.

"I wish I could have written down his story, but he wouldn't let me. You're really like your great-grandfather – you're smart, quick with detail, and you even look like a younger version of him. He's the reason I became a writer, the reason I named you after him. Even though your father thought it was a bad idea, he named you Malik after his father."

She went quiet after that, and they went back to focusing on breakfast. Malik had never heard this much about his great-grandfather before; it felt different than those other times his mother talked about him. Malik didn't think he looked like his great-grandfather, though he had to admit he didn't look much like his father and had distant features from his mother.

He was wiry, not all muscles everywhere, though he wished he was, from being an active kid who loved to run and skateboard. He had dark brown skin that seemed to absorb the sun – he could thank his family for keeping him from sunburning too badly. His thick curls were in a constant messy hairstyle that could never be fixed into any position, which was why he wore twists. He was only sixteen years old, about five-nine, and still growing. He had a strong chin, striking eyes, and a nose that seemed to be made to fit his face perfectly.

So lost in thought, he didn't almost hear his mom say in alarm, "Oh crap, you're going to be late to school! Let's go before you lose another day."

Dragging himself slowly out of his seat, staring at his unfinished breakfast in disappointment, he got up.

She grabbed her keys. "Come on, Anomos, I'm not gonna wait forever for you to finish the food, hurry up."

Malik finished quickly and put the rest of the food in a bag for lunch. He rushed out to meet his mom in the car, and she drove him to Olympus High in silence. Malik took that time to gather his thoughts and think back to everything that had happened in the past two days. It was a mix of amazing things and bad feelings, but he was now finally going somewhere where things would just be normal in high school. His mom pulled up to the school parking lot. She looked at him in concern, hugged him, and wished him luck. Getting out of the car and walking to the doors of the school, he waved to his mom as she drove off. He took a deep breath and opened the school doors, only to be thrown back by a towering giant.

The giant in question was a completely jacked teenager, Daniel Miller, who wore his lacrosse lettermen jacket as he leered down at him, his voice deep and booming.

"Stay out of my way, Blackwood."

Having been away from civilization for a while now, he forgot the rule of dealing with potential bullies. "A pleasure to see you too, Miller."

Daniel looked furious, and Malik knew that one of them wasn't going to walk away from this without a black eye or losing a tooth. As they stared each other down, hearing laughter coming from behind him, they turned around to find Jaden with his oversized vintage sweatshirt and designer jeans.

He acknowledged Malik with a nod but passed right by him to tap the giant on the shoulder. Malik could've sworn that when Daniel looked at Jaden, fear crossed his face, the first time he'd seen any guy as big as him look that scared.

"Go on Danny, get to class before the teacher counts; you're late again, and could get suspended from the team, but they need you. You know how Nico will get," Jaden casually told him, leaning forward as if he was announcing the weather and not threatening anyone at all.

Gulping loudly, all Danny could do was nod and briskly turn to leave but stopped to give Malik one last hateful look. Malik watched Danny leave, till his big frame was out of sight. Then Jaden turned to Malik and smiled.

"Nice to finally see you Malik, I thought you'd never get out from the place of yours."

Standing shocked, then he just started to laugh like a maniac. He didn't know how exactly they had become friends, but he was glad it happened. He gathered himself and he started to walk with Jaden. "What did you do to that guy?"

He just shrugged. "When you know everyone in school, you tend to gather their secrets as well. Danny boy just has some problems with grades and being on the lacrosse team."

In an almost conspiracy-like whisper, Jaden asked, "What, did you think I was some sort of drug dealer that needed his customer to behave?"

Malik was unsure how to answer that question; after the past few days, he didn't know anything about anyone. He laughed uncomfortably before answering, "No, but that's good to know."

Jaden grinned at him as if he knew something Malik didn't. He didn't know how to feel about that, but he went along with his friend.

"Whatever let's just get to class before we're late, too," he dismissed, trying to move on from the topic.

They walked together toward the school in solidarity, heading to their first period. The day went on pretty quietly with no one to bother him. They finally entered

History class, where he once again saw Bianca sitting where he had seen her previously just a few days ago.

Mrs. Taylor smiled when seeing Malik enter, though she looked troubled as well. "Well, it's a pleasure to see you, Malik, why don't you sit beside Bianca again?"

Pointing to the very pretty girl that looked at Malik with a bright smile, he smiled back and moved to sit across from her. He felt better about his day already. The lesson started soon after sitting down.

Leaning close to him in a hushed voice, she asked, "How are you feeling?"

He turned to her in confusion. How could she know what had happened to him without being there?

Seeing his hesitation in answering, she explained, "I meant I heard that you had an accident, and you were out of class for a couple of days. Just wondering if you feel better now."

His heart stilled for some reason. Why was he so nervous all of a sudden? Was he still thinking about what happened as something that was a big secret? The man Andy probably had family as well; they must have known what had happened to him. He felt like he should have told his family over the weekend, come clean about what he'd experienced, but he felt like if he did, he'd somehow put them in danger.

Malik sighed, unaware she was paying attention. "I'm sorry, I'm doing good now, just still processing what happened. You know how some stuff takes time to heal from?"

She looked at him closely as if she knew something about what he was experiencing. She reached over and grabbed his hand, squeezing it softly. "Yeah, I have some experience with that, if you ever need someone to talk to, I'm always here. Okay?"

Staring at her hand for a second, she blushed and pulled back slowly. Malik smiled at her; his chest felt a little better, not as terrified about his secret.

"Thank you, I appreciate that and if I ever need someone to talk to, you'll be one of the first people I turn to," he warmly told her. He appreciated her going out of her way to tell him that.

They focused on the rest of the class in silence; he tried not to look at Bianca unless it was required. The class ended and he went through the day feeling a little better with the reassurance he got from Bianca, even though she didn't know anything that had happened.

Lunch came after the fifth period. As he walked around to get his food, he noticed Nico pointedly looking at him as he walked by. This wasn't something accidentally this time, but full-blown attention as Nico walked toward him, with Daniel right behind him with a cocky purpose to his step.

Where was Jaden when he needed him? Malik was starting to get tired of people coming at him– first the three that had tried to kill him, then this morning with Daniel. If Nico turned out to be some monster, he wouldn't even be surprised at this point. Malik apparently just attracted assholes for some reason.

Nico spoke to Malik once he got closer. "Daniel tells me you're being unsportsmanlike toward him today."

The way he said it was more like an answer than a question, which irked him for some reason. He didn't know what he had done to earn this attention, but he wouldn't accept it.

"Well, I don't know about unsportsmanlike, like since we just met outside and not on the field," he retorted back at Nico, falling for Nico's bait.

Nico looked at Malik for a minute before letting out a small laugh that sounded more like a growl. He looked at his giant friend. "Well, Daniel, you didn't tell me you were talking to the idiot?"

Daniel just looked away in embarrassment, shrugging his broad shoulders. He looked embarrassed to have Nico come back him up, which Malik even thought was dumb.

Turning back to Malik, Nico suggested, "You should just stay out of our way next time, pup, before you get yourself into something you'll regret. Not even the great Jaden Williams can save you then."

The second after he said that Nico turned away as if Malik was as important as a bug. That made him angrier than he realized, reminding him of the guys from a few days ago. Just when Malik went to confront Nico, he looked back, and what Malik saw scared him. Instead of those disdainful eyes of deep emerald-green, he saw the glowing, piercing red eyes of a monster. Malik backpedaled out of the way, suddenly terrified once again. Nico offered a wolfish grin when he saw Malik's reaction and walked away with his hands in his pocket. Daniel followed, as well as other guys; to Malik's eyes, they moved as a pack.

Malik hadn't realized when he had backpedaled that he had run into someone until he heard a noise behind him. Malik was drawn into a pair of deep brown, beautiful eyes, accompanied by a girl who was equal parts beautiful and terrifying.

He recognized those eyes belonging to Maya, Jaden's ex; she didn't seem to notice Malik at all, but watched the group walk away. Once they disappeared around the corner, she finally took notice of him. Malik was able to get a good look at Maya, and he felt like he had seen her before in a dream.

Maya looked him over and, in a voice that seemed used to commanding people, she said "You should be more careful, Malik, you don't want to make enemies before you truly understand whose side you're playing on."

As he stood there, mystified by what she said, Maya just walked away in the opposite direction of Nico's group.

Malik collected himself and tried to act as if nothing

had happened. There were too many unanswered questions, like if the things he saw were still out there and wanted to hurt him. He felt powerless and alone, questioning everything, and wondered if he was going to survive.

He had to get answers, and he only knew one person that seemed to know everything about everything. He stood straighter and with a determined look set off to find him.

CHAPTER 4

Malik found Jaden sitting with a group of people in the hall and was surprised to see one of them was Nico, talking to Jaden adamantly as he faced him. Nico perked up as if he could see Malik coming without turning around. The rest of the group noticed Malik as well; they all got up and walked away. The only person left sitting there was Jaden. Malik steadied his breath, which he didn't realize was shaking, and walked over to Jaden with the resolve he had earlier.

Letting Malik get to him without moving a muscle, Jaden just watched him walk toward him. He took a seat next to Jaden, who seemed to be chilling and lost in his head.

He cleared his throat to get Jaden's attention, which seemed to work. Jaden looked at him with some concern. "Are you okay, man? You look a little shaken up."

He had to think for a minute about how to respond to that, and shaking his head, told him, "I have some questions I wanted to ask you if that's okay."

Looking at him closely, Jaden gave him his undivided

attention. Malik steadied his racing heart, scared of what may come out as lunacy. "I know this is gonna sound crazy, but I feel like I should tell someone, or I'm gonna feel like I'm going insane."

He shared what happened to him at the park a few days ago, everything but the dream he'd had about the shadows. Jaden took it all in without saying anything, occasionally encouraging him to continue in some heart-wrenching places, like Andy's death and the last words he spoke. When Malik finally finished telling his story, he expected Jaden to run or to call him crazy, but he just looked concerned and worried.

"Well, that sounds like a lot, I'm not sure how to react," he finally answered. It felt like he believed him for some reason, which was more concerning than everything he had said.

Still shocked that he hadn't run away, Malik inquired, "Why aren't you telling me I'm crazy or something?"

"Trust me, I've heard and seen crazier things, but this does deeply worry me since they were just outside the Sanctuary lines. This could be an act of war."

"War! What war is going on?" Malik yelled in shock, staring at Jaden as if he had gone mad. Did he somehow stumble into something much bigger than himself? All of this could have been avoided if he had just decided to stay in that night.

"The war that's been going on for centuries, unknown

by mortals," Jaden answered, grimly frowning at him.

Mortals? What was Jaden going on about? He was acting as if he wasn't even human as well. Malik felt like he might pass out from just a few words. Jaden reached out his hand and squeezed his shoulders, and Malik felt an instant calmness wash over him.

"I'm sorry that you had to go through that, Malik," Jaden continued, "I wish I could reassure you that everything is gonna be okay, but I have to tell you that the supernatural beings are as real as you and me. I know you have many questions and I'll try to answer them the best I can, but I can't right now. What I can promise you is that once you get those answers, you won't ever go back to the way life was for you."

Malik's dry throat started to itch, and he grabbed some water left behind by the group. Whatever calmness he had felt went out of the window the more Jaden talked. He took a sip and thought hard about it–was it better to stay in the dark about everything? Then, remembering the demon's last words, it seemed like it was a warning that they would come back for him. He needed to know everything to protect the people he loved from a fate just like Andy's, which would haunt him for the rest of his life as well.

Resolve coursed through him as he told Jaden in determination, "I can wait, I'm not gonna be able to let this go until I have answers."

Willing to wait however long it took to get answers, he

wasn't going to run away from this. He owned Andy that much at least, to fulfill his final wishes; maybe he would find the wizard that was supposed to help him out.

Jaden must have seen his friend's silence as concerning because he asked, "Are you okay?"

"I'm fine, I just have a lot on my mind right now, and I don't know what to do," Malik replied in a serious tone.

As if Jaden understood, he sympathized with him, saying, "Sometimes that's all I ever feel, like I'm grabbing for air, and I don't truly have the answers for everything. Maybe that's why I want to know what's going on with everyone, because if I don't have the answers for myself, maybe I can provide some guidance for others instead."

Malik stared at his friend, feeling like he was seeing him for the first time. Jaden had always seemed so strong and dependable. Maybe everyone had their demons they were trying to face, even his best friend. He wanted to be there for Jaden as much as he had been there for Malik these past few weeks.

Noticing Malik's quietness, Jaden shook his head and laughed, a sad, melancholy sort of laugh. "What are we doing? Let's live as much as we can because there's no reincarnation for us. We'll find the answers, not all truths are revealed in a single moment in time."

They went back to sitting with each other, trying to occupy their minds with something else besides the doom and gloom. That was when they heard the scream, turning to each other in alarm. They quickly got up in search of the scream, which sounded like someone in fear for their life. They ran to find the source; it sounded like it was coming from the school entrance.

By the time they got there, no school administrators were in sight; they had a quarterly meeting in the big upstairs office around this time. Malik and Jaden saw a girl who Malik recognized from his English class as Elinam Johnson; she was also a junior. She was surrounded by four men who didn't look like they belonged at the school. She looked at Jaden and Malik from the bottom of the steps of the entrance of the school. Her eyes seemed to plead for them to save her.

Malik's body moved before he could even think, landing right next to them. A big man that looked to be in his late twenties jumped down the final step and Malik attacked him, slamming his fist into his face. The guy staggered back, mostly from surprise rather than pain, but it was enough time to follow up with an uppercut that sent the man to the ground for a moment.

Now moving to the second guy, Malik grabbed the rails at the bottom of the stairs to propel his legs upwards to kick him in the face, throwing him off his feet and causing the attacker to slide several feet away from them. Malik felt as energized as he did the night he had been attacked; he felt the most alert and dangerous as he had in days, as if he was made for this moment. He reached

Elinam and pulled her out of harm's way, pulling her to a higher position on the stairs.

****

Jaden, who Malik hadn't realized was right beside him, attacked the last two guys. He moved quite well given the circumstances, using a combination of moves as they attacked him at the same time. Jaden took down the guys without any effort on his part.

One of the guys got up and shrugged off his pain to look at both Malik and Jaden in disdain. "Give us the girl who speaks to Death, and we'll let you live," he said in a raspy voice, as if unused to speaking. He looked at them as if he expected them to listen to his demands.

"Bro, you need some water and vocal lessons before you start making threats like that," joked Jaden, as if not remotely scared of the man's threats. Maybe he knew something Malik didn't.

Why was he so relaxed against these guys? Jaden muttered something under his breath that Malik couldn't understand. The man just looked at Jaden with a twisted grin and started to step forward but was stopped by an unseen force. The man tried to beat at the air in front of him as if something was in his way. Jaden just grinned, strolled up to the man, and stood right next to him. The man now seemed terrified of Jaden or whatever he was doing.

"I'd go before things get really ugly, pal," Jaden advised, "go back to whatever hole you crawled right out of, and stay there, because next time there won't be anything left of you but that terrible breath of yours."

The man shook in visible terror, but Jaden calmly walked back to Malik and Elinam as if nothing had happened. Both looked at Jaden as if he had grown another head. Jaden looked over at them, perplexed, as if he was flabbergasted as to why they were staring so hard. "What, I got something in my teeth? Do I have bad breath, too?"

He sniffed his breath using his hands, searching for the reason he was being stared at. Malik just shook his head; Jaden was indeed off his rocker. The assailants all watched with wide-eyed expressions; the man that had spoken seemed to be the leader of the group, and the others all looked to him in confirmation.

Before he could make a decision, students flooded to the entrance, about thirty of them. Most looked ready for a fight, having grabbed makeshift weapons like brooms and forks. Among the students, Jaden noticed Nico, Maya, and Bianca.

Bianca noticed Malik and just grinned as if she was excited about the fight. The attackers took in all the new students in confirmation that it was best to leave. The leader gave one last look to say it wasn't over and ran with the other guys. Many of the teachers were heading to the entrance as well with security right on their heels; it was dumb luck the students had arrived first.

"What's going on here?" Principal Monroe asked a middle-aged man, staring at all the students with weapons in their hands. He looked down at the three of them in confusion, then saw the four assailants running away. He quickly instructed the teachers and administrators to take care of the students, then hurriedly went down the steps to follow the assailants. He walked by Malik and the other two with security, trying to catch up to them as they ran away.

The other administrators and teachers started to move the kids back into the school, toward their next class. Most of the students dispersed, but the three students Malik had noticed before stepped up to Jaden, Malik, and Elinam.

Maya was the first to speak. "So, does anyone want to tell me what just happened?"

Jaden shrugged. "Elinam was in danger, Malik and I stepped in. You know how I am with damsels in distress."

At that last part, Jaden looked directly at Maya, who blushed slightly and looked away. Malik knew there was something between them than what they were letting on, but now wasn't the time to discuss it.

Staring after the four men being chased by the principal, Nico asked, "Should we follow after them?"

"They won't come here again and besides, I already took care of them. Plus, we're still students, we should be in class right now and not standing around like delinquents," responded Jaden, shaking his head.

Malik didn't know what that meant but chose to trust his friend. Nico seemed to like his answer, too, and just nodded in agreement.

"So, what do they want with you, Elinam?" questioned Bianca. She looked at Elinam with curiosity, which made everyone turn toward her to find out the same thing.

Suddenly realizing all the attention was on her, Elinam nervously avoided the question. "Oh, um, I don't have a clue."

Everyone knew instantly that she was lying, but decided to ignore it, letting her keep her secrets for now.

"Hey, Nico," Jaden said, trying to steer the conversion in a different direction, "could you make sure Elinam gets to class safely?"

Nico agreed, which made Malik raise an eyebrow, surprised he knew how to take commands. Nico turned, looking at Malik as if he knew what he was thinking.

"You got a problem with that, Blackwood?" Nico challenged, ready to fight him right there.

"Nope, no problem, hombre, you go take care of our damsel. We're all counting on you," Malik stammered, instantly putting his hands up.

Jaden fake-saluted Nico, which seemed to make Nico even madder; Malik couldn't blame him. Jaden was being ridiculous at that point. Thankfully, Nico quickly talked to Elinam, helping her get to class. Malik knew it wasn't over with him and Nico, but he could handle that another day.

"Oh, he's gonna rip your head off one day, I can't wait. I call dibs on front-row seats." Bianca laughed until tears filled her eyes as she watched Nico go with Elinam back into the school.

Everyone else just looked at Bianca in shock, but even Maya nodded. "She's crazy, but not wrong. I told you to know your enemies before you decide to challenge them. One day that's gonna leave you in a world of hurt."

Malik shook his head. What kind of school was this? How much was he in over his head, and why was everyone agreeing that he'd get beaten up by Nico, as if he automatically could beat him? Malik had some moves too. All protest deflated out of him as Jaden patted him on the back in comfort.

"At least you're still alive today, there might be hope for you yet, young Padawan."

He made a face, looking at Jaden in disbelief at the Star Wars reference. "Padawan, really? Then what are you, oh great Yoda?"

Trying to act all wise and sagely, which failed miserably as his grin destroyed the whole illusion with a bad Yoda voice, Jaden said, "You have much to learn, oh so inferior one."

Maya and Bianca both snorted, then headed back into school. "I guess that's our cue before this turns into a nerd fest," Maya stated, looking at them in disgust.

Much to Malik's delight, Bianca excitedly joined in. "Ooooh, let me be Han Solo – or wait, Chewbacca!"

At that moment, he knew that he liked Bianca, against all rational thought. She had chewed right to his heart, and he grinned at her, bowing. "Oh, majestic Han Solo, let us ride away."

She grinned at him and was about to reply, but Maya dragged her away, with Bianca saluting like a captain. He had to laugh at that; it felt good to laugh after having so many dark things in his head lately.

"That girl's crazy, I'd be careful," Jaden said, back to his old self. Malik had to agree with him, but he undoubtedly felt like he could get used to her type of crazy.

"Well, come on, we still got the school to survive. I think we've had enough fun for one day."

Malik agreed and followed Jaden back inside, spending the rest of the day going through the motions of boring, normal high school. There weren't any new revelations or big events that happened; the principal and the security had given up on finding the men after an hour. There were plans on having a school meeting with faculty to plan for any future incidences, and even talk about canceling school. Sadly, they had decided against it at the last minute due to testing coming up soon.

After their last period, Jaden told Malik to come by his place to explain more of what was going on. Malik was extremely excited and nervous to find out what was happening while he waited for his mom to pick him up from school. The car ride back was long and awkward because his mom kept asking about his day, even though she could tell he didn't want to talk about it.

As they walked into the house, the scene before Malik turned his stomach in so many ways. Jaden was there, talking to his dad and playing with his sister. With him was a man that resembled Andy so much, it caused Malik to flash back to the memory of him dying in his arms only a few days ago, murdered by the monster he'd been fighting.

A cold sweat crept over Malik; he'd never felt this terrified before in his life, besides the time he had almost died. His mom waved him in and, seeing him stand there, grew concerned. Malik wondered why these things kept happening to him without his input. He just wanted to sit down and suddenly felt dizzy. He was about to fall over when suddenly the man came out of nowhere to steady him.

The man looked at Malik closely, with the most intense eyes Malik had ever seen. They seemed to search into his soul for answers, and for an instant, the man's eyes glowed yellow for just a moment, so unlike the eyes of the werewolf that had glowed blue that night in the park. He instantly knew that these were two different men, but they could have been twins.

Breaking the silence, his mom asked, "Sir, what can I

do for you?"

The man broke away from Malik's gaze and looked at his mom with a charming smile. "You must be Mrs. Blackwood. I'm sorry to interrupt your evening, but I am Sergeant Oscar Gonzalez of the Portland Orem Special Affairs."

His parents gave each other a strange look that Malik couldn't identify, though it seemed like fear and anger.

If Sergeant Gonzalez noticed, he decided not to comment, and continued, saying, "I'm following up on an attack that happened approximately one week ago at eleven-thirty, inside a clearing in the Crimson Woods."

"I'm sorry, but what does that have to do with us?" his dad interjected for the first time, curious as to why that mattered to them.

Sergeant Gonzalez looked at both his parents before answering. "I'm sorry, but I was told that your son was one of those attacked, and I just come to get my report."

His parents looked over at Malik in shock and he groaned inwardly. He knew he should have told his parents, but with everything going on, it had slipped his mind. He knew it was because he wanted to keep them safe from whatever had attacked him. Not only that, but he didn't know what to say to not get in trouble. It seemed like his mother did, though, since she went into full lawyer-mode before he even had a chance to speak.

"Well, this is the first we heard of it, but I do recall his friends bringing him back after this so-called attack," Sergeant Gonzalez was met with a business-like tone, "Are you sure that it wasn't just made up and lead by adolescent behavior?"

The Sergeant looked impressed at her quick response. He replied, "Well, there is the fact that someone else had also been there, and now they are currently being buried."

That quickly alarmed them–who would be? Their only son being the prime witness for someone's death wasn't something you'd want to hear, especially from someone that wasn't their son. They looked completely scared for the first time.

Malik's dad looked over at him and in a shaky voice, asked him, "Malik, what happened out there?"

All the adults looked over at Malik, who felt there was no more hiding, so he told his parents, "I'm sorry, I wanted to tell you, but I was so scared and didn't know what to do."

He told the story of what had happened but left out the parts of the demons and werewolf, only telling the clean version he had planned out while the adults talked. He didn't want to seem crazy just yet, not before he had answers.

The officer, all the while, looked at Malik closely and wrote down notes. When Malik finally finished, the man nodded and put away his notes in his breast pocket. His voice was gentle. "I'm sorry that happened, Malik, but is there anything else you can remember, what the attackers looked like or anything?"

"I'm sorry, Officer, it just happened so fast I don't know what to say, I blacked out shortly and somehow made it back here," explained Malik, shaking his head to show that there was nothing else left.

"Is there anything else you need, Sergeant?" Imani asked, clearly thinking her son didn't need to answer any more questions.

The Sergeant could tell he had overstayed his welcome and quickly shook his head. "No, that should be it, but Malik, if you could recall anything else, please give me a call, and I'll help in any way possible."

Sergeant Gonzalez gave Malik his card, shook hands with his parents, and talked to Malik's dad a little more before heading out. He took one last look at Malik before heading out, and as he left, Malik could tell that the officer knew the true story but had chosen to say nothing.

Once the officer left, Malik's mom came over to him and hugged him tightly. "If anything happens again, please let us know, you could go to jail or worse."

"It's already started," his dad whispered fearfully, worry etched all across his face after the Sergeant left. There was an awkward silence as both his parents stared at Malik, questions and worry written on their faces. He could tell they wanted to talk to him about everything, but with Jaden there, it was difficult to bring up.

Jaden cleared his throat. "Well, this isn't the way I wanted to be introduced, but hi, I'm one of Malik's friends from school."

Seeming to remember herself, his mom flashed her bestseller smile. "It's great to meet one of Malik's friends, I can't thank you enough for bringing my son back."

"It wasn't anything, Mrs. Blackwood, just doing anything a friend would do," Jaden said, blushing. "I'm sorry that my mom hasn't come by to welcome you officially to the town. She has this tradition of going out to dinner with every new resident."

Imani smiled. "That's completely fine, she welcomed us when we first got here. She's the town mayor, she must be busy! She's such a nice lady, helping us get all situated for our move here."

"She loves to get her tenants the proper greeting; she likes to think she's the mayor and Sheriff all in one," Jaden agreed. His tone turned suspiciously innocent. "May I bring Malik with me to my house? My mother would love to meet him and give him the proper introduction."

His parents were slightly hesitant, as they just found out that Malik had been hiding things from them. Somehow having Jaden with him seemed to convince them to let him out; maybe it was because his mom was the mayor or that he had brought him back that night, but whatever it was worked. Malik promised them he'd be back before it was dark. He grabbed his spare board and gave it to Jaden; together they skated over to Jaden's house, which was thankfully only a few minutes away, right around the Crimson Wood's area as well.

CHAPTER 5

When they finally arrived at Jaden's house, Malik was quite impressed with the place. It was a big three-story home, with a nice view of the city. A few minutes away from Malik's house, it was the complete opposite style to his own, with a more modern look to it. It reminded Malik of the impressive homes he would see in big cities, with its white and gray colors, polished marble floors, a sprawling kitchen, and a beautiful minimalist living room. He had never entered a home as beautiful as this one.

No one else was home, as Jaden explained his mom most likely had a town meeting that night, so they headed up to his room. It was pretty simple for a sixteen-year-old, though Malik didn't see a gaming set or anything, just a wall full of books and movies. For some reason, Jaden had a stick laying across his bed, which he moved to his lap once he sat down on a couch he had in the left corner of his room, just across from the bed. Malik took a chair from the desk on the far-right corner, dragging it over to where Jaden sat.

"Yeah, this is my place. Think of it as my kingdom," Jaden proudly stated as he watched Malik look around his room.

He nodded. He was quite taken with the place himself; it felt simple and big at the same time. Malik rolled to a stop next to him.

"So …" Malik began, "what's going on?"

Jaden got himself comfortable before beginning. "Well, as I told you before, supernaturals do exist, and everything else in-between."

"In-between?" Malik asked.

"Yes, in-between, but I'll get to that later. Right now, let's focus on the supernatural," Jaden interrupted. "What do you know of it?"

"Um, just the textbook stuff – werewolves, vampires, demons, fae," Malik answered.

"Well, that's good to know, and you should know those are all very real, too, and pretty petty, annoying creatures to deal with," Jaden said.

He'd seen demons and werewolves already, so he had to at least believe in their existence.

"But there are more creatures that you don't know about," Jaden peered at him to see if he was understanding everything before continuing, "and unless you encounter them, I'd rather not talk about them right now. All you need to know are the essentials to supernatural's and beyond, so, starting my supernatural 101 class, I'll give you a history lesson.

"The supernatural world at one point wasn't so secret. You know, when the time of man used to worship gods and the like, but with time, science came to be what we all feared and hated. There were many wars and persecution, and we slowly lost our numbers and were forced into hiding in plain sight. Some decided to live side by side with man, while others decided to go to places a man could never reach. Portland became one of the many homes and sanctuaries out there for those that wished to live in peace; many groups try to maintain the peace, such as the officer you met today."

Malik took this all in, noticing how Jaden talked as if he was one of those creatures. He decided to let Jaden keep talking, for now; he had time to ask questions later.

"The demons you fought a few days ago didn't truly invade our home, but they did cross a truce made long ago. The man that fought for you was a werewolf that most likely worked for the Orim Council … and so do the people that helped you get home that night," continued Jaden.

He paused for a minute to get a glass of water from his nightstand before continuing. "You see, there are currently four different groups in this town that police the place. The Paladins are people imbued with supernatural gifts, but aren't supernatural themselves, believed to be chosen by some goddess or angels; in other words, they're knights. If the Orim can't handle it first, they go, and they're the 'stab now and ask questions later' type of people. A pack of were-shifters, from werewolf to were-cat or such, they're the supernatural police during the day; they fight crime and at night they hunt the bad guys. The Covenant is just a council of all different types of supernatural governing and handing out justice as they see fit." Jaden laughed darkly.

"And then there's me, well, me and my mom," he explained, "we're what you consider the witch council, even though we don't fit the numeric requirements for it. My mom and I are powerful enough to equal one. Every group has their witch or wizard, but they regularly call on us when they have a problem or need a statement others can't give."

"Wait, you're some kind of wizard?" Malik gasped. Was Jaden the wizard that Andy had wanted him to meet?

With a single gesture, Jaden's stick instantly appeared in his hand. Malik was so shocked; he didn't know what to say.

"Well, I happen to currently be one of the most powerful wizards of this century," Jaden jokingly admitted.

"That's so cool, man, but why aren't you part of these other groups? Seems like anyone would welcome you."

Jaden's smile fell. "Well, I'm technically not allowed to, since I'm an illegitimate child of my mother; they have a very warped idea of children and their lineage. They don't like who my father is, which hasn't been too much of a problem with me so far."

"Oh, I'm sorry I didn't know," Malik apologized, on behalf of everyone that treated him poorly.

"It's okay, it actually makes being a wizard a lot easier; I just do my job and then go home. They think she made a deal with a demon to conceive me; even her sister, who is part of the big coven in New Orleans, won't look at her."

"Coven?" Malik repeated.

"A coven is when a group of witches and wizards come together to practice magic; it makes channeling magic a lot easier for some people. The Western Coven is the largest witch and wizard council of today. My mother was one of their best before she had me, probably could have run the whole thing. They think of me as a warlock, a creature born of dark magic." Jaden's tone turned sad and hopeless.

"Don't care about what people think of you, I think you're pretty cool, Jaden," Malik assured him, trying to cheer him up as much as he could.

"Thanks, Malik, I appreciate it," Jaden said, his trademark smile coming back. "Enough about me, though. I think what happened to you crosses many lines, and we'll get to the bottom of this soon."

"I hope so, I don't want any more attacks happening to me," agreed Malik.

"You wouldn't be some type of supernatural yourself, would you?" Jaden asked innocently, looking at him sideways.

"If I was a magic user, I'd be the kind that sleeps and eats a lot," he answered, shaking his head. He remembered that moment where he had heard that voice, but he wasn't ready to say anything just yet. He still wanted to know more before saying anything else.

"Trust me, you'd be one of a kind." Jaden roared with laughter at his joke.

"Oh, I don't doubt that!" Malik uncontrollably laughed.

They laughed for a minute and forgot all about their problems. Jaden showed him some things he could do, explaining that there were different types of magic.

"Every magic user has a specific gene that enables them to access the magic that normal humans can't access. Some magic users can never activate their dominant power without some guidance, while others will open it accidentally. Thing's people find weird, such as telepaths or technopaths, came out into the world; some can join the world, but others aren't able to make it. Some general magic users go with the basic elements. But due to certain bloodlines mixing between magic users and other magical species, odd new magic types have slowly emerged throughout the years."

Not all beings could use the same magic; humans only had access to a certain range of magic, while higher beings like demons had higher-level abilities, sometimes even on top of human ones. The one he had personally came from within him; Jaden had told him that human magic practitioners had access to something called "mana," the very source of magic, and they could access it in multiple ways. The greater the connection, the more powerful someone's magic.

"What's that stick for?" Malik asked.

Jaden picked it up and showed it to Malik. It glowed with green runes all around it. "That's my staff; think of it as a wizard's wand, like in Harry Potter. I wouldn't need it – I'm better with my hands – but being a magic user, my power sometimes becomes too much to handle. Using this allows my body to not go through too much of a struggle when handling difficult magic. That's one of the many drawbacks to all types of users unless you've lived for centuries to cultivate your power; there's always going to be a problem of using too much power or taking too much power, to the point of death."

"So, it's like a conductor of sorts. Where's your grimoire or familiar?" Malik asked.

"One, I'm not a wizard like in Harry Potter, I don't cast spells, the magic is *me*. It's the essence of me. And second, I don't do familiars – too old-school. I got a phone and that's good enough for me. I don't have a grimoire yet, which I doubt will happen. A grimoire chooses its champion, not the other way around, but for most human practitioners, it's nearly impossible to gain more power unless you have a grimoire or there's someone around to teach you magic," Jaden explained, looking crestfallen at the words.

"Oh, that's cool, I'm sure you'll get it one day," Malik said. Jaden already seemed to be doing so well on his own. There wasn't any chance he wouldn't get one.

"It's actually forbidden for me to get one; the witch's council made it a rule. They'd kill me if I did, and I doubt there's a grimoire able to choose me since I'm already powerful and only growing, maybe a little too powerful." He smiled a sad smile.

Malik saw his friend struggle and was mad for him. How dare some pompous people think they could do that to his friend, strip him of the chance to do something great with his life?

For a minute, Malik had a flashback of his childhood, always being the outsider because he moved around so much. He could relate to Jaden on some level. They'd both been outsiders most of their lives; he felt like he'd known Jaden his whole life.

"Don't worry, bro," he reassuringly stated, "you'll get the grimoire one day."

"Thanks, Malik, it means a lot to me that you said that. Well, you should probably get home before your parents have an aneurysm or something."

They finally headed back to Malik's home. Malik's parents were asleep, so he said goodbye to Jaden, they made plans to see each other in the morning and make plans for figuring out what was going on. He headed to his room; all the energy of the day drained from him. He was barely able to change and get ready for bed, completely forgetting to set his alarm as he simply crashed after the long day.

The sound of singing woke him up in the middle of the night. Rolling over, he looked around the room to see if he had let his phone play music somehow but found that nothing was playing. It was still dark, barely three in the morning; he couldn't figure out where the noise was coming from. He got himself out of bed, groaning; knowing he couldn't go back to sleep now, he figured he might as well find the source. Going down the stairs slowly to avoid waking his family, he reached the bottom. The radiance of the beautiful night sky was on display, the skylight letting in the moonlight that seemed to give it an otherworldly look to everything in the house. He wanted to see if the TV in the living room was off.

That was when he heard it again, but this time it felt different. As if it was calling his name, some old friend that he should have remembered, on the tip of his tongue. He remembered their smell, of the cookies he used to bake with his mom, the summers spent running around in the backyard playing superhero. The sound was even louder now; it called to him as if it wanted to come home. Now he was blindly searching, not completely aware of what he was doing, as though the house wasn't there anymore, but hearing the noise, searching with his heart, and listening to the yearning he felt inside him.

Malik found a room that he hadn't been in before; he should have questioned it, but the singing was a roar in his ears, and he felt he would go mad if he didn't find it. As the noise came from below him, he got on his hands and knees groping for the source. Suddenly the floor crumbled beneath him, and he fell, screaming, into darkness.

It was a long drop, and he couldn't see what was in front of him. He didn't know what was coming. Was he going to die today?

He flailed helplessly in the darkness, but the singing was coming from here, so Malik calmed his nerves, thinking if that sound was from here, then there must be a bottom. Before he had enough time to process it, he hit something that broke his fall. Getting up, he found himself in some kind of chamber that shouldn't be possible. There shouldn't be something this far deep right under his home. Not knowing what to think anymore, just that he wanted to go to his room and wake up to it all being a dream.

He didn't know if it was possible anymore – he was somewhere under his house and he had to find a way out, and maybe that sound he heard was near an exit.

Brushing himself off, he saw a wide chamber that led to two far exits on opposite sides. The sound was coming from the left, and his feet uncooperatively headed in that direction. He wasn't sure what his body was doing anymore but felt that the exit must be in that direction as well. As he walked, he looked around, there were pictures depicted on the wall of monsters and god-like men, much like the mural in his school. This one seemed to be telling a story, but where the story ended, he didn't know. The chamber itself didn't seem so old; it felt like it had been cleaned just previously for some unknown reason, making his spine crawl, as he felt like he wasn't alone but being watched. He didn't pay much attention to where he was going but found a room pulsing scarlet light; inside the room, the light illuminated a sigil of some kind. It seemed to be from another century, with words and pictures he couldn't even describe.

It was then that he saw it, a glowing scarlet light coming from a rock on the wall. The sound finally stopped, but the rock pulsed even brighter. It called to him … as if it was meant for him.

It drew him in, even against his will. Finally, reaching it, he wrapped his hands around it. Malik saw words surrounding the rock and read them aloud. *"In our darkest hour it is not a man that prevails, but a monster that wears the mask of man and heart of a beast, who's willing to stand amongst the shadows to cast a light brighter than those before him."*

As he read those words, he felt an even greater urge to pull the rock out. As he did, the light coming from the stone poured onto him as if a tidal wave of power crashing down on him; as it did, he felt only warmth and comfort from the cascading energy. He felt the rock move in his hands for a moment; it seemed as though it was alive, understanding how he felt that very moment and somehow knew to make him feel safe. He felt as though he had finally woken up from a drowsy dream, he'd had all his life, as though colors and images could all change, somehow become more alive. After what felt like an eternity, Malik Anomas Blackwood collapsed onto the ground.

Standing over him was a man with a ball, a glowing reddish sphere in his hand which he quickly put away in his pocket. The man looked at him in concern; he was handsome, the definition of an angel reborn. With his chiseled bone structure, his hair perfectly brushed and combed, even his eyebrows seemed to be perfect. He looked like he was in his late thirties, and his striking blue-green eyes analyzed Malik.

"Well, mister, isn't it past your bedtime?" he asked in an amused voice. His voice even sounded perfect. As it was made to be heard and nothing could stop it from emerging from his lips.

"Where am I?" Malik asked as he got up slowly, remembering that he was in a chamber beneath his home–which shouldn't have existed, much less have a man be down here.

"You're in one of the chambers that used to be a form of secret bunkers for people running against prosecution.

You tripped one of the many alarms while stumbling onto this place."

"Oh, I'm sorry I didn't know," Malik said. He instantly knew the man was lying but didn't want to call him out on it.

"What did you say your name was again, young man?" the man asked as if they were having a conversation at a park and not in an old room.

"Malik Blackwood," he answered, uncertainty now creeping upon him. He wasn't sure if he was safe just yet.

The man's eyes gleamed for a minute with what seemed to be true menace, but before Malik could react, they were back to their cool and collected expression as before.

"Ah, well you must be the infamous Malik Anomos Blackwood I've heard so much about," the man said, his tone hinting he knew everything about Malik.

Malik was creeped out by this man – only people in his family knew his given name was Anomos.

"Well, I'm sorry to have bothered you sir, but I should start getting back now. My parents must be worried sick," Malik stammered. Rushing to leave, his fingers still gripping the rock, his eyes desperately searched for an opening to leave.

"Of course, I forget what it means to be a child sometimes, it feels like a lifetime ago," the man spoke in a reminiscent voice, studying Malik for a minute.

Then the man started to walk in the opposite direction that Malik had arrived. He didn't know what to think of this man but being left in this dark and ominous place was the last thing he wanted. Instead of listening to his better judgment, Malik quickly tucked the stone in his pocket and followed the man. For his part, the man didn't even stop to see if Malik would follow him; he just kept on moving.

"You know, dear Malik, that your namesake carries a lot of weight in our world. Names have power if you truly believe in such a thing," the man said, speaking as though he expected Malik to follow him without even asking.

Malik rushed to catch up to him. For some reason, even though the man gave him the feeling he was being sized up, he could tell that he could trust him to at least get him home.

"What do you mean, sir?" Malik asked. The man didn't seem to be interested in him anymore, which resulted in him lowering his guard.

"Well, take your name Malik, for instance. It means king in Arabic and other old languages. While your true name, Anomos, means violator of the law or godless man in some old tongues." He appeared to enjoy saying the last part.

That caused Malik to pause before answering, thinking about it for a minute as they turned down another unidentifiable tunnel. He knew that some old religions and cultures put names high, naming their children good names worthy of kings. Names had a way of describing a person's character and true nature. He knew his father called him Malik so he wouldn't deal with cruel kids, but his mother named him Anomos after his great-grandfather, and he turned out to be a great man overall. He could only hope that he lived up to that name; sometimes he felt like his mom put so much pressure on him because of who carried the name before him.

He just saw himself as Malik Blackwood – a kid in way over his head.

The man quietly waited for Malik's response. "I don't think it's a big deal. At the end of the day, I'm still just me."

The man's chuckle put Malik's spine on edge; it felt as though the man knew an inside joke that wasn't being shared with him. The man collected himself. "I guess that's true, Mr. Blackwood, I guess we have personal views on life and destiny."

Uneasily he smiled, not knowing what to say to that. They finally reached a corner where a light shone from overhead. A set of stairs lead to the light.

The man extended his arm to him, and he grasped it for a shake. The man pulled him slightly closer, looked him deeply in his eyes as he whispered, "Sometimes our eyes can look into the deeper parts of the soul, as much as our names sometimes forsake us for being among the corrupted. Mr. Blackwood, I advise you to look into the eyes of your fellow man and see if they truly have good interest in you before letting your heart be broken."

The words chilled Malik and made him wonder what he was truly talking about; why was this man down here? Had he been waiting for him? The man finally let him go, patting him on the back, and waving for Malik to move up the staircase.

Not even looking back, he started his ascension up the staircase. When he was halfway up, he looked down and saw the man still watching him in amusement. It only made him speed up his departure. Somehow, he found himself back in his home, or at least the garden area. He walked halfway to the house, then for some reason he turned around to double-check that there wasn't any chance of him being crazy. He walked back to the same spot that he exited to find it completely covered in plants. His breathing became labored as he got on his knees and dug out the ground, trying to find the hole that existed. Fingers covered in dirt and knees bruised from the garden's environment around him covered in rocks, his shallow, ragged breath was all that remained. Frustration bled out as he stared at the ground; no hole existed, even after he had dug a few inches deep.

The brilliance of the half-moon cascaded over his body and the surrounding garden. He shivered as the wind blew across his body, the night filled with the cacophony of creatures prowling the night. Across the distance he could have sworn he heard a wolf howl as he took everything in, deciding at that moment that he was done for the night. His mind and body seemed to agree as he was exhausted once again, his body moving on autopilot as he numbly got up, found his way to his room, and shut his door, locking it.

He shivered once again, not from the cold, but because the feeling of being watched every step of the way was stronger than ever. He washed his hands and changed his clothes once again. Now on his bed, he stared at the rock, which softly glowed. As his eyes closed, the face of the man stared back at him in his mind. It reminded him of a predator, watching and playing with its prey before finally pouncing.

CHAPTER 6

Alight hit Malik's face, making him feel home and welcome. He opened his eyes, thankful to find himself in his bed once again. His first thought went back to the chamber and the strange man within it–how had the chamber even appeared? How could he be sure it wasn't a dream?

He rolled over to get out of bed, reaching to grab his phone, and froze. Sitting on his nightstand was an amulet that wasn't there before, along with a card. He couldn't recognize it as he grabbed it. Looking at it in his palm with the chain dangling, it was now a light red gem, cut to fit a chain that had somehow been attached overnight. It was beautiful, somehow giving off a pulse; it looked remarkably like an eye. Next to it was a card, the only thing written on the envelope was *"Malik."*

He read it out loud. *"I'm sorry that we had to meet under such circumstances, but I hope you can forgive me, and we can look forward to formally getting to know each other. I am a friend of your family – we are family in a sense. This amulet you found has been passed down through your family line for generations;*

while you have retrieved it a little earlier than planned, you are its rightful heir, and I'm sure you will know best what to do with it. Sincerely, The Keeper."

He stuck on the last part the most–The Keeper. What did that even mean? Was he the Keeper of the family line, like a butler? He reached for the amulet and put it around his neck, it made him feel calm and at peace – like it was meant to be there.

As he stared down at it, his mom yelled from the bottom of the stairs. "Anomos, get up and get ready, you have an hour to get ready before you go to school."

"I'll be right there Mom, just let me get ready first," he yelled back, as he got up and looked around to find something to wear. He finally got up and started getting dressed; he chose to wear a graphic tee, gray hoodie, and green flannel with black jeans, decked out in a pair of sneakers. He added the necklace to his look; it now felt complete. Staring at himself in the mirror, he tried to fix his hair as best he could, but he never could get it the way he wanted it. He felt ready to face another day, with hopefully no new surprises.

Taking his time down the stairs today, his dad seemed to have already left for work and Nina sat in the living room, watching cartoons. He walked into the kitchen and grabbed some cereal out of the fridge, poured himself a bowl, and sat down. His phone chimed–a text from Jaden saying they needed to meet later in school. His mom sat across from him with her coffee in her hand, looking outside.

She let out a slight gasp when she saw the necklace around his neck. "Anomos, where did you get that necklace?"

Completely forgetting that he had left it hanging out, he almost choked on his breakfast in surprise. He swallowed roughly before replying, "I found it this morning on my nightstand. There was a card saying it belonged to our family."

"Yes, it's been in our family for generations, it's said to be an object of a very old king somewhere down our family line. I've heard stories of it, but I've never actually seen it myself, just in pictures." Her eyes became watery at the corners, as if she was remembering something from the past.

"Then why do I have it?" asked Malik, looking up at her, intrigued with the story.

She looked at him closely. "I guess it finally found its rightful owner. Someone must think you're worthy of it. Keep it safe and it will protect you."

Not sure how to take that, he chose to stay silent. He looked down at the amulet now in wonder. How could something so small have a big impact on his family history? There had to be a reason; why else was it underground in some dark and dungeon-y room, seeming to be waiting for him to find it? Though, it left the question of, why him? What made him so important?

The sound of keys being jiggled jerked him out of his thoughts; his mom, having finished her coffee, had grabbed her keys and now looked at him. "Come on, Anomos, I'll take you to school."

"Actually Mom, I'm going to take my board today, I need to clear my head and I don't need a ride home today either. Love you guys!" he said, stating the last part to both Nina and his mom.

Grabbing his board, he wanted to take his time to get to school, to truly enjoy the scenery. He was at school after only a few minutes, taking shortcuts to make sure he wasn't too late.

When he finally arrived, he searched for Jaden, but couldn't find him anywhere. Malik went over to his locker and started collecting all his books. Once done, he turned around and bumped into a girl, causing all her books to fly, and she went tumbling, too. Thankfully, his reflexes were fast as he caught her before she fell on her face. He slowly pulled her up, trying not to injure her in the process. When she was facing him, he recognized her from the events just a day previously– Elinam Johnson.

Realizing that they were both close to each other for too long, they blushed. The day previously he hadn't paid much attention to her appearance but now that she was with him, he had a better look. He noticed that she was only an inch or so shorter than him, she was wearing braids that fell to her shoulders and had an average high schooler build. She was an African American girl who he had heard was originally from Ghana but had been raised here almost all her life. She had an oval shaped face with flawless dark brown skin, she had dark brown eyes and brown lips. Eyes that seemed to be in a constant state of stress. She was wearing jeans and a shirt with a jacket.

He let her go, both of them backing away embarrassment written all over their faces. Elinam finally seemed to snap out of it and picked up her books. Still a little embarrassed, he helped her collect them. This was probably his most normal interaction in the past couple of days, and he smiled to himself, realizing that at least he was helpful to someone.

When they finally collected all her stuff. She was examining him, but for some reason, she didn't like what she saw and ran away with a scared expression.

Standing there dumbfounded, someone shook him, and Malik turned around to find Jaden looking at him in concern.

"You good, man? You look like you've seen a ghost." Jaden grew worried. "Don't tell me you can see ghosts? Because necromancers are forbidden."

Why would he be seeing ghosts all of a sudden? He shook his head. "No, Elinam just looked at me and ran away, and I didn't even do anything besides help her out."

Blinking at him, Jaden laughed at him for a few

minutes. He finally got ahold of himself and wiped away his tears. "I'm sure our problems don't deal with love and crushes right now, Malik."

"Wait, what problems?" he asked, anxious that some other disaster was about to happen, and life was officially out to get him.

"Well, our demon problem seems to be making every supernatural creature in our cozy home spooked and they're wondering what ties they have with you," Jaden answered. His voice had an edge to it that Malik hadn't heard before. Was Jaden worried about him?

"Am I in trouble or anything?" he asked fearfully.

"For now, all they can discern is that you're a regular who was in the wrong place at the wrong time, but I should let you know, ever since you've walked in today, I've been picking up an odd power coming off you, as though there's another person with you. Is there something you're not telling me?" Jaden asked.

After thinking about it for a moment, he decided to tell Jaden about what had happened the night before with the stone and the man that still made Malik's spine tingle whenever he thought of him. When he was all done, Jaden asked to see the necklace; when Jaden touched it, the color seemed to disappear, as if it was dying. Malik felt a sharp pain in his chest and his knees buckled. Jaden put it back on Malik's neck and the pain went away. Malik breathed a sigh of relief, though he had no clue what was happening.

"Well, that's undeniably a magic stone that's somehow bonded with you. Are you sure you're not supernatural?" Jaden asked in a defeated voice.

"Not that I know of, why? Am I gonna die if something happens to the stone?" he asked nervously. Was it some type of virus that slowly stole his soul or something?

"No, nothing like that, but you said the stone was passed down your family line, so at some point, someone in your family had some sort of supernatural connection," Jaden reassured him, seeing him start to panic a little.

Suddenly realizing who this could be, he admitted to Jaden, "My mom always talks about my great-grandfather, something about battling monsters, but I never really believed it, you know?"

"Well, there's only one way to find out. We'll have to talk to your mother when we get out of school. Let's just get through the day without any other incidents, please," Jaden stated, seeming to come to a decision.

Malik agreed; the more he knew about his family, the more answers could be learned. As much as he'd like for things to be the same as a couple of weeks ago, in the back of his mind he had this itch to find out the truth. He felt as though he needed to know, no matter how weird things got. He was completely terrified, but as long as he didn't start to glow or even grow claws, he could live with knowing.

They set out to find their classes before they were late; on the way there, he felt a shiver run down his neck, as if he was being watched. He kept turning to see who it was, but he could never find them.

He got through most of the day without any problems, though he did notice a lot more stares than usual, especially from Bianca and Maya. You'd think girls noticing him would make him happy, but it just gave him anxiety, as if he had a big zit on his face or something. Lunchtime couldn't have come sooner, and he headed over to sit with Jaden as usual.

What greeted him at the table was a surprise– surrounding their table were a big group of kids from his year and higher. Some of them were the most popular kids: Nico the star baseball player, Ji-Hoon the star soccer player, and even Simon the theater kid. He saw both Maya and Bianca among the group as well, and he quickly found out that there was a reason for all the popularity.

"I don't care Jay, my father is breathing down my neck to find out what's going on. Your mother and the Covenant aren't giving any answers. I don't trust anyone else's judgment but yours." Maya impatiently told Jaden, her voice slowly rising to match it.

"I'm sorry Maya, but I'm still getting the answers myself. Can you please be patient till I find out?" Jaden asked. He reached out, squeezing her wrist for a moment before letting go.

As Malik finally got behind everyone, Nico noticed him, but this time he chose to stay seated. Nico sniffed at the air and sort of growled under his breath, causing everyone at the table to stop talking, turning to Nico with confusion written all over their faces.

"Why does he smell of magic, specifically something old and somewhat demonic?" Nico asked Jaden, in a threatening voice.

"Keep your voice down, Nico, no need to start a riot. That's Malik, remember?" Jaden told him, gesturing with his hands to calm down.

"Answer my question, wizard. I dislike that smell, and it wasn't there a few days ago," Nico demanded, completely ignoring Malik's presence.

"Well, that's harder to answer. Malik, come sit down, and we can talk about this." Jaden sounded tired as he rubbed his neck.

Quickly scanning the table, he decided to sit in the chair closest to Jaden and furthest from Nico, who looked at him with a vile, loathing expression. Jaden explained everything they had learned so far; most of the group already seemed to know most of the information, but the new parts about the chamber and the amulet set all of them on edge.

"This reminds me too much of the old times; mortals shouldn't be dabbling in this stuff," Simon fearfully spoke up for everyone at the table. He was one of the guy's Malik had met in his classes.

Tired of being told what he could and couldn't do, Malik rudely told them, "Well, I'm sorry that I got attacked and shit keeps happening to me. If any of y'all wanna trade, let me know right now or shut up and help!"

Everyone at the table looked a little shocked, Jaden and Maya seemed to look at him in approval as if he had done something amazing, but Nico snapped at him again.

"Well, one of my people died for your actions. So, if you want forgiveness, it's not coming from me," Nico snarled back at him.

"I'm sorry, I didn't know, but what are you?" Malik asked, his frustration at an all-time high.

"Oh, yeah, I probably should give introductions," Jaden, turning to everyone at the table. "So, for everyone that wasn't aware of this before, this is Malik Blackwood. For everyone else at the table–Nico is a werewolf, the next in line to be the alpha of his pack and part of the Orem. Maya, and you've already met her sister Bianca, are part of the Paladins, also next in line for command. The rest are part of the Covenant or the other two groups."

"Whatever Jaden, what's our next move?" Maya asked impatiently, tapping her fingers on the table as she stared across the table at him.

"The plan is to talk to Malik's mother and find out what's going on. I have a feeling we're being left in the dark somehow and his mother can help us fill in the blanks,"

Jaden confidently stated.

Watching their interactions, he quickly saw that even though they were all big shots, they relied on Jaden for guidance. He led the group, even as the outsider. Everyone sighed in relief at Jaden's answer; Malik guessed being a powerful wizard had its perks as well as its downsides.

"Well, I'm coming with you, I'm tired of finding out information this way," Nico grunted, not taking no for an answer.

"If he's going, so am I. And I'm bringing Bianca – we already met his parents, so it should be easy," Maya told everyone in a voice that said no one was going to stop her.

Malik didn't know what to say, particularly about the part where she had already met his parents. He just nodded – he didn't want the werewolf or Paladin to get mad at him. Likewise, he didn't feel like making more enemies just yet.

Noticing that neither of them was going to back down, Jaden, defeated, said, "I guess that's it then, we'll head out after school. Meet at the front doors, I'll wait five minutes."

The rest of the day continued as if their meeting had never happened. As he sat in English class, playing with his new necklace, Malik wondered what it was and what it could do. He felt a warmth coming off the necklace as if it was alive. He touched it and it glowed for a second. Malik looked around to see if anybody had caught it, but no one paid him any mind.

"Hello, Master."

He looked around to see who was talking to him, but everyone was focused on class. He just shrugged his shoulders as if hearing things.

"I am Ento, and you are in danger."

Now he was without a doubt going crazy–no one was talking to him, and he was hearing it all in his head.

"I see you need proof."

One moment, he was sitting in his chair, and the next, he was *watching* himself in the chair. Malik in the chair looked awfully tired and needed sleep. He then turned to look at his hands, shocked to find they were translucent. He turned and saw a woman looking at him; she wore a white dress and was beautiful, as if she was an angel herself.

"I am Ento, and you are my master."

The women spoke to him, but he could only hear the words in his head, the voice he'd been hearing. His necklace now glowed a blinding white light. Somehow Ento was in his necklace, though he didn't know how that was possible.

Before he could ask, the room went dark, as if it was the night itself. The shadows reached out for him. He started to scream uncontrollably; the woman tried to help but it was no use. The darkness forced him to lose all rationality. As suddenly as it began, it was all gone, leaving him shaken.

"You see what I mean now, Master? I'll take you back, you may speak to me through your head right now, as it's best to not speak aloud."

All he could do was nod, and as suddenly as it began, he was back in his chair in the normal world. He felt like he'd hurl; he didn't want to experience anything like that ever again. Curiosity got the better of him as he tried reaching out with his mind to the voice, but he could only hear his heartbeat.

After a few more seconds, Ento spoke to Malik once again. *"Master, are you all right?"*

Trying to connect to the bodiless voice, he responded with his mind, *"I'm fine, just going a little crazy here."*

"Crazy, Master? I do not believe I understand this term."

It weirded him out that the voice could understand him but didn't understand the word crazy. *"What are you?"*

"I'm a being that was trapped by my original master and passed down throughout the years. I only live to serve the blood of the King."

A sadness came from the voice, and he felt that echo through his heart. *"How do I release you?"*

"Release? I have never had a master that wished to release me. I am a being with immense knowledge and power; most would use me to take over the world."

He chuckled out loud, earning weird looks from the rest of the class. He quickly apologized before going back to answer Ento, *"Well, if you can just make me normal again, trust me, I'd release you in a heartbeat."*

The voice was silent, then she answered, *"I am sorry Master, but I do not believe that is possible."*

Well, Malik had given it his best and he didn't know what else to do. *"Well, Ento, since it seems like we're stuck with each other for the moment, just call me Malik. This master stuff is too weird."*

"Ma-lik? Ahh yes, Mas- Malik, I can do that," the voice of Ento stammered.

After that, she was quiet throughout the rest of the period. Once the last class of the day ended, he set out to find the meeting spot. He found Jaden, Maya, Bianca, and Nico all waiting for him. Jaden greeted him warmly and Bianca just grinned at him, while the others offered a nod of recognition, which Malik returned.

"Well, let's go crew," Jaden said, "to finding answers and maybe some food too. I'm starving."

Malik joined Jaden in his laughter, which he could tell was a way to make everyone more relaxed, and it seemed to work somewhat. They exited the school premises and headed to Malik's home.

They all walked in silence, most preoccupied with their thoughts and what they might learn. Malik was speaking to Ento about her origins and what she could do. Her basic description of herself was a sort of grimoire in the form of a red emerald. She had served only two masters; she didn't tell him what happened to them, but he could only guess.

She did let on something she had discovered about Malik – that he was truly a supernatural creature, but she didn't say what or who he was. He started to worry and wonder how that was even possible. Trying to preoccupy himself after hearing this, Malik decided to walk with Bianca to get to know her some more. For some reason, he was drawn to her.

"So, Bianca, what do you like to do for fun?" Malik asked innocently, brushing against her shoulder slightly as he got next to her.

Bianca cocked her head to the side; she looked adorable when she did that. She replied with a smirk, "Besides fighting, I like to watch the stars sometimes. I want to touch them."

Surprise written all over his face, he smiled warmly. "We have a great skylight in our house. If you ever want to come by and watch some stars, I'd happily accompany you."

"I'd like that a lot." She smiled back at him, looking into his eyes.

Blushing fiercely from her stare, he had to turn his head to hide the smile that threatened to tear his mouth apart.

"If you're done flirting, we're here," Nico said, amused as he came up behind Malik.

Malik glanced behind his shoulder at Nico to give him

a hard look but found Maya's eyes boring into him with so much force that he quickly looked back to the front. When they arrived at Malik's house, he got to the front door, noticing it was slightly ajar. With a puzzled expression to the others, he pushed it further open.

The sight before them horrified the group. There he found his family inside, surrounded by five demons. They looked and felt a lot more deadly than the ones from before. One of them looked particularly hungrily at his little sister Nina.

CHAPTER 7

efore he could say anything, one of the demons spoke. "It is high time you arrived, Anomos Blackwood, and it seems you brought some friends."

"Demons, you are not allowed in here, go back home before we destroy you," Jaden demanded, rushing forward.

The demons in front of them were different from the ones Malik had fought in the woods. For one, they gave off an air of power, as if channeling something otherworldly. Their bodies were each different in ways that stretched the imagination and horrors of those around them. One of them had long arms as though they were pincers from an ant, with a humanoid lower body; it could almost be described as normal if not for its eyes. As in multiple–it had dozens of what seemed to be eyes on its face, as though watching their every move.

As the demon spoke, the sound that emerged was like scratching on a chalkboard, sending a tremor through everyone. "But you see, little wizard, we are welcome here; actually, we were invited by this very couple."

Malik's mom looked terrified, holding Nina tighter and pleading to him, "I can explain, Anomos, I'm so sorry."

The first demon chuckled darkly, as if it was having the time of its life, smacking its lips. As its tongue lapped out happily, drool dripped on the floor. "Explain away dear, we have all the time in the world."

"Your father and I tried to have children for years; we even thought about adoption at some point. You know the stories of your grandfather hunting monsters? I somewhat believed it, but I didn't think it'd be real. When we found this group that worshiped this old being, we thought, what's the worst that could happen? We thought we could just call the cops or run and hide if they ever caught us. We thought it was a cult, some nonprofit organization that helped fund pregnancies at first, they said they could help us have a baby … but in exchange for it, we had to give them our firstborn. Not believing them, we decided to go through with it, we were desperate. But there was no cult; it was all just one man, hiring individuals to act like a cult to hide his plans."

Imani's voice cracked, tears threatening to break out as she continued explaining. "Almost all our money was gone from trying to have kids, my career was at a dead-end and your father couldn't find enough work to keep both of us going. But we knew we wanted you in our lives, more than anything, Anomos. We love you! The moment I felt you kick; I knew you were special. Your father and I ran away from the powerful man and hoped we'd never hear from him again."

Shock was all Malik could feel right then; it sounded like he was the child of a demon or the Antichrist himself. While his parents didn't mean for any of this to happen, they were responsible for how things ended up.

In his mind, he heard Ento say, *"You're not alone, your parents love you. They were willing to risk everything for you and your sister to be here. I can tell you that much."*

Malik didn't feel remotely reassured of that whatsoever. They still had demons surrounding them. He wasn't sure if he felt anything besides confusion and terror.

"Well, I'm sorry to cut this heartwarming stuff short, but you're ours now, little Blackwood, our bargain cannot be betrayed. Our master has great plans for you," the third demon interrupted, tired of waiting.

Jaden reached over, touching Malik's shoulder, and his head became a little clearer. He glared at them with contempt.

"No, thanks, I'm not looking for demon dinner again. It's okay, Mom, I forgive you. You didn't mean for this to happen." It was their fault he had been attacked that night; he was almost a hundred percent sure of it.

The demons hissed angrily; one of them bared its uneven teeth at him, grinding them as it angrily spat at him, "You will be ours, little one, or else."

Unable to help herself, Bianca asked the group with

barely concealed excitement, "Can I keep one if I capture it? Please, Maya, just this once, you know I've always wanted a pet."

Maya looked at her sister as if she had grown an extra head, which was what the others clearly felt as well. "No, Bianca, we're sending them right back where they came from."

Pouting and seeming to be a little mad at Maya's answer, Bianca slowly grinned as if she had a mad idea and brought out a sword from god-knew-where, looking at the demons with malice written all over her face. The demons in turn backed up slightly from the crazed girl as if she had some weird disease they'd catch if they weren't too careful, which he greatly sympathized with; he was thankful she was on their side.

Leaning back confidently, Jaden crossed his hands as he stared at them. "Well, I guess that's your cue to get out."

The demons looked at each other in anger, noticing they weren't getting anywhere with them. All hell broke loose when Nico transformed into an eight-foot-tall beast with thick black fur and glowing red eyes.

Malik rushed to his family's aid while the others went to stop the demons from doing anything else. Nico held his own in a blur of teeth and claws; Bianca and her sister were tearing down the second demon to shreds, and Jaden cast spell after spell.

Jaden created a barrier around Malik and his family in

between all of that. It felt as though it was an invisible wall between them and everyone else. They seemed to be winning–until more demons seemed to come out of midair. Ten more came and everyone became preoccupied with taking them down, but there were too many. Malik helped his family get into the kitchen area where the fighting wasn't taking place, but he saw his friends in trouble and wanted to go back and help them. He checked over his family, seeing they were all right; his mom sobbed quietly, and his father held Nina with a sad look. His dad saw Malik's expression and just nodded, like he understood Malik's need to help.

He turned back to his friends and reached out to Ento, hoping she had any advice.

"Know anything that I could use to help me out?" Malik asked.

"Well, Malik, I know many things, you would have to be specific," Ento answered.

"I mean a weapon or something." Malik was desperate for anything.

"Oh, well of course I do. Use this," Ento said in what Malik could describe best as glee; it made him nervous.

A dark blue sword with symbols engraved on it appeared in his hand. It felt natural in his hands, as though the sword was made to be lightweight. Everyone stopped what they were doing to look at him and the mysterious sword in his hands. They all seemed shocked, which he welcomed greatly as it gave him a chance amid the confusion, and he dove into the fight.

His body moved instinctively, swinging his sword around. The first demon came at him from the side; Malik sidestepped and swept his sword in an arc, slashing the blade across its chest.

Ento advised him, *"Go for its head, that's the best way to kill it."*

Taking her advice, he executed his next move in one fell sweep, cutting the leg down first and then bringing it down to the head. He felt a thrill come over his body and he continued to attack the other demons; everyone was back to action, able to move on pure instinct.

Malik and Jaden went back-to-back at some point and over the fighting, Jaden yelled, "Well, aren't you full of surprises!"

Laughing, having the time of his life, Malik shrugged. "What can I say? I aim to please and seem to be doing well."

"Well, let's think about that after we win," Jaden said with a grin, going back to taking down a demon with unnecessarily long claws that retracted and extended.

Even Nico and Bianca worked together to take down the tougher demons attacking them. Nico would throw the demons Bianca's way, and she would put them down. The only person that didn't seem to need help at all was Maya – Malik could tell she was an expert at killing, and he had a feeling if she had to put him down, she would without hesitation.

One of the demons bound for his family, but everyone was preoccupied with their problems. Somehow, the barrier had gone down without any of them noticing. His dad tried to protect the family but was thrown into a wall and fell to the floor, unconscious. The same thing happened to his mom. His sister was scared and started crying; the demon wrapped its hand around her, holding her tightly.

"MALEEK!" she screamed at the top of her lungs.

The demon looked straight at Malik and venomously hissed, "If we can't have the firstborn, I'm sure the master will prefer the second one just as much."

Immense rage filled Malik, and his body felt unbearably hot before going cold. All around Malik, the shadows around the room flickered and reached for him. Malik remembered that feeling he had the first night, but it was unlike what he was experiencing right now; this felt alien and detached, as though something else was trying to take him over. All he cared about was getting his sister back, no matter what it took, and he quickly lost all reason. He brought his sword up, and it was wrapped in a black impenetrable mist; he swung it in a slash and the shadows followed that movement as if it was an extension of his arm. The slash left a great big scar in the middle of the room, destroying everything in its path.

"Try to calm down," Ento told him, *"Please stop Malik, you don't know what you're doing, you're going to hurt someone."*

In a voice he didn't recognize as himself, Malik snarled aloud, "That's exactly my plan, Ento. Either you help me or stay out of my way."

The demon had started to fade out from existence. From behind him, Jaden tried to stop the disappearance with a lightning bolt that seemed to touch Malik's sister but didn't do anything to stop the disappearance.

Then a ghost appeared in the room and grabbed her before she disappeared. The ghost, for his part, had an arm that belonged to the demon, its blood dripping on the floor with a dark red pool emerging. His hand also sported a large, jagged cut from the demon he had assaulted to retrieve Nina. Malik was shocked to see who the ghost was – Andy, now holding Nina as she cried in his arms.

"Andy! How are you alive?" Maya asked in confusion.

The man smiled weakly at them before collapsing with Nina in his arms. Malik's mom, having just become conscious again, quickly reached for her crying daughter and held her as Nico took care of Andy, holding him up.

Malik's heart broke; he couldn't handle the power anymore. He had all this power but felt completely powerless; even with all these other people with him, he wasn't able to save the one thing he cared more about than his own life – his family. He barely even noticed his power was overflowing and seeping out in every direction. All the remaining demons ended up taking the brunt of it, silently screaming in agony as they were pulled down by the shadows, their screams quieted with their disappearance.

The shadows reached for Malik again, but instead of attacking him, they seemed to caress him, as if to comfort him in his time of great need. Before the shadows disappeared, they whispered "Anomos" to him.

Everyone stood there in shock as if they couldn't believe what had happened. Jaden rushed over to his side. "Everything's going to be all right."

"How do you know, Jaden?" Malik whispered, defeated. "They might come back for me or Nina again."

"We'll make sure that doesn't happen, I promise," Jaden assured him, his tone comforting. It seemed he meant it.

Somehow that made him feel a little better; there were people out there that would fight for his family just as much as he would. He let out a sigh of relief; he was going to protect his family and find out who this master was – and teach them a lesson they would never forget.

He rushed over to his family and helped them get back on their feet. Imani looked broken, and Virgil looked just the same. She looked at Malik as if she didn't recognize him.

"Will someone please tell me what's going on?" she demanded, looking around her house at all the damage they'd caused.

"Well, we would also like to know too," Nico added, having turned back into his human form. His clothes seemed to be back as well.

Maya and Nico appeared back in the living room after taking care of Andy. Andy didn't come up behind them, making Malik wonder where went. Jaden waved his hand and the damage to the house disappeared, as if it never happened. His parents looked at Jaden with terror.

Jaden looked over at Malik's parents. "Why don't you start again at the beginning, Mrs. Blackwood? I think we can fill in the rest of the blanks from there."

Inside Malik's mind, Ento seemed to be intrigued as well, and even told Malik to get something for his parents' nerves for the story to be told. He made some tea for them.

Imani, after calming her nerves, said in a more leveled tone, "You may want to sit for this, Malik, your friends are going to be here for a while."

She took a deep breath before beginning. "I guess I should tell you that this all-started thousands of years ago."

Everyone got comfortable. Jaden sat on the edge of the counter, while Nico sprawled on the mini couch. The two sisters sat on the last empty couch, while Malik decided to sit on the floor. Virgil held Imani's hand while she told the story, with Nina in her lap.

"My side of the family has always had some influence in the supernatural world. I guess you should know we came from a long line of knights previously known as the Knights Templar; we did a lot of good, but all good things come to an end. When your great-great-great-grandfather defeated a witch, we were placed with a curse that we couldn't have children from any females in our line, and if we did, any male child would die by the age of seventeen. We're currently the last remaining line of Blackwood's that still have the curse; most went crazy with grief and couldn't handle living anymore."

Imani stopped speaking to wipe away a tear. Her voice was filled with so much grief and sadness. Malik now thought back to why he didn't know anyone from his mother's side of the family.

"Your great-grandfather somehow was able to skip the curse; it was said he had almost died, but somehow came back to life when he was just the age of thirteen. He had almost drowned; I guess when you're at Death's door, it takes a part of you. He lived to old age and somehow was able to pass down that mark to my grandfather, though they both had Alzheimer's in their old age."

She took a moment to squeeze Virgil's hand, and they shared a loving look between them as she continued.

"When I met your father, I fell in love instantly and knew I wanted to be with him. I thought it was only right to tell him our family history and let him decide to spend his life with me or not. I'm grateful that he was so understanding and deeply in love with me, just as I am of him. We tried to have children for two years to no avail, and when all hope seemed lost, we were approached by a man that said he could help us have children.

"At first, we didn't trust him, but his silky-smooth words wore us down. We ended up believing him, and with his help, we were able to have you, but this man seemed to be obsessed with us, or more with you, before you were even born. When we found out that this man had a clinic that wasn't meant for sperm research, but sacrifices, we contacted the authorities, but the authorities seemed to be in the pocket of this man. We knew there wasn't much for us to do, so we just packed everything and left.

"The reason we always moved around a lot was that we thought if this man was coming, we would pack up and leave. I found out about this place, where both the supernatural and humans are protected. My family had ties here, so we contacted the mayor and told her our situation. She promised us she could protect us – she had a powerful wizard with her and would make sure the man wouldn't even touch us." Imani breathed deep, indicating she'd finished the story.

Everyone absorbed all of it. Bianca went up to her and hugged her deeply. "You must have been terrified, always having to look over your shoulder."

Malik's mom nodded while she sobbed in Bianca's arms. Jaden and Malik looked at each other; they both had unanswered questions.

"Mom, can I ask what this necklace is?" Malik in a quiet voice.

Imani got ahold of herself. "It's something our family has been protecting for thousands of years. It's said to have been imbued with the soul of a fallen angel and gives the owner immense power. Somewhere down our line, someone used it to stop a great war, but that's all I know. It was originally the possession of a demon king. I don't know why it chose you, Malik, but please be careful. All great power eventually corrupts."

"So, let me get this straight, you're from a family of the old mystical order of knights and have a magical amulet that was originally owned by some demon king? Does no one else see how dangerous Malik is?" Nico asked in alarm, sitting up straighter and looking at everyone.

"Until I see him doing things that make me question his humanity, you will do nothing, werewolf," Maya commanded.

"Ento?" Malik reached out.

"Yes, Malik?"

"Are you a fallen angel?"

"Yes, the reason I fell was because I fell in love with someone I shouldn't have," Ento admitted in a sad, pained voice.

*"*Malik?" Jaden asked, alarmed.

*"*Yes?"

"I called your name four times now, you looked

spaced out. Are you okay, man?"

He looked around the room. There was no point in hiding Ento anymore. He cleared his throat. "There's something you guys should know about my necklace."

He proceeded to tell them what he had learned from Ento and could tell this all made them unsettled, especially his parents.

"I've never heard of the amulet ever speaking to its host like this," Imani said in a scared voice.

"It sounds to me like she's more of a grimoire than an instrument of evil. Just advises and helps you in any way possible," Jaden said in an assuring but sad tone. Malik remembered his best friend didn't have his own grimoire.

"Well, what's our plan of attack, guys?" Malik asked to preoccupy them with something else to do.

"You have to find the demon king's tomb," said a voice from behind them.

Everyone jumped in fear, having completely forgotten about Andy; he must have come through the side door. His arm had completely healed, no longer bleeding, and he stood raggedly at the edge of the living room. He leaned on his sword for support.

"Excuse me, what?" Nico asked, genuinely dumbfounded.

Andy stepped forward, obviously in pain, but ignoring it as best he could.

"Wait, how are you still alive? I thought the Sergeant

had confirmed your death?" Malik was bewildered by the man, still feeling like he was talking to a ghost.

Andy gave a small smile to Malik. "Sorry for doing that to you, but I had to make sure the demons didn't come back for sure to attack you. It was best to hide until Jaden had given me the signal."

Malik then turned to Jaden, who just shrugged and looked away. How had Jaden hidden something that had been tormenting Malik for days now? Malik shook his head, thoroughly surprised by his friend's secrecy. He had to ask Jaden some other time when they weren't busy.

"So, what about this tomb?" Malik asked, making sure to direct it at Andy.

"Jaden and I have this theory, which is greatly boosted by the fact that you have one of the pieces of the Demon King's grimoire. You're the intended incarnation of this demon; if you can find the tomb, then you'll be able to put a stop to the demon attacks," Andy reluctantly admitted to everyone.

"Wait, who is the Demon King? My mom mentioned it but not much else," Malik asked everyone, hoping for an answer.

"All you need to know right now about the Demon King is he commanded legions to his cause, and like most cases, the more someone believes in something, the greater the losses," Andy explained, a pained expression on his face. "He's infamously known as the King of Darkness, for taking in all and any creatures of darkness in his crusade."

"How can you be sure that he is this so-called incarnation?" Virgil spoke up for the first time, looking at Andy in curiosity.

"Well, we did some research on the cult and the man who promised to give you a kid, and we found out they were trying to bring back the Demon King," Andy said. "They've been actively working toward bringing him back, possibly to gain power. I believe that they somehow found a way to reincarnate him using his bloodline, and seeing that Malik is the only living male relative left, he's their only choice. Who knows if they'll give up on obtaining the most important part of their plan?"

"So, you're saying they'll keep attacking to get Malik or his family to go to him and to be their savior, or we go on the offensive to find the tomb first and what, make Malik the Demon King for them?" Maya analyzed out loud.

Andy shook his head. "It's better if we find it and destroy the tomb ourselves. I don't think they know where the Demon King died themselves, or they wouldn't have come after Malik's family so carelessly like this."

"I say we just kill him now before it's too late," Nico suggested, which everyone chose to ignore.

"They say that the tomb of the Demon King has many wonders, even the power to give immortality," Jaden said in wonder, looking away as if imagining something.

Nico looked at Jaden intensely. "Even bring back the

dead?"

That caused both the sisters to look at Jaden as if he was the most important person in the world. Jaden slowly nodded. "Possibly–at the prime of the King's reign, he was able to bring many of his warriors back from death. There might be something there that could do just that."

"How do you know so much?" Malik asked, curious as to how Jaden was so well-informed.

"Well, I've been looking for something that I need for myself, and I was always interested in the history of our world, especially the hidden one," Jaden explained.

Once again, Malik could tell that he wasn't saying everything. Maya, Bianca, and Nico all nodded as if they knew something Malik didn't, which greatly irritated him, but chose to let it go, telling himself everyone had their right to keep secrets.

Andy cleared his voice. "I think all of you guys should go with Malik; he needs all the help he can get, plus you might come out stronger than what you are now."

That seemed to solidify everyone's commitment to helping Malik. Malik, for his part, was dumbfounded as he absorbed everything around him. Was he really an incarnation of a Demon King, who had possibly killed many people? All Malik wanted was to make sure his family was safe, not go on an adventure that might leave him worse than he was now.

"Malik, we have a problem," Ento urgently said.

Malik jerked in alarm, and everyone watched Malik in confusion, unsure of what was happening.

"What's the problem?"

"During the fight, you expanded quite a bit of energy, allowing me to see into your source and there's a demon in here. If you can find the tomb, then maybe I could help you get rid of it. It seems they did indeed implant a demon inside you."

Malik groaned. So there *was* a demon in him, confirming Andy and Jaden's theory. Now he had another big problem on his hands; he needed to get rid of whatever was in him before it grew to be a problem. Everyone seemed to be invested in the tomb; hopefully, they would do something that could save him. He didn't want to become a monster that would attack his own family.

He looked at Andy with determination in his eyes. "I'll do it, I'll find this demon king's tomb and destroy it. All I want to do is live in peace. If I can live in peace after everyone gets what they want from this place, then I'll go, but someone needs to protect my family while I'm gone."

Andy nodded. "I'll be here to watch over them as well as others; nothing will happen to them while I still breathe, I promise that."

Andy brought out his sword and a wave of power rushed through everyone. The most shocking thing then happened – the sword spoke, at least in their minds.

"We will protect your family child, for we are the Guardians of this city. I have had many wielders throughout the century,

but each has the same goal, in the end, serving the people of this city. We are the blade that sings in the day and shines in the night, the Guardian." The sword spoke with a voice so ancient and immensely powerful, it felt like the voice was all-knowing.

Andy put his sword away, nearly passing out, but Nico caught him. Malik was now sure his family would be safe from harm. He quickly thanked Andy, who just nodded his acknowledgment.

Malik looked over to everyone else in question, unsure how to proceed. "What do we do now?"

"Well, first we need to get some rest and energy back up. Tomorrow we'll go to the Covenant with the information we now have and plan a strategy for how to get to the tomb, as well as stop that master of theirs," Jaden advised them, getting up from the counter.

"Why can't we go now?" Malik's concern for his family outweighed everything.

"Because, Malik, we have to weigh our best options without anyone getting seriously hurt, and you need to be better trained before we can do anything before you become a liability to us all," Maya said.

"I'm sorry, Malik, but they're right, we have to leave it to the professionals at this stuff," his mom agreed.

Malik shook his head in anger; he wasn't being put on the sidelines now. "I'm sorry, but if you're going to this meeting, then so am I. I'm not going to let some pompous people decide my fate without me having some input."

Everyone nodded as if they understood and got up, ready to head out. Maya turned around to Bianca. "Bee, you stay behind, protect Malik and his family while I turn in my report."

Bianca just nodded and settled in to help Malik's mom make some dinner, while the others went to the door. Nico looked at Malik grimly. "Well, it was nice to fight with you, little pup, maybe you're not bad, after all. I'll let the pack know that I stand with you on the plan."

Appreciating Nico's statement, he reached out to shake his hand. His grip was firm. Malik realized having a pack with him when it came down to the fight would be great, especially after seeing the power he had displayed earlier.

Malik turned to Maya and saw her serious expression. "While it may not seem that I care, I greatly do," she admitted, "when all of this is over, we're going to find out why you're so important to them and whether or not you're a threat, but for now we'll side with you."

Saliva got stuck in his throat, causing him to gulp deeply; he didn't want to think too hard on it. All he cared about right now was finding the tomb; whatever problems he had, he'd face later. He nodded to Maya, and she went on her way, disappearing into the night as if she was never there to begin with. Jaden and Malik stayed at the doorway, watching her go.

Jaden looked back at Malik. "She's not too bad once you know her, she just cares deeply for everyone in this town."

"You guys used to date, right?"

"Yeah, but her father didn't approve of it – something about tainting the family tree. It has nothing to do with my father, surprisingly, but more to do with the fact that I have witch blood in my veins."

Malik patted his friend on the shoulder to comfort him. Sometimes life had its way of letting you know your life truly sucked. Jaden shook his head and said with a smile, "We'll figure this out, Malik, don't worry too much about it."

Malik nodded back and looked at his friend knowing he truly believed it, too. Jaden stepped outside and with a wave of his hand, disappeared in thin air.

"I gotta learn how he does that," Malik chuckled.

"You can do that too, Malik, and more."

"Really, how?" Malik asked.

"Well, one thing I don't know is what exactly you are, but I can tell you have great potential in learning something like that. It's up to you on how you use it," Ento excitedly commented.

He turned around to find Bianca watching him with concern. His cheeks flushed when he saw her looking. She looked away with an awkward smile.

"Not today Ento, another day," Malik replied.

Walking up to Bianca, he noticed his parents had gone

back to their room and left them alone.

They both stood there for a moment in silence before Malik broke it. "You want to see the sky?"

CHAPTER 8

She nodded enthusiastically and he led them to the room where they could see through the skylight. There was a staircase on the side that led to a railing that let people have a better view than the one from the ground. They walked up there and watched the sky for a while in silence. The stars were out tonight, as well as the crescent moon. He threw side glances at her to see her watching the sky, memorized in wonder. It was nice to see someone admire something he was used to seeing at this point.

Turning her head away from the stars, Bianca, looking over him, said, "It makes you sometimes wonder, if others are also looking up and looking back at us, too."

He raised his eyebrows in surprise. To find that she had more than one side to her made her an interesting person to be around. That was something he couldn't say about most people.

"I didn't think of that, always thought we were alone out here," he admitted, not believing that aliens had ever existed. There was only so much you could believe in before you outgrew it.

"You never know, there are parallel worlds, maybe there are worlds out there just beyond our reach," she said.

Parallel worlds? Now he didn't know what to believe, but maybe he could ask her some other time. He shook his head in wonder at the things she could possibly know that existed that he'd never even heard of.

"You haven't been out there yet?" he jokingly asked, surprised a little that she didn't try to go to find out for herself.

"No, I haven't. Possibly once Maya takes over, I can just quit this life and begin my search," Bianca spoke wistfully.

Curiosity made him ask, "What exactly are you guys?"

"Oh, I thought Jaden already told you. Paladins are a large group of individuals, each with some ties to supernatural descendants, that work to make sure the Veil between the human and supernatural stays a secret. Don't you ever wonder why there's never a big news story about a Kraken destroying a big city?"

He had never really known monsters existed or seen proof of them. Sure, his mom talked about his great-grandfather seeing them, and he read about them, but seeing was believing, and he hadn't seen anything that could confirm they existed–till now.

"I guess you're right, I never have," he admitted to her.

"Exactly, we're the ones that clean up any unnecessary messes that the public could know about. It's something that we take pride in. Personally, my family has direct ties to one of the fallen angels, so we take it as part of a responsibility to clean up the messes. Our dad is currently the head of all of North America branch, so our family will probably inherit the legacy after him."

"Wow, I didn't know that, is it something you want?"

"No, it's something I've always wanted to avoid. I'm not the firstborn, so I'm not riddled with the responsibility of possibly taking over the role. I honestly think Maya was made for it; she seems to be able to do everything right. You'd think a sixteen-year-old could have trouble adapting to this, but ever since our mom passed away, she's taken on so many roles in her life. What's one more to her?" she told him, shaking her head in wonder at the type of sister she had.

He nodded at her, thinking it was kind of sad that Maya didn't get to live her life either, but he understood where she was coming from. Some people were born for certain things; some could naturally be leaders, while others would have to learn on the go. She was just unlucky in some way–at least Bianca got to live her life instead.

"Is it hard being here?" he asked, trying to find another topic to talk about.

"It's not that I hate it, but if I had a choice… I want to be able to look at the stars more freely, but duty calls."

Malik saw what she meant, to be able to be free to choose the life you wanted and not have others decide it for you.

"Don't you just want to let go of all your problems and just lose yourself to the stars?" Bianca asked.

"As a kid, I used to imagine myself as the man on the moon," Malik answered.

"Trust me, the moon's even beautiful up close," Bianca assured him, sounding as if she knew from firsthand experience.

He stared at Bianca; she had a look of pure bliss on her face as if she truly had gotten to see the moon and visit it. Right now, this girl, with so much training to kill monsters and protect the people of this town, looked like any other girl hanging out with a guy.

"Well, maybe next time I can go see it with you."

Bianca looked at him and smiled the most beautiful smile Malik had ever seen. Malik was so struck by her look. He liked this girl.

"I'd love that." Bianca smiled brightly.

They made some small talk about their lives, the things they loved and feared in life. The places Malik had been to fascinated Bianca, who had never left this town. Malik found himself truly at peace with this girl, as if she was like him, an explorer at heart.

"One day, when this is all over, I'm going to show you the most amazing place to look at the stars. They feel like they're right next to you, you could reach out and touch them," he promised, both to her and himself that he would do that.

"Wow, I can't wait, Malik!"

She turned back to look at the stars, and Malik couldn't help but watch *her* watch the stars. It was the most perfect and peaceful moment he had in so long. He tried to hold on to that feeling for just a little longer.

Her head snapped to the left. "My sister wants me back," she cried out in disappointment.

"Oh, okay." Malik was disappointed as well.

After another moment he led Bianca to the door, and before she left, Bianca kissed him on his cheek. "Thank you for letting me see the stars. I hope I can see them again."

All he could do was stand there and blush fiercely, the lingering feeling of her lips remaining. They felt so soft and warm on his cheeks, and he wondered what it would be like to kiss her.

"Well, you're always welcome to come back whenever you want," Malik earnestly answered.

Bianca's cheeks flushed pink, and she nodded, disappearing into the night. Malik watched her go for a minute before closing the door. He headed to his room, thinking about the moments he'd spent with Bianca, and fell asleep with a smile on his face.

After Malik fell asleep, he went back into the darkness like before, but this time the shadows seemed to have crept closer and were waiting for him. The shadows surrounded him as if they wanted him. Malik recalled having experienced this a while ago, and he still felt edgy from it all.

While the shadows reached for Malik, he noticed a figure, which looked oddly like himself, but was far away for some reason. It seemed to be wrapped in a cocoon of darkness itself; he noticed a bit of black substance leaking from the figure.

"Well, when they say we all have a monster in us, it wasn't meant to be literal," a woman said next to Malik.

He was shocked he didn't notice her before and looked at her closely. He felt like he knew this woman for some reason, then realized she had the same voice as Ento.

"Ento, is that you?"

"Yes Malik, it is in your subconscious, I'm able to fully manifest myself into a form that I previously had."

The form in question was vivid in detail, the perfect picture of a woman who claimed to be once an angel. She even had wings that were silver, with gray tips at the ends of them.

"Why am I here?" Malik asked.

Ento looked at Malik in concern. "When you reached out with that power from earlier with the shadow calling, you somehow beckoned your own demon forward."

"*My* demon?"

She flourished her hand toward the darkness and the

mysterious figure surrounded by it. "This is your Source, your own realm in a sense. It's a type of house for your soul, though it does seem to be fractured in some way. Your house of power … my theory is your parents didn't know that when they agreed for you to be born, the man implanted a demon seed inside you to one day take over you and eventually rule the world."

"A what?" Malik asked.

"It's a demon, I noticed something odd while getting a read on it. It almost felt like you, but not you at the same time."

He wanted nothing more than to get as far as possible from this place. A demon seed sounded like bad news and if the others ever found out, he'd be dead in less than a week.

"How bad is it?"

"Well, it hasn't taken you over yet, though surprisingly, it already seems like it's fully grown."

"How do I stop it from taking over?" Malik asked.

"Well, through will alone. Don't let the power consume you and never for a second let your guard down," Ento advised him.

He thought it was easier said than done. He reminded himself of the feeling he'd had when he used its power, overwhelming and intoxicating.

"How can I stand in my power when I have nothing?" Malik rebutted.

Ento remained silent for a minute. "Well, this is your source of power, it's not coming from the demon, this is all you. You shape it how you see fit."

He stared at Ento as if she was crazy, but maybe it was possible to shape something. Malik considered how he wanted to see his Source and imagined being back in New York, the bustling city that never truly slept. Slowly started to notice the darkness recede and the image of New York appeared in front of him. Too shocked by what he did, the image disappeared. Malik tried again, this time holding on to the image in his head, and finally, Malik was back in New York. Malik was beyond happy with his discovery. Ento was next to him, smiling the whole time like a proud parent.

Turning his face toward Ento in a childish giddiness, he asked, "What else can I do?"

She smiled wider. "So many things, Malik. You're almost as powerful as your friend Jaden in your own right, even if it is in a different aspect."

Ento continued to tell him things and showed him some things he could do. She explained that while he had a great Source, it didn't make him utterly powerful and godlike; there were many beings out in the world with power just as great as his or more. Not many people could access their house of power, especially people like Malik, who were supposedly not altogether supernatural. Malik needed to learn how to fight and harness his power if he ever wanted a chance for peace in his life.

Ento explained that Sources were usually something great to learn about, but he could still run out of power and energy if he didn't learn how to gain more power, actively adding more into his Source as well. Actively adding more power was dangerous – if it led to an imbalance of energy, it could outright kill him, but if he learned to give and take energy, then he would be at a great advantage over others. She believed Malik had a closer connection to demons than she'd originally thought, especially since one now housed within him.

Ento explained that demons came in different levels. "You see, demons long ago fought each other to gain power, much like werewolves and other shifters. They gained power after taking down alphas; the demon world is much the same. It's a bloody give and take of power; before the Courts were established, many demons died or were enslaved to one another."

Malik was curious about demon history. "What changed?"

Ento looked away. "The Demon King did, when he took control of the demon realm, he established rules and guidelines, which I believe are still active to this day. The King realized he needed to create a system to unite the demons, creating four different classes: lesser demons, greater demons, arch-demons, and princes of hell. The Court of Hell is ruled by the Princes of Hell, who are politicians overseeing everything, while the lesser demons under them are their charges. Other demons are considered to be equal to the Princes, but they have no sway in the courts. While in the demon realm, no demon is allowed to kill a demon two grades below them but allows them to be servants of those demons. But if demons of a lesser grade attack each other outside the realm, it's free game. Though that doesn't mean lesser demons won't attack stronger ones, as long as the lesser demon attacks first, the stronger demon is allowed to defend itself, allowing for the loophole to kill or worse to the weaker one."

"What's the difference between the demons?"

Ento smiled, her purpose being fulfilled by helping the young master. "Ah, the lesser demons are ones such as imps, fiends, shadows – weak creatures with almost no intelligence. Greater demons are more intelligent, even cunning; they range in size and abilities, but the most noticeable attribute about them that separates them from the archdemons is the fact they can't change shape. Archdemons are something to be terrified of, they are almost equal to the Princes; they are one of the best strategists and schemers and play the long game. They are usually the ones that make humans sign away their souls and much more. If it wasn't for the rules set in place, they would have probably rebelled against the princes a while ago. The Princes of Hell are nine, much like the nine levels of Hell from many religions; they are the dictators of the realm, second only to the Queen. They usually play games with humans and other creatures; they are considered to be stronger than the angels, sad to say."

"Queen? I thought you said there were only Princes." Malik stared at Ento in confusion.

"It's considered an unspoken rule that the Queen keeps the Princes in check and makes sure earth isn't overrun with them. Though they sometimes slip out; I'm not sure if they have a Queen currently, as they tend to get killed regularly. Demons don't like being ruled, something of a problem for them. Must be from the Heavenly War days."

Malik was stunned, lost to what she was saying.

"There's also the Fallen, but they don't count, honestly. After the war, most of them left this world, though some of them stayed and remained hidden for some unknown reason," Ento mused, mostly to herself.

"Do you regret it?" Malik asked, remembering Ento's previous life.

Ento looked longingly at the sky before answering. "Some days I miss my home, but in the end, it worked out. I got to meet you and that's worth the sacrifice."

Malik smiled at her; even though he knew she missed her old life, he hoped to one day repay her by giving her a new one.

"Enough about this, let's get back to training you," Ento cleared her head, emerging from her thoughts.

As she explained it, his Source may be immense at this

moment, but he hadn't used it for almost sixteen years of his life. Since his connection and ability to draw any power from it would be slim at best, she suggested to not do anything too big, especially with a demon so close to his very house of power. She explained that early in learning about his Source, he should be careful to not become too unbalanced in his life because it would affect the growth of himself, and it would then harm his source as well since it was a reflection of him. Malik was a fast learner, trying his best to absorb everything he could and Ento explained to him even if it felt like days, he was only asleep in his room for a couple of hours.

"Unlike your friend Jaden, who uses himself as a medium to influence things, you're able to impose your will on and shape things. If you wish it to rain, just direct your will outwards, and it will rain," Ento explained. She paused, appearing to listen to something too far away for him to hear.

"Your mother's going to wake you up soon, Malik, I'll leave you to practice. You should know this is a form of training called dream-walking; many magic users use this to train their young during times of war, and they need to pass down the knowledge."

"Are we going to war, Ento?"

"I don't want to be the bearer of bad news, Malik, but we need to protect your family and find the tomb. We may have to rely on that demonic side of yours, and if others find out, we'll have to fight for our lives."

"I don't want to hurt anyone, Ento," Malik admitted.

"I know you don't, but I refuse to let anyone hurt you, Malik. I'm sorry, but you're not just a master to me, but a friend. I'll do whatever it takes to protect you," Ento proclaimed with force.

With that, Ento opened her beautiful wings and disappeared into the sky, leaving him alone for a minute processing it all. It might take him and the demon in him to survive everything. What did it truly mean to be a monster?

Malik heard his mom calling to him and started to fade away from his Source and back to reality. Malik didn't notice that under his feet, his shadow twisted and grew in the form of a monster, rather than his usual appearance.

With a start, he jerked awake. Opening his eyes completely, he saw his mom and Jaden were next to him, trying to wake him up.

"Wake up, we got a big day ahead of us." Jaden was cheerful, wearing a bright smile.

"What's going on?" Malik asked.

"Jaden came by earlier this morning to give us the news from Covenant, but he wanted to let you sleep," Imani explained.

Malik sat up, his mind now fully awake and paying attention to everything. This was the news he'd been dreading to hear all night.

"The good news is that they're willing to hear us out, but they want to talk to you specifically. I guess I couldn't expect Maya to leave out the shadows coming out of nowhere out of her report to her group." Jaden groaned, shaking his head in frustration.

Sweat started to drip off him, as he grew nervous; the shadows weren't a part of his power, but the demon in him. He couldn't tell these people that without having a mob come at him with pitchforks or whatever supernatural beings used, though. Malik could tell he needed to tell someone, and Jaden was trustworthy.

"I agree, Malik, we need allies," Ento agreed wholeheartedly.

He looked around and saw the clothing he wanted and willed the idea of having the set of clothing on his body. His body ached as if he was using a muscle he had never even used all his life. It was like moving his toes individually while simultaneously balancing on a board with one foot. As a few more minutes passed, he felt his vision blur; he guessed he couldn't expect perfection on his first try.

One minute he was half-naked; the next, he was in his usual attire of cargos and graphic tee, sporting an old-style coat that he didn't remember willing on him, but surprisingly felt like a natural look to him. What he didn't expect was his shirt to be inside out and his socks to be mismatched. As he looked down at his clothes, he felt something drip out of his nose. Looking at his hands as he watched something bright red splatter on his hand in surprise, and he quickly wiped it away.

Jaden just stared at him with an eyebrow raised in slight amusement as if he knew what was going on and grabbed a tissue from his desk. His mom, on the other hand, looked shaken from his display of power.

"Well, you have something to tell me?" Jaden asked in an amused tone.

"Mom, can you leave me and Jaden alone for a minute?" Malik asked politely.

His mom nodded her head and headed out of the room, but not before casting another glance at Malik, as well as his attire.

"Well, how should I put it? I have magic, too," Malik sheepishly remarked, rubbing his neck.

"Malik, I know magic and that wasn't even remotely it. I can detect magic users when it flows through them. No, you bent time and space in some way. That's close to god-level or in your case, demon-level," Jaden disagreed, shaking his head.

He gave Jaden a wide-eyed look; he could tell Jaden knew, but not for how long.

"I've been able to detect it ever since you got the amulet. Remember when I touched it back at school? I was able to separate it long enough to look into your soul with soul sight. It's something I've been working on creating myself. I noticed immediately that there was a being in the necklace, as well as something dark and murky inside you as if it was trying to evade my sight, but after the fight yesterday, I've confirmed it," Jaden stated.

"So, what are you gonna do now, report me?" Malik asked.

Jaden just looked at Malik and laughed, shaking his head in disagreement. "No, I'm not, it's your life. You get to choose who you want to be in this world, not something inside you."

"What if it wins … my demon, I mean?"

"We all fight our demons inside us, they can win today, but that doesn't mean they'll win tomorrow. We just have to find the strength we had again to keep fighting." Jaden seriously told him.

He was shocked by his friend's words; he truly did understand things in ways Malik never could. Malik got up slowly and went to Jaden, reached over, and hugged him tightly. Malik felt like a weight had been lifted off his shoulders since his late-night dreamworld session.

"But I recommend not letting anyone else know what's inside," Jaden advised, smiling as he pulled Malik off him. "Everyone would just make a big thing out of it as far as they know you already have some magic. Let's just say the shadows are a manifestation of some old-style magic that's been forgotten. I'll say this–you don't have an ounce of Templar magic, especially since it's dead magic, but we can use that to our advantage."

"So, what's our next move school or do we go to the meeting?" Malik asked, letting go of Jaden.

Jaden groaned. "Sadly, it's school, the council set the meeting at five so we can all have a full day of class."

Laughter bubbled out of Malik, now at ease. Jaden was hilarious even without trying sometimes. He quickly fixed himself and said goodbye to his family. He reached for his bag and headed out with Jaden right on his heels, walking together to the school in silence.

While they walked, he tried to absorb everything he'd learned while in his dream session. His ability to bend the universe felt like he had to will both his mind and whatever his power was, into doing what he wanted. Sometimes when he "pushed" something to happen, he didn't feel anything, but other times he felt a pressure build up inside of him and then go outwards to manipulate whatever he wanted to happen. He figured if he started pushing things that he wasn't ready for, his body would drain itself and he'd be left defenseless against his enemies.

He was so lost in thought, he didn't notice they had reached the school grounds already. Jaden was saying something to Malik, but he had tuned him out while deep in thought.

"So, when we get inside, you should know that most of the school knows about what happened at this point; if they're not regular humans and have heard anything, it's going to be an edited version of it."

Malik had figured people would talk, especially in a small town like this one. It wasn't anything different than what he experienced with already moving a lot, but this time involved monsters and the tomb. That immediately brought Malik's mood down, but he was here for a reason. Right – putting his family back together was most important.

"So, just don't make a big scene if anything happens and just let me handle it," Jaden continued looking at Malik for confirmation, which Malik did. He didn't want to make it a big deal and mess things up like he did at his last school.

They had finally walked into the school at that point. He could tell already that everyone was watching them and giving Malik pointed looks. Malik thought it was best to ignore it all, but even the teachers were watching them carefully. Was the whole town this weirded out by what had happened?

Malik saw Elinam, smiled and waved at him as if he was just some old friend. Malik smiled at that; it was nice not to be a pariah, even if it was for just a second. He'd only just helped her pick up her books the day before, but it felt like so long ago.

Seeing who he was smiling at, Jaden raised his eyebrows. "Hmm, Elinam Johnson, interesting?"

Malik laughed at Jaden. "No, it's not like that, I guess

she just remembers me from earlier in the week."

Jaden nodded coyly as if he understood him, but Malik wasn't thinking about love or anything. Malik didn't have room for that right now, and even if he did, his thoughts went back to last night with a certain Latina whom he'd been thinking about kissing for a minute now. No, Malik told himself to stay focused on finding the tomb, then get the girl.

While Malik and Jaden were talking, he hadn't noticed that the whole gang was back together. Nico, Maya, and Bianca had somehow appeared by their side and were watching them talk with disapproval. Malik saw Bianca and blushed, remembering what he had been thinking about just a second before she had appeared. Bianca, not knowing what had happened, just smiled at him.

Maya cleared her throat before speaking. "So, I'm sure Jaden has already told you of the plan for today. The council will meet with us today after school. I'll warn you all the kids, mortal or not, are on edge right now. The Sheriff and mayor are going to hold a town meeting tomorrow for the mortals in case anything else happens but be on your best guard right now. No one's going to mess with you with us by your side and especially since you're close to Jaden, this is the safest place right now. More than half the school is supernatural in some way. If something happens, the demons won't be able to do anything."

Truly glad to have someone who took command so

quickly and well, Malik didn't have to worry about anything. Nico also nodded and added, "My pack will be watching you from every point of school and will report to me instantly if anything happens."

He appreciated that as well. Jaden nodded as if he also agreed with everything they said. Malik, with a lump in this throat from all his emotions welling up, said, "Thank you guys for everything, I wholeheartedly appreciate it."

Smiling, Bianca reached out to Malik to comfort him. "It's okay, we look after our own. Now let's get to class, it's going to be a long day."

Like a puppy, Malik followed her, and after that, everyone else disappeared and went their separate ways. The day continued like any other, besides the usual stares and whispers about him. Malik chose to ignore it most of the time but felt weird that people were watching him. He was sure that it was an invasion of privacy, but it was for his own good.

He could tell that Nico's pack of athletes were watching his every move and there was always one within eyesight. There was also Maya's group, which Malik didn't know how, but could tell them apart from the rest because they gave off this warrior mode vibe whenever Malik walked by them. Lastly, Jaden, who seemed to be the most on edge; Malik noticed quite a few people gave him a lot of room all day long through school, which Malik was later told was because Jaden was authorized to be ready to do serious magic if needed, so everyone was getting as far as they could so as to not be caught in his crossfire.

Surprised, he made it through the rest of the day without anything going wrong. Bianca was great company, distracting him for the most part by keeping his mind occupied. If she wasn't, then Ento would share things she thought he might want to know about the supernatural world.

"So, the supernatural world isn't really what everyone makes it out to be. Yes, there are vampires, witches, and werewolves. But there are even more beings and worlds out there than I could know. The demon in you could be from one of those worlds. Maybe one day you could travel to those worlds."

Malik finally understood he was only just beginning to unravel this world within a world. He felt outclassed in so many ways but made up for it with the people he was with. He was thankful for everything they had done so far.

CHAPTER 9

In the last period, someone unexpectedly approached Malik. It was Elinam Johnson, who seemed too shy to talk as she stared at Malik for a couple of minutes before Malik decided to help her out.

Malik tried to find a conversation topic while at the same time trying to figure out what she wanted. "How are you? Since that attack happened at school?"

She stared for a minute, open-mouthed, then closed it, and in a small voice said, "I'm okay, just a little shaken up."

Smiling a little, he figured that she wanted to thank the people that helped her out earlier.

"How are you?" Elinam asked in concern.

Staring blankly at her, he remembered the whole school knew about an abbreviated version of what happened at his house.

He rubbed his neck, not entirely sure what to say. "I'm good, just a little nervous if anything else will happen."

She seemed to understand, nodding. "Well, thanks again for what you and your friend did. Nico said that you guys were the first to notice anything was happening. If you need anything, just let me know."

Malik smiled warmly at Elinam. He appreciated her going out of the way to tell him herself. "You're welcome, and thanks for checking up on me."

Finishing saying what she wanted to say, they exchanged goodbyes. As she walked by him, she tripped. Reaching out to catch her before she fell, he grabbed her hand and wounded up somewhere completely different. He was standing in a dark and abandoned graveyard. It was lined with dusty, old tombstones with holes; some graves were dug up as well. In front of him sat a tombstone that chilled him to his core. It read "Malik Anomos Blackwood, beloved friend, son, and brother."

Malik was ready to read the rest of his tombstone when he was suddenly pulled from it to find himself back in the school halls once again. Elinam was in his arms, supporting a nosebleed that poured profusely with no end in sight.

Malik, while concerned as to what had just happened, steadied Elinam and looked into her eyes, which were fully glazed over, as if she wasn't there. Before he could ask her what had happened, Nico appeared out of nowhere and grabbed Elinam, giving him a look as if to say, "don't ask any questions." He just stood there, dumbfounded as to what was going on as she was carried away from him. After that, Malik walked away with many things going on in his head, with no possibility of answers from Elinam at the moment.

By that point, the end of the day had already passed, and Malik found himself surrounded by Jaden and the others once again. Nico didn't even acknowledge his presence; whenever he looked at him, all he got was a stony look. He knew he would have to talk to Jaden after the meeting to figure out what Nico was up to.

They all looked at each other and nodded. Jaden spoke first. "Well, the council is set to happen in five minutes, so let's get going to the gate."

"The gate?" Malik asked in confusion.

"Yeah, the gate to the meeting. You think they'd hold a meeting of this importance right here in town, but it's on a different plane, so time runs differently over there." Seeing his expression, Jaden explained while they walked away from the school grounds. "Think of it as a place where you hit pause on everything and only you are truly moving through your perception of time."

While Jaden talked, he waved his hands in the air, creating a blue energy that rotated around itself, as if it was a clock going the opposite way.

"Malik, think of it like what we did in the dream session, time wasn't moving the same as everywhere else," Ento explained.

He got the idea somewhat–maybe he could stop time himself? He thought about it and asked Ento.

"I don't see why not, though I doubt you are ready for that

level of power without paying a price. You truly only know the basics of your power."

Slightly flustered by her statement, he saw everyone watching him, as if they could tell he was talking to Ento.

"When he does that, it sets me on edge," Nico remarked.

"I've met people that speak to their grimoires, but seeing Malik speak to the thing in his head is not a good sign," agreed Maya.

"Her name is Ento, she's more important to me than just something," Malik angrily told them, trying to defend Ento.

The others nodded in surprise, as they were unused to him being so defensive. Jaden redirected everyone's attention to a blue pulsing door in the middle of thin air.

Seeing his stunned face, Jaden grinned at him. "Yup, that's a gate. Now let's get through before anyone sees us."

Maya went through first, then Nico. Bianca squeezed Malik's hand and walked through the glowing light. Malik felt something in him wanting to run away because he knew the minute he walked through the gate, he was going to trap himself with people that he didn't know.

"You can walk away from all of this," Ento suggested, *"if you go in, and they find out what you are, you might not make it."*

That set him even more on the edge, but he wasn't doing this for himself. He needed to become stronger for his family, even if it meant surrendering his life.

Watching Malik closely, Jaden didn't say a word. Malik turned to him and took a big deep breath before moving toward the door. When he stepped toward the gate, his body felt weightless for a moment, as if he was being separated by an invisible barrier. He could have sworn his shadow flickered into a different shape for a second, but when he looked again, it was the same. Shaking his head, thinking he was crazy, he walked through the gate, and possibly to his death.

He found himself in a room full of strange creatures. It reminded him of a grand courthouse, except there were big differences. Everything felt like it was moving on its own; he could have sworn he saw a moving staircase. In the courthouse, there were five levels of seating, each with its assortment of creatures seated there. One level hosted a few people he assumed to be some type of werecats, given the tails and cat-like ears. What was most impressive was the glowing orange globe floating in midair, giving the feel of being bigger than the room itself.

Everyone was watching his group's every move, and it made him pretty uncomfortable. A woman walked up to them. Malik automatically recognized her as Jaden's mom; they looked too much alike to not be closely related.

She smiled at the group, and it was warmer than Malik had expected, but there was a calculating look in her eyes, as if she was measuring their worth. It was an odd combination that sent Malik on high alert; he knew automatically that this woman was completely dangerous. It felt like he was seeing a version of Jaden that he'd never expect to see.

Jaden's mom spoke. "It's nice to see everyone together again; it feels like forever since I've seen each of you come together."

She paused as if she was going to say something, then noticed Malik. "You must be Malik. I've heard a lot about you."

He smiled sheepishly at her. "Hello, ma'am, it's nice to meet you."

Jaden's mom laughed, and he found it surprisingly warm. "Please, call me Regina, I'm not that old just yet. Maybe in another century, I'll let you."

He followed her, laughing at her joke uneasily. Did she mean that she had lived for a century, or was it a form of expression?

Jaden cut in. "Mom, what's the game plan?"

Regina looked at her son and for a moment Malik saw something dark come over her face, but it passed so quickly that he couldn't tell if it had been just his eyes playing a trick on him. "Well, Jay, it probably won't be a big deal to find the tomb, though it's still a risk. I don't know why Andy wants to do this. But the main problem is if they figure out what your new friend really is."

"Yeah, we know he has an amulet from some old

demon king," Bianca spoke up. "It's not a big deal."

Regina smiled sadly. "It would be if I didn't recognize its aura of the original owner; it's going to shake things up once they find out there's an heir to that damn bloodline."

The group all looked at Malik, but he was just as lost as the others. He didn't know if she was referring to the Demon King or someone else. He could tell Regina knew more than they did, probably even his mother, but protecting his family was more important and right now nothing else mattered.

"It doesn't matter what or who I'm descended from. I need to make sure my family is safe," he told them, stepping forward to get everyone moving.

Studying him carefully before deciding on something, Regina seemed to agree as she then turned briskly toward a corridor. "The plan is simple, you just state what happened again. You already have the go from Maya's and Nico's groups; you just need one more, and they'll follow. Don't do anything stupid, and you'll find the tomb and be back by the end of the week once we get the location," Regina explained as they walked. "Nobody knows what to do with you, because you still seem to be almost human, but you show a power that hasn't been around for almost centuries."

"Should we be worried about his safety?" Jaden asked, concern showing in his face.

Regina didn't stop moving but did incline her head.

"Once we destroy the tomb, he's going to have to get stronger, because there will be legions that will want him dead before he rises to his full power."

"Wait! Why? I haven't done anything wrong." Malik was scared, alarm in his voice.

Stopping before a door, Regina looked back at Malik with sadness before responding. "It's not my place to tell you, Malik, just know that power has a price."

Regina turned and walked into the big room. Malik, dumbfounded, finally snapped out of his shock, and walked into the area. It reminded him of a massive courtroom, with sections made for observers and a big area for someone to stand. There were sections up high, so people could look down on them, and Malik could feel the amount of power in the room. His legs shook slightly. Everything rode on convincing these people with a hell of a lot more power than him to say yes to the plan.

Ento tried to calm him in his mind, but it wasn't truly helping. They had already walked into the room; he could spot people from school, as well as other people. Many of them looked human, but some weren't. He could have sworn he saw a six-foot-tall brown bear in armor.

He was so busy looking at everything that he didn't realize a man talked above them. The man's face seemed to be everywhere, floating in the middle of the building. "We are here to question the worth of finding the tomb of this so-called Demon King. Here to advocate for this mission is human Malik Blackwood, the wizard Jaden Williams, werewolf Nico Gonzalez, and Paladins Maya and Bianca Cabello."

"Why should we help find this tomb?" one of the people in the crowd asked. "We should just leave it alone so no one can gain its power, it would breach the Accords."

Jaden stepped forward, his voice projecting everywhere. "What makes everyone so sure that the Accords haven't already been broken? Malik has informed me of being attacked by demons on the outer borders, and the Weres can verify that information."

The room started to buzz at hearing this; Jaden stood there letting everyone talk for a moment and Nico then confirmed his story. Jaden continued, "If they start trying to abduct one child, who's to say they won't take more, especially ones of influential families?"

The room couldn't be quiet for a while after Jaden spoke that line. Now Malik saw why the others followed him; it wasn't because of his magic, but his way with words seemed to move people. Malik was sure he would find the tomb. No way they wouldn't want to save their own families from danger.

A man stepped forward and everyone instantly quieted down. The man oozed power; it felt as if he was an immovable mountain and everything fell to him. There was also as a strange familiarity, with his deep, velvety voice. "Why don't we let the kid talk?"

Realizing all eyes were on him, Malik nervously said, "Um, please, I don't know what's going on, but you have to help. I'm told I'm one of you, and I feel it's only right that you do this."

"One of us, what do you mean?" someone yelled.

"He means that he's from a line of long-forgotten Templars, whose family has a curse laid on them," Jaden spoke for Malik.

Malik nodded. "Please help us."

The man from early on stared at him directly in his eyes. Malik's body felt like it was sinking into the ground, until he finally looked away. The man said, "If you can prove you're one of us, I'll agree to help you."

Regina must have prepared for this before they even entered, because she gestured to some people standing on the side to grab a strange machine. It looked like it was a tablet onto a pedestal. It glowed dimly as if it wasn't something remotely normal. She instructed Malik to put his hand on the tablet and keep still.

Sweat started to drip off him as he waited for something to happen; Jaden had said all the tablet did was show what he was. It showed his strongest distinction of bloodline or level; he told him to not worry, and that everything would be fine. Malik was stressing now, sure the demon inside him would be registered or that his mom's family would show up.

Finally, after what felt like forever, his hand felt a soft, warm heat coming from the tablet. Strange symbols appeared on the tablet; someone read the results out loud while his heart still beat fast. He didn't know whether to be happy or fearful in what he read.

All the person said was, "It reads as unknown, it seems the tablet can't determine what he is."

Everyone speaks over each other again. Malik's anxiety and fear started to creep up, and his shadow seemed to only grow with each waking moment. Malik couldn't contain it anymore.

"SHUT UP!" he screamed. It was as if his very voice crept through every crook and cranny of the room, it echoed with so much power.

Everyone stared at Malik in silence; the guards that Malik hadn't noticed in the wall were suddenly at his throat. Jaden and the others were instantly on the defensive, ready to protect Malik, when a girl came rushing toward them: Elinam.

Elinam yelled, "Stop, please! Malik, you can't go, or you'll die if you do!"

The entire building turned toward her in surprise, especially since they weren't even in Portland anymore.

"Um, what's going on, Malik?" Nico asked as if he had all the answers.

Shrugging in reply, he barely knew what was going on these days. Regina waved her hands and instantly was bathed in a brilliant golden light. "It looks like we have a new development, let's get a five-minute break."

"No, we will not, I sensed some magic interfering with the divining tablet. There was demon magic in it!" an old man spoke angrily, stomping his cane in protest.

Someone from the stands threw a glass and when it shattered, a red mist leaked out into the air. While the vapor disappeared, no one seemed to be hurt by it. The guards seemed to make their minds up and rushed Malik. Before anyone could do anything, the vapor finally entered his nose and he felt like he was about to throw up, like something was crawling out of his body. It acted on its own; his arms reached out and darkness swept the floor and the guards disappeared into it, screaming for help.

All he could do was stare at his hands, not knowing what had happened. He noticed his shadow for a minute – there was a silhouette of something not human, and he remembered the demon in him. Fear came over him. Was he already losing control?

He felt even sicker, as if everything he had been feeling the last couple of days was starting to overwhelm him. All he could think about was not dying at that moment, completely forgetting about everyone else. The darkness continued to pour out, seeping into every part of the floor; Malik could have sworn he saw faces in them. A cold sweat came off of him, and he felt lightheaded. As if the shadows themselves were alive and wanted to taste the blood of the master's enemies.

"Malik, calm down and stop this before it's too late!" Jaden yelled at him. He heard his voice, but it sounded so far away, as though he was drowning in the dark.

Malik was helpless as he watched the shadows start to attack the people in the room. The guards that the shadows had swallowed up reappeared from the ceiling as they free-fell to the ground with astounding speed. Everyone watched as the guards nearly had a gruesome death before Regina cast a spell that stopped their imminent death in midair, and Jaden somehow made a portal, so the guards appeared on the other side of the room on the floor.

Malik was terrified of what was going on, but he knew he couldn't stop whatever was happening.

"Malik, you need to let go of all of your negative emotions, the shadows are feeding off it," Ento demanded in the back of his head, but she seemed too distant and far away.

He tried his best to do what she suggested, but no matter what they didn't seem to disappear; actually, the opposite happened – the shadows seemed to be gaining even more power. Some of them even appeared to be taking on a solid form.

That was when Malik saw a blinding light and was suddenly thrown across the room, where he lay unconscious. One minute it was dark and then Malik found himself in a room on a bed. He got up with a start, and Elinam rushed out of the corner of the room.

"Are you okay, Malik?" Elinam asked in a worried

tone.

He found himself woozy for a moment, his head ringing; he rubbed his head before responding, "I'm okay, what happened after I blacked out?"

She looked around anxiously, as if someone else would save her from answering Malik. When no one came, she spoke. "Well, after you were back to your old self, some people there wanted to kill you, but Jaden stopped them. I've never seen him like that before; heck, I've never seen magic before, but he protected you and transported us to this place and we've been here since."

Malik took all of that in. Was the demon in him the one that caused it or was that himself? He remembered Ento saying it was a demon seed. He felt the demon wanted to protect him for some reason other than the fact it was in his body, but Malik felt that the demon wasn't the cause of the manifestation of the shadows. Maybe the glass that was thrown had caused his body to react like that? Malik needed answers, but importantly, right now he had to escape.

Looking over at Elinam, he raised an eyebrow. Why was she here? This was supposed to be some secret place that wasn't even supposedly in this world, not that Malik even believed that.

"Sorry, I know I don't know you that well, but how did you even get here?"

Elinam tried her best to keep a straight face, but she

couldn't. Her expression showed panic. "I, um, sort of followed you. When I saw you today, I saw things happen in my mind that I knew didn't happen but felt so real. I told you I saw you die; I was there."

She seemed to have lost her voice; she was scared and shivering. He didn't know what had happened in her head, but he didn't believe his death happened. He went over to her, sitting close to Elinam. He reached over and wrapped her in a hug, Elinam didn't try to get away; she leaned in and just let him hold her until she could control herself again.

"I was going to tell you at the end of school, but you and the others left. I thought it was odd that all of you hung out to begin with. Maya and Nico are the popular kids and Jaden's cool with everyone. I think Bianca has a crush on you, so I figured it was Breakfast Club meets the Goonies."

He just looked at Elinam as if she was losing her mind but let her continue.

"I followed you, and then you disappeared, so I stood there for a minute. Then something came over me, screaming inside me to warn you and, well, you know the rest. I jumped forward and wound up in here."

There was something wrong with this girl. "Were you always like this?" Malik asked.

Elinam looked at Malik, pushing her fallen hair behind her ear. "You mean, could I always tell when people die?"

"Yes, could you always tell?" he asked, intrigued to find out the answer.

"I've always been able to tell when someone is close to dying. It's like being able to read someone's fortune. I was adopted when I was young; my last family found out and abused it. That's why I don't let anyone find out about it."

"It wasn't until I bumped into you that my 'gift' changed. I've been seeing things, I guess you could call them ghosts, for better terms. I've been having nightmares of your death for two days now, and today was finally the day I decided to tell you."

He took in everything she said. She was like him but seemed to be different at the same time.

"Are you human?" Malik asked in a concerned voice.

She looked lost and scared, but Malik could tell immediately she didn't know as much as Malik. He didn't even know what to call himself, was he human or something else?

"No, she's human, but not like anything I've seen before." Malik and Elinam both jumped to find Jaden leaning against the wall in the corner.

Jaden stepped into the light. "I know what you are. They call you sirens, or in some cultures, banshee, depending on your power. Usually, they're mostly human. We can discuss that later; we have more pressing matters."

Staring at Malik intently before concluding, Jaden took a deep breath. "We were able to calm most of the frenzy after you left. I'll be frank, they want to kill you, Malik, and they might very well try while we attempt to find the tomb."

He wasn't even remotely shocked that they wanted to kill him, but if everyone else was safe, he could worry about it another time.

"Does that mean we're going to do it?" Malik asked in a hopeful voice.

"The council agreed to let you go but said that if given the slightest hint that you were going to be unable to control, they would hunt you down and kill you themselves," Jaden admitted, his voice betraying his concern for Malik.

He took all of that in without even arguing; he didn't care what these people thought of him. He had a feeling that they were nothing compared to the monsters that threatened his family.

"So, does that mean they'll help us?" Malik asked, hopeful at Jaden.

His friend frowned. "They said they wouldn't kill you, but they refused to help us search for the tomb."

"I guess we'll have to do things our way then," Malik angrily stated.

After this was all over, he would show those people what he truly thought of them. While he didn't like this demon that was in him, he knew that he needed all the power possible to survive whatever came next.

CHAPTER 10

Elinam looked as scared and lost as he did when he first got introduced into this world. While he still didn't have a full handle on everything else, he wanted to help her as much as he could.

"Hey, is it possible to track demons if you have something of theirs?" he asked Jaden.

Jaden looked at Malik in surprise and nodded. "If you can find something that still connects them, yes, there's a way I can use my magic to have a location."

They'd have to do this a way to find the tomb on their own, he realized he'd come a long way to that night where things changed and recalled something – there was a knife there. He wondered if it had a clue to possibly finding the place.

Standing there, a plan formed in his head. It was still cloudy, but tangibly there. Malik got up and looked at his clothing and saw that he had dirt and other things on him. He reached out and put an image in his head; one second he was in his old clothing, and a second later he was in a fresh set of clothing.

Elinam looked at Malik in shock. "Malik, you can do magic, too?"

"That's not magic, at least not any magic that's in this world," laughed Jaden.

Giving Jaden a questioning look, Jaden met Malik's eyes and just winked.

"We should get going, the others are waiting for us," Jaden said while turning around. The iron doors swung open and with a squeak, Elinam followed after Jaden.

Malik got ready to follow when a buzz sounded in his head.

Finally, Malik, I've been trying to call you for a day or so." The voice in his head, Malik realized, was Ento. He hadn't been able to reach her when he was spiraling out of control earlier.

"Where have you been, Ento?"

"Something happened that made your body react strangely, I couldn't reach you. I'm so sorry, Malik," Ento said, defeated.

"It's okay, I'm still alive." Malik forgave Ento immediately. It wasn't her fault that it got out.

"Now we have to be ready for whatever it does next," Ento assessed, believing that there was more to come before it was all over.

He nodded to himself; behind him, Elinam gave him a side-eye as if he was crazy. Malik just smiled at Elinam. He needed to figure out everything fast before anyone else got hurt or worse, and he had a feeling someone else might have the answers.

"We'll deal with everything one at a time," Malik declared to Ento, but more to himself.

Following Jaden and Elinam down the hall, each step got him closer to going home and putting all of this behind him. They started down a path that seemed to be aimlessly going nowhere, but they trusted Jaden to get them wherever they needed to go. Finally, they reached a corridor that had a couple of people waiting. Malik saw the others sitting there, mostly quiet. The only person that seemed to be adamant was Bianca, though Malik wasn't surprised in the least.

As the others watched Malik, Elinam, and Jaden as they came down the corridor, they all got up to know what had happened to them.

"Are you doing okay, Malik?" asked Bianca.

He looked at Bianca and smiled sadly. "I'm better now, how are you guys?"

She smiled back at him before looking around. "We could be better, but we're good for now."

Maya looked at the interaction before looking at Jaden. "What's our plan now?"

"For now, we go home and come back together again at school tomorrow," Jaden told them.

Maya interjected, "Actually, Jaden, if that's your next step, then we need to do something else first."

Everyone looked at Maya in confusion. Malik realized

he didn't know this girl, besides the fact that she had saved his life multiple times. Maya walked away from them without even waiting to see if they would follow. Malik turned to Jaden, who just shrugged in confusion as well, let out a puff of air, and followed after Maya, so everyone followed her down to a room.

They were led into a training room. It was beautiful; the walls were adorned with weapons of different types and a strange sigil on the floor that seemed to move by itself. It was intimidating, to say the least.

Having finished examining the room before looking at Maya, he asked her, "So why are we here?"

Stripping off her shirt, she had only a tank top on. Maya was covered in more scars than Malik would expect from a girl his age, especially two big ones around her upper back. Maya stared at Malik straight in the eyes, as if daring him to say anything about them. He looked away sheepishly, too embarrassed to say anything.

"You're an unknown asset and I dislike unknown things. It's best to train you and gauge your strength for myself before proceeding with this quest of ours," Maya explained.

"Um, quest? What quest?" Elinam interrupted, looking at everyone in fear.

Grabbing Elinam's hand, Jaden led Elinam to the corner. He looked over his shoulder to Maya. "Try not to kill him too hard. We need him at least coherent enough."

Only giving a simple small smile, Maya looked at Jaden, sending a shiver down his spine. It seemed to him that Maya resembled a demon at that moment.

Maya shrugged. "No promises."

Nico laughed at the exchange. "And they call me the monster."

Watching Maya carefully, Malik started to slowly back away. Sadly, he wasn't fast enough – in just a second Maya was right next to him.

"Relax, we call this the Death Zone. It's a training place for noobs when they first start. You can't really die here. Yeah, you get killed and might have a splitting headache after, but you're not dead." Bianca came up next to Malik as well, grinning ear to ear.

He wasn't the slightest reassurance by that. "How is that possible?"

Maya once again shrugged. "I don't know, like everything else I guess, magic. Don't ask for the specifics, Jay's the magic expert, not me, so take it up with him why you don't simply die. All I know is in the next two hours, we're going to see just how skilled this old Templar magic of yours is."

Bianca grinned as if she'd found the best new toy, while Nico shrugged and started to stretch. They left them alone, deciding to stand on a corner on the other side of the building.

"We're going to start with hand-to-hand combat, that's

simple enough," Maya stated.

Motioning to Malik to stand six feet across from her. Malik reluctantly did it; he hadn't trained in martial arts for a couple of years now. He knew he still wasn't a match for Maya, who was built for war.

Getting into a fighting stance, he waited for Maya to make the first move. Maya didn't even waste any time, rushing at him with what he knew wasn't even her top speed. Malik was able to dodge the first punch to the face but was caught by the punch to his left side, leaving him winded and in pain. As he moved to step back, Maya followed, not letting him even gain a marginal amount of space. Malik started to get peddled with punches and kicks until he lost count. For his part, he managed to keep himself mostly safe, even though he was only retreating and losing badly.

He saw an opening ten minutes into the fight. His body was too close to her once again; he saw that Maya's leg kick wasn't timed to protect her and he knew he had her right there. When Maya started her next spur of attacks, Malik made his move, and when her leg came up to hit his heart, he grabbed it and twisted it forward. Maya couldn't get away from his grip; she tried to punch him off it, but Malik knew that would happen and proceeded to spin to get her into a lock. While he partially succeeded, he wasn't able to get her body fully locked down. Maya stopped struggling with her leg and put the full weight of it on Malik, who couldn't release his grip, or he'd lose his advantage. Maya then punched Malik in his kidney, leaving him to let go of her leg and clinch his side. Maya spun out of his grasp and sent a mean hook to the side of his head, knocking him out completely.

All he remembered was going down and getting back up again, and the experience left him very nauseated. Malik found Maya talking to Nico and Bianca when he came up again.

Watching him for a moment before speaking definitively, Maya congratulated him. "Not half-bad, Malik, definitely need to work on some things, but I can work with what I got."

"Please tell me we're done?" he begged, not feeling up to fighting anymore.

Sighing as if she was dealing with a child, she said, "Yeah, we're done, Jaden just chastised me for going like that."

Frowning at her, he looked around, wondering where the mighty sage wizard was, anyway?

Seeming to read his mind, Nico told him, "Oh, Jaden left to help Elinam learn some things. Something about a wizard's secret cave, that dude's a weirdo."

He hated to agree with Nico on something, but this one couldn't be helped. Malik still didn't understand why Jaden was so pressed about finding the tomb.

"So, what do we do now?" Malik asked sheepishly.

They only had an hour left before they were set to leave.

"Now we review footage from our fight and I'm going to offer advice, as well as possibly teach you some new moves. Nico and Bianca can go train somewhere else," Maya explained.

Gathering their things, Nico and Bianca left the room as well, Bianca sending him one last look of pity before leaving. Then Malik was once again left alone with his very own terrifying Angel of Death.

Turning back to stare at the footage on the screen, Malik walked up next to her.

"Do you know why I'm doing this, Malik?" Maya asked, still facing the screen.

"To help me get better?" he responded, giving a mild guess.

"Nope, the council would rather see you die than get more powerful. No, I'm doing this for myself, isn't that selfish of me?" Maya asked, turning to Malik giving him her full attention.

Her eyes showed a life filled with impossible choices and unbending resolve; he found her stare unnerving. How could someone only sixteen experience so much in their life? It was unthinkable. Nobody had ever looked at him this way before, not even his parents. Like she counted on him to save her or something.

"What's so selfish about it? You want me to stay alive," Malik declared, having to finally break away from her gaze.

Silent for a moment, Maya told him, "I grew up too fast, having to stop my father from sinking into a downward spiral and keep my sister from losing herself. Sometimes we can't be our own person; sometimes we're forced to throw away our own identity in order to save others."

He looked over to Maya once again and saw someone else, a girl trying to find her own way, but burdened by others. Malik didn't understand what she meant, as he had grown up sheltered. He may have been friends with people that had later joined gangs and died, but his family had earned enough money to move away from that life before it could have consumed him. He had never really struggled for anything, but he understood on another level that she was just as alone as him or Jaden.

"Why do that to yourself?" Malik's curiosity got the better of him.

She looked away as if trying to remember something. "I made a promise to someone important that I'd take care of everyone they had left behind, but in the process lost everything."

"What about Jaden? He seems to care for you."

"I care for Jaden, don't get me wrong, he's always been there for me when I needed him, but I couldn't give him my own burden when he has so much more than me. That wouldn't only be selfish, but wrong," Maya answered.

"I think he could handle it," Malik tried, though he was unsure what she meant by Jaden's burden.

She gave him a sad smile as if she knew something Malik would never know. "I don't know why I'm telling you this. Even though I can clearly tell you don't have Templar magic; it may be there from your ancestors, but you didn't inherit it. I don't know why Jaden chose to lie about it during the council, but I think he sees something in you that I couldn't see until now," Maya uttered in a solemn tone.

"And what is that?" he inquired.

Taking a deep breath, she admitted, "I make idiotic mistakes, and I'm oblivious to the pain of others because I'm too used to pain myself. But you're not like that, Malik. Even though the mistakes you've made have been big, you do it from the goodness of your heart. That's something not many people can do, you have a positive impact on people. I even see Nico being more open, that's the kind of presence you have. You're so, so many of the things I'm not."

Standing there shocked, he absorbed what he had just heard. He had no clue what mistakes she had made, but they couldn't be that bad. Malik noticed that Maya looked ready to fall right there, but he had to say his piece.

"I think you're looking for the wrong person, I'm not someone to look up to or trust. There's something in me that wants to break free and destroy everything in my path.

I'm not a leader, maybe you or Jaden are, but I'm nothing but a scared kid that just wants to go home and play with his little sister," Malik finished in a huff of breath.

It suddenly felt too tight in the room, like everything was closing in on him. Malik needed to get away from there before Maya tried to change his mind, or worse, he had another episode. Malik grabbed his things, not even sure where he was going, and rushed out the door, leaving Maya standing there sad and lost. As much as he wanted to help her, he knew it couldn't be from him. Broken people had a way of finding each other, but that didn't mean they could help fix each other as well.

"Was that a good idea, Malik?" Ento asked in his head.

"I don't know, but I needed to get out of there," he expressed, having finally reached the halls.

"I know you don't want my answer, but I think she may be right," Ento, with some hesitation, answered.

"How can you be so sure of that? I feel like I've caused nothing but problems for everyone so far," Malik asked, burying his head in his hands.

Ento was silent for a moment before speaking. *"You know, before you I was always treated like a tool and nothing more, but with you, I feel as though I'm a friend, maybe even a second mother for you. Let me just say that I've watched how the others are around you; while they may fear you on some level, they are willing to fight their own superiors over you, and doesn't that say something?"*

He had no response to that. Earlier they had protected him when the council had been ready to attack, even Nico, who he was surprised to see do that for him. That didn't mean anything really, they possibly just did it on instinct.

"Maybe you're right, but that doesn't mean I'm going to be some big hero. I just want all of this to end," Malik told Ento in earnest.

After that, Ento left Malik alone to gather his own thoughts. It wasn't before long that Andy turned back up. The man didn't say anything but just sat down with Malik for a couple of minutes.

Andy finally spoke. "I should officially say I'm sorry for what I put you through. I never meant for this to cause all these events to unfold."

He looked at Andy; he seemed so much bigger now than the time Malik thought he'd died in his arms.

"Well, you certainly do know how to make a dramatic exit," Malik weakly joked to him.

Andy grinned. "Trust me, Ant was chewing me out for traumatizing you for days on end."

"Ant? What is that your imaginary friend?" he asked, raising an eyebrow at Andy in confusion.

Andy barked a laugh. "Don't let him hear you say that, or you might find a sword hunting you down."

Blinking at him in surprise, Malik asked, "Wait, the sword's name is Ant? Wow, you have issues."

Staring at him with a straight face, Andy didn't say

anything, which caused Malik to start to laugh more freely than he had in a while. It felt nice to laugh again.

"There we go, there's the kid I met that night, I thought he was gone with all that doom and gloom I see you got going on," Andy cheerfully remarked.

"Well, I'm sorry to have kept you waiting," Malik said, making an awkward bow while staying seated.

Andy just raised an eyebrow in his direction, and Malik made a wave with both his brows. Andy snorted in his hand before laughing hard. Malik had to join in after seeing Andy's response. Once they both calmed down, Andy spoke. "If you must know, I named him because he never gave me a proper name. And since he's kind of an ass sometimes and tends to just scream in my head about me being dumb, he always reminds me I'm an ant inside a small hive."

Malik snorted. He remembered Andy fighting; this man was indeed reckless. Malik was almost sure Bianca was trained by Andy himself.

"So, he talks to only you usually?" Malik asked curiously, given he had someone in his head as well.

"Usually he does, but only to nag or say I'm doing something wrong. That night at your house was the first time in centuries that he spoke through me," Andy mused, in astonishment himself.

Malik shrugged. He was getting used to the impossible happening even though he knew he shouldn't be. "So, what now?"

"Now we save the world." Smiling, Andy got up.

His saliva felt thick in his throat for a moment. "Save the world?"

"Well, yeah, the reason we're trying to get to the tomb is to stop the other demons from getting there and releasing god knows what out there," Andy stated.

"You'll be coming with us though, right?" Malik asked in a hopeful voice. He was here to protect his family. Saving the world wasn't part of the deal, and it would be nice to have Andy, an actual responsible adult, instead of just teenagers.

"I'm going to personally look after your family," Andy promised to him.

That settled his fast-beating heart; he was happy Andy was watching over his family himself. "Thank you, Andy, I truly appreciate it."

"It's okay, we help those that can't help themselves. It's what I was born and chosen to do," assured Andy, as though it wasn't something difficult to do.

He stared at his hands for a moment, wondering if he someday be someone as selfless as Andy.

Clearing his throat, Andy told him, "There's something I need to tell you. It's almost my time soon, I want you to promise me that you'll make sure both Jaden and Nico will finish completing the mission."

Pulled out of his thoughts, he glanced at Andy, was he

talking about his death or something? Panic made his voice quiver. "Um, what are you talking about?"

Kneeling till they were eye level, Andy gripped Malik's shoulder, staring into his eyes, and keeping an even-leveled tone. "We all die; it's something that must happen. We all must pass on at some point. I believe I've been given enough time to help you in righting some terrible wrongs that have been done to your family."

"What about my family and me?"

"I'll protect them to my last breath, I promise you that, but I just need to know if you'll take care of my boys after I'm gone. Nico has never wanted to be the alpha of the pack. While I've shouldered the burden for him, I'm not sure I can protect him from the world much longer. Jaden is very much like a son to me; I'm proud of the man he is becoming, but he'll need you to lean on as much as you'll need him, so please look after each other like brothers for me," Andy's voice was now shaky and thick.

He remembered experiencing Andy's death the first time. He couldn't imagine the pain Jaden and Nico would soon experience. He didn't think it was right that they had no clue as to what was about to happen.

He agreed with Andy. "I've never had any brothers, but I'll look after them like my own siblings, though I'm honestly not sure what I can do. They're both pretty capable of taking care of themselves."

The expression Andy had seemed to say he knew that

they would be all right. "I know, but that doesn't mean anything, they're both still kids and they've each endured so much pain in their short lives."

He once again wondered what pain they had endured but chose not to ask. It wasn't in his place to ask such painful questions about someone's past.

"I'm still a kid, you know," Malik pointed out to Andy.

"Sure, you are, but I have a feeling you're going to grow up faster than them, you've seen the world for what it is already. You don't have any delusions of what is out there," Andy remarked, as if he was sure that Malik had some kind of advantage over them.

Once he finished telling him everything, Andy got up, and Malik quickly followed. Before things could get any more awkward, Malik rushed in to hug Andy, though it felt as though they were saying goodbye.

After a minute, they separated and Andy ruffled his twists playfully, then walked away. Andy's shoulders never slumped or appeared sad; the man walked away from Malik for what could be his last time with a powerful posture that spoke of his conviction to whatever pushed him forward.

Watching Andy walk away, Malik knew what it truly meant to be a leader and a hero. Malik hadn't realized that tears had spilled down his cheeks; he wiped them away and steeled himself to go meet the others.

CHAPTER 11

Malik found all of them once again together. This time, Malik noticed Maya pointedly looking away from Malik, as if embarrassed at what had occurred earlier. Jaden talked excitedly with Elinam and Nico, which didn't surprise him. Bianca seemed to be training because she kept counting out loud but just stood there, shaking her arms out in front of her.

When everyone saw Malik, they all paused what they were doing. Malik glanced around as no one uttered anything, then pointedly stared at Jaden as if to silently tell him to say something.

"Oh yeah, we should be heading home right now, it's getting late," Jaden announced. "Malik might give us a lead, but until then, best rest up, it's been a long day."

Nico snorted. "Oh yeah, no thanks to Malik. Should we really trust this guy?"

Everyone turned to Nico, shocked as to why he would say such a thing. Jaden looked angrily at Nico, who looked at Malik with loathing. Even Malik was shocked as to why Nico would say such a thing. "What's your problem, Nico?

What did I do to you?"

Nico looked at Malik. "Oh, you don't know, do you? The night those demons attacked you, the guy who saved you was my uncle."

At the time, Malik hadn't known that Andy was related to Nico, but Andy had turned out fine. Why was Nico still harassing him over something that was in the past?

"I don't trust that you're all good man, you're bound to break, to be corrupted at some point, and when that happens, I'll have to put you down," Nico declared emotionally.

Malik sort of understood where he was coming from then; he could already feel it after what the demon proclaimed to him, that hunger for blood. He knew the more he used his power, he'd end up worse than those demons that attacked him. He didn't want to risk his family's lives if he couldn't trust everyone in the room to protect them from everything, including him.

"If you ever feel like I might try and turn against you, I understand, just protect my family," Malik professed solemnly.

Everyone looked at Malik in disbelief – here was a sixteen-year-old acting like a grown adult. Even Nico was taken back and looked sheepishly at Malik.

"Hey, don't say stuff like that. My emotions just got the best of me, let's just go stop whatever is going on and go home." Nico frowned, weirdly looking at Malik.

"Malik, I for one forgive you for my brother's fake death," said a voice behind them. They all turned to see Sergeant Gonzalez, Andy's twin brother, and Nico's uncle. "He was just doing his duty, though I do think he was an asshole for not telling the rest of us what he was planning. I don't know what my nephew was gibbering about just now; besides, Andy is perfectly able to take care of himself."

The Sergeant walked up to Nico and tousled his hair before turning to Malik and giving him a big smile. Malik, thinking he wanted to shake, extended his hand. The man slapped it away and came in for a hug, wrapping Malik in tightly enough to crush him.

"Thanks, Sergeant Gonzalez" he wheezed out, trying to breathe.

Letting him go out of the hug, he said, "You're welcome, call me Oscar. No need to be so formal."

"Honestly, don't beat yourself up too much. He's the Guardian, he knew the risks when given the job," Oscar continued after putting Malik down. "Y'all should head home now, it's getting late." He shook hands with Malik, hugged Nico, and fist-bumped Jaden before making his way out.

"Is he always like that?" Malik asked.

"No, he's usually worse. He's the most serious and funny weirdo here. Andy is even worse," Jaden said with a small laugh.

The others, besides Malik and Elinam, joined in agreement.

"He truly is one awesome weird dude," Maya surprisingly agreed.

Jaden cleared his throat. "Well, let's head out."

Jaden proceeded to bring a pocket watch out to look at it before putting it away. He waved his hand in the air in front of him and a portal of swirling green and blue colors appeared.

"Wait, what's a Guardian?" Elinam asked suddenly. It was something Malik was wondering himself, but he'd forgotten to ask Andy.

"I'll explain on the way there, now get in, children. I'm not able to hold this all day, you know," Jaden answered in a strained voice.

Everyone got in line as they all stepped through, but Nico, in an arrogant voice, started to tell them about Guardians.

"A Guardian is a title. We have a certain definition of one – for us, it's a Guardian at the gate. The Guardian at the front gate is by definition a protector looking in, never truly one of the group. He's the monster in the night that other monsters fear."

Malik shuddered, both from the portal and the way Nico told it. He didn't think Nico cared about anything, but he was wrong.

"The Guardian is chosen every generation to protect our home. It was my uncle Andy who was chosen; a lot of us thought it'd be Jaden, since he seemed to be the most likely candidate and I think he will be again once this is all over," Nico explained.

They were now at a park near the back of the school. Nico walked them a little further and decided to sit on the bench. Everyone followed after him, Nico then look around everyone and asked, "Any questions?"

Malik shook his head, but Elinam still didn't understand and asked, "How do you choose a Guardian?"

Jaden beat Nico to it. "We have someone that does it for us."

Looking at both Jaden and Nico in suspicion, Elinam just nodded. Malik felt she didn't understand but had just agreed.

"It's time to go home and figure out what our next game plan is," Jaden continued, "Maya and I will decide on something. Then we'll let you know."

Everyone nodded and began to depart. Elinam looked around. "How do I go home?"

"I'll take you home, no need to worry. Do you need a way home as well, Malik?" asked Jaden, turning to him.

He looked around and decided he wanted to run home alone. "I'm good, I'll see you guys tomorrow. I need to clear my head."

Everyone agreed and said their goodbyes. Bianca

hugged Malik tightly before leaving. Nico and Maya just waved. Someone appeared by the school as if they were waiting all along; Nico huffed and went to meet them. Bianca and Maya walked away in another direction. Jaden and Elinam said their goodbyes and stepped through a hole in space.

Malik shook his head, still amazed by his friend's power. He started running home, remembering how the last time had almost resulted in him dying. Malik made it to his house, breaking out in more sweat than he normally did; he knew that he wouldn't sleep and needed answers, but there was so much he needed to be ready for tomorrow. He went to his room, his body ready to pass out; he couldn't even get himself to take off his shoes, and the minute he closed his eyes, he passed out.

He turned over in his sleep and felt the wind blowing in his face. Tiredly, he opened his eyes thinking his window was somehow still open. Instead of seeing his nightstand next to him, he was facing the window outside his room. He found himself free-falling fast toward the ground, with only his pillow in his eyes.

Panic started to hit, his eyes completely opened. All he could see was the concrete ground of some type of floor fast approaching.

"Ahhhh, Ento! Anyone, please save me!" he sobbed out loud, tears in his eyes as the wind hit his face. Dust pelted his face repeatedly; he could barely see what was in front of him. Was gravity going to win today? Who would save him before he became an omelet?

"Please, I'll do anything, just save me!" he begged out loud, to anyone that would listen to his pleas.

"Take control of yourself, Malik, how dare you act this way. Get ahold of yourself and concentrate on the lessons I just taught you," Ento demanded, embarrassment and fear mingled in her voice.

As he flailed through the air once more, he felt ready to pass out from all the blood rushing to his face. Just when he was about to give up hope, he remembered Ento telling him he was the master of his own body; he wasn't just human, and that meant he didn't have to live by their laws anymore.

Remembering her lessons, he was able to survive the drop. Instead of falling this time, Malik remembered he could exert his will on things. Malik, with Ento's guidance, suggested he wrap himself in a mental image of being carried down in a way that supported him, and the wind didn't harm him anymore.

He was breaking out in a sweat by the time he got to the bottom. Huffing as he exerted so much force on himself, he got up and internally asked Ento, *"I need you to take me back to where I found you."*

He could feel Ento was surprised by his question. *"Are you sure? I think you should get some rest."*

"I need answers about what's happening to me, and I got a

feeling that there are some answers down there," he said.

Ento, seeing that there was nothing she could do to stop him, agreed. *"Okay, I'll show you the way."*

He was once again in the labyrinth, with his memory and Ento searching for the location of where he found the stone.

Instead of going to the stone, he went to the far wall, which had depictions of monsters and an army. Sure enough, once Malik looked closely, he saw a picture of a man, just the back of him, but he felt like he recognized him from memory or something. What undoubtedly scared him was that in the same picture stood another man that looked similar to Jaden. Malik was shocked beyond his wildest thoughts. Malik wasn't sure if he was safe anymore; he quickly pulled his phone up and took a picture of the walls.

"Oh, I see you're back, my boy."

Malik jumped so high, he felt like he was flying. He turned around to see the same man from before, looking at him in intrigue. He once again felt like he was being watched by a predator that loved to toy with his victims.

Finally, being able to force his heart back into his already-weak heart, he took a breath. He needed to have his head on, or he'd end up regretting being here again.

"I have a question for you once again, Anomos. What do you think makes you human?" the Keeper asked.

"Human?"

The Keeper laughed. "What separates humans from being like other things?"

"Other things? What are you implying, exactly?" inquired Malik, narrowing his eyes at the Keeper.

The man just smiled coyly and shook his head. "Oh, nothing, just trying to figure out the age-old question that still hasn't been solved. I thought you would understand since you're on the crossroads to answering that for yourself."

"I think it's our emotions and thoughts, we feel empathy and kindness toward our fellow people," Malik said in contemplation, thinking about his question thoroughly.

The man grinned at Malik's answer, showing off sharp canines that felt unnatural in the light. "But don't you also feel rage, lust, and sin? Can't it be that humanity's greatest enemy is each other, as time has shown repeatedly throughout history?"

"What are you?" Malik asked.

The man stared at Malik, almost in disappointment. "What do you mean, Anomos? I'm just a man talking to a kid."

He once again wondered why he had come back here. He must be going insane. "I think you're lying, there's no way you live down here by yourself."

"So what do you think I am?" The Keeper peered into his eyes as he asked, as though searching for something.

He had to mull it over for a minute. This man seemed to know things about Malik that shouldn't be possible. Plus, he *had* claimed he was a keeper of some sort, meaning he'd been around for a while. Malik had a nagging suspicion that this man, or whatever he was, knew where the tomb was located.

"I'm not entirely sure yet, I'd say some type of supernatural."

The man looks at Malik in disappointment. "Well, I guess until you figure it out, I should give you a tour."

He was shocked by the way the man blew off Malik's accusations. Before Malik could say anything, the man turned and walked away.

"As you probably know, your family were knights, of sorts, but what you don't know is that you're from a direct line of demons, in more ways than one," the Keeper mysteriously added.

He stopped in his tracks. Did that mean the demon in him was more than just a demon seed? Malik was so lost in thought that he didn't realize the man was walking away, still talking.

"At some point, the demon was betrayed and was left bleeding with a knife in his back. It's believed that when he died, he swore he would return to avenge those that had wronged him."

"Is that true?" he asked, in between breaths, as he struggled to catch up. Had getting down here really drained all of his energy?

The man stopped and looked at Malik carefully. "You tell me, Anomos, wouldn't you want revenge on those that wronged you in such a way that it drove you mad?"

Malik was transfixed with those eyes; they felt inhuman. As though they had lived thousands of lives, had watched nations and great men fall before them, immovable as the storm tearing through all things that were weak before it. They seemed to know things about Malik. "I see it behind your eyes, Anomos. You have a hunger that you're barely able to conceal, and if you don't find what's wrong, it's gonna eat you alive or kill everyone you love."

Malik was shocked that the man could see that, wondering who this man truly was. "What do you suggest I do?"

"Follow the clues – find your connection to the demon from the past, find the knife, and possibly the scrolls as well."

"What knife and what scroll?" Malik asked, though with a sinking feeling that he knew exactly what knife the man referred to.

The man pointed to a stone depiction of the demon, and in that demon's hand was the exact knife that Malik had held that night of the attack in the park. Malik felt something stir in him, like righteous anger, even though Malik knew it wasn't from him. He was still in shock and felt himself going over the edge.

"Well, this is where I take my leave. It's been a pleasure, Anomos, I hope to see you again." The man smiled wickedly before walking off.

"Wait, what about the scrolls?" he yelled at the man.

"You'll find out soon enough. I hope next time you'll know my name, Anomos. If you don't, I fear I'll have to do drastic things to make you know it." The man, still walking away, waved a hand in goodbye. Malik watched him for a moment, walking away until he disappeared around a corner.

As Malik stood there alone in the catacombs of a labyrinth, he felt something brush against him and whirled around to find nothing. He needed to leave, and so he called Ento. *"Help me get home, please!"*

"Malik, are you okay?" Ento asked, concerned.

"I'll be fine once I'm back home."

Ento led Malik back out to his home, taking the same staircase as last time that led to the garden. He didn't even turn around to check if it was still there, he just hurried inside. His parents were already asleep and Malik went to his room and got in his bed. He nodded off the minute his head touched the pillow.

He woke up feeling like he was once again being watched. This time, instead of Jaden, it was a crow perched on the window, looking at him with intense fascination. Malik was sure it was no ordinary bird but just shook his head. He didn't have the time to dwell on it. Malik got up and changed his clothing quickly, deciding to do it the old-fashioned way, since he wasn't in a rush this early and still needed to process what he saw last night. Malik realized there were more secrets that his family and friends weren't telling him.

As Malik got dressed, his dad walked by his room to his study across the hallway. "Are you okay, Malik? You look lost."

He shook his head. "I don't think I have what it takes to be able to do this anymore."

"Do what exactly?" Virgil very carefully asked.

"You know, save the day, be a hero," he answered with an edge to his voice. Malik realized he was throwing his frustration at his dad, who just wanted to help.

His dad nodded, then stepped into his room and sat on his bed. He motioned for Malik to sit across from him.

"I remember when you used to play hero all the time growing up, Power Rangers, then on to superheroes like Superman. You always loved them for what they represented," Virgil started.

For his part, Malik looked away in embarrassment as he remembered running around in a cape.

"You don't think you have what it takes to be a hero, so what?" Virgil asked.

"What if I can't stop another attack or save all of you from anything? I don't even think I can do this quest right without messing up," Malik confessed, tears starting to roll down his face.

Virgil put a hand on Malik's shoulder and squeezed. "We all make mistakes in life, and there's no shame in admitting that whatsoever. What's really bothering you, son?"

Malik finally blurted out his real problem. "I think there's something wrong with me; there's this darkness that threatens to surface whenever I'm pushed to the edge. What if I hurt the people I love and care for?"

"There's nothing wrong with having a dark side to yourself," Virgil said, "no one is truly perfect, as long as you don't push yourself too far to the edge. But that's what we're here for and your friends as well, to keep you from going too far. There's always going to be dark parts in life, but that doesn't mean there isn't any light in it either, you just have to find it. Life is balanced like that, sometimes the darkness wins and sometimes the light does, but it's never one side forever."

Tears rolled down Malik's face, and he wiped them away. His dad was right, like always. Malik couldn't let himself be overwhelmed by his doubts, not as long as he had the courage to at least commit to the quest. If there were moments of darkness, he'd rely on Jaden and the others to pull him back up.

"I'm sorry you feel pressured to save us, but please don't forget we're your parents. No matter what, just know we always want what's best for you. If you can't do this, we understand, it's our fault you're in this mess," Virgil assured him.

He shook his head. "I took your mother's maiden name instead of my own because I love and respect the culture of her family. I have no problems with the name Anomos, especially since now you know about the supernatural world; you'll find more history around that name and be proud of its significance in society. You're still finding your place in life; don't rush growing up. Go have adventures, save the world a couple of times, and you'll see that it's not so bad having different aspects of life. As you grow older, you'll encounter a new you … who's to say that side of you won't save your life one day?"

Malik had to ponder for a moment. He never really saw his given name as something he could fit or look at with pride. For some reason, in the back of his mind, it didn't feel like it belonged to him at all.

"I guess you're right, Dad, thank you for talking to me about my problems."

Virgil just smiled and left Malik alone to ponder his thoughts. What was going on in this city? There was something no one was telling Malik, and he could tell that there was a big hole in this adventure, but no clue how to approach finding the answer. Were Jaden and the others hiding something from Malik? The part about the scrolls and knife seemed to say that it was right in front of him.

That was if he even believed that man in the underground area.

"What did you expect, to be openly welcomed as one of them?" a voice in his head taunted him.

Malik, with a start, realized that the voice wasn't Ento; it felt like it was speaking to him in the darkest corners of his mind.

"Relax, I'll let your pet speak again real soon," the demon promised in a carefree tone.

Malik felt queasy and wondered if he should call for his parents.

"I wouldn't recommend that unless you're ready to hear the truth of why you were attacked."

Malik's blood went cold, as if something was shutting him down. Did the demon have something to do with the attack as well? Malik sat there trying to figure out all the jumble in his head. His brain took him back to the moment his sister was almost taken, and his inability to act. Malik felt his uncontrollable anger pushing him, to blow him to the point of wanting to destroy everything.

"Malik, you need to stop right now!" Ento's voice begged him.

Malik finally broke out of his moment of rage and with a startle, saw his mother wrapped in shadows, struggling to breathe while being suspended several feet in the air. Malik saw his hand reach out in a choking motion, his fingers unconsciously tightening around her throat. His mother had one hand trying to grab the tangible wisps of darkness that held her, while her other hand reached toward Malik; she looked at him in pure terror, as if he wasn't her son.

Malik finally snapped out of it and his mother dropped to the floor with a loud thud. Virgil rushed in to see the scene unfolding. Malik felt his anger subduing and realized with disgust what had just happened. Malik reached out for his mother, hoping to apologize and explain what he had done. Imani flinched, which made Malik's heart cold. His own mother was fearful of him. His dad knelt down next to her, looking at him with uncertainty as to what he should do. Malik saw the bruising on her neck.

Malik wanted to be anywhere but there. He felt something cold and dark twist in him, as if tugging him along to a place where he knew he wouldn't be a danger. It was as if a door that wasn't supposed to be opened finally started to creak wide open to welcome its newest victim.

Malik opened his mouth. "I promise I'll stop this, even if it kills me."

After saying that, the darkness took him. Malik wandered in the dark. It felt strangely lonely but welcoming at the same time, as if it was where he belonged. He had finally found the light again. Malik found himself in Jaden's room, but before he could do anything he was attacked. Malik was thrown off his feet and pinned to the far side of Jaden's room. When everything cleared, Malik saw both Jaden and his mom looking at him in a hostile manner, Jaden with his stick, looking ready to end Malik, and Regina also looking to murder him with just her glowing hands, along with an old, black book.

CHAPTER 12

Once they realized it was just him, they lowered their weapons while still looking uneasily at Malik.

"What are you doing here, Malik?" Jaden asked.

"What I want to know is *how* did you get here? This place has so many protections and wards up, you should have been fried the minute you got inside," Regina demanded to know, still looking ready to end him if he answered wrong.

Fearful of being turned into a toad or worse, he stammered at them sheepishly before saying, "Um, I got in from the back."

Both Williams looked at Malik as if he spoke gibberish. "I, um, somehow slipped into the shadows and wound up here."

"Malik, I think it's best if you started from the beginning. I think there's more to the story," Regina stated.

Malik, with a look at Jaden, decided to tell them what had happened since Jaden and the others left. When Malik told them the part about his mother, he became rather emotional.

"Why is there a man in your basement?" Jaden asked.

He shrugged, not even knowing what to say. "I have no clue, he just seems to show up whenever I'm there."

"We need to figure him out soon, I think he might be the key to all of this. But the most important thing right now is making sure you and your parents are all right," Jaden said.

Regina peered at Malik as if trying to see just how dangerous he was. "You need to find the tomb fast. I don't think the demon in you is trying to take control–I think it's trying to *corrupt* you."

Malik had had similar thoughts and said as much.

"To gain control means to rid your body of your soul and leave it a husk to take over," she explained. "When a demon does that, they become powerful, but only for so long before they wither and the body dies. But to corrupt, it means to consume your soul to the point of no return. They'll be in charge, and you'll helplessly watch as they destroy the world around you."

His body shuddered just thinking of what could happen to him. He remembered something that man revealed from the other night. "That man shared I have demon blood running through my veins, what does that mean for me?"

This time Jaden answered. "It means you're a lot more subjective to the influence of the demon, but it also means you should be just as capable to stop its advancement on your soul."

Malik mulled this over. "So, what do we do now? I can deal with my soul being taken over another day, we need to find the tomb and the only clue might be a knife and I also find out about the scrolls, which I have no idea how to find."

"Scrolls!?" the Williams uttered in unison, staring at him in bewilderment.

Looking back and forth at them, he was wondering on why they acted surprised.

"What's the big deal? Are the scrolls important?" he excitedly asked them, hope starting to spring up in his voice.

"No they aren't, or they would be, but the scrolls are considered to be a myth. A sort of bypass to get into the tomb. Let's just deal with the facts for now," Jaden told him, trying to not get his hopes up.

Jaden and his mom looked at each other for a moment. "Well, I guess you're bound to find out anyway, I think it's time to bring my father back."

Malik looked at both of them in confusion, unsure of what that meant.

"We'll need to contact the others and meet up," Jaden told him. "This isn't going to be a pleasant trip for any of us."

Pulling his phone out, it read eight-thirty. Shouldn't

they be going to school?

"School's been canceled for the next couple of days, to make sure nothing else happens, plus it's almost break, so we'll just give everyone an extended vacation which I don't think any of the students or teachers will mind. We'll make sure everyone still gets their standard pay as well, the council wants to use it as an excuse for why all of you might not be around," Jaden's mom explained as if somehow reading his mind.

"That gives us more than enough time to find the tomb and solve the problem of the missing knife," Jaden assessed.

They talked for another moment, then Regina excused herself to deal with council matters as well as make sure Malik's family was all right. Malik watched Jaden gather things up to take with him in a satchel. Jaden pulled out his phone and checked for messages. He nodded to himself, then looked over to Malik. "Everyone's ready, let's get this over with."

Quickly getting up out of his seat, still slightly confused as to what was happening. "What's the big deal about your dad, Jaden?"

He wore a pained expression on his face. "You'll see."

He stood there for a moment and a glowing golden portal appeared before them; they stepped through it and found themselves outside the house.

"I really need you to teach me that sometime," Malik

enviously informed him.

Jaden just looked at Malik and laughed. "I'm pretty sure you don't need my tricks when you've got your own that seems to be working just fine. For one thing, it can get past any magic defenses, which could be useful later on."

Malik blushed and just shrugged, trying to act like it was no big deal. Malik followed Jaden, who then made another portal, which they entered to find themselves in a clearing in the woods. Everyone was already waiting there, including Elinam, who he was shocked to see. Elinam smiled sheepishly at him before looking away.

"Oh, yeah, I invited Elinam to come, she could be useful if a death is about to happen. We'll know for sure," Jaden said.

"Why are we here of all places, Jaden? I have things I need to do with the pack," Nico grumbled.

"We've had some developments that make things more urgent," Jaden explained in a serious tone.

As Jaden turned to Malik and nodded to him, and Malik explained everything again. The others just sat in silence, taking in everything. Maya's expression didn't change at any point; Nico's unsurprisingly darkened by the time he finished; Bianca had a look of pity and sadness; and lastly, Elinam looked horrified and scared.

"I guess it was bound to happen, we knew you have a demon in you. It was wishful thinking, to think you could control it long enough to stop it," Maya stated, no emotion evident in her words.

It felt as though a knife was pressing in his heart with each word she imparted, as though she hadn't had any hope in him since the beginning; it hurt him a lot more than he expected. Maya was one of the few people he didn't want to disappoint, as she had revealed a side to him that he doubted many knew. He felt as though he had let down someone that wanted him to be everything she saw him to truly be.

Nico just looked at him in disgust. "Every time something happens, you're always losing control."

"Like you've never lost control of the wolf," Jaden admonished him.

Nico rounded on Jaden, his hand transforming into claws. "Yeah, when I was a kid! You're all throwing everything at a guy who's passed the point of maturing and expect him to be able to handle everything. Mark my words, he's gonna be our downfall, it's better to cut our losses before it's too late and skip the heartache."

Elinam and Bianca just watched it all unfold. Bianca looked long and hard at Malik before deciding on something. "Guys, there's no point in fighting right now. It's obvious his emotions are what pushed him to do that to his mother, I don't think he was even aware of what he was doing. I can tell he's ashamed of what happened, so let's find the tomb and get done with this, the faster we do it the better."

Seeing that he wasn't going to win his argument, he quickly quieted down. Nico looked at Malik, who understood what his eyes were saying–that this wasn't over.

Clearing his throat, Jaden told everyone, "Now that the drama is over, we need to call my father."

All the others besides Elinam gasped and looked visibly scared. "Do you think it's a wise idea to do that, Jaden?" Maya asked in a shaky voice. "The last time we did that, things didn't turn out so well."

He had never seen Maya shaken before and realized how much he didn't know what was going on in the group. They had obviously associated with each other more than the occasional lunch meeting.

"I know, but we don't have much of a choice," Jaden answered in a defeated voice.

The others said nothing after Jaden finished speaking; not even Nico responded back.

"What's going on? Who's Jaden's dad?" Elinam asked, worried.

"Well, you're about to find out why Jaden is a pariah in this town. His father's a demon and not just any demon – a Fallen," Maya said.

"A Fallen?" Malik asked. Did that mean what he thought it meant?

"Yeah, my dad was one of the good guys, but turned dark," Jaden nonchalantly told him, as if it wasn't the biggest news in the world.

"The stories are all different in each version, but just know he followed a bad demon and wound up on the losing side," Nico clarified for them.

He thought back to the painting in his basement and of the man that looked eerily like Jaden. Malik slowly pulled out his phone, showing Jaden a picture. "Is this the guy?"

Jaden froze the minute he saw it and quickly threw Malik's phone on the ground.

"Why did you do that?" Malik asked, shocked. "What if my parents call?"

He quickly picked his phone up; all he saw was a black screen and looked at Jaden in annoyance. Jaden looked at Malik with regret. "That picture was of my father, I'm sorry, but that picture shouldn't be on your phone. They can track you with that."

"They? Who's they and how can they track a picture?" Malik asked, already starting to lose his patience.

"Having an object of a demon, whether a picture or something that represents them in some way. It can be used as an anchor into our world, that's why a lot of religions value idols to show a visual image of someone they worship, for demons it's the same way with pictures. You give something a meaning behind it, if there's even a small amount of value placed on it, it's enough for them to cross over, some demons only need a weak connection. Luckily, my dad is the nicer type, but paranoia still got the better of me. I'm sorry for that," Jaden explained to him.

Malik just stood there mystified but nodded. That was all he could do at that moment.

"Let's just get this over with," Jaden grumbled, seeming to dread his reunion.

With that, Jaden turned around and pulled out a knife, and knelt to the ground. With a swipe of his hand, he parted the grass, leaving a visible engraving for all to see. Jaden cut his hand, poured his blood on the engraving, and spoke some words in a weird language.

"Whatever happens, make sure my father doesn't touch Malik, it could trigger his demon and cause a confrontation," Jaden commanded.

Everyone agreed with him. Malik and the others watched with awe and fear as a red ominous hole appeared on the ground where they stood. A few seconds later, a man appeared. Malik knew instantly it wasn't a man; he could feel the power oozing off the demon. It felt as though they were looking at a creature that had been born from living energy, the air visibly crackled red around the man.

He looked slightly like Jaden, but an older, darker version of him. His body was similar to Jaden's in some ways, he was taller and most muscular than his son. He sported a simpler haircut, unlike Jaden's skin he was a few shades darker with eyes that watched everything and left nothing for assumptions. A version that had seen and lived too much to be called human, he wasn't visibly imposing, but his presence left a sort of pressure that if someone wasn't too careful, they could suffocate from it. This demon surprisingly wore designer clothes seemingly crafted to every inch of its body to look its best; Malik could see where Jaden got his style from. He was so unlike the demons they had met in his home who just looked like demons, and the demons he met before that in this very park who looked like teenagers.

It just watched them for a couple of minutes, as if to see they were worth his time. Jaden said a couple more words and stepped back quickly.

"Why did you bring me here, Jay? I doubt it's for a father and son reunion." Its very voice felt like a mountain was speaking, it seemed to make everything shake.

"Can you stop that, Dad?" Jaden asked in an irritated voice.

The man just grinned. "No, I will not, now answer my question, or I'll leave. You've already rejected my power, what else could you want?"

Malik could tell Jaden didn't like his father and could see why he wouldn't. This was a true demon, nothing like the ones they faced before. It could destroy their whole town without even breaking a sweat; this was a being that had lived for centuries, and it didn't see them more than a simple moment in time. By the time it blinked, they would be old and gray, while it was forever young and unchanging. Why would it care about something as insignificant as them? Malik could just feel the power coming off this one. He was sure, if he had an inch of that power, he could save everyone without help.

"Malik, snap out of it," Nico reprehended roughly, pulling him back. Malik didn't realize he had unconsciously moved toward the demon.

The demon turned to Malik with mild interest. "This is what you're doing now, son? Taking in demon-ridden children? I thought you were better than this."

Through his better judgment, words escaped before he could stop himself, "What's your problem?"

Everyone held their breath as if waiting for things to blow up, but the demon just stared at Malik and burst into laughter.

Shocked, Malik took a step back, scared he was going to be blasted by the demon.

"You have guts, I'll give you that. Come closer, so I can see just how special you are."

Against his better judgment, Malik stepped toward him. The closer he got, the more he felt a weird sensation, as if he was once again reuniting with a lost friend.

Once Malik was close enough, the demon reached out, its once-masculine hands now with claws that touched his forehead. Malik's hand shot up and gripped the forearm of the demon, and when Malik turned over his own hands, they swirled in a black mist, and what seemed to be claws outlined them.

The demon withdrew his hand as if puzzled by something. "So, you've seen the portraits of us, hmm, that's very unfortunate."

The demon looked at Malik and bowed his head before backing away, leaving Malik feeling weak and used. It felt like he was in a far corner in his mind and watching everything happen around him.

The demon composed itself, stepping out of the circle as easily as crossing grass. The others stood there gasping, as if shocked that he escaped their circle so easily. It sat down with a chair that appeared before them from thin air. It looked at them, annoyed. "Well, are you going to stand there, or do you want some answers?"

Everyone looked at each other, and they cautiously followed the demon by sitting on the ground, arranging a semicircle around the demon.

"We're here Dad, tell us what's going on," Jaden stuttered, he struggled to say those words clearly.

The demon looked at Jaden as if saddened. "I should start from the beginning, everyone should know the story of the Demon King and his Nine Legion. I'll keep it short. When we first started, it was just a quest to make every creature equal. We were all tired of the everyday prejudice we faced from other beings that walked the Earth.

"No one truly knew where the Demon King came from; we all figured he was part-celestial, like some of us. We united so many different races; our dream of a perfect utopia was almost bearing fruit. That was until the Demon King was betrayed by one of our own. This droves a wedge between all the nine generals because they wanted to kill this person, but the Demon King loved the attacker and chose to let them go. You see, the attacker was none other than his beautiful wife, the Demon Queen."

"The attack didn't kill him, but it did lead to other gods from a different place banding together to attack us; many of us wanted to destroy these gods. But our king saw that with himself weakened, even if we were to win, it would be at a great cost. So the two other right hands and I laid a plan to bring ourselves back from death, essentially a reincarnation. We created a way to bring forth most of our generals and the power we lost by creating a prophecy because everyone knows prophecies are done in two ways."

"Either it's natural or you create one that's self-fulfilling. You just have to let the course be laid out to happen," Jaden interjected.

Everyone was distracted from the deep telling of the story by Jaden's interruption. The demon just looked at Jaden, waiting for him to finish, so he could continue. Jaden realized he interrupted and sheepishly nodded to his dad to finish.

"Like I was saying, almost all of us did something to come back to our King once he awakened. We didn't want to live in a world without him. He each sealed our power away in some way, whether it was an amulet, painting, or a creature."

Malik fingered his amulet, realizing this might be one of the demon's sources of power.

"We did everything we could, to wait for the right time for the King to come back."

"Why were you around then?" Maya surprisingly asked.

"If you'd let me get to that, I'd happily tell you. I couldn't put myself to sleep, since I was one of the original fallen and happened to be the one who did the ritual as well as others. It was simple, go to sleep. Make sure to have followers and build up our power in secret through our bloodline so one day we could all come back and finish what we started.

"I waited centuries for my best friend to come. I even gave up a quarter of my power to one day bring my incarnation to be around the same age range as the new King to help advise him."

Jaden and Malik shared a look. Could they have been destined to be friends no matter what? It was weird to think they were meant to meet in life, that something as flimsy as destiny existed.

"We followed everything, but what I didn't account for was one of the original demons to have its own plan. It was a true follower, it wanted to bring the Demon King back. I think in the beginning it waited, but one can only wait for so long before they're forced to take matters into their own hands. He wanted to take revenge on the world; probably figured if he could control the Demon King's return, he could get the outcome they originally wanted."

"That's the person who tried to take my sister. What are they?" Malik asked nervously.

"I'm getting to that," the demon irritated, shaking its head. "Someone interrupts me one more time, I'm just going to head back, and you can figure it out yourself."

That shut everyone up.

"So as I was saying, this demon was around for a while and laid the groundwork for something big. I believe in the beginning, it wanted to have its master back, but after a while, it became just as twisted as it was. It seeped into the lives of many and built its own lies just for the return of the King. The rest I can only guess to know what's truly going on.

"What I do know is that it's following the prophecy to the letter and not straying from it, so you can use that to your advantage. It wants the new king to either get its power or to wreak havoc, it's easier to break something than to build it up. It's pushing faster to reach its goal, meaning it's under a time crunch."

No one spoke for a long time, and the demon prompted them. "I'm done now."

"So what exactly is the prophecy?" Elinam asked, intrigued.

Jaden answered. "It goes like this," and began to sing:

"For death's greatest regret is to have lived, the coming of the promise land will bring about the destruction of life.

For the son of the sinner will rise, his brothers and sisters, to lead the greatest and loneliest wars imagined.

The brothers who walk in two worlds will rise to claim his true heart and be whole once again.

The sisters that rise to the heavens shall bring the crown of death.

The sons that howl at the moon will once again dance in harmony.

The generals of death will each claim their title before their Age of Enlightenment or die by the hands of their greatest beloved.

For the world will feel the sorrow of the King and rejoice in their coming death.

For the King shall come risen to bring his vision, at the cost of what he holds dear. Who shall conquer who, only time will tell whose blood spills in anguish to madden Nightmare?"

Everyone just sat there trying to process everything. Bianca started talking. "Wait, I think it's–"

"Bianca, be quiet," Maya commanded sharply.

Bianca's mouth snapped shut at Maya's outburst.

"The prophecy doesn't matter right now, just tell us how to find the demon, so we can stop it," Maya demanded.

Jaden's dad just shook his head. "I've already told

you, but I guess I'll break it down. The demon can invade others' nightmares, or dreams, to be exact. Malik's already been around it more than once now." It looked over at Malik in a knowing manner.

Malik thought back to the moments where things couldn't be explained. No matter how many times he thought back, his head went to the house and meeting that man. The man did say that he knew Malik and somehow was watching after the family. Malik suddenly remembered that the man had two sharp incisors for teeth. Malik told the others and they all inhaled sharply.

"Malik, that's a type of demon, possibly S class or higher of some kind. That explains it now, why Malik told us of the place he thought was under his house," Jaden said, seeming to piece things together that Malik didn't see.

"So you're saying this demon planned everything to the point of Malik's attack at home, all just to make Malik go crazy?" Nico skeptical asked.

"That explains his family's connection to everything, he must have been the one that implanted the demon in Malik when he was an infant," Maya added.

"No, that's obviously not what they want. They wanted revenge, having Malik go crazy won't help them do anything. I think they just want a way to control Malik without having to do a lot of work. It's easier to make someone follow your orders when they have nothing else to live for," Jaden countered. His idea seemed to be more plausible than Nico's.

"Well, I guess you don't need me anymore since you've figured everything out," Jaden's dad said. He got up and the chair disappeared. The demon started to walk back to where it originally came from.

CHAPTER 13

Wait, I need to know. What makes me so special?" Jaden asked, scrambling toward his dad.

The demon turned around and, its eyes glowing a golden red for a minute, then slowly only one eye glowed red while the other showed a dull purple.

"I think you already know, Jaden." Staring into Jaden's eyes, the demon seemed to not seem as powerful anymore, but looked like a man that was tired of living, who had experienced so much that it had worn down not just his eyes but his life, making him age right in front of them.

"You gave up your own power, didn't you? You imprinted your power into me, a piece of your very soul. I'm not an incarnation of you but literally, carry a piece of you."

The demon nodded, looking up into the sky as if searching for something. "I tried so hard to have children for centuries; I had a few successes, but their demonic side would always win and the only way for them to pass on their power is to have their prodigal children kill them. It wasn't what I wanted; I had given up until I met your mother. She didn't know I was a demon the first time, she just thought I was an awakened mortal, but I fell in love fast, and I realized she was the one that spoke of my death and the child I would bear to fix my wrongs.

"I finally told her what I was, but by then it was too late. We were deep in love, but I didn't know that I was expecting you for a while now. Your mother was pregnant for a while until something happened that brought you here. To save you, I gave a piece of my power, which inevitably led to me slowly dying. I guess in some way you are my incarnation, you'll fix the mistakes I made so many centuries ago."

"Wait, I'm lost now," Elinam asked, puzzled. "Are you a wizard or demon?"

"I thought it was obvious, he's a warlock," Nico answered, surprising everyone. "Since he's part celestial, and his father wasn't originally a demon, he can be on their side of the realm."

"I still don't understand, but I think we're wasting time talking about it," Elinam defeatedly admitted.

They watched as Jaden and his demon father walked away from them to a corner, talking in hushed voices. Malik could only imagine what he felt, to find out his father's true origins and his as well. He was lucky his parents weren't directly supernatural; he didn't know how he'd be able to take it. Everything was beginning to fit, and he wasn't as lost anymore.

"So we're just gonna stand here and talk all day?" Nico questioned all of them.

Bianca looked annoyed, but Maya shook her head at her sister and that seemed to calm her down. Bianca walked toward Malik and went in for a hug. Malik greatly welcomed it; he needed a hug badly, since he still felt responsible for what had happened in his parent's house.

"Are you doing okay?" Bianca sincerely asked.

Malik sighed melodramatically. "Yeah, other than the fact that I might be the incarnation of some big bad demon king who probably has a gripe with everyone that caused his downfall, plus one of his equally messed-up followers is causing all of this. Yeah, I'm doing great."

Bianca laughed the first laugh Malik had heard in a while, and he loved it. He didn't want it to end.

"Well, you're definitely right, you're doing great. Let's do more stuff like this again," Bianca applauded him, she gave him a mischievous smile.

"Oh yeah, summon demons regularly and find out stuff that could lead to the world ending. That's what I do for all the girls I think that are cute." Malik blushed, realizing what he'd just admitted.

Bianca just arched an eyebrow at Malik as if she'd caught him tripping up. "I wouldn't say that in front of

Maya, just know I'm expecting a date after this is all over." Bianca smiled.

He almost choked on his saliva right there and then. Malik cleared his throat profusely, then spoke in a scratchy voice, "Yeah, I'll definitely remember that once this is all over."

Looking around, he saw everyone was starting to regroup. Jaden was done talking to his father and now conversed with the others.

"I think we should get back to everyone," Malik recommended, clearing his voice once again. Why was he this bad at talking to her?

"Okay, good, everyone's here, so my dad told me we don't need the knife necessarily at the moment. We just need to find the demon and defeat it," Jaden announced, as everyone gathered around him.

Nico just looked at Jaden as if he was joking. "How do you propose we do that with no clue how to find the demon?"

Maya now looked at Nico as if he was joking. "It's obvious where the demon is – every time Malik went to his house. He saw the demon under his home in a supposed catacomb, which now that I think about it, it's probably the tomb we've been looking for this whole time. But I looked into Malik's home blueprint and while there is a basement, there's no way there's a catacomb that big under his home, unless …"

"Unless it's by magic," Nico finished Maya's sentence.

"Exactly, or at the very least, a dimensional rift that leads to another plane," Jaden added.

"I'm sorry, what?" Elinam asked, once again looking lost.

"Well, you know how we go through my portal? I'm ripping a hole through one place in space to another, so just think of that but on a bigger scale. It's almost impossible to make unless you're powerful or have something that connects you to that place," Jaden explained.

"So how did Malik get there in the first place?" Nico asked the group.

"It's simple, the amulet called to him the first time, and it led him there," Jaden explained. "The second time and maybe the first time as well, the demon had somehow brought him into the tomb himself. Malik had left an imprint of himself there, so it was easier to enter the next time. It was a nightmare demon he did meet down there, so possibly it invaded his dreams, he possibly dreamed it all. Once Malik was there, it allowed a door into his mind to leave and enter whenever it wanted to. If Malik strongly felt like visiting the tomb before he slept then he most likely had opened the doorway himself especially with his shadow walker ability he used in my house, I could see that happening. I do believe this time, with us and who else is going, we need something more than just the amulet. We need to find the door or maybe a demon to get us in."

"How about the knife? I have a feeling it could get us there," Malik suggested.

The others all shook their heads. "When we first got you, the knife, as well as the Guardian's sword, was missing. We just assumed the sword went to the next in line, but we've seen that Andy still has it," Maya stated.

"So, let's see what we have. We know where the tomb technically is, but we can't go without the knife that supposedly gets us there. Well, things could be worse," Nico reiterated for everything.

"Actually, my dad did tell me that we could use the scrolls to find the tomb ourselves; I currently have one of them from my dad, and it's telling us to go somewhere. I didn't think it is possible for most of us, but luckily we have our own resident kid, or should I say, girl wonder." Jaden cheekily smiled at Elinam as he pulled a scroll from his bag.

"Elinam's connection to the dead is something above anything I've ever heard of, it's like she's the Reaper himself," Jaden admiringly told everyone, which in turn caused everyone to look over to her in surprise. Was she that special?

"What are the scrolls and what are they supposed to do?" Elinam asked in a way to deter the attention away from her. Nico protectively reached out to her to pull her back from the scroll as if it was a bomb.

"Well, according to my dad, there were originally

three scrolls to lock away the tomb of their King so that no one would try to find it so easily and destroy it. If we find the other two scrolls and put them together, we should be able to bring the tomb back to our own world instead of wildly searching to find it. It's a precaution in case we find it and don't throw ourselves into outer space or anything." Jaden weakly explained it, as if he wasn't completely sure of himself. That didn't give them much confidence, especially since Jaden wasn't even sure.

"Yeah, I think things can definitely go wrong now," Maya stated, bringing everyone's moods down again.

"Oh, I don't know about that. I'm sure we can help you on that front," a female voice from the clearing told them.

Everyone immediately sprung into defense mode, swords and claws drawn, and staffs at the ready.

Malik tried calling upon his power but couldn't seem to find anything. He just felt empty. Before he could panic, the voice and the body that belonged to it appeared – it was a Asian American girl wearing a robe as dark as midnight, with a blue crest of a raven on the left side of its chest.

"I see you're still talking to your demon father, Jaden, even after we warned you last time," she spat at Jaden.

"Nice to see you too Vy, what do you want?" Jaden asked, grinding teeth in annoyance.

"Why, to kill your little new pet demon, I thought you

would stop asking stupid questions now after so many years," Vy said, not bothering to hide the malice in her voice.

"I'm sorry, but that's not happening, the council already gave him amnesty, so you can't touch him until we found the tomb," Maya said, peeved at the girl.

"Well, good thing I'm not in your stupid council, isn't it?" Vy asked, smiling in triumph, as though she was in on some big secret they weren't privy to.

"Can we just take her down now? I'm tired of all of this," Nico chimed in.

Jaden warned them, "Unless she does something to us, we can't attack her."

The girl Vy reached into her pocket, causing everyone to tense up. She brought out a piece of paper and tossed it to Maya, who in turn passed it to Jaden. Jaden read it, and Malik could tell from his face that things didn't look good.

"We have only twenty-four hours to destroy the tomb, or we'll all be tried for treason. This is by the witch coven and the high council," Jaden revealed in an uneasy voice.

"The high council? What exactly are they?" Malik asked in a worried tone.

"The big international one that all supernatural creatures follow," Jaden said. "They want you gone; they think you'll bring about the next apocalypse. But they're giving you one day to stop it."

"Okay, that works for me. Why is she here then?"

Malik asked, wondering why they didn't just send a letter message.

Everyone looked at the witch as if she'd share why she was here. Then he heard it, first low, then it got louder. Malik saw eleven or twelve more figures wearing weird masks and the same clothing as Vy.

Nico could barely conceal his excitement. "It's an ambush, everyone, get ready!"

Then it just happened so fast – one minute they were standing there and the next, Malik was fighting witches.

The witches came from all corners of the woods. Malik had no clue how many of them were there. When Malik looked around, everyone was busy fighting.

Nico moved in and out of wolf form so fluidly, it was like he was stepping into thin air and transforming without a moment's notice. He was so busy flinging witches and taking down any sort of magical attack that he failed to notice a group of witches chanting just behind him on a mound. He rushed to give out a warning, but before he could, Elinam did the weirdest thing–in her hands were dark spheres seeming to be some type of energy. She threw beams of energy at the witch. Not only that, but he felt the power from where he stood; luckily it wasn't pointed in his direction, or he would have been hurt.

Quickly he gave her a nod and she gave one back before she rushed to cover Nico. Now all he could see was a girl with energy blasts and a beast creating a massacre in her wake.

Jaden was literally a one-man army, taking down witches as if batting flies down. He would create portals and simply send any objects after them one after another, sometimes even sending other witches through a portal to end up trampling on their friends. With no end of power or ammunition to take them down, Malik could tell the witches were getting weary of everything.

Turning the other way, he saw the sisters being badass as well; they truly looked like avenging angels as they moved as one to take down the witches' accomplices, which seemed to be made of mud. He could have sworn he saw wings on both sisters' backs, but before he could make out the details, they disappeared.

Vy moved to attack Malik, and he fended for his life. Malik instantly knew he was outclassed in every way. He couldn't bring his magical air sword to a legit magic fight; he even tried to make one and all there came was sparks. His death would just be comical, and he had a feeling Nico wouldn't let him hear the end of it, even in the afterlife.

"Hey Ento, any ideas to help me survive?" he called to his ghostly friend from a different century. He could feel her in the back of his head, almost bubbling up to the surface.

He waited a couple of seconds, but had no answer, and went back to the task at hand. Currently, he had Vy and two others taking him on. Malik was able to keep himself from getting annihilated, mostly by luck. Maybe he could somehow slip through the darkness and take out the girls one at a time.

The last time Malik had done that, he'd ended up in Jaden's room with no clue how he got there. He reluctantly recalled back to the feelings he felt after seeing his parents hurt, and it left a great pain in his chest.

A small black hole appeared in midair, and Malik began to understand he needed to fill his power with emotion to make things like that happen.

"Oh, you're finally starting to figure it out?" the demon in him suddenly taunted.

"Shut up," Malik growled in his head as he stopped one of the witches that threw a vine at him. Malik hated to admit it, but the demon was right.

Not only could he make portals, but he could also enter other people's shadows. The first time he did it, it had been by accident. Vy had cast a fireball at him, which he thankfully ducked. Then he was being pulled under, he thought it was by one of the other witches, but instead, he sank into a shadow and appeared behind her; luckily, he recovered fast or the lightning bolt that came after him would have fried him faster than he could disappear again. After getting the hang of it after a couple of errors, he was able to barely survive each attack.

He couldn't seem to get close to them long enough to land a hit; if he attacked one girl, the other two backed her up. It was starting to get frustrating not being able to do anything; everyone was too preoccupied. He slowly noticed small patterns in the shadows, like they were giving him precognitive awareness of where they would attack. It wasn't completely correct, which he sadly discovered after burning his new coat on accident. He decided to stick to his instincts instead of something that wasn't reliable.

Even though he was somewhat trained to create fireballs and other types of stuff, he hadn't been able to do anything since being in that dream state.

Malik was lost on how to push himself, so caught up in the thought that he didn't notice the sneak attack until it was too late. The witch on his right whipped a vine around him; he sidestepped the vines but didn't realize Vy was right next to him until it was too late. She brought out a knife that looked oddly like the one used to attack him a few nights ago.

The knife went into his side and Malik met insane pain. Malik doubled over, blood already seeping out of his mouth. He flashed in and out of consciousness, saw a shadow in front of him. His eyes slowly cleared up, and he stared at himself, but he knew it wasn't truly him.

He was wrapped in a cloak of shadows but sported just a T-shirt and jeans. The other him looked at him in disgust, as if he truly didn't believe Malik was this pathetic.

"Well, I see you're still lost," the other Malik grinned. The voice sounded just like his, but colder and left a heavy emptiness in the air afterward.

Malik, still in pain, asked, "Who are you?"

"Oh, I think you know, Malik, you've known all along."

Realization dawned on Malik. "You're the demon inside me, aren't you?"

The other Malik offered a wicked smile. "Yes and no, oh, how much I despise you, Malik. You could have it all, but you're still not giving in to your true power."

He was starting to completely lose consciousness now. Demon Malik reached out and grabbed the hilt of the knife; Malik thought he was going to take it out, but he twisted it even more.

Excruciating pain raced through his body as every nerve was aflame, but the more pain he felt, the more he stayed awake. The demon was now at eye level to Malik, and it grinned in satisfaction.

"Good, we got some catching up to do. First, you need to survive this, and then we'll figure it out," the demon Malik told him.

"I'm not really in a position to survive, if you hadn't noticed, I can't do anything!" Malik yelled at himself, feeling stupid as well as groggy.

The demon laughed. "Maybe because you're not doing it right. Let me take control, and I'll get us out of here. Your wizard friend has the power to stop this, but doesn't want to," he claimed, ticking his head over to a suspended Jaden.

He just realized everyone was frozen in midair as if time itself had stopped. Malik didn't have much of a choice right now – whether he liked it or not, he had to give in to the demon.

Demon Malik grinned again as if he already knew Malik's answer. It was like it could smell his defeat.

"Well, what's it gonna be? You possibly die without protecting your family, or just let me take your body for a spin for a couple of minutes to save you and your pathetic excuse for friends?" Demon Malik asked innocently.

Ready to give in, he sucked in a deep breath, but before he could speak, Ento came out of nowhere. *"Don't do it, Malik!"*

Shocked to see her, all he could do was stare, unsure what to say anymore. He felt like he had no better options; he couldn't access any of his power besides making a portal, and he wasn't going to use it to leave his friends. He was bleeding out and useless to everyone there. Jaden and the others deserved someone who could contribute to the group in a fight, so what if he gave his body to the demon– it wasn't like it could do worse than him.

"Why not? I need him to get out of this!" Malik desperately asked, pain rushing through his entire body.

Rushing to him, Ento bent down and spoke softly, "If you do this, there's no going back. You're letting a monster take you over. It's going to mark your soul and lead you down a dark path."

Even though Malik was scared, but he was willing to do anything to survive this knife wound and protect his family.

Looking away in shame, he said, "I know, but it doesn't matter. I can only save myself if I use the demon."

"Just know I warned you."

All he could do was nod, then look upon demon Malik; his eyes told him everything that needed to be said. The lookalike of him smiled in a sinister and twisted way before reaching to pick up Malik. It held him by the throat and looked in his eyes.

"This is going to hurt a lot, but I hope you survive this because I wanna have more fun like this," the other Malik gleefully told him.

All Malik saw were eyes made of a swirling of red and gold. He could feel the power and rage coming off of them with just a look. Malik had to look away. When he looked back at the demon, he decided at the last minute. He'd rather fight to the end as himself than give away his humanity to some demon.

Trying to wiggle out of its grip, but it was like trying to fight an iron wall. The other Malik raised Malik high.

"Wait, I changed my mind!"

The demon Malik just laughed. "Hell no! It's my time to rein in terror."

It slammed Malik down hard, but when it did, Malik passed through the floor and tried to get up but was blocked by a barrier. Malik was suspended right next to the floor, but he couldn't get out.

Demon Malik looked down at him and grinned. "Well, let's have some fun."

He pleaded to Ento with his hands, who stood there doing nothing. Malik went to call for his friends' help, but Ento, defeated, said, "It's too late, Malik, now you'll know what it truly means to be broken."

All he could do was watch as the world in him slip away to only see demon Malik transformed into something twisted.

He woke to feel the knife still in him, but when he tried to look around, he couldn't. It was like he was still in his body, but he was disconnected, not fully submerged with his physical body.

"Now you know how I feel," demon Malik expressed to Malik in his head.

He was shocked. This is what they felt while he was living? This was a cruel and sad way to live.

Unable to do anything but watch as the scene unfolded before his eyes, demon Malik pulled the knife out and just looked at Vy with a grin.

In a voice that sounded just like Malik's, but with an edge to it, he cheerily told her, "Thank you, darling, but I'll be keeping this."

Then Vy looked mystified, as if she thought it was supposed to kill him. Demon Malik just stood up and stretched, as if he'd been asleep for a couple of hours. Everyone stopped for a minute to see the bizarre scene.

Demon Malik looked at the knife and said some words Malik didn't understand. Before Malik's eyes, he watched the knife turn into a long, thin sword.

Everyone was shocked by what was happening, or at least that's what Malik thought. One of the attackers pointed at Malik and shouted, "His eyes! It's really a demon. Everyone, run!"

CHAPTER 14

All hell broke loose. The demon controlling him just laughed and started to attack everyone. It didn't care if they were a part of Malik's group or not – it rained fireballs on witches, while at the same time throwing arches of shadows from the new sword. Malik was amazed at the demon, and how it seemed to know how to exactly use his power.

The one thing that surprised him was that it didn't kill any of the attackers. Malik was grateful for that. It was one thing to kill in self-defense, but another to kill in cold blood.

Once most of the witches were taken down, demon Malik turned to Vy and grinned at her. The girl stumbled backward; Malik had to give credit to the girl, she seemed stronger than the others for not passing out in terror.

The demon Malik spoke, "So who really sent you?"

Vy, with a shaky voice, "I don't know what you mean – the witches sent me."

The demon Malik shook its head. "I'm truly disappointed that you think I'm that naïve, it really wounds a demon such as myself. It looks like you're going to die."

The demon Malik walked slowly to Vy as if it had all the time in the world.

"Wait, I'll tell you, please don't kill me. It was a Prince, a Prince of Hell sent me! I swear that's all I know," Vy cried out.

The demon didn't stop his stride toward Vy, seeming to ignore whatever she proclaimed.

Out of nowhere, a sword came at Malik's head, though the demon easily blocked it. The demon Malik looked to his sides to see the sisters attacking him–Bianca on his left and Maya on his right.

"We can't let you do that, Malik, or whoever you are," Maya firmly told him, not caring who it was that was in front of her.

The demon Malik laughed. "Oh, really? So you let me take down everyone for you, but once they're gone, you want to take me down?"

The sisters just looked at each other in agreement, then pushed at Malik's body, but the demon was easily able to take them on. They attacked persistently, but no matter what they tried, they could never get the demon to drop his guard. Malik, inside his head, was mildly impressed; the demon controlling him was incredibly skilled.

While the demon Malik fended off the sisters, a claw came out of nowhere and tried to tear off his face. Malik from inside screamed at the demon to watch out. The claw was followed by the rest of the eight-foot-tall beast he recognized as Nico. Malik thought Nico in werewolf form was scary when he was attacking him and not fighting for him. The demon controlling Malik didn't even seem to mind the big wolf. The werewolf couldn't get any hits, and Malik's body finally got tired of the games and threw Nico across the woods.

"Malik, I need you to come back to us before we both do something we regret," Jaden urged him, completely ignoring the demon controlling him and trying to reach him inside his mind.

He tried to call out but couldn't say anything. The demon Malik spoke instead. "Aw, you care, Jaden, well, it sucks for you that you're not getting Malik back."

Jaden just snorted. "It seems like you don't know Malik that well. He's willing to do what it takes to for everyone, but what about saving them from him?"

The demon looked puzzled for a moment, then it grinned. "I guess we'll just wait and see."

Elinam threw one of her blasts once again in his direction. It threw Malik to the ground and caused him to howl in pain. It felt as though his life was being sucked out of him.

One minute the world was moving, then it froze again. Malik finally broke through the floor and saw the other Malik watching in annoyance.

"I can't believe you're the one they chose, you're truly pathetic," demon Malik disdainfully said.

Getting up as quickly as he could, Malik composed himself, and walked over to the demon. "I'm never letting you have control ever again."

The demon Malik just laughed. "Stop lying, little king, you know you enjoyed the power, even if it was secondhand. You'll come back, they always do!"

"I think that's enough, Malik, let's get out of here," Jaden told him.

Malik whipped his head around to find Jaden a few feet from him and wondered if he was really losing his mind. Jaden was there, in his head with both Maliks, but it wasn't the same guy he was used to, given the fact that this Jaden was a six-foot-something creature with black feather wings and a small horn on the left side of his face. The strange tattoos that he saw on his body were the most surprising thing, continuously swirling and changing shape.

Confusion was on his before realizing what Malik was staring at, but Jaden flickered for a moment and Malik saw the regular Jaden that he knew.

Jaden blushed. "Sorry, not many people see my other true form. I guess it's not normal to be part-celestial and witch."

"Oh, ah, it's cool. I was just shocked to see it, but it was cool," Malik awkwardly admitted. It was pretty impressive, but he wasn't sure how to process that his friend had another form that looked demonic. It made sense, given his dad was a demon, but it made Malik wonder if he had a demonic form in him.

Jaden walked toward both of them, nodding to the demon version. "I guess this is your source of power, it's pretty impressive. Most people can't access it for decades, and it seems to be pretty immense. I believe that you have a lot more power than the Demon King did at your age, you just have to learn at some point."

It was Malik's turn to blush. Quickly changing the subject, Malik asked, "So how did you get in here?"

"Oh, you know, magic." Jaden grinned.

Laughing a little at his small inside joke, Malik cluelessly laughed with him.

The demon Malik just groaned at both of them and started to walk away, while a hammock appeared out of nowhere. The demon jumped on the hammock, its sword still in its hand. The demon Malik looked at both teenagers. "If you're done making terrible jokes, go away, I'm going to take a nap."

They just looked at the demon in confusion. Malik asked, "That's it? No fighting for power or anything?"

The demon Malik turned to both and just grinned. "Why would I need to do that? I've already won, you've had a taste of my power, and you'll always come back for your fix."

He frowned. As much as he hated the demon for saying that he could already feel the hunger to destroy more. To have utter mastery over his powers was something he'd wanted ever since finding out he had any. After seeing the way the demon handled everything, it showed that he needed to get better, until the point where everything was instinctive.

"Let's go, Malik, we need to deal with the present problems. We can deal with this one another time," Jaden suggested.

He moved to follow Jaden when the demon interjected, "Oh if you want to find the tomb, I'd strongly suggest contacting a demon to do it."

Surprise rang through both Malik and Jaden, who looked back at the demon and just frowned.

Malik asked, "Why are you being helpful?"

The demon just huffed and shrugged. "I want my family back together too. I've grown fond of the people in your life, plus I'll get to fight some more, so it's a win-win."

He was shocked. Maybe the demon did care about him and his family just as much as him.

Malik opened his mouth to speak. "I appre–"

Before he could finish, he was on the ground, coughing up blood, and discovered Maya standing over him. "Get up, Malik, we need to talk."

Still in pain, he stood up, looking at his hands covered in his blood. Maya stopped a couple of feet away from him, waiting for him to get up. Jaden walked over to Malik with the demon's knife-turned-sword.

Jaden threw it to Malik, who caught it in midair. The instant his skin touched it, his mind started to clear, and he watched to his amazement as the wound in his side closed in on itself. Once finished examining himself, he was greeted with the others watching him closely.

"So you really are a demon?" Jaden stated as if he was finally confirming a suspicion.

"What are you talking about?"

"That's your weapon; any wound inflicted by your own blade can be healed. It's officially become bonded to you in the old ways of bonding weapons with the wielder's own blood. It'll keep you alive."

Malik still didn't understand what that meant. He looked over the knife and saw swirling symbols etched into it. The symbols slowly crawled off the knife and onto his arm. Malik tried to drop the knife, but it was impossible. The symbols finally settled onto his right arm. The knife that was once there disappeared, as if it was never there, and the symbols disappeared, as if made from invisible ink.

Bewilderment was written all over his face as he looked at the others watching him closely again. Malik looked around and saw all the attackers had left. It looked like a war zone. Malik slowly got up. "What happened?"

Nico got up, and for the first time, Malik could see Nico was wounded. He had a nasty gash on his shoulder and he nursed the wound with his shirt.

"You happened, Malik, mind telling us what the hell you did?" Nico grunted in a slightly pained voice.

Malik looked around. Maya was okay, but Bianca seemed slightly dazed. Elinam didn't seem hurt but shaken, and she was huddled where Nico had been sitting.

"I'm sorry, I let the demon in me take over," Malik apologetically answered.

Nico growled. "Why do you keep doing this? Don't you know we're all here risking our necks to protect you, and you decide to endanger us with your idiocy once again?"

Malik started to see what he had done was bad. "I thought y'all were in danger and I wanted to help."

Nico just shook his head in disappointment, and walked away, deeper into the woods. Elinam got up and went after him. Malik and the others all watched them disappear.

Maya walked up to Malik. "We were never in any real danger, Malik, Jaden is here. Next time you want to do something like that, please give us a warning. We're all friends with lives outside of this. This isn't some adventure where we risk our lives for you. We could die helping you, trust me when I say we know what it is to lose someone you love."

Malik just nodded. Maya then turned to Jaden. "So, what's the plan now?"

Jaden got up as well, walked to the middle, and motioned the rest to get closer. "It's simple – we need to get to the tomb. Now we know the demon entered through his dream state. We have the knife; we need to just find a way in now."

"Hmph, easier said than done, how do we get in?" Bianca asked.

"Well, it's simple, we need a demon with similar abilities to get us in. Since Malik is technically their king, I'm sure someone will be able to help us, and I know just the place to get one to help."

"You sure there's not another way?" Malik asked, they all stared at Jaden as if he had lost his mind.

"I know this whole demon business is bad, considering your history with them, but to help Malik, we have to go deeper than we've ever done before."

Wondering who Jaden was talking to, he looked over to see Bianca and Maya giving each other what appeared to be pained expressions.

"What happened?" he asked Bianca, looking back and forth between the sisters.

He saw sedated eyes meet his and Bianca said, "Our mom was killed by a demon when we were kids."

He stood there, shell-shocked, not knowing what to say. Here he was letting a demon control him, while he should have understood why they didn't want to be around them in the first place.

"I'm so sorry, I didn't know," Malik apologized to both sisters, his head down in shame from what he had done.

Maya shrugged. "It's not a big deal, it's life. We all die in the end, our mother was just earlier than most."

All he could do was stand there as he was blown away by Maya's response. How could she be so cold about her own mother's death?

"I'm still sorry about me going all demon on y'all," Malik apologized once again.

Maya turned to Jaden as if she was done with the conversation. Malik opened his mouth to speak but was stopped by Bianca grabbing his hand and shaking her head.

"Okay, we're going to the Underworld to get ourselves a demon," Jaden said. "Everyone rests up for a couple of minutes before we head out. It's going to be a long day."

Everyone splits up and grabbed all the gear they had with them. As much as Malik wanted to talk to Bianca about her mother, Malik knew there was someone he needed to talk to more at that moment.

Malik walked up to Nico, who had his back turned. Once Malik was a couple of feet away, Nico asked impatiently, "What do you want, Malik?"

"How'd you know I was behind you?" Malik asked, surprised that Nico could tell it was him.

Looking him directly in his eyes, Nico shrugged. "Werewolf, remember? Plus, you're not that quiet, anyway. You need to work on your stealth with Bianca."

He looked away embarrassed, not even knowing the reason why he did that. "Can you turn people into werewolves?"

Nico searched Malik's face for a minute before answering. "Yeah, there are ways to turn people, but it won't work for you since you're already a demon or whatever."

"Not for me, just wondering in general." Curiosity getting the better of Malik, it was something he'd wondered since meeting Nico.

Annoyance evident in his voice, Nico told him, "People can either be born or bitten. But being bitten gives you a fifty-fifty survival rate if you survive the transition. Sometimes the body rejects the transformation. But you should also know that if you're a supernatural person and a wolf bites you, if you can't heal in a matter of hours or days, you'll die, but won't ever turn."

Absorbing all of this information. He figured it was because of the way Elinam followed Nico around that she wanted to turn into one herself, but it wasn't possible because she was also supernatural.

"So, is being an alpha like the same thing? You're one or you're not?"

Sighing, Nico explained, "That's more complicated,

you can be born an alpha, but you can lose it as well. You can take being an alpha from another alpha by killing them."

Malik was shocked about this; he figured all the myths weren't true, but he was wrong. Malik looked at Nico; he assumed he was an Alpha, given the color of his werewolf eyes. He remembered the first werewolf he'd met had glowing yellow eyes.

"What about eye color?" Malik asked.

"Um, it's simple, yellow is the purest one, blue means you've killed an innocent, and red is usually alpha. There are stories of gold-colored eyes, but those haven't been around for centuries."

"Gold-colored? Like what?"

Finally finished with his packing, Nico sat down facing Malik. "There are stories of weres that had gold-colored eyes; they were the most powerful of us. They were said to be great ancient spirits with abilities unlike any other. I personally think they're stories like the Boogeyman."

"Oh, that sounds cool," Malik whispered in awe.

"But there is an even worse Boogeyman story – weres that would kill other alphas in rituals to gain their power. It was considered forbidden because it takes a piece of their soul and traps the weres that were killed from fully crossing over to the other side. If you ever see a werewolf with black-colored eyes, run, " Nico quietly told Malik, who had just barely heard his words. "But let's table this for now, right now we've got to find your Boogeyman and put a stop to it."

"Wait, can I ask you something else?" Malik nervously asked Nico, scared of his reaction.

"What is it?" Nico asked tiredly, already getting up.

"Why did you help Elinam that day?" he asked, peering into Nico's eyes.

"I don't know why you feel you have to know, but if it's that important to you–she reminds me of someone I once knew. I feel like it's my responsibility to protect her. Like you would with Nina. Are you happy now?" Nico stared directly into his eyes as if to challenge him before brushing past Malik to meet the rest of the group. Malik watched him go for a minute before rushing after them.

Once everyone was once together again, Jaden opened a portal around the area where they first spoke to Jaden's dad. Malik remembered something from earlier before the fight.

"Hey guys, what about that scroll?" he asked with uncertainty, feeling like they were rushing to their doom.

Standing there shocked, Jaden looked at him for a moment, then hit his head with his palm. "Damn, I really am slow, I completely forgot about that. I think we can hold off on going to the Underworld City just yet."

Everyone let out a sigh of relief, which caused Malik to think about why they were all scared about that city in the first place. He chose to let it go and watched as Jaden pulled out the scroll.

His hands shaking, looking at the scrolls, Jaden said, "If this doesn't work out, we could find ourselves anywhere in this world or another."

The alarm was evident in all their faces. Nico groaned, "Wait, you're not even sure?"

Aging before them, Jaden appeared haggard and tired. "Hey, I can't know everything, and it's not like there's a manual for this type of stuff. This is legit centuries-old magic that no one is really taught these days. All I know is that it's supposed to unlock the way to the tomb, wherever it is."

He couldn't expect Jaden to know everything there was to know, but he completely trusted him. Taking a deep breath, before he told everyone. "I say we go."

"Are you crazy?" This time it wasn't Nico who asked, but Elinam.

Malik felt the demon in him stirring as if tired of being judged. Forcing himself to not lose the smallest ounce of control, he barely could, and turned toward everyone.

"What's the point of *not* going? I thought we were on this quest to stop the demons that wanted to resurrect their old overlord. If we're not willing to push ourselves toward the next stage of this journey, then we might as well just turn back now and let the world as we know it to be destroyed. But I know none of you will do that, so let's stop pretending to be scared and just go do the job that needs to be done instead of wasting time."

"Well, look at you becoming a hero. I guess we can't let you go off and die alone." Jaden applauded him.

They all wore smiles, some more reluctantly than others.

"I guess we have to go now." Elinam accepted the decision.

Walking up to Malik, Jaden clapped him on the back, getting close to whisper in his ear. "You might just have what it takes to be a leader one day man, I'm proud of you."

He gazed up at Jaden, smiling weakly as he recalled his conversation with Andy from earlier that morning.

Turning his attention to everyone and rubbing his hands together, Jaden reiterated, "So just to be clear, there are three scrolls we'll have to gather to get the upper hand on the demons we're up against. We have one that leads to the spirit realm; the other two are believed to be in the demon realm and somewhere right in this city."

Bianca perked up. "Did you just say spirit realm followed after demon realm? We're definitely going to die. You can count me in."

He broke into a smile at her joke, which also let everybody loosen up as well.

"So how do we get there? There's no way there is a portal that is directly connected to that place," Maya asked Jaden.

He turned to Elinam. "Our biggest advantage right now is that we have Elinam here with us. Since her powers come from death, she has a direct link to the spirit realm. We'll need her skills to get us there and back. Do you want to help?"

Elinam, who had been quiet with them the entire time, spoke the most Malik had heard since she came with them to the woods. "I'm not sure how I can help. I once accidentally stumbled upon it, but I don't know if I want to go back there again. The spirit realm takes a piece of you when you leave it, are you sure you want to go there?"

Jaden seemed to understand Elinam's hesitation but nodded. "Yes, I'm sorry, but we need to go. We'll protect you when we're there, I promise."

Everyone else showed their agreement in different forms, even Malik. Elinam stared at them and finally signaled her agreement to Jaden's request.

"Well, we'll have to go where death is the closest to the living," Jaden suggested.

"A funeral?" Elinam asked him, puzzled.

Jaden shook his head. "No, that'd be nice if we there were, but we can't wait for someone to just die for us. We can go to a graveyard where souls are last tied to their physical form."

"Oh, that's just as weird, but I guess there's nothing to do about that." Disheartened, Malik shrugged, even though he was unsure if he wanted to cause the dead unrest. Malik wasn't super religious, even though he'd grown up with a somewhat spiritual family.

"Let's go before we lose our conviction," Jaden said.

A portal opened and Malik could clearly see tombstones before him. Everyone looked hesitantly at the graveyard, and Malik figured it was only right that he went first, since he had proposed the idea. He took a deep breath, jumped into the portal, and was instantly greeted with the cold, which he found to be peculiar since he wasn't cold before.

The others quickly came through after him, and Malik saw he wasn't the only one feeling the effects of the temperature drop. It felt like it was creeping through his bones and trying to claw him, searching to see if he was part of its collection or not. Elinam seemed to be the only one that was barely affected, her hair moving as if it was happy to be back home.

"You know, there were nights when I'd sleep and wake up to find myself curled up in a ball on one of these graves. That was before my foster family found out and started to lock me in my room at night, putting up locks as well as bars on my window," Elinam told the others sadly.

They turned to Elinam. No one was sure what to do, but it was Maya that surprisingly came up to Elinam and gave her a hug, followed by Bianca. Malik and the rest of the guys just stood there, unsure what to do. Each of them weakly murmured words of encouragement.

Stepping forward, Jaden opened the scroll, and it glowed an unworldly green color before disappearing. Everyone waited for something to happen, but when nothing did, they stood there mystified.

Frowning at the scroll, Jaden sighed. "I guess that's a bust."

Everyone murmured their agreement to that statement. Nico started to walk away until he stood at a tombstone that read: *Sarah Gonzalez, wife and mother, the cycle of the moon is only as transcending as her beauty.*

"Was she your mother, Nico?" Elinam asked. She had seen Nico stop over the tombstone and connected it to him, just as they all did.

All Nico could do was mumble a yes, wiping a tear from his face while turning away from the others. He quickly cleared his throat. "She was amazing, I think all of you would have loved her. She was caring, compassionate, and fierce to protect the innocent."

Coming up to Nico on each side of him were Jaden and Elinam. Each gripped his shoulder in silent comfort.

"How'd she die?" Malik asked quietly.

"My dad was jealous of her; he was also an alpha, but he paled in comparison, and he didn't want me to one day inherit her power, so he killed her. I don't know why he left me alone, but I think he wants to wait until I'm old enough to gain my power as well. I've heard he's been gathering a pack of murders full of alphas as well." Nico's rage was barely concealed.

Malik couldn't believe he hadn't heard this yet. He realized Nico was just putting a front of a big, bad werewolf this whole time; but in reality, he was just a sad and broken kid.

"I think she's at peace, and you shouldn't have to worry about it," Elinam spoke. Her voice sounded as if she was speaking through something and wasn't fully there.

Nico looked over at Elinam and smiled as if he believed her.

Jaden turned to Malik. "Hey, don't you have a relative that died here?"

Malik frowned, not sure where this was going. "Yeah, my great-grandfather, I think, Anomos Syer Blackwood. Why?"

"I think we've been looking at this wrong the whole time. It's obvious you're descended from the Demon King, but what if there's a clue tied to your family line?" Jaden asked, rubbing his chin thoughtfully.

Staring at all the tombstones, Malik wondered about his family. His great-grandfather supposedly fought monsters at some point, so it would make sense if there was a clue to get to the other place through him.

"I guess that makes sense, but I have no clue where it's

at," Malik admitted.

Stepping up to him, Elinam turned to Malik and touched his hands. Her eyes glowed white for a moment before she let him go.

"It's over this way," Elinam addressed everyone, still not sounding like her usual self, and she walked away before anyone could stop her.

They all looked at each other, then back at Elinam's disappearing figure in the dark, and rushed after her before something bad happened.

When he caught up to Elinam, she appeared to be silently crying at a gravestone. Malik was surprised to see the others staring at it in shock.

Pushing through everyone, he saw what had caused them to look shocked. The tombstone read: "Anomos Blackwood, beloved son and brother. *'A thousand suns burned bright'* 2006-2022."

Muttering words from the tombstone, he read it twice, but nothing changed. He stumbled backward, his eyes blurring. He started to hyperventilate uncontrollably, unable to believe what he had just read. There was no way he was dead. He didn't *feel* dead, but there was a tomb with his name and death right in front of him.

"Malik, please calm down, it's possibly a prank or something," Ento dismissively assured him, trying to comfort him.

He wanted to believe her, but his head was still

spinning and there was nothing she could do about it.

Putting a hand on his shoulder, Jaden calmly told him, "Malik, please breathe. I know you can't process this right now, but we need you."

Breathing in and out slowly, he got himself under control and, with shaky legs, went to his tombstone once again. His voice was barely audible. "There's no way that this is possible."

"Yeah, it's not, unless we're in the spirit realm," Elinam agreed.

They regarded Elinam with shock and disbelief until they noticed the sky. It was as if they were seeing the northern lights right in front of them, which wasn't possible since they lived in Portland. The sky overflowed with colors more mesmerizing than any sunset or sunrise. The colors flowed effortlessly to emerald, gold, and scarlet. Swirling rivers and shapes of hues of colors they could barely describe other than supernatural. They stood there transfixed by the sky for what felt like hours.

"Wow, that's amazing," Maya gasped in breathless wonder. All Malik could do was silently agree. He had never seen something as beautiful as this.

"So, what does this mean about my tombstone?" he asked, unsure what to even say.

"In the spirit realm, death and dying things are all present," Elinam explained. "It's simply showing a possible death; it's not completely set in stone until it comes to pass.

But you should know Death hates being cheated; she's a cruel mistress."

He feared dying like everyone else, and he remembered Elinam's warning, of him dying if he went on this search for the tomb. He felt uneasy about being in this world that crossed to the next.

"If it happens, just know I'm not going down without a fight," Malik told everyone, but mostly it was to himself because he was completely petrified of his death.

"Well, now that we're here, what do we do? The scroll got us here, but what was the point of it all?" Maya asked.

"I think we're supposed to activate it somehow and bring it back," Jaden answered.

"Why am I not surprised?" Nico snarled at Jaden. What was with this guy? One moment he was vulnerable and open, and the next he was hostile to everyone.

"Hey guys," Elinam tried, but everyone ignored her.

"Okay, Nico, I've had enough of you and your attitude, if you wanna go home, just say that. It's not like we need you, we can always ask another were," Jaden spit back with venom.

Eyeing the two of them, all he did was watch them. Jaden and Nico looked ready to throw down right there and then. He turned to see Maya and Bianca even arguing, which he didn't think was possible.

"We should tell them, what are you so scared of?" Bianca yelled at her sister.

Which caused Maya to yell back, "Shut up, you battle-crazed demon!"

The only person who wasn't arguing with anyone was Elinam, who instead stared at the bodies rising from the surrounding graves. Malik and Elinam looked straight at each other and yelled, "Zombies!"

Everyone stopped their fighting to turn toward the noise and saw zombies coming from all the surrounding graves.

Quickly closing up the scroll, Jaden yelled at the top of his lungs, "RUN!"

Everyone didn't need to hear the warning twice. They all ran as fast as possible away from the horde coming right at them.

CHAPTER 15

Running from the graveyard, they ran aimlessly outside the area. Once they stepped out, the view of the surrounding area changed. Before their eyes stood two contrasting locations, as if they were standing on the edge of the world. To their left, they felt the dry, humid heat hit them in their face. The feeling of rough sand caressed them like soft kisses from the vast desert before them. The sun sat high, beating on them as though they were lost travelers who had never felt its touch on its strongest days. Their throats begged for water, as it slowly dried up, staring at the endless sand and dunes before them. It was beautiful, unable to even fathom the depth of the oasis.

On their right was the cousin of the desert, just as beautiful and peaceful as the golden sands. Mountains stood as kings, as majestic as unbending warriors standing before their inevitable doom. The trees they swore to guard with their lives swayed, singing their tales of valor and honor. They stood proud to be welcome in the domain of kings, rising high into the heavens that whispered glory and gave breath to a new world. The moon rose, shining its beautiful light down on the creatures of the night.

"Where the hell do we go?" yelled Bianca.

"I say we go there," Elinam pointed to the right as she gasped between breaths.

"Yeah, I definitely agree with her." Jaden looked over his shoulder to see if the zombies had caught up to them.

Catching their breath for a moment, they heard the horde coming closer. They could just make out something in their gurgling, broken, undead jaws. "El…ie."

Against his better judgment, Malik looked back and he saw one of the undead's arms fall to the ground. The arm continued to move on its own, crawling forward as it used its fingers to slither toward them. He shuddered at the sight, forcing himself to look away.

"Yeah, let's go anywhere but here," Malik agreed.

Leading them to the mountains, Jaden led them deeper through the high trees, into a clearing. Now they could see it was thick with vegetation; trees and roots seemed to aimlessly be everywhere.

"I'll make a path for us, so everyone follows me," Jaden declared without slowing down. He brought out his staff from somewhere into his hands.

"How do you do that?" Malik stared in wonder at the piece of wood that came out of nothing.

Jaden grinned at him. "Oh, this is something not many people can do. It's like a little locker where we all store our personal things–remind me to teach it to you someday."

Malik nodded. "So the tattoos have nothing to do with it?"

Jaden continued to make a path through the trees by waving his staff to push whatever magic it contained to clear room for everyone to go through.

"The tattoos are something else; they are tied to me. Every magic-user has some sort of mechanism to help them do amazing things. Since I can't use a grimoire, I'm following an unusual path of magic myself. I've learned to use living tattoos as a sort of backup. When I told you I was a wizard, I was technically lying. Most wizards need a specific element to connect to focus their magic, plus a grimoire. I'm the odd one out, so to help my body adjust to the power, I've learned to use tattoos, or runes as they're formally called, to do my heavy lifting for me."

Finally, they came upon a rocky clearing lit up by the moon above. He gazed up to the moon, realizing with unease that, unlike the moon from home, it wasn't white, but a bright green. He marveled at it; this was the first sure sign – besides the zombies – that they weren't on earth anymore, or any world for that matter.

"So, does that mean your magic is better?" Elinam asked Jaden, also intrigued by his explanation.

"Yeah, you noticed how I can do portals and other things, it's not similar to magic that you'll see from other wizards. Normal wizards require something to draw their magic, which is around us everywhere. They just need something to influence their environment; mine works differently, so I guess you could say so," Jaden explained.

"Oh, that's pretty cool," Malik agreed.

"Yeah, I guess it is," Jaden remarked.

By that point, they were all able to find somewhere to sit down. Jaden sat in the middle, having put away his staff, and was busy creating a fire for them. Maya and Bianca chose to sit at the far right; each of them had weapons ready in case danger lurked behind the thick, dark trees. Nico sat down on the left to watch out for any danger as well, but unlike Maya and her sister, he sat there and meditated. Elinam was the odd person out, pacing back and forth. Malik chose to help Jaden start the fire by looking for wood.

"So, are we just going to sit here until the zombies come back?" Elinam asked in a panicked voice.

"There's nothing we can really do right now, Elinam, but wait it out, I don't think we're in any danger at the moment," Jaden told her.

Kicking the dirt hard, Nico grunted in frustration. "Damn it, why are we here? I can't even feel my wolf right now."

His outburst caused Maya and Bianca to look at each other in panic. They both closed their eyes, seeming to concentrate on something. Each of them grunted for a moment before they both gave up.

"Yup, no access for us here, either. I guess only Jaden's powers work here," Maya dejectedly admitted.

Glancing away, Jaden rubbed his neck in embarrassment. "Actually, I'm not able to access anything either. I've been just using my reserves at the moment, I'm barely at fifty percent."

Alarm showed on all their faces. He was their only way out and if he didn't have any more energy to get them home, they'd be here for a while.

"So what does that mean? No one here is even remotely powered enough to get us out?" Bianca asked in amusement.

"What's so funny, Bianca?" Nico asked in irritation.

"Well, I've always wanted to explore another world, and it seems like I have all the time in the world. If I die here, I'll get to explore it longer." Bianca now smiled to herself

Malik shook his head; he didn't want to be stuck here. He had to get back to his family.

"Wait, Elinam, how are you feeling?" Jaden asked, ignoring Bianca completely.

All attention turned to Elinam who stopped pacing and faced them. "I feel good actually, the most energized I've ever felt, why?"

"Okay, that's great, I figured since you were most closely tied to the dead, this place must be powering you up, like how Nico here gets more powerful during a full moon." Jaden grinned.

They all regarded Elinam with hope. They all knew that Elinam barely understood her power, much like him, but still were glad someone at least had power here.

Searching inwardly, Malik tried to reach for Ento, but couldn't feel her presence, either. It may have been because they weren't on Earth anymore.

"How does that help us, Jaden? No offense, Elinam, but the powers of the dead can't get us back to the world of the living," Maya asked, something they were all thinking subconsciously.

Choosing not to answer Maya, Jaden instead turned to Malik. "You remember when we first met Elinam? When we rescued her from those men, they said something about the Dead?"

He recalled what had happened that day and nodded. "It was so weird, but now knowing what your power is connected to, those men wanted something from you. What was it?"

"I, um, once raised someone from the dead," Elinam stammered, now nervous and looking away from them.

Completely shocked, gasps could be heard all around him as if they didn't understand what was going on either. He was so overwhelmed–Elinam could raise the dead! That put everything in a different perspective about death and the afterlife.

She rushed to explain. "I didn't mean to; this little boy

was so nice to me and one day he got hit by a car. I was standing over him, wishing he had never died. I felt a part of me weaken and the next thing I knew, he was alive again. His parents were happy for a while, but it didn't last, because he started to fall apart and wanted to eat and hurt other people.

"I found him one day trying to eat his own mom in the kitchen. I stopped him, but before I did, I heard him say 'master' in his little voice. I swore then that I'd never do it again, but my secret was out by then. People called me the devil, tried to hurt me, and later on, a cult somehow formed. They wanted me to be their master and worship me. I jumped from foster home to foster home since then, they didn't want me around them. Those were the same men in that cult you found that day."

Everyone processed what they had just heard. It was Malik who went up to Elinam this time to consult her. He could feel her pain rushing off her – someone who had to shy away from friendship, connections to a life, knowing she'd have to leave again. It must have been lonely for Elinam to bear this burden.

Not saying a word, and he knew Elinam would somehow feel what he was trying to say from action alone. Malik wrapped his arms around her, feeling like he had to protect her from the world. Elinam cried into his shoulder for a moment, and when her tears were all dry.

After what felt like a long time, Malik let go of Elinam,

who had put herself back together remarkably.

"I think I was wrong about Elinam, which is my fault. I thought you were a banshee or siren, but I was obviously wrong, as you did something I didn't even know was possible, and that something gives me hope that you could be our ticket home," Jaden in uncertainty explained.

"So, how do I get us out of here if I'm something else?" Elinam asked with a raspy voice.

Jaden looked at the fire as if deciding something. He turned to Elinam and motioned for her to sit down across from him. When she did, he addressed her. "Remember how we practiced your scream? Even it didn't work out, you did something else, and we'll try to find a way to succeed in some type of way. Since we're in the spirit realm, your power should be ten times as powerful. I want you to reach out and grasp that power and pull it in toward you in a slow and steady stream."

They all watched as Elinam did what Jaden instructed. Her body seemed to be glowing brighter and her breathing more labored. Jaden told her he was trying to find a way to have her create a portal for them to go back.

Choosing to leave them both in peace, Malik sat down a couple of feet away. Bianca decided to move away from Maya and sit next to him.

"How are you feeling now?" Bianca asked in curiosity.

"Weird actually, now that I've become a demon. I'm more worried about what the demon will do once I sleep, but I'm kind of thankful that I can't feel him right now watching me, thanks to us being here," Malik answered honestly.

"You know this is gonna cause imbalance to our power structure," Bianca stated, lost in thought.

"What do you mean?"

"Well, think about it, we're a group of what, six total, minus all the extras you got in your head. Before you or Elinam joined, it was Jaden, Maya, Nico, then me, though I think I should be higher than Nico for sure." Bianca looked over at Nico in disdain. "Now I think we're all lost as to who is gonna lead us or who's the most powerful."

"Why does it matter?" Malik asked, not seeing the point she was trying to make.

"Think about it, if we have more people that are as powerful as you and Elinam, we become unnecessary characters in your life. Who are we supposed to follow anymore?" Bianca asked.

"I don't believe that," Malik disagreed, thinking Bianca was crazy.

"Believe her, Blackwood, she's the one with the genius IQ, even though she should be just considered mad," Nico spoke up, causing Malik to nearly jump a foot because of how close Nico had gotten without him knowing.

"Well, I'll definitely take mad genius then," Bianca grinned, all smiles at Nico as if she wasn't remotely shocked to find him there looming to Malik's left.

Malik just turned to Bianca and was utterly surprised. If she was a genius, why did she act the way she did?

"Oh I see, my secret is out. Don't look so surprised, we all wear masks that we don't want to show people. I just want to be the crazy sister for a minute longer," Bianca grumbled in disappointment.

"Trust me, you're always the crazy sister," Nico assured her.

Bianca beamed at Nico. "Aww, that's the nicest thing you've told me all year."

Embarrassed by her praise, Nico looked away. Malik shook his head to clear it; now wasn't the time to ask about her brain.

"So what were you saying about the structure?" Malik asked, trying to bring the conversation back on track.

Bianca looked away from Nico to look down at Malik. "Oh yeah, just me wondering who's powerful and whatnot."

"That's simple," explained Maya behind his ear, causing Malik to jump in terror once again. "Jaden is a powerful magic user, with Nico being the strongest of us, and Bianca being the fastest. I'm a mix of both Nico and Bianca. Once Malik and Elinam get their powers figured out, it's obviously going to be Malik at the top, especially if he gets the power from his own ancestor, and it doesn't corrupt him. With Elinam being the unknown in all of this, we've never seen anyone like her."

"God, can y'all stop doing that?" Malik held his heart to prevent it from jumping out of his chest.

"Sorry," Maya apologized, but Malik had a sneaking suspicion that Maya was lying to him and actually enjoyed torturing him. It didn't help that he saw the corner of her mouth twitch for a moment. Malik let it go; it was nice to see the ice queen break down her walls, even for a moment.

Before they could talk more on the topic, Jaden stood up suddenly, causing everyone else to be acutely aware of it.

"Everyone, I think we're going home," Jaden told everyone in excitement.

Excitement was evident around their circle, as they left their position to come over to Jaden.

"What's going on Jaden?" Malik curiously asked, looking at what seemed to be a pool of power coming off Elinam.

"Remember when Malik came into my house with his shadow portal of his power? I'm hoping if Malik could do something like that, then Elinam could as well. Malik told me that he was pulled by the darkness to find the safest place for him, maybe she can do the same."

All he could remember was that sickening moment to what had accrued before going to Jaden. He looked at Elinam and sure enough, she was creating her own portal. While Malik and Jaden's portals were always in the air, hers was on the ground. It slowly started to grow from the size of a pebble to a hole big enough for one person.

Speaking to Elinam, Jaden was whispering to her when the ground began to quake. They were all thrown to the ground. Elinam's portal was closing, now just a small crater of dirt in front of her. The whole woods seemed to shake and howl as though an earthquake had struck. They all got up trying to figure out what was going on.

That was when the earth started to fall apart. The ground split in two right in front of them. The force of the split caused everyone to be thrown in opposite directions.

They were split up, Malik and Nico thrown to the left side, while the others were thrown to the right. The left piece was starting to fall. The shaking had caused a cliff edge to form, and Malik looked down to see a big hole that seemed to lead on endlessly for miles.

"Jump guys, jump now!" Jaden yelled at them.

He didn't need to be told twice. He ran for the already falling piece of rock free-falling at a fast speed, but when Malik saw Nico, he was instantly worried. It seemed that Nico had been hit harder than Malik by the split; rocks had hit Nico in the head, causing a shallow stream of blood to flow down to his temple. Nico seemed to be dazed by what had happened.

"Nico, grab my hand!" Malik yelled.

He got to the edge of the rock that wasn't falling and then turned to reach out to grab Nico. Nico grabbed his hand, but Nico's hand was mired with blood that had traveled to his arms. Malik tried to hold on as long as he could but wasn't able to keep his grip tight enough.

"Maya, Jaden, someone help me please!" Malik shouted.

"We can't, I'm trying, but I'm out of magic and Elinam is unconscious. If we even move, there might be a worse result," Jaden's pained voice broke through to Malik.

All he could do was look down at Nico's bloody face. Nico looked up at Malik. "It's okay, go save the world without me. I can finally see my mom again."

"You're crazy if you think I'm letting go. What about your own family here? Your uncles and your pack. What about me? Aren't you gonna be the one to put me down if I go crazy, who's going to be around to keep me in check?" Malik choked on the tears that started to come out.

Just looking into his eyes, Nico smiled. "If you can cry for someone as bitter me, then you'll be all right, Malik, trust me."

Realizing this was the first time, Nico had called him by his first name. Nico yelled loudly to everyone, "It was nice hanging with you guys again, come visit me when this is all over!"

He stared at him in confusion, wondering why he had said that. That was when Nico's free hand hit Malik's arm hard enough to make him momentarily lose his grip. Malik watched in horror as Nico fell backward. He could have sworn that Nico smiled as he fell, swallowed up by the hole in the earth.

Watching him disappear, Malik couldn't stand it; this was no way for someone to die. If only Malik wasn't so weak. Malik no longer felt the rage that came with being a demon coursing through him. Malik begged his body to bring it out, to let the demon in him once again take control and save his friend, but nothing came, only sorrow. The greatest sorrow Malik had ever felt; it brought him back to the day when everything had all started. Malik's heart broke a little again; there was nothing to comfort him now. He had known that people would die; even Maya had told him before, but Malik never believed it. Everyone seemed so invincible and unstoppable.

It was then that he heard them, the whispers; they tried to comfort him and tell him everyone was going to be all right. Malik did something he hadn't done since agreeing to the quest. He decided to listen to them. They seemed to only want him to be safe; they'd do anything to make sure he did.

Maybe it was the whispers from the shadows, but a crazy idea formed in his head. If everything worked out, then he'd be okay, but if not, he'd be very dead, trapped in this spirit realm.

"Jaden, everyone – thank you for everything you've done. I really appreciate it. If I don't make it back, please tell my family I love them," Malik pleaded, appreciating told them.

Looking up from Elinam in his arms, Jaden gave him a look as did Maya and Bianca, as if fearing what Malik was saying.

"Wait, let's talk about this, Malik." Jaden lowered Elinam, rushing to Malik before it was too late. Malik had already turned to the hole, with the hope that his friend was still alive. Malik smiled at the others and waved at them before diving off the edge.

CHAPTER 16

His stomach turned cartwheels as the force of gravity pulled him down. For a moment he felt weightless as if he was a bird soaring free, effortlessly existing with the wind pulling at his face, bringing tears to his eyes. He almost regretted his decision before remembering Nico was down there, plummeting to his death. He steeled his resolve to save Nico.

Yelling to no one in particular, he knew they were listening. From the first encounter he had with Andy, he had heard their voices, begging for him to claim them as their master. To the moment when he felt his emotions go haywire, he knew that they were simply following his reaction when they had attacked his mom. All the shadows wanted was to be recognized. They were creating a cloak around his body at that very moment.

"If you care about me, then you'll care about my friends, too. Either I die with him, or you save both of us!"

He heard no answer but could feel within his body that the shadows had decided something. Malik felt his body being improved, which he took as a yes from them. It felt easier to breathe now, as though he was wrapped in an invisible bubble. His body felt more durable against the winds and gravity itself. He found Nico almost at the bottom; he conformed his body to be rigid and dove, going faster and faster. Malik barely felt anything anymore, with the shadows now supporting him. He made it to Nico in a matter of seconds.

The minute he got to him, he grabbed Nico's arm, yelling loudly at him. "You really thought you'd get rid of me that easily? Come on man, we're in this until the end!"

Surprise was written over Nico's face, as well as relief. "Are you crazy? You're worse than Bianca, and that's saying something."

Once they were closer, he could hear Nico perfectly, as if he was right next to him and not an arm's length away. He could once again thank the shadows for that, he really wanted to figure out how they worked. They seemed to have their own intelligence and independence, but somehow still working for him.

He had to laugh at Nico's question. Maybe he was, but he didn't plan on someone to die on his watch. "Takes one to know one, now hold on, I'm not sure how to get us out of this just yet."

With a solid hold on Nico, he looked up and was shocked to find how far they had fallen. To compare it would be diving into the deepest part of the ocean, to a place where people couldn't even survive the pressure.

Hopeful things would work out, he called to his shadows. He wanted some type of rope to get back; the shadows somehow knew what he wanted, but did instead of rope, tentacles made of shadows and other things erupted out of his back, four total, all seeming to follow his command. They were weightless and very durable.

Pointing one arm out toward where he wanted to go, two tentacles surged forward to follow his command. He didn't feel anything, then he felt a tug as if to let him know they had grabbed onto something.

He willed himself to move back up and, with astounding speed, Malik held onto Nico tighter as they rode the tentacles back up. Within a minute, they were back to where everyone was waiting.

Standing over Elinam, Jaden looked as though he was grieving. Elinam was still unconscious. Maya and Bianca were processing everything; Bianca had tears in her eyes and Maya tried to console her grief. Maya didn't appear any better, as she was banged up from the earthquake she appeared numb with only a somber face, she hugged Bianca with overflowing tears. They looked up at them as they rose from over the edge, not believing what they were seeing. Jaden got up and rushed to Malik and Nico, to get them away from the edge. Bianca quickly wiped away her tears, but a small smile broke out on Maya's face.

"Never do that again! Next time you feel like giving me a heart attack, at least warn me," Jaden demanded from both of them.

Even though Malik knew everyone would still be mad at him, he couldn't help grinning from the adrenaline rush. "Sorry Jaden, I had to go. I knew you'd all try to stop me."

Rising from her sitting position, Bianca walked up to them, who he'd thought would hug him from his safe return, but instead spoke to Nico. "Malik only did this because of you, what do you have to say for yourself?"

Embarrassment was written on his face as he turned away, realizing how much everyone was hurt because of his decision. "I feel terrible, but I didn't think there was anything else to do. If I hadn't let go, Malik would have gone down with me. Malik's the important one, the rest of us are expendable."

Hearing Nico's words, Maya spoke up before anyone else could. "Stop disguising what you did as a noble reason. I know you're still hurting inside, but that doesn't give you the right to give up. I thought you'd keep living till you finished your quest. Has your heart finally given up as much as your brain has? We're all getting through this no matter what."

Her words were so cold to Nico; all they could do was stare at her in shock. Nico looked away guiltily as if he knew Maya was right. Before Nico could say anything,

Elinam groaned. Nico rushed over to Elinam, Jaden standing next to her. Elinam's eyes fluttered open, and she saw everyone looking over her in worry. She started to get up but moaned and grabbed her head in pain.

"Why does it feel like I was thrown around like a doll?" Elinam asked.

That caused everyone to laugh, and the tension that had started to build up between Nico and Maya faded. Jaden reached out and grabbed Elinam's arm; she gasped and tried to pull back until she realized who it was. She slowly let Jaden hold her hand.

He gently examined her, staring into her eyes as if he'd find answers there. After a few moments, Jaden put her arm down gently so as not to disturb Elinam's fragile state.

"So what happened?" Elinam asked.

Nico looked up at everyone quickly, as if to silently tell them to not mention what he had done. Malik gave a slight nod in affirmation of Nico's request.

"Oh, well an earthquake happened, and we all were thrown everywhere but luckily no one else was hurt, at least only you were hurt," Jaden answered for everyone.

Even though they had no real clue what had caused it, they could make a guess it involved Elinam but not to what extent.

They all breathed a sigh of relief when Elinam seemed to believe Jaden. They didn't want to explain what had happened with Nico; she would have blamed herself.

"How do you feel, Elinam? You think you're up to another try doing a portal?" Bianca asked softly, concerned for Elinam's health.

"I can try," Elinam weakly told her. Trying to get up, she wobbled and swayed, then stumbled forward. Luckily, Jaden and Nico were able to catch her before she fell.

"I think it's best if you rested, you probably spent a lot more energy than necessary," Bianca suggested.

Getting up and walking over to the side, Jaden looked down at the ground. "I think we should all rest, it's been a long day. Who knows what else could happen? We can't do anything without Elinam being at full power. Let's make camp for the night, we can set up a watch for a couple of hours in rotations."

Malik realized just how tired he was at that moment; the adrenaline was starting to wear off now. His body seemed to have exerted a lot more energy than he thought possible. He was ready to sleep it off. Malik looked around and saw everyone was exhausted as well, many of them with their own scrapes and bruises.

"I'll take the first watch, then I'll wake up the next one," Malik proposed, figuring if he took the first shift, he'd get the most sleep later that night.

Everyone nodded, not even trying to argue. Jaden suggested taking the next one, followed by Nico, Maya, and Bianca. Elinam tried to be added, but Jaden flat out refused, saying she needed her energy more than anyone for what had to happen in the morning.

"Okay, let's all get some sleep, we should be safe for

the night," Jaden assured them, then proceeded to sleep at a safe distance from Elinam in case she required anything.

Walking a good distance from the edge, Malik found a high enough rock and sat down. Nico chose to stay close to Elinam as well, deciding he wanted to make sure she was all right. The sisters each went to a corner and laid down to sleep.

He finally had a moment to himself in what felt like so long. He could still hear the whispers of the shadows just on the edge of his mind. Malik chose to thank them quietly for helping him out. After that, they ebbed away into silence.

Malik thought about everything he had gone through to this moment. He wasn't sure what he truly was anymore, whether he truly was a demon or a Templar. Malik felt sure his mom had lied about the Templar ancestry, but he decided to ignore it for now and ask her in private later on.

He had no clue what to do once they found the Demon King's resting place. They were supposed to destroy it, but he certainly had no clue how to do even that. Malik wondered what made him so special to even be considered the incarnation of that monster, but even Malik could see the signs. Andy hadn't been lying about believing he truly was that. Did that make Malik a monster as well? Malik had never really done anything evil himself – maybe mischievous, but not evil.

He really didn't know the history of the Demon King except what the Keeper had told him, but he wasn't sure if he could trust that creature. He knew he had an ulterior motive.

The catacombs didn't really exist in his basement; somehow, he was transported there subconsciously.

Stifling a yawn, he looked up to see lights that reminded him of the northern lights. The sky was filled with orange, red, and green swirling colors that led aimlessly to somewhere beyond. It was so beautiful to watch, he didn't even realize that this was a whole realm to explore outside his own. He wondered how many places he could explore and people he would meet. Malik smiled, recalling his conversation with Bianca; maybe they could explore it together. The others were filled with obligations to the town, besides Elinam, but he doubted she would come unless Nico came, too.

He wondered what quest that Nico was living for–perhaps he wanted to avenge his mother. It made Malik wonder, what did *he* even live for? It wasn't like he had some big dream to chase after, even though they were going to be seniors in the following year. He had good grades, but he didn't know if he even wanted to attend college much like the rest of his class. He just lived for the moment.

Malik figured it was true what people said, that broken people tended to find each other. He didn't think he was technically broken, besides the fact that he had a demon for a roommate for who-knew-how-long in his head. Yeah, Malik was starting to rethink his thoughts on brokenness for sure.

His eyelids closed more frequently; it had only been thirty minutes since he started his shift and he still had another thirty to go. He looked over to Jaden sleeping peacefully; he wasn't going to wake him up now, but before he could think about a way to stay up, he was already falling asleep.

As his eyes started to close forcefully, he could have sworn he saw a skeleton with a long dress come up to him and kiss him on the cheek. "Sleep, little shadow, when you wake on the 'morrow, you'll be gone from this world."

He slumped over and was out. He quickly opened his eyes again in panic, seemingly finding himself once again in the spirit realm, or what he perceived to be it.

Furthermore, he quickly looked around and was surprised to find himself alone. Not only that, but he was in a grassy field, with a large, ancient-looking oak tree sitting alone, swinging its branches aimlessly.

A pond sat a few feet in front of him; he decided to sit by it and was shocked to see his own reflection looking right back at him. He immediately thought this couldn't be a dream– you couldn't see yourself gazing back in dreams.

But there was something wrong with this reflection. It grinned at him as if it won something.

Then his reflection's eyes turned black, as if there had never been any warmth or humanity in them. The irises had a ring of red, begging him to look closer to grab him and pull him in the abyss of darkness.

"You like what you see?" his reflection spoke to him. Malik jumped back and looked around wildly as if someone was playing a prank on him. There was no one there but him. Malik slowly gazed at himself once again.

His face once again wore a grin. Malik knew now that this was just some twisted plot from the demon in him.

"What do you want?" Malik asked himself, which would have felt odd if he hadn't known this wasn't truly him.

"Nothing, just thought you could use some reflection on yourself. Was getting tired of being ignored anyway," it answered back.

He watched his face, studying him closely. He had never realized how much he had changed through all his life. His own body seemed to be different through the reflection; it was like the progress to his perfect self. Malik's hair in the reflection was cut shorter in the back, with the top hanging; some twists even covered his eyes somewhat. His face had more of a chiseled physique than his current baby-faced self. Malik could almost describe himself as handsome in some regard, but the eyes ended this conclusion, empty and hollow. It was looking at someone who had been through trauma and chose to look at the world in contempt, as though it had personally hurt them. These were the eyes of someone who had lost a piece of themselves along the way.

Sweat appeared on his brow from fear of not knowing if this was the future him or just a version of what the demon looked like.

"Well, I'm done reflecting, so send me back," he demanded.

His reflection simply shrugged. "Wish I could, but that walking, talking pile of bones almost killed you right there. If it wasn't for my interference, you'd be dead."

He studied his reflection for a moment, shocked that he had almost died, but more shocked that it seemed to care for him. Maybe he had been wrong to assume it wanted to do him harm.

"Oh, well thanks."

"Don't thank me now, you're stuck here for the time being. I couldn't pull you into the source at the moment, I'm too low on power, this was the best I could do," the demon admitted, surprised by his gratitude.

"How were you able to even reach me? I couldn't feel you or Ento since I entered here."

The demon sneered at Malik. "You can thank those freak of nature shadows of yours, I could feel them at the edge of our mind. Never accept them again, they'll eat away any part of you they can take. Luckily, I was able to keep them from completely taking you over."

"I thought that was your power?" Malik stared at his reflection in alarm.

"Hell no, those things are an abomination. You really don't know what we are, do you?" the demon, almost in pity, asked Malik.

In response, all he did was shake his head.

The demon snorted. "Figures, Jaden and company send you on a fool's errand without telling you the whole story. Even I can tell from just the feeling I get from them."

Malik thought back to the first time he had been in contact with the shadows; they were there when he was angry and sad. He remembered the feeling of sadness and desperation after Nico fell off the edge.

"They feel cold, empty, but alive," Malik answered.

"Oh, they are very much alive, believe me, they're creatures worse than demons. They feed off of your worst moments, grow stronger until they can use you as a tool. A simple instrument, a piece in their little perfect machine," the demon told Malik in a voice that sounded terrified.

Malik shivered; he felt as if he had been used. He remembered the whispers even now as if they were brushing him across the cheek with words as though they were a lover, but now that he knew it was probably as a meal, they were tenderizing their next course.

"Where did they come from?" Malik asked.

"No one knows exactly, they say they somehow slipped in through one of the other realms, most likely the

Abyss. They eat worlds, millions die from their very touch. Each whisper they utter is a thousand blades cutting through you. No one survives after they leave a world to go to the next," the demon spoke those words with such sadness and terror as if he had experienced them firsthand.

It caused Malik to shiver down his spine. The pain the demon spoke of scared him in so many ways.

"How do I have them?" Malik was scared of the answer, even though he had suspected it from the moment the demon started talking.

The demon, with its eyes that spoke of darkness far wickeder than the darkest of nights, looked at him as if it was saddened by telling him.

"It's from the Demon King, our so-called ancestor." It spoke without emotion this time.

Sitting there, he couldn't feel anything for just a moment. Malik, the inheritor of the Demon King, was truly a monster in every sense. If he ever let himself give up, the shadows would take him over and destroy everything that he loved.

Malik's emotions finally broke, and he started to weep for just a moment. "Why? Why me?"

"Because we're the best of his bloodline. With our demonic ancestry, we can hold back the shadows, even control them someday, so no one could ever be harmed by them," the demon told Malik without an ounce of sympathy in its voice.

"I'm not a demon, stop saying that" Malik, now somewhat hysterical, yelled at his twisted reflection.

"Oh, but you are. I'm you, and you're me, I'm the part of you that you kept locked away from yourself because you were ashamed to admit what we are. Every self-doubt, insecurity, trauma that you could have experienced, you dumped it on me. You selfishly lived life, blissfully unaware that I even existed. I hated you for it; you take your life for granted, while I just watch it pass by without ever saying or doing anything." The demon's rage could be felt in each word it spoke, it was bitter and envious of everything he had. That caused him to finally come to his senses. He stared at the face that was so much like his. Was the demon lying? Had he purposely locked away a piece of himself, and he had been the one to cause this demon to hate everything?

"We're not the same, I've never once felt you were next to me, or I would have said something. That crazy demon put you inside me?"

"Oh, how they misled you. I suggest asking Jaden the truth about how to create demons because you'll learn something interesting," the demon retorted back.

"Haven't you ever felt like you were missing a piece of yourself? Don't you wonder why you always felt alone even when you're surrounded by people that love you? You always knew subconsciously that something was missing–that's me."

Shaking his head, not wanting to believe a word it was saying but knew it was all true. He had always wondered why he never left like he had belonged anywhere, or why he chose to not make many friends. Believing he had been this way because his parents moved around a lot, but maybe this was it.

"I'm sorry-" Malik started to say.

"Sorry? You lived my life, I'm the shadow to your Peter Pan. But you left me in a box at the depths of your mind. You never cared, I watched you grow up. I watched Mom love and care for you, I watched Nina play with you. I was never a part of it; you're the reason I'm the way I am. Stop trying to run away from who you are – so what if you're a monster? There are worse monsters out there; sometimes we need to be one to stop a greater one. The sooner you accept that, the better."

Looking at his reflection, his true shadow, he started to wonder if they were just two misunderstood creatures that each wanted to exist. He would never accept the demon truly without knowing everything; this was someone that had been broken from not truly existing in the world of the living.

Reaching out toward his reflection as if to touch it, and the reflection mirrored his movement. As if it longed to be recognized, to exist, to be seen, and it wanted to know that it wasn't fading away. Just as Malik's fingers were about to touch the water, he faded away into black.

Jerking up, he woke to find Jaden shaking him awake. Malik was groggy from his dream until he recalled what had happened.

"Where did it go?" Malik yelled in a dazed state.

Staring at Malik as if he was crazy, Jaden looked around and sighed as if he was the only sane person left. "What the hell are you talking about, Malik?"

"The skeleton, it was here just a second ago," he answered Jaden, finally clearing his head.

Acting as if he was searching for something. Jaden then looked back at Malik. "There's no one here but us. Besides, we have more pressing things to worry about, like getting home. Who knows how long we've been here?"

Completely forgetting about the skeleton for a moment, he sat up straight and looked at Jaden in alarm. "What do you mean 'how long we've been here?'"

Looking over at the destroyed ground, Jaden admitted, "Time works differently in the spirit realm. For the dead, it could feel like they just got here yesterday, when in truth they've been here for hundreds of years. For us, it's worse, we're still living beings. We're not tied to this area, so time could have literally stood still from the moment we entered this area, or it could have been weeks, if not months since we arrived."

He just stared at Jaden bug-eyed; there was no way they'd been trapped in here for that long. Trying to imagine having been here for months, if not more; he could have missed a whole year's worth of a life. He could have missed his seventeenth birthday by now.

"Oh, we have to get out of here," Malik urgently told Jaden. Worry about his family increased.

Jaden's face showed the same urgency. "No kidding."

After a moment of silence, Jaden changed the subject. "So, I saw you fell asleep on watch. It's cool, I'll just tell the others I took over and let them sleep through it. Next time, just let us know you're tired it's okay to just sleep, it's better than putting us all in danger."

Embarrassment was written all over Malik's face, realizing how much harm he could have done to the others if anything had happened. It was partially his fault, but that skeleton was somewhat a part of it. He didn't want to admit what had happened to put him to sleep; he had a feeling Jaden wouldn't believe him.

"I'm sorry," Malik somberly told Jaden.

"It's cool, just glad you realized your mistakes. Better to know now than next time."

He remembered what his demonic half had told him and wondered if any of it was true. The truth seemed to have become blurred since the minute Malik had joined up with them on the search for the tomb.

"Hey Jaden, how are demons made?"

Snapping his head to Malik, Jaden studied him for a moment as if searching for a reason behind his question. He seemed to mull everything over before answering carefully.

"I think I don't need to say the birds and bees of how demons are made."

He studied Jaden for any sign of deception before asking his follow-up question. "I meant how are demonic children made?"

Jaden looked down at the ground in front of him as if scared to answer him.

"A half-demon child can be conceived in multiple ways. While there are lots of demonic children, most of their parentage is from lesser demons who somehow won a piece of their human soul. The problem with those demons that come from lesser demons is that most children have abnormal features as if they never fully established who they are. That's where the legend of Rosemary's baby comes from. Higher-level demons can supply the energy required to have demonic children with no abnormal features at least, in the beginning, most of their children show signs of demonic features in puberty. The child can have an ability to switch between their two halves; not many can achieve even that because it takes skill. "

He looked at him to see if Malik was keeping up with everything he was saying, once sure he was, Jaden continued his explanation.

"In the demon realm, there's a constant stream of demonic energy, which we call Animus, which is basically living energy that hangs in the air slowly being absorbed by the demons in that world. If a demon isn't fully demonic, they have trouble collecting the energy and storing it for themselves. Think of it as photosynthesis – we gain energy from the sun, and they gain living energy from the surrounding air. Some demons need their parents to constantly feed them to fully become demons."

He sat there for a moment, absorbing it all. "So, am I a demon seed or not?"

Jaden shook his head. "Andy and I worked on figuring it out and concluded that you're not. We don't know how you're a true half-breed, but you're not a demon seed. You're not going through the ascension of one; a demon seed is just a piece of an older demon put inside you to corrupt everything you are. To me, it seems like your very soul was split from a young age. I've been developing this technique which I've told you about soul sight which isn't perfect, it allows me to better understand people's powers specifically and their potential but seems to me like there's damage from someone you personally know that did this to you."

Slumping down as he finally accepted what he was. His demonic half was right – they were truly the same.

"So, I'm really a monster," Malik whispered, dejectedly staring at his hands, not recognizing himself.

"No, you're not. I'm a half-human, but I haven't done anything monstrous, have I?" Jaden spoke to Malik in a stern voice. "Let me tell you something, there will be two or three moments in life where you'll make a choice that will define who you become. In those moments, remember that you aren't who they see you as, you're the same you. No matter what you look like or act like. The choices you make in life are who you truly are and nothing else."

He nodded, seeing his logic, and he appreciated Jaden's help to make him feel better. But Malik knew, deep within his veins and body, there was a part of him that was worse than a demon. Malik didn't know how'd he survive it all but chose to focus on one thing at a time. Jaden didn't need to know everything right now.

"Okay, thanks man, I appreciate it," Malik truthfully told him.

Giving him a small smile, Jaden clapped Malik's shoulder before going over to the others to wake them up. He took a deep breath, then went over to help the others wake up as well. Malik saw his reflection in a puddle, and black eyes filled with red stared back at him for a moment. Putting his foot into the puddle, the image rippled and disappeared.

CHAPTER 17

After the two of them woke everyone up, the group was grumpy but got up nevertheless.

"Damn, how long were we out?" Nico asked, yawning as he got to his feet.

"Wait, who was the last one on watch?" Maya asked, remembering that Jaden wasn't supposed to wake them up.

"It was me," Jaden admitted, looking tired. "Malik woke me up, and I decided the rest of you needed the sleep more than I did."

Maya looked at Jaden angrily. "That's not your call to make, we need you at a hundred percent for when we get home."

"Trust me, the minute we're home I'll be at full power. For now, we put ourselves in Elinam's hands," Jaden reassured her.

All she could do was shake her head in disappointment, not saying another word. Malik had a goofy smile after seeing Bianca's bedhead. She looked adorable with her hair all over the place. Bianca saw Malik looking and gave him a wink as if she knew exactly what he was doing. Malik looked away, blushing; he could never tell when Bianca was playing around or being serious.

The rest of the group saw their exchange. Maya and Nico both groaned as if they were tired of them.

"Just get a room already," Nico told the both of them.

Feeling embarrassed, Malik saw the look Maya gave him as if she planned on murdering him right then and there. Malik looked at the ground, trying not to antagonize her further.

"No one is getting any room, let's get out of here. We got things to do," Maya loudly told everyone.

"I'm still not sure how to get us out of here, but I can try," Elinam admitted she seemed to have fully recovered.

"We need to go home before it gets dark again," Jaden suggested. "I'm afraid that we've been here too long already, and the inhabitants of this realm won't take kindly to living visitors."

"What do you mean 'inhabitants?'" Malik asked. "Like the zombies we saw?"

Jaden shook his head. "No, much worse than those, the gods or whatever beings ruled this realm."

Gods! Gods existed as well, beings so powerful they were only talked about in mythology. Why was he surprised–he'd met demons, werewolves, and even fallen angels. There should be nothing that surprised him at this point, but here he was with Elinam, both of them with their mouths hanging open in shock.

Choking out his words, Malik yelled, "Gods?! They're real, too? You really should give me an encyclopedia of this stuff."

"Didn't I already give you that? Well, never mind now, just know that demons, angels, and even gods exist. And trust me they're not the fun kind, these are the old ones who have been around longer than most present gods," Jaden explained as if it was everyday information.

Things so old as civilization itself existed, and Jaden had conveniently forgotten to mention that. Malik was going to have a serious talk with Jaden about telling him everything that existed in his world or another.

"So we're probably gonna run into them if we don't leave?"

"We've probably already run into them one way or another. They knew we were here from the moment the undead chased us in. When you're a being of immense power, you tend to tell what belongs in your world and what doesn't. I'm just hoping they're not hostile and let us leave as quickly as possible." Jaden didn't seem to be too worried about it for some reason.

"Should we be worried about a fight or worse?" Maya asked Jaden, already thinking about the bigger picture.

"No, we probably won't fight them because there are rules and such for mortals traveling into places like this, but that's not going to stop them from trapping us in here for who knows how many years."

"Should I try another portal?" Elinam asked, now gnawing on her fingernails.

"No, we can't try that just yet, you need to wait, and I'm worried that the earthquake was the product of that portal practice earlier. Until we understand your power and how it works, we'll wait," Jaden stated.

Everyone sat there trying to understand their best options. Malik knew that he could call on the shadows again, but at what price? Was it worth saving his friends to damn himself in the process?

"Yeah, y'all are definitely going to die," an unfamiliar voice said next to Nico.

They all whipped their heads toward that direction to find a kid about twelve years old eating a biscuit; how he produced the biscuit they had no clue. The kid was in little rags covering most of his lower body, his shirt in tatters. Everyone looked at the strange kid eating without a care in the world.

"How long have you been here?" Maya questioned the kid suspiciously.

The kid smiled at her before finishing his biscuit. "Oh, me? I've been here since the beginning. Some advice: don't waste time here, you don't know who else is watching from the shadows."

The kid stood up and started to walk away. "Well, are you coming or not? The Lady in White requests your presence, and I suggest you don't keep her waiting."

They all looked at each other as the kid waited for them, tapping his foot impatiently. Malik looked toward the thick trees and, sure enough, eyes were watching them, each all in different sizes and colors. They watched with interest, but an unnatural hunger that Malik couldn't describe seeped off of them.

There was no way they were going to blindly follow a kid they didn't know to someone who might hurt them. Malik looked at the others' faces and saw they all agreed.

The kid growled at them unnaturally. Malik and the others were immediately on high alert for a possible attack. The kid started to grow and foam at the mouth, reaching his hand out to them and dropping it in agony. His body grew four more feet until it towered at nine feet tall. His body went through an unusual transformation of what looked like a mix of a werewolf and fox. He had two arms on each side, with his face resting on top of a wolf-like head. He was covered in red and orange fur, with a tail that whipped viciously back and forth. He had claws for two sets of arms; the fingers looked bent and jarred. His other set of arms were trunk-sized human arms, and his transformation looked like a true abomination.

They all looked away for a moment to collect themselves. Malik felt sick to his stomach. He could tell the kid was in pain and tortured throughout his change, but Malik couldn't move; it was like his body was stuck.

"You did this to me! I'll kill you! I'll kill all of you!"
The kid's voice seemed to be in so much pain trying to
speak through his wolf head and his own.

Before the kid could even step up to them, a big white
wolf appeared in front of it; it wasn't as muscular as Nico
was in his wolf form, but it was leaner and built for speed.
The eyes of the wolf were red, filled with specks of green; it
growled at them as if to tell them that the monster in front
of them was all theirs. Malik and the others didn't even try
to fight the wolf on its prey, the wolf and the monster
started to circle each other as if sizing up its competition.

The kid monster jumped first; he reached his claw
arms out to end the wolf swiftly but was too slow. The wolf
jumped around the monster, attacking its legs first. The
monster didn't seem to understand what was going on
before it was too late. Its legs were the first to go; the
monster tried to stand, but the wolf had somehow
immobilized its legs to the point they couldn't move. The
monster reached out, finally able to grab on the wolf's hind
legs; he grabbed them hard enough to hear an audible pop
from their distance.

The wolf yelped in pain, as it was thrown off its feet
and thrown around repeatedly before it reached out and
ripped its leg off. The wolf landed unevenly on its now
three feet. The wolf jumped back from the monster's grasp
once again. It was bleeding openly, as was the monster. It
seemed to still have the energy to make its kill. The wolf

jumped high enough to reach the human head, and the human portion cried out as the wolf viciously dug into its face. The wolf grabbed the neck of the kid, and before they knew it, the head flew right next to Nico's feet.

Everything happened in a matter of minutes; everyone watched in awe as the wolf howled at the sky as the body of the monster lay dead under its feet.

"Wow, did we just witness a fight between titans?" Bianca just watched in utter shock as she asked. No one argued with her analogy; it was true, for the lack of better words.

The wolf finally broke away from its victim and approached them; as it moved, the leg that was previously lost started to repair it before their eyes. Its movement as it approached them seemed to change from awkward to that of a predator.

The wolf stopped just a few feet from them, as if waiting for something or for them to understand it. As Malik looked at the others, unsure what to do, Malik was surprised to see Nico approach it.

"Nico, what are you doing?" Jaden asked, concern laced in his voice.

Nico looked at everyone over his shoulder; his eyes had somehow turned red, even though that was supposed to be impossible.

"I think she wants us to follow her," Nico told them, with a voice that spoke of untold conviction.

"She? How do you know it's a she?" Maya asked in bewilderment, staring at Nico as if he was crazy.

"I don't know, but I'm going. I think we'll be safe with her. Maybe it's the wolf in me, but I'll bet my life on it," Nico told the others as he turned back to the wolf.

The wolf stared at Nico for a moment before looking over at the others, stopping for a moment to look at Malik before deciding on something. It tilted its head at them to indicate that it wanted them to follow. Nico followed the wolf without any worry.

The rest of them looked at each other and, unable to stop Nico, followed after the two of them with unease. They walked for a while, with Nico leading them and Maya taking up the rear. After a couple of minutes, they came to a new clearing that was surrounded by two trees that looked ancient, as if they had been around for centuries.

The wolf growled as if to tell them to stop, which they did. The wolf then went to the trees for a moment, standing in front of it as if conversing. It then went behind the trees and didn't appear for some minutes.

"So what do we do?" Elinam asked. They all just shrugged, unsure what to make of their situation. Malik turned to his left and saw a guy there, a few years older than them, come toward them. He wore jeans and a T-shirt, but what stood out most about him was that he was carrying a scythe over his shoulder. He seemed to be completely calm as he walked toward them.

"Hey guys, should we be worried about him?" Malik pointed at the strange guy.

Turning to the direction he was pointing, everyone stared at him. The guy hadn't slowed down at all; he was just a few paces away from them. Jaden stumbled backward, and Maya grabbed his hand before he could fall. Malik watched it all unfold with concern.

As Jaden stood upright again, he looked at the rest of them in fear. Malik had never seen Jaden scared before this whole time. What could cause him to be scared now, especially from this guy?

"Everyone, let me do the talking when he comes to us," Jaden fearfully told them. They all watched Jaden in concern; this must be something serious.

The guy finally stopped just in front of them. He looked about their age. He was wearing cut-up jeans and a Metallica shirt. His face resembled an African American kid that could pass for someone Malik might see in his neighborhood.

The guy just stood there, grinning at them for a moment. "Wow, aren't you guys a little far from home?" Even his voice was like multiple people layered into one; there were so many pieces of culture stemming from his voice.

"Oh, I'm sorry, my Lord, we didn't mean to be here longer than necessary," Jaden groveled.

Silence hung in the air as they all walked Jaden act this way. It was weird, to say the least.

"No need for all of that, Williams, just called me Omen," Omen told Jaden.

Omen stepped up to Malik and grabbed him into a hug. Completely caught off-balance from this display of affection, Malik awkwardly hugged the guy back.

"Nice to see you too," he laughed, awkwardly patting Omen on the back.

"It's nice to see you again," Omen told Malik happily.

On his part, Malik was concerned for this man. Omen must be delusional. "We've met before?"

All Omen did was just shrug, as if he wasn't entirely sure himself. "Maybe in the last life."

Omen then proceeded to act like nothing had happened and walked over to each person to look them up and down.

"So, would you mind explaining to me why there's a cliff's edge in the woods down there?" Omen stared at them as he asked his question, specifically at Elinam and Jaden, who looked away guiltily. Malik was confused; he figured it had been an accident all along.

"That's partly my fault, I thought we could leave if Elinam here could open a portal just like Malik, but it ended up backfiring on us," Jaden explained nervously.

Omen rubbed his chin. "What do you mean by 'a portal like Malik's?'"

"The way Jaden explained it, Malik could step into the shadows and move through any shadow that he found. He figured I could do the same thing but find graves or something similar to that." Elinam explained for Jaden, flustered by Omen's gaze on her.

"The only problem with that is that you and Malik are completely different; if you had noticed, when you tried to summon the portal, you actually summoned the dead that had already passed over to the next." Omen shook his head, disappointment showing in his face.

Staring at Omen in shock, they all dumbly gawked at him. Was he saying what they thought he was saying? That Elinam somehow was reaching for the dead that had gone to the other side past the spirit realm? There was no way to be sure, but Malik had a feeling this man wasn't the type to lie about this stuff to make them feel better.

"No! You don't mean...?" Elinam, barely able to speak anymore, started to shake as if she was a branch about to fly away at more words. Maya came up and held Elinam steady. Elinam somehow stopped her shaking.

"I'm sorry, but yes, if you had been in the human realm, you possibly could have opened a portal, but in the spirit realm, your power is five times stronger, if not more. If you don't have any control, you could have caused ten percent of this realm to collapse under your power. Luckily, my brother cut you off on the other side and I sapped some of it here when I located you," Omen explained.

"Wait, you knew we were here all along? Then why didn't you try to locate us from the beginning?" Malik blurted out.

Shrugging, Omen didn't speak until he found a tree to lean against. "I knew you were here the instant you walked through. Though, I lost you for a moment when a powerful magic was cast over all of you. I found Elinam the instant her power went crazy. After that, it went dark for a moment, like a World Eater had escaped from its trap and come here. All the spirits ran in panic, so I couldn't get to you guys until after that. When I found out that the Lady in White was trying to intercept you guys, I sent my second-in-command to retrieve you. Sorry, it's been a busy couple of days."

From Omen's perspective, it *had* been an eventful couple of days. They all seemed to agree on that as everyone murmured their understanding.

"So what exactly is a World Eater? I've heard of the Ancient Ones as well as a few others, but not that name before," Jaden asked, finally back to his normal self.

Omen looked around as if to make sure no one was listening in, which Malik found strange. "A World Eater is a class of species much like the symbiote from Spider-Man. Instead of one invading the minds like Venom, it's a collection of them. They give their hosts unimaginable power, but they slowly consume and kill them from the inside. It's a closely guarded secret, but the only other species that are known to survive it all are the Ancient Ones. Everyone thinks that the Ancient Ones were originally a war race that someone came in contact with, resulting in them forming hospitable forms. But we haven't seen them in a millennium, thanks to one of their kind betraying them and throwing away the key to unlock them. Another name for the World Eaters is Eldritch Terrors if that helps," Omen explained gravely.

Malik stumbled back. Was that what was inside of him? The ones that whispered in his ear just a day ago. The World Eaters sounded like them, but until he knew more, he had to keep quiet.

Thankfully, it was Bianca that saved him. "How do you know so much about Spider-Man?"

On his part, Omen acted as if it wasn't a big deal. "I may be the Reaper, but even I get downtime. We have a great collection of comic books and an excellent cable connection. I also get to talk to all my favorite dead comic book authors."

"Wait, did you just say you're the Reaper? As in the Grim Reaper?" Nico yelped.

Glancing at them all funny, Omen sighed. "Is it not obvious? I thought the scythe was enough. Man, I need to work on my introductions better. Yeah, I'm the Reaper. At least one of the four aspects of Death."

Maya stumbled at the words. "What do you mean, one

of the four? I thought there was only one."

Ignoring her, Omen looked at Jaden as if disappointed in him. "You didn't tell them?"

Raising his hands, Jaden tried to look innocent, but failed utterly when his eyes had a laughing expression.

All Omen could do was rub his eyes as he answered, "Kids. I'm dealing with children here. Okay, listen closely, because I'll only say this once. There was only one Death in the beginning, but as the world grew, so did Death. He saw, though I'm not even sure it was a male, that the world was changing. Growing tired of it, he chose to split his consciousness into four separate parts. Furthermore, he tasked each of us with a job and certain abilities from his original form. So besides me, there's the Jackal, Saint, and Oracle. You don't need to worry about any of the others for now. Though if you do meet my sister Jackal in the human realm, tell her I said hi and I want my Nintendo back."

They all just stood there for a moment before Bianca started laughing. They all turned to her in bewilderment. Bianca laughed even harder when she saw everyone's attention on her. "Oh, I'm sorry, but you sound like characters from a comic book or anime."

"Sorry, we just like pop culture references. It's a bad habit of ours; a few years ago, we were seen as the four horsemen of the apocalypse, and I would like to say it was my idea. We do have other names, but that's what we're calling each other this century." Omen laughed a little before changing the topic. "I'm actually interested in Elinam, where exactly are you from?"

"Who, me?" Elinam pointing a finger at herself.

"Yes you, is there another Elinam around here somewhere?" Omen playfully looked around.

"Oh, I don't really know, I know that one of my parents is from Ghana, but the other was born and raised in the states all their life," Elinam nervously answered.

"Hmm, makes me wonder what you are exactly. You're not a banshee nor a necromancer … or could it be …"

"Could what be?" Maya asked, now concerned for Elinam's sake.

"Is it possible you have a birthmark? An unusual one at that, shaped like a crescent moon?" Omen excitedly asked Elinam.

She nodded slowly, unsure what to make of it. "Yeah, it's on my left breast. Why?"

"I thought your whole lineage was wiped out centuries ago," Omen told her in disbelief.

"Excuse me, but what the hell are you talking about?" Nico was now irritated with the way Omen looked at Elinam as if she was a rare animal at the zoo.

"My apologies, I just thought your family had died out. You, Elinam Johnson, are a Champion of Death!" Omen explained proudly as if they all knew what that meant.

"I'm sorry, what?" Malik asked, completely out of the loop.

"Oh yes, I figured many people forgot about them in this century. A Champion of Death is a sort of extension of Death itself; many people confuse them with banshees or necromancers. The original Death, when splitting us into four different aspects, bestowed a tribe of people the power to command death at some levels.

They could range in many aspects, from seeing a person's death to calling up the dead. Doing the work for us in the beginning, guiding the dead to the next life, or finding those that abused death and stopping them. Not only that, but they were the tribe leaders and shamans of the people. I figured all of them had died out with the colonization of Africa," Omen explained.

Then the weirdest thing happened–Omen got down on his knees and bowed his head to the ground in front of Elinam.

"I'm sorry we weren't there for you in your time of need. You were the heart of everything we do. I can't apologize for the ancestors you lost, but if you ever require me, know that I will come, and not even The Scepter can stop me," Omen humbly pledged to her.

Elinam looked scared as she reached down to touch Omen. Her eyes once again glowed purple as she spoke, sounding just like Omen, as if speaking through multiple people.

"Lord of Death, we do not blame you for what happened, for it was our people that let it happen. Hold on to yourself, as we will avenge the brothers and sisters we have lost; our home was taken from us without a fight. We simply gave up; we will not let this Child of Death meet the same fate, we promise you that! For we are the Speakers of the Dead, they will hear our words as the mother earth weeps for our fallen." Elinam spoke in a voice that sounded as warm as a mother speaking to her child as she put them to sleep, and as cold as a mother that had her child taken from her.

It was amazing and terrifying at that moment. Malik shuddered; he had never seen something so beautiful in all his life. Elinam finally lost the glowing purple eyes as she smiled at Omen, helping him to his feet.

"I think I need to find my true family and heritage for myself, thank you for your words, Lord of Death." Elinam smiled as she thanked him.

Thinking about Elinam's life, a person without anything to call home, thrown away into a foster system that didn't love or want her. Life truly was cruel, but beautiful at that moment; she now had a chance to find out who she truly was in the world. Malik felt the same way; he wanted to know who he truly was and his place in the world.

"So, now to get down to business, are you guys ready to go home?" Omen rubbed his hands together.

"Yes!" They were all ready to get out of here and finish the quest.

"I don't usually do this, but you all have a choice after this. One of my abilities is seeing your future and your possible deaths. While the future is not set in stone, I can usually see the outcome of a person, and I think you should all be given a choice. Do you wish for me to tell you?" Omen proposed.

It was quiet for a moment as they all each thought about Omen's proposal. Malik wasn't sure if he wanted to know his future, especially from a guy that was the Grim Reaper personified. This wasn't something to take lightly; it would probably affect his choices moving forward, and Malik wanted to have his own free will and choice of what to do with life. But the other part of him thought it was a good idea to at least know how it was going to all end.

"I think I like how my life is going, I'm going to sit this one out," Maya gave her answer to Omen.

"Same here, I'd rather live in ignorance than know. I already have a good idea of it anyway," Jaden added.

"I'd like to know, actually," Elinam admitted, raising her hand.

Feeling the urge to join, Malik agreed to do it and was quickly followed by Bianca. Nico was the only one that hadn't given his answer yet. He looked at all of them and in the end shrugged, raising his hand. Omen looked at everyone closely as he came to a decision.

Bring his hand up, Omen's eyes glowed a bright red, almost crimson. In a voice that truly felt like death itself, he spoke.

"Elinam Johnson, you walk the path of death. Your life hangs in the middle; your end will come blissfully protecting which you love."

Sighing, Elinam looked relieved to hear that, as Omen continued, "Bianca Cabello, you live your life hoping death will come fast. You shall meet your end doing which you love."

Folding her hands as if expecting that, Bianca just nodded in acceptance.

"Nico Gonzalez, you've lived your life for only one purpose. You shall find what you pay a heavy price for it."

Satisfied with his premonition, Nico stepped away from Omen. Malik stepped forward nervously.

"Malik Anomos Blackwood, you have many weaving elements in your life. I see two souls struggling with dominance. Who is the true you, only time will tell. You have two choices: you can choose a happy life filled with love and no regrets or a path filled with pain and misery; you will find your world utterly changed. I cannot see the end of your journey, just that it is a great one. For you, there is no true death, just the void of nothingness."

There was a moment of silence as they all stared at Omen, who looked like him again. Malik stood there numbly as he took it all in.

Was he going to truly die this year at any point? He wouldn't live to see seventeen at this rate; he couldn't live with putting his family through that pain. If he left now and never looked back, then he'd be all right.

There was this feeling coming to the surface that he wanted to know who and what he truly was, but did the risks outweigh everything? Was it right for him to simply walk away? He had a dark part of him that he felt he owed to set things right.

He found everyone watching him in concern. Giving them a weak smile, he said, "Thanks for telling me, I guess only time will tell. For now, I just want to get out of here."

Seeming to understand, Omen walked up to the tree that stood alone in the field. He waved his scythe in front of it and a portal opened.

"I understand that you must all feel somewhat changed from knowing your futures, but I hope you all find the right paths for you."

There was a general murmur of thanks then, and as they all got together without a word toward the portal, they heard footsteps.

"Ah, my partner has finally arrived," Omen said in exaggeration to no one in particular.

"Oh, shut up, Omi, you can never do things right without me," said a woman with a strong voice.

They whipped around toward the voice. What greeted them was utterly surprising. The woman in question looked exactly like Nico, minus a few features, but it was definitely her.

There was a loud thud as Nico dropped to the ground, looking up at the woman.

"Mom, is that you?" Nico whispered as if scared to say it louder, or she'd disappear.

"Who?" the woman asked, staring at Nico as if he was crazy.

"I'm sorry Nico, but if that was your mom at some point, she's already gone. When someone takes over the job of being my partner, and they've died, they lose their memories from their living years; it's very rare to retain any previous memories," Omen regretfully told him.

Nico shook his head in disbelief, as if Omen was lying to him. Malik and Elinam walked up to him to try to comfort Nico in some way. Before they could, Nico jumped up and grabbed ahold of the woman's hand. As if a switch had been flipped, the women smiled at him.

"Hello, my little Prince," the women told Nico in an affectionate tone.

Looking deep into her face, tears started to roll down Nico's face. "I'm sorry Mom, I wasn't strong enough to stop him."

Nico's dead mom grabbed his cheek and wiped away the tears. "It's okay baby, don't blame yourself. It was just my time to go. I want you to stop holding on to that guilt and live your life."

"I can't, I'm not strong enough. I can't do anything right, I never wanted to be the alpha. I'd give it all up to be with you." Nico sobbed quietly, gripping her hand tightly.

His mom pulled his head closer to her and kissed his cheek, wiping away his tears. "You need to give it up, go be a kid. Don't fall like Atlas."

"I love you, Mom," Nico told her, wiping away his tears.

She replied with tears running down her face, "I love you too, my Prince."

Determination brimming in his eyes, Nico declared, "I'll avenge you, I swear, even if it kills me."

She jerked, trying to say something. "Please … don't."

That was all she could say before she seemed back to the woman who'd first arrived.

"What just happened?" she asked, puzzled as to why she was crying and holding Nico in her arms.

Finally, Nico composed himself and let go of his mom for possibly the last time.

"It seems that Sarah somehow held onto a piece of her previous self and left a sort of imprint in case Nico ever came to find her. I guess it's all gone now," Omen explained.

It was amazing what had just happened. It did seem like Nico's real mom was truly gone, with a different person in her place.

"Let's go, guys," Nico declared, having finally put

himself back together.

He jumped into the portal without waiting for anyone else. Maya, Bianca, and Elinam all followed after him. Only Malik and Jaden were left standing.

"I should warn you that after you get out of here, you'll face incredible challenges and I do hope we see each other again," Omen told them both as he handed them a scroll.

"Wait, what's this?" Jaden questioned Omen.

"The scroll given to you was only to get into the spirit realm, which you honestly didn't need, given you had Elinam with you the whole time. But now you have two scrolls, which means you only need one more."

"Wait, I thought the last one was in the demon realm?" Malik asked, glancing down at the scrolls.

Omen just laughed. "Well, that's technically true. You currently hold the first scroll and I gave you the second one now, but the last one is in that demon city that you call Underworld."

"Then when did we get the first scroll?" Jaden pressed Omen.

"Oh, you've had it for days now, it's currently resting on Malik's neck at the moment. I'm sure you'll figure out how to take it out when the moment's right," Omen casually stated.

They both looked at each other, then at the amulet around Malik's neck. A dim glowing red light came off it as they spoke, apparently attracted to the scroll in Jaden's hand. That alone confirmed it; they really did have the first scroll since the beginning.

"Well, thank you for your time, Lord of Death, it's been a pleasure," Jaden said to the Reaper.

"The pleasure's all mine. You really should look into your problem Jaden, or I'll be seeing you again soon," Omen pleasantly told them.

Painstakingly smiling at the man, Jaden walked inside the portal. Malik stared at his friend for a moment, but he was ready to get out of here as well.

As Malik stepped into the portal, he heard Omen say, "Until we meet again, Prince of Darkness."

CHAPTER 18

Once Malik stepped through, he found he was back in the woods that they previously fought in. He could tell everyone was mulling over what had just occurred in the spirit realm, especially Elinam and Nico, who'd had big revelations.

He felt his phone buzzing; he'd completely forgotten about it. It was okay, even after Jaden had thrown it. Malik opened his phone up and saw fifteen missed calls, all from his mom and dad. He saw everyone was looking at their phones except Elinam.

"Everyone got calls and messages, too?" Malik asked, even though he knew they all did.

The others all nodded in agreement. Jaden looked at his phone and gasped. "That's not possible."

"What is it?" Maya snapped her head over to Jaden in concern.

"We were gone for three whole days and while we were gone, an attack happened," Jaden answered.

"I'm going to call my mom," Malik told everyone, worry all over his face.

They all nodded, each of them going to do the same thing. His phone rang for a moment before finally, his mom picked up.

"Hello, is that you, Anomos?" his mom asked in a shaky voice.

"Yeah, Mom, it's me." Malik was instantly worried.

"Baby, they took my baby," his mom cried through the phone.

"Mom, Mom, they took who?" Malik asked, trying to hear her answer through her cries.

"They took Nina," his mom finally managed to say.

He just stood there for a moment stunned, and his hands shook uncontrollably. They took Nina? His little sister, who always wanted to play princess and knights.

He saw only red at that moment. He didn't know how long he was like that until he heard his mom on the other line calling out to him.

"Anomos, are you still there?"

"Yeah, Mom, I'm still here."

"They also killed Mr. Gonzalez and your father is now in a coma. They both fought but lost in the end," she explained, once again breaking down.

Malik crumbled to the ground. His father, Virgil, the man who raised him to who he was today, was in a coma. He didn't know if his dad would ever wake up.

He remembered moments of his dad being there for him and telling him great wisdom.

"*The dead always speak to us, it's up to those living to hear their voices and speak for them.*" His dad always loved to say that about his work.

"*We are just men made in the image of other men, if we cannot accept that gift, then we will only see ourselves as the monster they depict us to be.*" His dad's way of living was truly philosophical and unique. Malik hadn't just lost a father, but a teacher as well. He swore he'd find those that had his sister and find a way to bring his dad back. He'd end them with everything he had.

"Mom, I'll get her back, I promise!" Malik declared to his mom, even while holding back tears.

"Thank you, Anomos, I love you!" she told him.

After that, he ended the call and just sat there.

It's going to be okay, Malik, we'll get her back, Ento told him.

He had completely forgotten about her until now. Malik only nodded his agreement; he didn't want to talk about anything at that moment.

It was several more minutes until everyone had gotten off their phones. They all got together to talk about what they had discovered. Nico was wiping away tears as well; he and Jaden consoled each other. They must have looked up to Andy more than anyone else. Bianca hugged him, as well as Maya and Elinam, gave him words of comfort. Nico was going through more than Malik was, first seeing his dead mom to finding out his uncle was dead as well.

"It's true, demons attacked Malik's home the minute we left to the spirit realm. They killed Andy when he tried to shield Nina from a demon attack. Oscar was there as well and fend them off for a moment, but in the end, he lost his arm. Malik's dad was hurt and is currently in a coma being treated with the best medicine we have," Jaden reported to all of them.

"How could they have known?" Maya asked, frustrated.

"They could have been watching us from the beginning, who knows how they found out. That doesn't matter anymore anyway, what do we do now?" Nico asked.

"My mom told me they left a video on Andy's phone after the attack. Do you guys want to see?" Jaden asked.

When they all nodded, Jaden played the video. It depicted the destroyed living room of Malik's home and bodies were everywhere. It seemed a lot of the supernaturals in the city had tried to protect his family. They could see Andy's body on the ground bleeding out, and Nina squirming to get out of a demon's grasp.

The camera panned to the main leader and Malik gasped. It was the Keeper; the one Malik had met under the basement.

"Hello everyone, especially you, Malik, or should I say Anomos. I feel that I need to send this video to justify my reasoning for why I did such a horrible thing. I was the one who started all of this in hopes it would awaken my forsaken king. While it seems to have partially worked, I'd like my true king to return. If I have to forsake my purity to let him return, I must do so. Understand that there are no hard feelings, truthfully. I'll give you five days to find me before I do something even more drastic to reach you. Much love, The Keeper of Dreams."

"The Keeper of Dreams? I feel like I've heard that from somewhere," Jaden mulled over out loud.

"That doesn't matter, we're going to find him and destroy him for good. Let's go," Malik angrily stated.

"Slow down Malik, let's think for just a moment, this could all be a trap," Maya cautioned.

He whipped his head at her. "I know it's a trap and I don't care. He has my sister and my dad is in a coma. I'm going, and if any of you try to stop me, I'm taking you down."

"So, what are you going to do? Do you think you can just storm in there without the third scroll? Who knows how many people are guarding it?" Jaden quizzed Malik.

He stood there for a moment, tears coming down his face. He was so frustrated at his weakness; if only he'd been stronger, maybe he'd have stopped all of this from happening in the beginning. If he had figured out that the man he kept seeing was the demon that orchestrated it all if he had enough power to stop being used by everyone in this world. He wanted to be able to stand on his own and protect everyone, not to rely on others and no one sacrificed their lives for him.

"Power comes with a price, but powers make sure the strong can protect the weak," the demon whispered in his head.

"Shut up!" Malik yelled at the demon out loud.

The others all stepped back from Malik as if in fear, and the shadows started to sweep him in waves. Malik couldn't control his emotions anymore; everything was threatening to explode and, with it, Malik himself.

Something in his body switched, and the shadows disappeared at that moment. The demon in his head was somehow offsetting Malik to the point where he only felt a small piece of his emotions. It was like using noise cancellation, but instead of the noise, it was his emotions. Malik had to thank the demon silently for stopping him from doing something dangerous.

"I didn't do it for you, I need your body to save our sister. I just need you a little longer, nothing more," he told him in disdain.

He didn't know how to feel about the demon's declaration but still appreciated it. It seemed to care for Nina just as much as Malik did and that was all that mattered.

"Okay, so what's the plan?" Malik asked after he calmed down.

"We're going to the demon city, Underworld City, just

a few miles outside of our territory," Jaden said, "we should be able to find answers there and the final scroll. After that, be prepared for anything when we enter the enemy's area."

"Wait, there's a demon city here?" Elinam asked.

"Yeah, it's full of half-breeds, some can't live in the regular world because they look more demon than human. There's a lot in this world, but the one we need is this one," Jaden explained. He opened a portal around the area where they first spoke to Jaden's dad.

The first to step through was Maya, sword in one hand. Nico followed after her with Elinam right behind him. Bianca grabbed Malik's hand and squeezed it before following them in.

Before he stepped through it, Jaden demanded, "No matter what happens, don't use your demon side. It might make things difficult for us."

He agreed and walked through the portal to find the most unusual scene before him. They were in a part of a dark town where it seemed to be a miniature Chinatown. Shops and weird attractions were everywhere; he saw adults with scaly faces and kids with small bat wings.

"Malik and Elinam, welcome to the Underworld, one of the largest demon towns in this side of the world. Even though we call it a city, it's too poor to call it a true one. We're just a few hundred miles from the border of our own," Jaden boasted in a touristy host voice; it seemed that he had been here before.

"Wow, I can't believe we're really here," Elinam said, stunned.

Malik could only mumble in agreement. It was hard to not look at everything as a tourist–there were stalls where people yelled prices for peculiar-looking objects. Some shops sold jewelry, while a crowd formed in front of a building as someone put on a show with fire coming out of their ears and mouth at the same time. It was like a normal city, but it felt as though they weren't as progressed as the city they lived in. it looked run-down for the most part as they walked in the streets.

"Yeah, we know, just stay close to us and don't take anything they offer to you. We're here on a mission to get in and get out fast before trouble finds us," Jaden asserted.

"Hey, what did you mean by a high-class demon? Like he was an archdemon or something?" Malik asked Jaden.

Heads turned as everyone looked at Malik in curiosity.

"Why did you say archdemon and not its class?" Nico asked, looking dangerously close at Malik.

He was worried as to why he was getting so many stares. "That's how Ento classified them. I'm sorry, is there something wrong with that?"

Jaden shook his head. "No, that's okay, we should have probably explained things earlier. Most demons are classified in that sort of ranking, but it's only down amongst their own people. We just generally stick with the general classification for all other supernatural creatures; while it's similar to the setup of demons, it's not as narrow. For the general classification, it starts at C rank being the lowest to S rank being the highest. There are other ranks above S, but that's on a whole different level like they can go toe to toe with literal gods and be all that. We don't have much time to explain, but I'll let you know more once everything is settled."

With that, Malik chose to not say anything else. Everyone weaved in and out of places until they reached a building that had a sign saying *'Mad Dogs Only.'*

"Mad Dogs Only? That's a weird sign," Malik read, laughing.

Everyone turned their heads to look at Malik in confusion, except Jaden. "You can read demon tongue?"

"Um, sure, I guess. I don't really know, it just sort of happened."

"Well, just be careful, if demons catch on you can read their language, they might figure out what you are," Maya warned.

Getting in front of the group, Jaden reminded them, "Just remember, let me do all the talking, and no weapons displayed."

Everyone put away their weapons and walked in after Jaden. They met the receptionist at a desk. The place had an eerie vibe to it but was well-lit compared to the outside.

Walking up to the girl at the desk, Jaden asked, "Is

Lawrence in right now? Tell him Jaden wants to see him."

The girl looked up and smiled; she looked like a regular girl compared to others outside. She spoke with a soft voice. "Oh, of course, I'll let him know you're here."

The girl got up and grabbed her clipboard. What Malik didn't expect to see was her tail with a spade-shaped tip.

"Stop drooling, Malik, she's just a demon, most likely half," Nico reprimanded him. Malik just grumbled, embarrassed. This was the first time he was seeing half-demons, why was he being hard on him?

"Wow, that's amazing," Elinam said in awe, staring at the spot the girl sat in earlier.

"Is it though? We're usually discriminated against in the demon *and* human world because of our appearances. Not all of us can look normal like your friend Jaden here," a deep male voice said.

Everyone looked over to see a guy about their age with horns on his head. He was a brown skinned African American kid, about six-one in height, though he was lanky. He dressed in casual streetwear but the energy he gave off was someone in charge. All the demons in the room seemed to respect him, as they all whispered greetings.

"I'm sorry, it's just the way I am," Jaden apologetically.

The guy just waved his hand dismissively. "It's not a big deal at the moment. What can I do for you and your crew?"

"I'm sorry to ask this Lawrence, but I need your help," Jaden urgently told him.

The guy's eyes narrowed for a minute, and the air around them seemed to shimmer for a moment before settling down. Malik could automatically tell this guy was powerful and he probably wouldn't stand a chance against him. He could feel the demon in him just jumping to fight someone worthy of its attention. He had to clamp down on its hunger before it got both of them into trouble.

The guy turned his eyes to Malik as if knowing something was going on before turning back to Jaden. "Oh, another favor. And I told you to call me Law from now on."

"Sorry Law, can we talk a little more privately?" Jaden asked as he looked around. The demons in the room were looking at them in curiosity; Malik figured they must not see humans come into their city frequently. Some children hide behind their parents in fear of them. Many of them looked at Maya and Bianca in a hostile manner.

Law gestured for them to follow him to a back room. The room was spacious, well-lit with a few chairs and tables. It seemed that it had been prepared for their arrival, with condiments set aside for them. When everyone got situated, Law turned to them and asked, "What do you need?"

"We need a way to get into a different dimension that

only a terror demon can access."

"You're crazy if you think I can do that. I'm only able to do small things" Law stated, staring at Jaden funny.

"Stop lying, Law, we both know that you have more power than you let on. We just need someone that can get us in, you know everyone," Maya angrily stated.

Staring blankly at Maya, Law shrugged, answering her, "I don't think I can do anything, but I might know of someone. But if we do this, you have to help us over here. We're already running out of clean water, and we need constant medical attention."

"I can't do that, and I hope you understand why," Maya disagreed with his request.

Law nodded. "Then I guess I can't help you and I hope you understand why."

Jaden tried to maintain peace before Maya and Law started fighting. "Okay everyone, just relax, let's work out a deal."

"You know what, I think I'm done," Law angrily declared. "I've been asking the council to help for years. While you watched us suffer, I've been giving back to mortals and demons under my protection. So go back to your little net you call your town and turn a blind eye to our struggles once again."

"It wouldn't be like this if you gave us full access to your town," Maya spit back at Law.

"Get off your high horse if you can't see what they're

trying to do. They want access to our land to use us and the minute they drink up every inch of resources we have, they'll leave us to die or worse in the name of being a savior," Law said.

"What savior? We're just trying to help," Maya asked, enraged.

Law just snorted. "Whatever you wanna believe, *Hermana*. I'll let you have whatever you want if you agree to have them at least listen to our terms."

Before Maya could say anything, Jaden stepped in. "What terms?"

"We want full amnesty to whatever your bad demon does and access to water. Also, we want a seat at your council," Law stated.

"Okay that works, I'll make sure to let my mother know," Jaden agreed.

"Well then, I know just the person to help you out. You can come out now, Ash." Law gestured to someone they didn't see before.

They all turned to see a girl in ragged clothing, looking like she had barely slept in days. She held a sword that strangely resembled Andy's sword. She seemed to be around their age, but underfed and malnourished.

"Give me the sword now, demon," Nico in barely concealed anger.

"That's going to be a problem since she's bound to it," Law grinned at them. "I'd like to formally introduce you to

Ash, half terror demon and your new Guardian."

Everyone looked at the girl in shock. The girl walked up and tripped, but Jaden went to her slowly and helped her to her feet.

"Hi, I'm Jaden Williams, it's nice to meet you, Ash," Jaden softly greeted her.

The girl, for her part, just looked at Jaden with wide eyes. Jaden waved his hand around and a minute later, the girl was cleaned up. Malik could make out her details more.

She was an African American girl with the oddest color of pink hair, with small baby horns on her head like that of a goat.

Stepping forward, Bianca offered an apple from her bag to Ash. She looked at it in wonder, as if no one had ever offered her anything.

"Are we really gonna believe she's the new Guardian?" Nico asked in disbelief.

Reaching his hand out for the sword, gave it to Jaden who looked at it closely. "I'm sorry Nico, but we're going to have to believe it because it's already bonded with her. We need to train her as soon as possible."

"That's going to be a problem because she ran from her previous master and father, the same demon you're after. She's been sealed; unless one of you plans on helping her out, she probably won't make it past this town without dying," Law told them.

"Sealed? What does that mean?" Elinam asked.

"They didn't tell you? The demon world is cruel and vicious, where it's all about survival or become enslaved. From the minute a demon is born, they're hunted to gain power or status; it's a broken world where creatures wish to escape into ours for just freedom or to feed," Law explained. "Demons are usually born from a collection of Animus or a cloud of magical particles somehow magnetizing and magnifying till they take a sentient form. When there's a demon hybrid, it requires more to sustain them into adulthood sometimes. This girl has been tied to her master for so long, she doesn't know how to sustain herself outside of being with him."

"But what does that mean to be sealed?" Elinam asked, still confused.

"It basically means that she won't ever get to her full growth as a demon because of her father blocking her progress. He controlled everything and never let her develop; she was just a tool he used for his own personal gain," Jaden answered angrily.

"So which one of you wants to do it?" Law asked, turning to everyone present.

"I'll do it. I'll help her break her seal and ascend. Do you want to live, Ash?" Jaden asked as he stepped forward to volunteer.

The girl grabbed the sword and held it to her chest tightly looked at Jaden with determination in her eyes.

Smiling and clapping his hands, Law got up with a mischievous look in his eyes. "Well, let's do this. We have a world to save."

CHAPTER 19

Jaden and the girl Ash walked to the corner of the room. Jaden looked over to Law and said, "We need room to work."

Law nodded and snapped his fingers; immediately, demons came rushing into the room and helped clean everything away. Maya and Bianca just watched what was going on, not moving yet. Nico and Elinam chose to walk away and sit down. Nico grabbed one of the demons and ordered them to bring a lot of food. Malik decided to follow the sister's example and wait for someone to tell him what to do.

"Watch what's going on, you'll have to do something like this someday." Perking up to hearing Ento's voice in his head, Malik was glad for some company.

"What do you mean, I will do this someday?" he asked.

"Well, for when you start building up your numbers. You'll need a way to connect with your people, you'll share power and information. It's something the King used to do regularly," Ento explained.

He was silent; would that be something he would do,

too? He didn't want to have any more beings in his head; he could barely handle one of them. Nervously he told her, *"I'm not sure I want to do that but thanks for the information."*

"It's okay, Malik, you don't have to, but it's good to know. It's something a leader must know."

After that, Ento went silent and Malik went back to watching Jaden do his thing.

Sitting down on the floor, Jaden seemed to be deeply thinking. The girl Ash sat next to him.

Deciding to get a better view, Malik walked up to Maya and Bianca. Jaden was saying things under his breath.

Jaden didn't look like himself anymore. The version that Malik had previously seen in his mind was before them. Though in his mind, Jaden hadn't looked nearly as powerful as he did now. Symbols swirled all over his body and he even seemed to have wings that moved on their own. The girl Ash looked at Jaden in awe as she handed the sword to him.

Speaking in a voice that didn't seem quite like his own, Jaden asked, "Do you, Ash, wish to serve and protect the people that in turn serve to protect you?"

The girl opened her mouth and in a calm voice answered, "I do, I will protect you and your people until my last breath."

With everyone watching in fascination, Jaden glowed for a minute before one of the symbols on his body disappeared and moved to the sword. He handed the sword back to the girl. "Be one with yourself and never let anyone else take from you what you're born to be."

The minute the sword was in the girl's hand, something changed. She grew to her full height and the person in front of them disappeared completely to show a girl with lightning coming off of her, giving off the power so immense, it was blinding; she had black wings of a crow and her horns were fully curved out to the back of her head. Malik was amazed and transfixed by the display before them. Instead of her previous image, her features seemed to border on over worldly with her body no longer seeming to be underfed and ragged. She had the glow of someone older and more mature, she even appeared like that to them. She should have appeared to be their age but instead seemed to look a year or more older.

When Malik thought he had seen it all, she disappeared, completely gone from their view. Jaden was back to his old self.

"What just happened?" Elinam asked, staring at the same spot Ash had been just a moment ago.

Answering for Jaden, Law explained, "He helped her ascend and she'll be able to help you guys out."

They looked at Jaden who nodded in agreement to Law's explanation. He looked slightly tired, but overall okay.

"Where did she go? Ash?" Elinam asked in disbelief.

"It doesn't matter, but if you must know, she's with me. I did something similar to connect to a familiar so she can be hidden from her father and be safe to recover for the moment," Jaden answered before Law could answer for him again.

"With you? I don't see her."

Pulling his shirt slightly down, Jaden revealed a tattoo that wasn't previously there. It was of a girl holding a sword.

Malik came to the wildest conclusion. "Is she inside your skin?"

"Something like that, but right now we need to get to your place and settle things with that demon," Jaden said.

Malik nodded; they had more pressing issues to deal with. They only had a few more hours to save his sister; if Jaden said she was good, he had to believe him.

Jaden turned to Law. "Can you get us out of here?"

Walking up to them, Law gestured to them to follow him. "Let's go before it's too late. I can show you a faster way out."

Everyone grabbed everything they had and headed out. Law and Jaden lead the group, with demons on either side of them. They went through a back door that led to a courtyard. They walked for a couple of minutes until they reached the edge of it.

"You should be able to do your portals from here, Jaden. It was good seeing all of you," Law told everyone.

Jaden went to shake Law's hand but was pulled into a hug for a minute. Law whispered something in Jaden's ear, but Malik couldn't make it out.

Once they said their goodbyes, Law walked up to Malik. Malik was taken back by his words.

"I know what you are, Malik, and if I can give you any advice, it's that no matter what you act like on the outside, they'll always judge us on what we are, so be careful of who you trust."

"What do you mean?" Malik asked.

Law ignored his question with one of his own. "You know what they do to demons?"

Shaking his head, Malik was completely lost. Why was he asking him something like that before they left?

"You know how witches like Jaden were hunted down by humans and burned to the stake? It's worse for us; demons like us have souls, unlike the demons in Hell. So people like Maya's would hunt us down and hang us like animals to die; imagine not caring if a half-demon was innocent or not even if it was a child. These people are sick."

He turned to Maya and saw her looking away as if she knew they were talking about her and chose to say nothing.

Malik didn't know how to answer. He hadn't known demons had it so bad; he had thought that they were just poor.

"For so long, all we ever wanted to be was left alone. It's not our fault who our parents are or what bloodline we come from. We're enslaved, dehumanized, just so some sick people could feel good about themselves. They fear us so much because they don't understand us, but still use all our customs and methods of survival. My demon ancestors are probably rolling in the grave right now in anguish," Law finished, looking ready to either murder someone or throw up.

Malik understood his position on it; even though humanity as a whole had advanced from barbaric traditions, there were still others in this other world who still believed in it. Malik was suddenly saddened by the fact he himself would be on the receiving end of it all someday.

"I'm sorry, I never knew," Maya apologetically told Law.

Law chose to ignore Maya, focusing on Malik instead. "You thought the prejudice you had so far from joining this mission was bad, wait until they find out what you are. I suggest you go home now and forget about this. Because if they kill you, there will be no justice."

All he could do was stand there numb from Law's words, but as much as he wanted to go home, he still had to save his sister. With that, Law and his group left them alone walking back inside their building.

After they left, everyone became quiet. Elinam and

Jaden seemed to understand what was going on; maybe they had both been on the receiving end of someone who didn't appreciate their existence as well.

Jaden cleared his throat and they saw he had opened a portal. He turned to everyone and asked, "Y'all ready to end this?"

Everyone wore determined looks on their faces and nodded. Jaden smiled and waved them all into the portal.

When they stepped through, they encountered the most bizarre scene before them. A few hundred people were waiting for them.

Someone stepped forward and they recognized it was Oscar, Andy's brother. The story was true as they all saw him without an arm; Malik had been hoping that was false. He looked tired but excited to be there. Nico walked up to Oscar and hugged him deeply, and they stood there for a few minutes as they consoled each other. Jaden came up to the pair and hugged Oscar. After saying everything that needed to be said, Oscar turned to the rest of the group.

"We're all ready for you," Oscar confirmed.

"Thank you! I appreciate you doing this for me," Nico bowed his head in gratitude.

"Of course, anything to help our Alpha; we even got some of Maya's people to come." Jaden walked up to Malik and said under his breath, "It seems like we weren't the only ones busy."

"What's going on?" Elinam asked. The others mumbled

a general consensus, their curiosity piqued.

"After the attack in the woods, I made some calls to my second-in-command to gather any people that wanted to support our attack on the demons' stronghold, and this is everyone who showed up," Nico explained.

"Wait, your uncle isn't your Alpha, it's you?" Elinam asked.

Nico had a pained expression on his face. "Yeah, when my mom died, I was the only logical reason for Alpha, my uncle was just the acting Alpha till I'm of age, which was last year."

Squinting his eyes; Malik started to piece things together now. It seemed that all along, Nico was leading all the Weres in Portland, not his uncle. He had assumed that Nico was just going to one day inherit the position, not that he currently *was* the Alpha.

Accepting the help, Jaden greeted everyone that had come, shaking hands with people. He talked to a couple of people that were with the officer. It seemed like everything was falling into place, and they were really about to save his sister.

Elinam came up to Malik and asked him if he was all right.

"I don't know, I can't believe we're really about to save my sister. I can go home and put all of this behind me," he whispered with emotion in his voice.

Elinam shared her opinion with him. "I feel the same

way, but you really think this is going to be over? I don't think people are going to stop coming after you, especially once they find out there are others out there that might still be alive from the time of the Demon King; they'll want their revenge."

He hadn't thought of that. Even if he saved his sister, there would be people that would want to harm her or use her to get to him again. He needed to make sure this was the last time it happened.

"Thank you for being here, especially since you could have gone home." Malik thanked her sincerely. She had stayed with them through everything that had happened, without even knowing her own story.

"I wouldn't have left–you guys are my friends now, too. Plus, Nico said he'd help me find my family. My power is hereditary. I need someone to train me to be better, I don't want to slow you guys down." Elinam smiled at him.

His heart was warmed by her commitment to stay with them. Jaden cleared his throat and spoke in a voice that reached everyone. Malik shook his head and smiled; he really needed to learn that skill.

"The six of us are going to head in first. Once the fighting starts, I'll be able to send you guys in from here with a portal. I'll warn everyone now, we're dealing with an old and powerful demon who can invade your minds and make you see anything it wants to. Whatever happens, don't let yourselves get out of the protection I put on you guys. I can try to save you, but you might be a danger to yourselves as well as us."

They all understood the danger they were about to face and were fully committed to the cause.

Quickly speaking under his breath, once Jaden did Ash appeared. The sword she held now glowed with symbols, it was slightly smaller than before and ended with a curved tip. Ash nodded at everyone else and walked ahead of them. She grabbed her sword with both hands and brought it high, followed by a single slash going down as if cutting a wire. Immediately in front of them was a giant gate that wasn't there before. It looked old, ancient, with deep engravings with words and drawings, and had a very forbidding vibe to it. Malik knew they were in the right place immediately.

Shocked to see such power used in front of them, Ash walked back to Jaden, everyone parting ways for her till she stood next to him.

Clearing his thoughts, Jaden asked everyone, "Well, let's go save Malik's sister. Everyone ready?"

They each shared anxious looks, but they knew the people around them would fight for them. This was the trust they had built for each other from all the obstacles they had faced together. The other people that had just arrived stood back but looked ready to go in as well.

Malik's skin glowed for a moment; the strange symbol

he had received last time appeared. One moment his hands were empty and the next, the sword the demon had used was in his hands. It felt comforting to know he wasn't entering empty-handed.

They all walked toward the doors, which opened wide for them. It showed a swift darkness which they all plunged into. That's when everything went downhill.

Malik found himself alone in a small room with no one around him. It was a dimly lit room with hardly any furniture besides a chair and a desk. There wasn't anyone there except for a man that seemed to be wrapped in darkness. Malik turned to the man waiting at the entrance, his very presence imposing. Malik could feel his body act as though it had known him all his life as if reacting to a lost limb and not a stranger.

"It seems we finally get to meet," the man expressed, seeming to be happy.

"Who are you?" he asked, even though he knew exactly who he was.

"I'm simply the master of this house, the question is, who are *you*?"

"I'm Malik Blackwood, but I think you already knew that" he answered, gritting his teeth at the man, who acted as though nothing was wrong.

The man was amused by Malik's response. "Well, I guess that's true in a way, but you're more than that, aren't you, my son?"

Malik's frustration was getting the better of him. The longer he waited, the more danger his sister was in. "What do you want?"

"I want to know you. You see, I'm only a shadow of who I was. I have no true consciousness; I've only been tied to this building, and after it disappears, so will I," the man answered.

"So are you really him? The Demon King?" Malik asked.

"The Demon King? Is that what they called me? I simply took the form of something that suited my purpose," the man told Malik.

"So what are you?" Malik asked.

"Hmm, now I am nothing more than a whisper in the night. The true Demon King lies within the young man I see before me." The shadow looked deeply into his eyes, continuing with his speech, "What do you think the point of your existence is? Why did the Demon King decide to die instead of staying alive till the end?"

He stood there a minute, trying to figure out what was the point of it asking him that question. Malik didn't know the answer, from all the things he had learned about the Demon King, it didn't seem like he was the type of man that would quit so easily.

"I don't know, okay? I'm just trying to save my sister, that's all," Malik answered.

"So you're a hero then. Maybe you won't go on the

same path as he once did," the man said, speaking more to himself than to Malik.

They looked at each other for a moment, each unsure of what to say next.

"What was he like? The real you?" Malik blurted out.

It seemed like the man knew he'd ask this question. "He was in the beginning much like you. He came to this young world he truly didn't know, but saw much devastation, just like his home world. He thought the world was still young so that he could change its ways before it could fall. With hope and renewed energy, he came about bringing as much faith and restoration as possible. But that hopeful kid soon started to disappear, until all that was left was a man wearing too many invisible scars."

As the man spoke, Malik was entrapped by his voice, which was filled with pain and sadness.

"He tried so hard to change their ways, but as you know, power comes with a price, and it was a heavy one indeed. We spent centuries trying to build our little perfect world, but that's the funny thing, sometimes the world doesn't want help. There has to be a balance to everything; all we could do was create realms or worlds to separate everyone's conflict. With the creation of these realms, we were no longer seen as the heroes, but the villains. The Demon King grew tired of trying to change the creatures of this world and sought a way out."

"So he gave up?" Malik clarified for him.

The shadow looked at Malik angrily. "Gave up? No, he saw that his existence was the problem. He wasn't of this world, and he knew that at some point when the others found out, all his hard work would collapse. He decided that he needed to be incarcerated, with the hope that the next generation could use that power a little better. Now you stand before me, on the crossroads to a troubling and pain-filled life, wondering if you have what it takes to stand against what's coming."

"What's coming?" Malik's nervousness was showing steadily.

"Everything, the end as we know it. The ones across the veil of time are coming to reclaim their lost world. Whether it's an era of peace or suffering, only time can tell. Do you think you can weather the storms that are raging to be let out?" the shadow asked Malik sincerely.

"I-I don't know, but I can promise you that I'll try. I'm not trying to be anyone else but myself, I'm already splitting at the very seams. Please help me save my sister!" Malik begged the man.

"I'm sorry, there's nothing for me to do unless you accept my gift. Your inheritance as the descendant of the Demon King and his incarceration. I'll become your shadow and master. I'll teach you how to use your power and guide you in advancing to the next stage. I'll even teach you how to mend your soul, as well as other forms you can take," the shadow stated.

He stood there for a moment, processing it. There wasn't anything the shadow of the Demon King could do. How could he? He wasn't even a real person anymore, just a last echo of someone that once was. Malik didn't want to take the inheritance; he felt with everything going on, adding more problems would only complicate things later on. While he wanted to save his sister, he felt that, at least with his friends, he still had a chance.

He shook his head to signify his answer. "No, thank you. I think I'll just figure it out on my own."

The shadow smiled at Malik as if it liked his answer.

"I personally think that was a good decision; it shows that you're not easily swayed by promises of power. I'll let you in on a little secret – if you decide not to take me up on my offer, I'm still willing to advise you on anything you need. You see, I'm nothing more than a piece of the Demon King's will; if you felt inclined to take me out of this prison, then I suggest you find the piece that keeps me here."

"What are you talking about?"

The man stepped forward and in his hand was a small glowing glass sphere the size of his palm.

"What you're about to enter is simply a pocket dimension; if you could retrieve the sphere I'm trapped in, then I'll be able to advise you whenever you want or just to tell you stories of the Demon King," the man explained, staring at the sphere in concentration.

"Oh, okay, I get that. Can I ask for the Demon King's true name?" Malik asked, his curiosity getting the better of him.

"I'm sure even he forgot his true name from his home world. Before he was named the Demon King, he went by another name." The shadow looked at Malik intensely for a moment before answering. "His name was Mo'Nomos, which is translated to what it is now as the moment of law. Though back then, it had a different meaning – the defender of law and justice, the punisher of sins."

Malik stumbled back, unable to think straight for a moment. There was no way that was a coincidence – Anomos and Mo'Nomos were too similar in wording, as well as the definition.

"Wait, there's no way!" Malik stammered out loud.

"So you're finally catching on. Destiny and free will are false chooses–it was an illusion to give you hope in the dim life you live. Everything was decided before you were even born. You will live to punish those that sinned against me and my people."

Everything spun as Malik started to disappear and all he could hear was the echoes of the shadow of the Demon King's laugh.

CHAPTER 20

Malik found himself back with everyone again as if he had never left. Once they all entered the area, it lit up. Malik and the others looked around, shocked to find this before them. Instead of the dirty and dusty catacombs, they were in a beautiful open labyrinth. They found themselves in a beautiful hall, time itself had been rewound. A myriad of emerald and gold was spread on the walls, on top of stone tiles. There were four pillars on each side of them, each had a snake or creature curled around them. It felt as though they were in a hall built for a god, not something they should see.

Malik almost felt like he was in a completely different place than where he had previously visited. If it wasn't for his gut feeling that he was in the same place, he would have suggested they leave.

Standing before them were multiple rooms, as well as different paths. Some lead into tunnels they couldn't see the end of in the ground. There were also paths up high where they couldn't tell either where it led.

"Where should we go, Malik?" Elinam asked.

"This way guys, let's go to where he showed me the painting," Malik stated before leading them through many turns and twists before stopping at the painting he had seen.

"Is everything okay, guys? I don't think my sister or the demons are here," Malik stated, after seeing all the looks of shock on their faces.

"Malik, this isn't just some random place the demon picked, this is the chamber that legends say the Demon King rested. It's said to house the most powerful objects and beings in the world," Jaden explained, looking around the room again in concern.

"So, what does that mean?" Elinam asked nervously.

"Oh, that we're in more danger than I originally thought possible," Jaden soberly determined, "and I don't know if we can bring in our reinforcements just yet. Who knows what kind of things guard this place?"

As soon as Jaden uttered those words, the room distorted and changed as if rearranging itself. The whole area changed to a different view. They were now in a big room, like a treasury of some sort. There were pictures and paintings on the wall, as well as books were lined on the walls going high. The biggest change was the three big foreboding doors that appeared before them.

"What the hell just happened, guys?" Elinam asked, panic in her voice.

"I think the demon knows we're here and is laying

traps for us. Everyone, be careful," Maya stated.

They didn't have to be told twice–everyone was being cautious, fearful they would be transferred into another room without their permission. They each looked at the three doors, unsure what to do.

Nico's eyes changed to red, and he was looking at each of the doors in great detail. Jaden was doing the same, with his hands waving in front of him as if to sense the danger.

After another moment, Nico pointed to the door on the far left. "Something is guarding that door, but I have a feeling we'll have a better chance if we go through that one."

Hesitating before agreeing with Nico, Jaden said, "Let's go through that door, just be ready for anything."

Everyone nodded and Malik moved to step forward, but when he did, he was no longer with everyone else. Now he was in a well-lit throne room that he didn't recognize.

Before him stood Ento, as well as the demon, who was clearly in a bad mood.

"Hello again, Malik, I think it's time we've talked."

He was about to yell at them that he needed to get back when he started to notice the room itself was starting to disappear. "What the hell is going on?"

They each looked at Malik in a saddened expression. "This is your space, the very core of your soul, and right now at this very moment, it's starting to fall apart."

"Fall apart?!"

"Malik, you're falling apart. Your soul has already been split apart for a while now. But since discovering you were the incarnation of the Demon King, that part of you is vying for control. The shadows inside you are slowly starting to carve more real estate within you. You were never supposed to be two halves of an individual. If you can't fix the imbalance, something will happen, I'm simply here because the demon asked me to help you understand," Ento explained in earnest.

"I'm lost, what's going on? I thought we were fine earlier?" Malik asked.

"Yes, you were, but that was before you stepped in here. For some reason, your soul is reacting to this place as if it's found its home. Be careful, it's going to suck you in and take everything that makes you special," Ento said. "I was supposed to be the first piece of the King for you to connect with and help teach you, as well as get you ready to Ascend to the next level before finding the remaining parts."

"Oh, shut up hag, I'm tired of your act," the demon snarled, interrupting Ento. "I'll do whatever it takes to protect this worthless vessel, even from the likes of an Ancient One and an ex-angel."

Ento ignored the demon, continuing, "Things went sideways because of your split soul. You can't fully merge with the king and gain all of his memories, I'm honestly at a loss because I've never heard of something like this, I'm currently looking for a solution."

Staring down the demon dead in his eyes, Malik gave him a look that said to shut up. The demon huffed but shut his mouth.

"There's something you should know. You need to make yourself whole, or you'll die," Ento stressed, looking in Malik's eyes. As she said that, the room started to shake even worse, causing him great pain.

"You need to figure out a solution, and fast," Ento begged.

"Wait, I don't understand what-"

In the middle of his sentence, Malik found himself right back to where he was before with the group, no longer surrounded by his other counterparts in his head. He was disoriented for a second, shaking his head to clear it. He felt better after gaining some balance.

"Everything okay, Malik?" Bianca asked in concern.

He knew nothing was all right, but he needed to push forward. He was almost at the finish line- he was going to get his sister home no matter what.

"Yeah, I'm fine, let's go," Malik said in a rush, his heart feeling like it was going to jump out of his throat.

Once everyone was inside, Maya led them further through the room. The door behind them shut loudly and disappeared in thin air. The temperature in the room quickly dropped, and they rubbed their bodies as the cold chilled the air. Malik breathed and watched his cold breath in front of him, as if they were in icy mountains, with the wind picking up the cold air swirling around them. They clenched their clothes tightly against their skins, shivering loudly. All that could be heard were their crackling teeth and the shuffle of their boots. Quickly walked further into the building, they hoped to find some warmth along the way.

They were led into a dimly lit corridor until they were in a grand room and a giant wolf lay sleeping there. The room before them looked like a fancy jail cell, as it was built like a throne room, but in the corner was a giant chain. Its fur was a different color Malik didn't think was possible. It had gold fur with slight silver pieces here and there. It was the most beautiful wolf Malik had ever seen, considering it was a towering beast; it took up almost the whole room itself, and Malik has a feeling that it wasn't even at its full length just yet. Staring at the wolf, he noticed as it had a scar on its left eye that went down almost to its nose.

"Is that what I think it is?" Bianca gasped.

"Yeah, it's a great spirit." Nico's rageful eyes were glued to the sleeping wolf, his hands already formed into claws.

"Nico has some history with this spirit – well, technically everyone does," Jaden told them all. "You see, that is the spirit that originated all werewolves; he's basically the father of all wolves and other wolf-like creatures. He's been gone for centuries; his people have been waiting for him for so long."

"We waited and waited, if it hadn't been for this pathetic excuse of a great spirit, maybe my mother would still be alive and my father wouldn't have done what he'd done to her," Nico snarled, something that was between a man and a wolf.

"It doesn't matter now. I'm sorry Malik, you're going to have to go on without me. I'm not leaving till I take this monster down."

There was no way for Malik to understand Nico's pain, but that didn't mean he was going to leave him alone to face it.

"That's okay, Nico, but you're out of your mind if you think I'm leaving you alone to deal with this. I know you're suffering, and I'm not going to let you suffer alone," Malik assured him, looking at Nico straight in the eye, it helped Nico calm down.

"Well, well, well, if it isn't some lost sheep in my little den."

He immediately tensed up; he could tell that this spirit was older than any modern country today. Its voice vibrated in his head and chest as if its claws were reaching out to tear him to shreds if it got bored with them.

"We are sorry to disturb your slumber, dear Great Wolf Spirit, but we wish to pass to save one of our own," Jaden said in that silvered tongued voice of his, bowing his head in respect to the wolf spirit.

The wolf growled, and the room slightly shook, setting almost everyone off-balance except Nico, Maya, and Jaden.

"I know what you are, child of the betrayer, silence before I silence you."

Everyone looked at Jaden in surprise and confusion. Jaden just shut his mouth and retreated backward till he was next to Malik. He looked at Malik and jutted his head out to the wolf as if to tell Malik to go talk to it. Malik shook his head; no way was he going to risk his life over some senile old spirit.

"I feel someone among you is different. Could it really be! The master is back?"

The wolf opens its eyes, bigger than humanly possible. They were a swirling of gold, while slightly murky. It was like looking at a primordial beast, something wild and free. It was never meant to be chained like a pet, but to hold dominion over all other beasts, the pinnacle of power.

The wolf looked at Malik as if it instantly knew he was there. When the wolf and Malik locked eyes, Malik was thrown into the wolf's memories of a time when he, or the Demon King rather, first met his dearest friend.

It presented Malik with images of him playing with the wolf, hunting, helping it cultivate its power, and how it had children for the purpose of protecting its master.

Stumbling as he was forced from the immersive memories to being back in the present. He wanted to throw up; he knew these memories were without a doubt real. He wasn't this Demon King, but Malik – why did people keep expecting him to be someone he wasn't?

"I'm sorry, but I'm not your master, I'm just a kid that wants to save his sister," Malik earnestly told the wolf.

The wolf growled, sending tremors throughout the room. *"You speak like a child; I feel my master ever so stirring within you. Claiming you bit by bit, till he swallows you whole."*

Malik felt a shiver go down his chest. Was that going on? Was that what the demon and Ento meant by him losing himself? It was coming to the point of Malik losing who he was and his humanity.

"He might be inside me, but that doesn't mean I'm him. It also means if you hurt me and my friends, you won't get your master back," Malik said, trying to find some wiggle room to stop the spirit from attacking him and the others.

The spirit's chuckle vibrated through all their chests.

"Ahh, you even have the master's way of words. I shall not fight you all, but you must leave one behind if you wish to proceed. I choose the wolfling over there. I am dying, just like every great creature must one day pass on, but if I die without leaving an heir, the energy left behind could bring legions of the Darklings on our doorsteps. I was the last line of defense after the War of the Gods to hold the gates closed."

Everyone but Malik and Elinam looked shocked as well as scared. Even Ash, who hadn't said anything, now looked like she was about to break out in a sweat.

"War of the Gods?" Malik asked.

"It's the greatest war to ever be recorded in history," Jaden answered, "many didn't believe it, but the Demon King had fought on the side of good that day and helped save this world, as well as millions of different species."

"Yes, now you know how serious I am. I believe the demon you're after is somewhere further down. Be warned, the further along you go, the more you'll have to face your worst parts and moments of yourself. The demon likes to make others see their own demons to break them."

"How did you end up being stuck here?" Malik asked, wondering how a creature as powerful as him was captured.

"My master asked me to guard its grave till the new master was to arise. I had always been able to come and go, but the demon somehow found a way to confine even a spirit such as me into this part of the room, and I've been here for centuries since slowly losing power."

Looking at the wolf; he suddenly felt sorry for it and reached forward to touch it. Malik suddenly felt some pain in his arm and looked over to a new piece collected on his arm. It looked somewhat of a yin and yang symbol, but it had the shape of a wolf instead, one howling at the moon while the other bared its teeth. It was moving on its own in a constant loop.

The wolf immediately changed into the shape of a

man. The man was only covered from the bottom. He looked like a great but wild prince; he was covered in scars but seemed to make him even more majestic.

The man nodded, and in his hand was a great spear. Malik turned to see Nico tense up and looked ready to attack the man. Malik looked back in confusion.

Before Malik could ask, Jaden answered for him. "He's seeing his father – while you may see the true form of the great spirit, everyone sees something else, even me."

It made sense; people perceived what they wanted to believe, not what was truly there.

"What does this mean?" Malik asked.

The spirit answered for them out loud and not in their heads. "It means, dear King, that you're one step closer to who you truly are, and you freed me from this rotten cage."

Malik was hopeful; with this powerful ally, they might be able to truly defeat the demon.

"Does that mean you can help us?" Malik asked in barely concealed renewed hope.

The wolf spirit frowned. "I'm too weak to help you now; I can't leave this room. I'm barely able to keep myself going. I shall help you by doing three things: give you a successor to my power; my last child; and I'll let all but one of you go."

"Your last child?" Malik asked.

The spirit reached into its chest and pulled out a piece of a claw, handing it to Malik as if he was something sacred.

"This is the last true spirit I could make; it should be greater than I ever once was. It's up to you how you wish to do with them, you are now its father and master, just as the one in you once was," the spirit said. "Your friend, if he can handle it, will inherit my power if he wins in battle; if not, he will die. That is the law of the wild."

Malik glanced at Nico, who just nodded as if he understood. Malik took the claw and put it in his pocket, unsure of what to do with it. Malik then walked toward Nico and asked him if he was ready.

"I know it's not my father that I'm facing, but I'm still going to fight it. Now knowing the reason why the spirit never came back for us makes me even angrier at my father and the demon," Nico answered, staring at the spirit calmly.

The spirit answered, "Parents have a way of disappointing and breaking us into pieces, all for the sake of their advancement."

"They sometimes do, but don't let them break you. As long as you have the will, you can undo the pain they inflicted," Malik disagreed, a shiver going down his neck at the amount of emotion in Nico's voice.

Gathering around each other, they said their goodbyes to Nico, who stood ready to fight the great spirit wolf. Jaden had decided to leave Elinam with Nico, possibly thinking that she could assist him in some way. Nico also said he needed a partner to take down the spirit in case he couldn't do it alone. They had always been a good team since joining up together, so it made sense.

Emotions were high as they all watched Elinam and Nico stand before the great spirit, who had turned back into his giant wolf form. Quickly steeling their resolve before it crumbled, they raced forward to the next room. Looking back, it looked like a clash between a Titan and a pup.

Another door appeared once they accepted the spirit's terms. Walking through it, they entered another room. The door shut behind them without a care in the world that their friends could lose their lives, and they could do nothing about it.

CHAPTER 21

As they walked, the group that was once seven was now only five. Their movements felt dragged and forced as everyone kept thinking about what Nico must be facing. Malik had to steel himself; he couldn't get distracted right now. He knew Nico could handle himself if Elinam was there to help him, so he should stop worrying.

Their footsteps echoed across the hall till they reached the next door. They all looked at each other and nodded. Jaden stepped forward, pushing the door open. What happened next was something Malik wasn't prepared for – they found themselves blinded by light. They were suddenly outside; they could see white orchids for miles, with no end in sight. Beautiful cherry trees swayed with a silent symphony only they could hear.

Malik looked around to only find Bianca with him; he turned his head multiple times but found no one else in sight. Bianca appeared lost as well, as if she too was wondering what had happened to everyone.

"Should we be worried?" Bianca asked.

"Oh, we should definitely be worried, but I have a

feeling this is exactly what the demon wanted," an anxious Malik told her.

In response, Bianca just put her sword back into its scabbard, sat down, and started to make a sandwich. Malik watched her in confusion.

"Oh, relax, Malik, I'm sure my sister and Jaden are tearing this place apart trying to find us at this very moment," Bianca said dismissively to the situation at hand.

Continuing to look at Bianca in disbelief, Malik came to the conclusion they were different, Maya and Bianca. She looked up and tried to offer Malik a bite of her sandwich, but when he didn't take it, she just shrugged and ate more.

"I thought you would be panicking right now?" Malik asked.

"No point really, people will come for us no matter what. Plus, I have an ace up my sleeve if I ever need to use it, so I'm sure we'll be fine," Bianca told him, with no sense of urgency in her voice.

"Oh, you think so?" a sarcastic voice asked from their left.

Spinning around to find themselves facing none other than Law. Why was Law even here?

"What's going on, Law?" Malik asked.

Bianca had already put away her sandwich and started to reach for her sword when Law raised his hands in surrender.

"Relax, I'm not here to fight you, just to give you a warning. This is the Hall of Dreams, where your subconscious pushes all of those bad memories and misfortunes that you wish to keep buried; each of these flowers represents memories that have been forgotten," Law explained.

He narrowed his eyes at Law. "You're not really him, are you?"

Law grinned a wicked smile that could almost pass as the real Law. "You're right, I'm not your Lawrence. I'm the guardian of this place. Picking a face that you're used to from your memories is the easiest way to ease the tension. I do have some interesting memories that both of you wish to keep suppressed; it'd be a shame if I shared them with each of you," Law said with a ruthless expression.

Bianca visibly paled, then she gripped her sword and brought it out, ready to attack. Malik reached out and touched her arm; he shook his head. He had a feeling if they attacked Law, or whatever wore his face, she wouldn't be able to do any harm to it. Malik stood there, thinking long and hard – what was the point of each of these challenges? Was it meant to send a message to Malik? The thing acting as Law said something about his memories and something being buried, maybe that could help him get a clue to what was going on.

"What if I want to see my memories, but not Bianca's? Is that possible?"

Sharply looking over at Malik, Bianca stiffened in disdain but chose to not express her opinion on the topic. He just waited for Law to respond to his question, silently thanking Bianca for not saying anything else that could cause them any troubles.

"Sorry, no can do, you must see each of your worst moments if you wish to see the memories. You can visit each of them together if that helps," Law disagreed with his request.

He looked over at Bianca, silently asking if she was willing to see each other's memories. Bianca looked solemnly at the floor before saying out loud, holding her sword at Law, "Go ahead demon, it's not like I haven't already experienced it before."

Smiling, the creature wearing Law's face reached down to pick a flower; the flower that was once white had now bloomed to a blood-red color, and it blew on it. As the petals flew into their face, the petals felt like soft kisses of air. They were once again transferred to another location, this time a memory.

Malik looked around, finding himself in a big, beautiful yard with two little girls playing with a mom that looked like the exact duplicate of Maya; she didn't have Maya's look of commanding authority, but Malik could tell immediately that many people would follow her leadership. She had a warm smile spread on her face and laughed at the two girls that played together.

Grabbing his hand so hard that he thought she might break it, Bianca pressed her other hand to her mouth, trying to stifle her tears.

"It's okay Bianca, this doesn't seem like a bad memory," Malik assured her, grabbing her hand in comfort.

"This is the day Mom dies – when a demon somehow escapes and kills her." Bianca softly shook her head, a sad smile on her face as she gazed at her mother.

They looked around to see Bianca's younger version playing around. Malik saw the oddest thing on her back.

"Bianca, are those baby wings?!" Malik asked, his breath caught in his throat. They were the most adorable thing he'd ever seen. They were small wings on her back; the colors were light blue with a hint of gold in them.

Bianca smiled warmly. "I had just started to grow mine at a couple of months; Maya, being perfect as she is, even though she was only born a year older than me, had already had her wings longer and could fly a little."

Malik searched for Maya and sure enough, he saw Maya smiling as she stood on higher ground and jumped. She looked so free and happy as she sort of glided across the yard. Her wings were the opposite, gold with hints of blue in them.

That was when Malik saw it – it looked like a big mix between a rat and a bat, but several feet tall. Young Bianca was the first to notice it and screamed at the top of her little lungs. Malik was shocked at how fast their mom responded; a sword made of light appeared in her hands.

Grabbing Bianca in one scoop, Maya saw what was happening and rushed to her family. The demon threw a weapon that Malik could almost smell and make him vomit. Before the weapon could hit Maya, Malik saw the most beautiful wings possible. It felt like he was seeing an angel, the wings were made of light of the sun itself. Bianca's mom blocked it and spoke to Maya.

"Grab Bianca, get into the house, and call your dad or any adult. Tell them we have a breach and need to get everything to safety," Bianca's mom told Maya, her unwavering voice having a great calming effect.

Maya nodded at her mom, grabbed her little sister, and ran into the house. Malik and adult Bianca watched them go away, then turned their attention to Bianca's mom and her fight. If it could be called a fight – it seemed like the fight had already been decided from the start. Their mom moved at a speed that Malik couldn't have believed was possible; she was like lightning, effortlessly moving and being everywhere all at once. Her attacks seemed to only be seen after she had already made her move, leaving flashes of light in her place.

Malik wondered how Bianca's mom could have died like this; she was so powerful and seemed so unstoppable.

That's when Malik noticed it – a piece of the demon had fallen off, but instead of just disappearing or laying there, the disgusting thing mutated and created multiple copies of itself. Some of them had reached the house; young Maya had grabbed a small sword that had probably been made just for her. She handled the brainless copies on her own, but she was so preoccupied that she didn't notice Bianca had disappeared from her sight. Once Bianca checked that her mom wasn't fighting anymore and had beaten the demon, she came out of her hiding spot and rushed to her mom.

Bianca's mom still looked ready to fight. She turned around and saw her daughter come rushing at her to get a hug.

Malik, despite knowing that he couldn't be heard, yelled, "Look out!"

Little Bianca's horrified expression at her mom must have been enough to warn her. Bianca's mom turned away, raising her sword for the impending danger, but it was too late. While her sword was enough to cleave the demon in half, it still had enough power to latch on to her neck and bite down hard. That was the last thing it did before dying; it wore a triumphant expression on its disgusting face.

He looked over to Bianca to see if she was okay. Malik was shocked at the expression, it reminded him of the anger he felt when his sister was taken that night. Her look said she'd tear the demon to shreds with her bare hands if she got the chance.

"That should be it. I remember Maya saying mom died

from the venom at the hospital and I passed out from everything," Bianca said in confusion.

They both turned to the scene unfolding in front of them. Bianca was next to her mom, who tried to stop her crying, and her mom hugged her tight, telling her it wasn't her fault and she loved her.

Maya came out from the house with her sword still out in front of her, looking around for more monsters. Maya saw her family and rushed over to them; Maya froze once she saw her mom. Malik hadn't noticed till then that the mark left after the demon was a green sickly-looking thing; their mom's arms were already green and looked like puss was about to come out, too.

"Mamá, we need to take you to the hospital," Maya said.

"It's okay, *hija*, I need you to do something for me," Maya's mom said in an affectionate voice. Maya shook her head as if understanding what her mom wanted before answering.

"I won't do it; we can still save you," Maya protested, her kid voice breaking.

"I need you to be strong for me and Bianca. One day, you will help right the wrongs this world has done to my siblings and family," their mom told her.

"What about your family now? We still need you. How am I going to learn to fly without you? Or celebrate me becoming a woman?" Maya asked.

Bianca, next to Malik, grabbed his shoulder and started to cry softly into it.

Fresh tears rolled down her mom's face as well. "I'm sorry, but it's too late dear, this wasn't a normal demon. If it was any other bite, I would have walked it off. Someone specifically sent this demon after us. You'll be fine without me, hija, you're strong. You know what to do – I erased some of Bianca's memories. The first thing you tell her she'll immediately believe, and it will alter her memories naturally.

"You're my beautiful children. Maya, you've inherited my looks as well as my power. While Bianca is so much like her father and grandfather, protect her, you don't know how much she matters. I'm ready, Maya, please, only you can do this before I succumb to the poison and attack the both of you," their mom said urgently.

Bianca, who had already fallen asleep, was moved to a nearby bush. Maya held her sword, the small sword flickering for a minute until it had the same light, though not as bright as their mom's. Maya walked up to her mother, who was already starting to change; her hands had started to turn into claws and her teeth into sharp needles. Maya brought her sword up with tears in her eyes, closed them for a second, and swung.

Malik and Bianca both looked away, Bianca buried her head into his shoulder, unable to watch. They heard the swing then a thud, and Malik was sick to his stomach at what he just witnessed. Malik thought that was it, but he was very wrong. After their mother's death, Maya glowed for a minute, then a blinding beam came from the sky. The beam hit both Maya and Bianca, and then it was gone. Maya's wings now had streaks of light coming off them.

Maya then did the unthinkable – she reached for her wings and made crude cuts, crying out in pain as she tore her wings apart. After doing both her wings, she reached for Bianca's, but stopped midway and gave up. Maya ended up passing out from the blood loss and exhaustion.

Soon, adults came to find three bodies: one dead, one covered in blood and missing pieces, and one sound-asleep child.

Watching everything unfold, they were quickly transferred back to the garden. The minute they were back, Malik immediately hugged Bianca. He regretted his decision to see the memories. What had happened was something private that only their family should have experienced.

"I'm so sorry, I didn't know that was going to happen."

She dug deep into his shoulders. "It's okay, I guess I didn't know, either. I can't imagine what Maya must be going through."

He thought about Maya. How could she be so strong? He didn't know how he would handle it if his mom or anyone in his family died right in front of him. It now made more sense what she had said to him back at the training center.

"Are you ready for the next memory?" Law asked with no ounce of remorse.

Malik glared at him; knowing it wasn't even Law facing them made him want to attack it.

"Can you just give us a moment, please?" Malik in annoyance asked.

"Sure, I'll give you five minutes. There are still other things you need to do and people to save," Law said absentmindedly.

"No, we can go now," Bianca pulling herself together told them.

"Are you sure? We can wait a minute."

"No, let's go now, the longer we wait, the longer we're apart from the group and your sister isn't safely home yet," Bianca said in a firm voice.

He turned to Law to reply, but it was already too late. Law had picked up another flower, and it bloomed red, the same thing happened as last time. The petals flew to them and hit their faces, they quickly found themselves in a new memory.

This memory showed Malik as a kid, back in Chicago, where he had been born. He was just six at the time; Nina had just been born a couple of months earlier.

He was playing in a clearing by himself, acting like a superhero. His mom couldn't make it that day, due to Nina needing a check-up. His dad was there at the park, but with a man that seemed to be similar to the demon they were supposed to fight in the present day.

"What's my dad doing with the demon?" he gasped in shock.

He pointed the man out to Bianca, who was just as shocked as Malik. "Is this the connection between you and the demon?"

"How was this memory kept away from me, was it the demon who did this or my own dad?" His voice trembled with each word he spoke out loud.

"Malik, calm down, don't think too much right now. We can figure this out," Bianca said in a panic.

Noticing the black wisps of shadow coming off him, Malik told himself to breathe, and little by little they went back into their hiding spots. Finally able to think clearly, he said, "I remember this day, but not my dad and the demon knowing each other. Then again, when the demon first introduced himself to me, he did say he was the keeper of the family."

"It's not like your dad knew that the Keeper was a demon in the first place, so it's safe to assume your dad's good," Bianca said, still trying to console his fears.

His younger self played around for a minute longer before running up to a steep incline, ready to jump. It reminded Malik of how Maya and Bianca were playing before something happened to them. Malik looked up at his younger self and smiled; he didn't remember himself being so carefree.

His younger self slipped at the top of the high incline. It was about a five-foot drop, which wasn't so bad, but Malik noticed a big, jagged piece of glass. Malik, even knowing that he survived it, looked in alarm at his father and the demon talking. He wanted them to stop his younger self from falling, but they seemed to be too absorbed in their conversation to notice Malik's problem.

Malik heard the loud thud as well as the snapping of a bone. He'd expected to hear himself crying or screaming in pain but heard nothing. Malik's dad looked up in alarm as if noticing the sound of his fall. The demon he was talking to noticed as well, and it moved with astounding speed toward Malik's unconscious body.

Malik's father was there in a moment as well. As the demon helped move little Malik to a safer place, Malik noticed just how badly he was injured. He was sure that one of his legs was broken so badly he wouldn't be able to walk for weeks, and the jagged cut on the side of his face would leave a scar.

Quickly getting to his son, his dad grabbed his little body from the demon. They looked at Malik as if he was a goner.

"I can't believe this had happened right under my watch, Imani is going to kill me, I need to get him to the hospital," his dad said in a worried tone.

"I can fix him right up Virgil, she won't even know,"

the demon said, even sounding the same as the demon he had met so many times.

"I'm not letting you touch my kid; I'll personally break you if you do, " Virgil said that in a voice Malik had never heard, so cold and filled with rage.

"Okay, Virgil have it your way, though I don't think we'll have to worry, after all. He really is your son," the Keeper said in amusement, jutting his head at Malik.

Malik and his father both looked down at little Malik to figure out what the demon was saying. Malik and Bianca, as well as his dad, all gasped in shock at what they saw happening. The terrible cut on his little face seemed to stitch itself up and even the once-seemingly broken leg made loud noises as it healed itself back together. What amazed him most was his eyes, though – they were a pair of pitch-black eyes, with specks of red in the irises. He realized this must be what he looked like as a demon.

Malik's eyes widened and looked at Bianca in panic. Did that mean he had been a demon this long? Why hadn't his demonic side ever come out before then? Like when his sister was being taken?

Questions raced through his head. He needed to see this through first. Malik calmed himself a little before going back to look at his younger self. He saw his dad looking at his son, expecting him to be fearful, but instead, his dad wore a big smile on his face.

"He really is my son, taking after his old man," Virgil

beamed at little Malik.

"Like I said," the demon said smugly.

"How are you feeling, Malik?" Virgil asked his child, who had just been through a traumatic experience.

"What happened?" his little self asked.

Virgil lovingly touched his face. "It's okay, you're all right, Malik."

"Who's Malik?"

Everyone froze, Malik started to piece it all together. This was when the demon inside him had first appeared.

"Then who are you?" Virgil asked slowly.

Little Malik slowly got up, shaking his legs to see if they were all right. With his little pitch-black eyes, he said in answer, "I'm Anomos, who else would I be?"

Virgil and the demon looked at each other, then the demon nodded and said his goodbyes. Malik's father watched him go and once the demon was gone, his face changed.

Both Malik and Bianca shivered, seeing the look his father had. Virgil removed his contacts to show eyes made of deep crimson red, eyes that seemed to come from the depths of hell.

"My plan actually worked! Eight thousand years of planning, now finally bearing fruit," Malik's father said absentmindedly to himself.

He wanted to take the younger version of himself and run as fast as he could. This person couldn't possibly be his father, but Malik knew deep down it was.

"Who are you, Dad?" Malik said to himself.

Virgil brought little Malik close to him, his voice full of rage and bloodlust. "One day, you'll be the most powerful being alive. All the work and sacrifice I made led us to this moment. I have so much to do, and you're going to help me."

All they could do was watch as little Malik disappeared with his dad. Malik and Bianca found themselves back in the field again; this time, all the white orchids were gone. Law stood alone with just a sword in his hand.

Malik was still trying to get over what he just learned. So far, he knew that the demon personally knew his father, and that was the moment that the demon inside Malik had awakened and even had its own name, Anomos.

"What are you?" Malik asked, frustrated.

"Me? I thought you knew by now. I'm sure you heard of my race's cousin, the Jinn, or Djinn, as some like to call them. We are the Baku, creatures of darkness that feed on the nightmares of others. We feed on the misfortune and dreams of individuals. I figured you'd know since Damien is a demon that goes by Keeper of Nightmares or Dreams; while we aren't demons, we still serve the dark master," the Baku stated in distaste.

They gasped as they slowly pieced it together. The Keeper title wasn't just for show. Damien had planned this out with Malik's father, to create this environment to torture him.

"Well, I believe it's time to go," Bianca anxiously stated when she looked at Malik and saw he was still processing everything. "We'll be on our way now."

"No, only one of you is going. I've been trapped here for centuries, and I want to see what the world has become," Law said in an angry tone.

"What do you mean by 'one of us?'" Malik asked.

"There needs to be a guardian here at all times. One of you will take my place."

"Well, that's not happening, we're both leaving," Bianca defiantly told the Baku.

The Baku raised its sword and looked ready to kill one of them to get out of there. While Bianca readied herself for the fight, Malik's anger threatened to blow over. He started to see red; all he could think about was all the people that had used and lied to him for so long. Who knew if any other people were out there manipulating him to do things? His rage finally blew over, and it pointed itself to the demon impersonating Law; that'd be the first person he'd direct his rage at.

In a fit of rage, Malik made a sword out of the wisps of shadow coming off him. Before Bianca and the Baku could react, he blindly struck at the Baku, hoping to wound it or scare it away. He felt a warm wetness drip on his face.

"Malik, please stop," Bianca's voice came out oddly

close to him and weak.

Pulling himself out of the rage by her voice, he found a horrific scene before his eyes. Instead of the Baku, his sword had gone through Bianca, who had somehow gotten there before he struck, possibly hoping to stop him before he made a mistake.

All he could do was watch as Bianca fell to the ground, blood coming out of the hole in her chest and out of her mouth as well. Bianca grabbed Malik as if to tell him something; still gripping the sword, he bent down to hear his friend's last words with tears in his eyes.

"Malik, I can't believe that you're a monster," Bianca said in a sad voice.

He stared into the eyes of someone he considered to be his first crush, as her life finally left her. He just sat there, with blood covering his shaking hands. Malik didn't know how long he sat there. All he could remember was someone coming to find him and taking him away.

CHAPTER 22

Days slipped by after that. Malik didn't even remember how they had gotten him out of the chamber. He didn't remember if Nico had been with them when they finally got out. All he could remember was the look Bianca gave him as she finally lost her tether to life. Malik had nightmares for days on end. He kept seeing weird dreams of being tortured and Bianca smiling, flirting with him, right before he killed her.

Malik remembered being taken in front of a counsel. They decided he would be meet judgment–his death–in three days. Malik didn't even care anymore; all he could think about was the pain Maya felt losing her sister and her mother to tragedy. Malik experienced torture he didn't think was possible, a form of mental torture. His mind would be torn apart, only to be repaired. Malik's mind started to drift away when that happened. There were moments he felt someone was trying to wake him from a bad dream; then he'd be pulled back into his living nightmare and experience even more torture.

That was the way it had been for the last two days before he was to be executed. Malik sat in the cell, having lost most of his clothing from his torture. While there, Malik was able to finally understand some of his power. The wisps of shadow had welcomed him during his time of need; they would wrap themselves around him as if to protect him from danger. There were times when he'd hear voices inside his head calling him to wake up, but after a while, Malik learned to ignore them. He found that he could play with his shadows to make anything he wanted but was sickened by what he'd done to Bianca, and he chose to not make any weapons. He didn't even try once to escape–he figured he needed to be punished for what he'd done.

For some reason, he couldn't remember why he had been in the chamber in the first place; it wasn't like anyone he cared for was down there. Why hadn't they agreed to go down there to stop the demon? Why should he care about some demon doing bad things? Malik was the demon that needed to be stopped. He thought he'd be a hero if he stopped the demon, but he'd not only made a big mistake, but it'd cost the life of someone he cared for deeply.

"Oh, I see you're still stuck like this, good."

The sound of footsteps stopped, and Malik stared up to see the voice belonged to none other than Law, or not-Law. He could tell it was the Baku – it wasn't a demon, but a creature that had multiple faces. Malik didn't understand how he knew, but it gave him some peace of mind.

"I thought I could leave you in here for a minute, but

it's time for you to come back to the real world," the Baku said.

With dead eyes, Malik just stared at the creature, wondering if he could kill it for what it made him do.

Instead, he chose to ignore it and went back to lamenting all his problems. He deserved to be here for what he had done, and there was nothing the creature could do to change that.

The Baku huffed and shortly after seeing Malik, disappeared to wherever it came from.

After that happened, Malik would get visitors who made no sense; there were times when he'd see someone like Maya was trying to talk to him, but he couldn't make out what they were saying.

On the day of his execution, Malik saw his other self appear before him. His demonic side looked pissed-off at him.

"You know how long it took me to get here? You're an asshole," the other Malik said.

He just shrugged. He didn't care what his other half had to say.

"You're pathetic Malik, I should have been the one to gain this body, not you," the other Malik said with venom. "While you're here wallowing in self-pity, our sister is out there, and she needs a hero."

"What sister? I don't have one! I'm no hero either, didn't you watch me kill Bianca?" Malik in anger screamed back.

"So? No one cares if you killed her – people die, it's a part of life, but are you going to let her sacrifice be in vain?" the other Malik asked.

He glared at his other half. How could he be so cold?

"You know it wasn't your fault, it's the people that tried to use us, it's their fault. They drove you to that point; punish them, not yourself," the other Malik said.

As much as Malik didn't want to agree with him, he remembered that this time, when Malik had made that decision, it was because his father and Damien had driven him to the edge. Malik decided then that he'd make them pay for pushing him to become this; then he'd find a way to give Bianca justice.

The other Malik nodded as if noticing the change in Malik and approved. He looked one last time at Malik. "By the way, my name's Anomos, and one day I won't help save you from yourself. Next time you fall, I'll take complete control."

Malik just snorted at his demonic half; over his dead body would he let that happen. Malik needed to figure out a way to get rid of Anomos at some point.

"Some advice, Malik – sometimes the world doesn't need a hero, sometimes it needs a monster." That was the last thing Anomos said before disappearing.

That left Malik thinking about a lot of things. Maybe he was going on this path the wrong way, but for now, he had to break out.

"How do I get out of here?" Malik asked himself out loud.

"I can help with that."

He whirled around to the voice, surprised to see Jaden standing there with the same gear he wore when they'd entered the chamber.

"Jaden, what are you doing here?"

"I'll explain later, right now we need to get out of here before it gets too dangerous," Jaden said in a hurried tone. While Jaden said that, a ghostly-like creature came at Malik. Malik dodged the attack; Malik didn't have time to think, so he rushed toward Jaden.

Holding out his hand, Malik grasped it and he lurched forward. One minute he was standing in his cell and the next, he was lying down, surrounded by friends once again.

His memories of why he was here in the first place suddenly flashed before his eyes. Malik was shocked. How could he have forgotten that he was here to save his sister?

What shocked Malik the most was seeing the eyes of someone he thought he'd never see again. Bianca kneeled right next to him, checking if he was okay.

Malik sputtered, not sure if he was seeing things or not.

"How … what … I thought-" Malik was just able to say before Bianca clamped Malik's mouth down.

"Okay, Malik, I'll say this once. What you experienced was just another version of the Baku's power. It was never real; you experienced a nightmare of sorts. The demon that took your sister set it up to happen once you entered your own memories; he wanted to break you, but as you can see, I'm still alive. We made a deal with the Baku – in exchange for your escape, I'd help it get out of here. So don't worry, I never experienced anything, you just thought I did," Bianca explained.

"But it felt so real, the pain and the memories. There's no way I didn't experience all of that in my head," Malik countered Bianca's facts.

Malik was about to say more, but Bianca leaned in quickly and kissed him on the lips. Malik melted into the kiss, smelling the scent of flowers and metal. This kiss felt real and so did Bianca's body heat. She pulled back, grinning at Malik.

He smiled back at her; he definitely knew that this was the real world this time.

"If y'all are done being cute, we have some things to discuss," Maya said in annoyance.

Bianca just looked at Maya with a grin on her face. "Whatever you say, sis." Bianca then got up and stepped away.

He slowly sat up. He looked at everyone and saw that some of them were tired. Maya looked like she'd been through the wringer as well.

"What happened to y'all?" Malik asked.

Maya flinched. "I'd rather not say anything right now. Maybe later."

"Each of us went through our own challenges, but that doesn't matter right now. I just got a message from Elinam that Nico is all right, but he won't be able to help us out facing the demon," Jaden explained.

Malik nodded; he knew that Nico would be all right in the end. Malik was ready to save his sister once and for all. "That's all right, I think we'll be fine with just us five. Jaden, can you still make a portal to get those people in to help us?"

"I think my power's coming back finally, but we have another problem. The Baku said that this place is going to disappear soon – it could be one to three hours, give or take," Jaden worriedly told them.

"Disappear?!" Malik yelled in alarm. Did they have time to save his sister and get out of here?

Maya answered this time, "Yeah, disappear, this place doesn't truly exist in our reality. Somehow the demon was able to anchor this place for this long, but it's been straining to return to its original place in the dimension."

Malik just raised an eyebrow at Maya, who looked back and shrugged. "I listen sometimes"

Jaden laughed at Maya's answer, he then turned to Malik. "So what's the plan, boss?"

"You're not going to take charge?" Malik asked, staring

at Jaden as if he had grown an extra head.

Jaden shook his head. "We've made it this far. I think you're ready to take command to save your sister."

"I think you're wrong, you and Maya are the better planners, but whatever you think is best. Here's my plan." Malik shared what he planned on doing. Once they knew everything, they got ready to head out.

He thought back to the nightmare he'd experienced, looked at the shadows, and made a silent command to them to bend to reform into something. Malik grinned; he knew now why his shadows didn't answer him. They wanted a master to wield them, not some lost kid lost who was scared of himself, scared to use their power in fear that he would hurt himself. That was the issue with his power—he had been fearful of using it but after living in that nightmare he had come to realize something.

A person couldn't live in fear of their potential, or they would disappear. No, a person must be fearful that their power would grow dull from never being used. Like a poet couldn't be fearful of the words they etched onto the paper, they existed for only one reason, to bring the words to life and nothing else. Malik knew what he had to do now to make sure no one ever hurt his family again. He had to become powerful enough to take down even a king or a god.

Tightening his hand to form a fistful of wisps of a shadow; he could definitely do something now. He no longer felt powerless. Malik turned to his friends, who were waiting on him to move, they moved on to the next and final challenge. A door appeared before them, they stepped forward together with no fear in their eyes. They got into the room and the door seemed to disappear within itself once inside.

"Where did Baku go anyway?" Malik asked in concern, worried the creature was planning something nefarious.

Bianca grinned. "Don't worry, I got it."

He just looked at her smile that said she was having fun. He shook his head. That girl undoubtedly was something else. Malik led the group to the last door, which was more of a gate than anything else, and pushed it open.

Everyone followed Malik, going with the idea he'd planned. Once they entered, they noticed multiple doors and rooms spanning throughout the space. Ash nodded and rushed off to search for the room that held his sister.

Next, Jaden had his staff out, having fully transformed into his other form. Maya and Bianca both had their swords out, ready to take anyone down.

"If it isn't about time, Anomos, I thought you'd never come," Damien said as he clapped his hands in applause to their arrival in the last room. The demon sat in a simple chair around a large rectangular table. There were multiple seats around the table as well.

One minute the demon was in his seat, then he was before them. It still had the form of what Malik was used

to, the beautiful face and perfect features. But Malik finally saw it for the true predator it was. Its eyes gave it away, the eyes that were void of any emotion.

"My name's not Anomos, it's Malik. Why are you doing this, Damien?" Malik asked.

"So you finally know my name. That's good, it'll help you understand me better," Damien said in a low voice.

"Well, why don't you come here, Malik, I think we need to talk," Damien commanded.

Before Malik could even think, he wasn't standing there anymore. He was right next to the demon, in its own personal bubble. Malik turned out to see his friends getting swarmed by demons of all sizes and shapes. Malik tried to get back to them but couldn't.

"It's useless to try to leave without my permission," Damien said.

He turned around to face the demon, but it didn't seem to be paying him any attention. It stared somewhere far off.

"You know, I've been in service to the Demon King for centuries, if not more. He saved me from being enslaved by the Dark Ones. Oh, my brothers and sisters could have made it with me if they had the strength, but they chose the easy way out. I served and served, but when he chose to die, I accepted it, knowing that I'd be reunited with my master one day."

Malik just watched the demon talk, unsure if he even

knew what was going on anymore.

"I watched as the world grew sicker and sicker; each century saw the creatures of earth destroy each other with their petty fights. All they did was destroy this world, even the lesser beings that count themselves supernatural were worthless in my eyes. They just let the human race destroy the world without even a fight, all stuck in their own self-loathing. Pathetic!" Damien said the last word with venom in his voice.

Was it really doing this just because the world was messed up? Malik understood the world wasn't perfect, but it didn't mean that he had to inflict pain on others to make it better.

"Stop doing this, you can find another way to handle the world's problems," Malik tried to reason with him.

He was hoping that he could convince the demon to back down before he had to fight them. Malik wasn't ready to end someone's life, but he would if he had to.

"You think you can take me down, Malik?" Damien asked, amusement in his eyes.

His eyes hardened. "I will if I have to. You never meant to take my sister, did you?"

"I thought you would figure it out at some point, but understand something, Malik. I'll do whatever it takes to get you to be the king again, even if it meant taking your sister at some point," Damien openly admitted.

He understood the demon's point of view. All it

wanted was its master back, but that was never going to happen.

Damien turned to fully face Malik. "There is no good and evil, only power; one day you'll understand that."

He could tell that their conversation was over – there was no one to convince Damien of his wrongdoing. Damien charged at Malik, catching him fully off-guard. Damien turned fully into his demonic form – the black armor he wore was dark as obsidian stone. His blade was fully out of the scabbard, ready to be drenched in blood. With a set of dark black eyes with a pool of orange swirling within them. His skin was as red as lava. His red, leather-like wings expanded, and they pushed Malik out of the bubble into the fight before him.

Jaden battled demons left and right; they appeared as if out of thin air to annihilate them. Along with letting Oscar and all the extra backup in through multiple portals, Jaden started to appear visibly tired. Maya glowed with white light as she moved effortlessly against the demons attacking her. What surprised Malik the most was Bianca, as she flew with wings he could only describe as angelic; she truly did look like the angel of death herself.

His friends and team were more than competent in taking down the demons by themselves. Malik didn't know what had happened to them through the challenges, but they had become stronger. They must have faced parts of themselves they weren't able to before and stepped out more tempered, like a sword was forged tirelessly to fulfill its only purpose, to fight. Malik knew that he needed to take down the demon Damien if he truly wanted to stop the fighting.

He snapped his head back in time to see Damien bringing his sword up to slam down on Malik once again. Malik was able to stop his sword from destroying him by creating a shadow blade; while it helped Malik not get torn to pieces, the attack sent him flying several feet away. Malik was thrown into a wall where he fell; he was in extreme pain, but he pushed through it. He summoned more shadows, this time to wrap around his body as a form of armor. The pain slowly dulled to nothing; Malik knew he was still injured, but for now, that would be enough.

Recalling all the training his mom made him endure all those years ago, this was the moment where it mattered the most. Malik once again reformed his sword, this time to a more solid form. He refused to access his demonic sword; this would be all him or nothing. Breathing deeply, then pushed off from where he stood at Damien, waiting for him in the air. He used every trick he had picked up from Ento to survive this fight. Bending the surrounding area to make him able to fly.

They met with a clash that sent a wave of power destroying everything around them. Whenever Malik would find an opening, Damien would cut him off from exploiting it. Malik knew he wasn't going to win this fight, but he could do everything in his power to stop him.

That was when Malik heard it, a voice he'd heard only a couple of hours ago. "Malik! Stop right now or your sister dies."

Down below him stood Law, leading Ash and a girl with a bag covering her face out into the fight. Everyone was still fighting; Damien raised his hands up and the demons all froze and stepped back, causing everyone else to stop in confusion until they saw the trio.

"Law, what are you doing here?" Maya asked in confusion.

"Sorry guys, but this is where we come to a crossroads. Malik, get away from my dad before I have to end you," Law said with venom in his voice.

Unwillingly, pulling his body back to the ground, he stepped toward Law with his sword still by his side. Malik started to piece together why they saw the face of Law in the challenge – it was both a warning and a way to gloat. Malik growled. Anomos wanted out to punish both the son and father for doing this.

"I'll kill you if you touch my sister, don't even think I won't," Malik said, a bit of Anomos leaking through.

He could see Law visibly taken aback from Malik's statement. *Good, let him know I'm serious, that way he doesn't make any mistakes.*

"Oh, relax, Malik, she'll be fine. We're only here for

you," Damien said in a dismissive tone.

"What do you want from me?" Malik asked, looking at the pair in loathing. How could Damien talk about all this, but still want to hurt him even more?

"It's pretty simple, we want your heart," Damien stated.

"Wait, Law, how come you're doing this? What about your Ash, if he's your father, then doesn't that make you her brother as well?" Jaden asked Law, ignoring Damien as if he didn't matter.

Law once again looked lost for words. Malik didn't care anymore about this demon family and their problems; he only cared about his family.

He was about to say something, but he saw Jaden motion for him to not do anything for the moment. Malik nodded back to acknowledge it, though he didn't know how long he could hold out from unleashing Anomos to rain hell on the pair.

"Yes, she's my daughter, and they're family. I don't know why you have so many questions, son of the Fallen, but ask something else, and I'll personally rip your heart out. Your father is an old friend, but I'm sure he can have more children again. Anything else?" Damien said in an impatient voice.

In response, Jaden just turned and smiled at Damien. Even though Malik saw that Jaden wasn't fully in his other form, he could tell power poured off him; Jaden wanted to take Damien down as much as Malik did. Damien continued to walk toward Malik, and as he walked, he transformed back into his human form in a fluid fashion. Malik gripped his sword tightly; this could be his chance, but before he could move, multiple demons surrounded him.

"Do this, Malik, and your sister can go away free, without any harm happening to her. As well as all your friends walk away from here, we won't even fight them," Damien suggested his ultimatum.

He looked at his friends. He knew that they'd fight till their last breath if it meant getting them all home. While Malik knew that, he didn't want to risk his sister getting caught in the crossfire. Malik let his body relax and pushed Anomos back down with some effort. Malik pushed the shadows back to the ground, though he set some precautions in case his friends and family were betrayed by the demon family, who he didn't trust to keep their word.

Gazing at Damien, he asked him the most important question at the moment. "Why do you need my heart?"

"Well, I guess your memories haven't fully resurfaced, but don't you wonder why you're able to have so many beings within you? Quite simply, your father, in his quest for his stupid vengeance, had somehow tweaked your heart to take as many powers as possible, though in your current state, you'll probably tear your heart and soul apart without knowing how to fully adjust to it. I could teach you how to use it, but what's the point? If I could just take it and put it in someone else that can withstand it, the Demon King will most likely come forth and be fully reborn, because you, Malik, are a sorry excuse of a vessel who won't submit yourself to him."

"Wait, what do you mean tweaked? Did my father experiment on me?" Malik asked, feeling sick to his stomach.

Damien nodded somberly. "That thing isn't your father. Trust me, he's worse than I'll ever be. Your demonic side must have suppressed the memories, but yes, mostly he did. Well, let's get this over with."

He was hesitant to do this, but he heard a voice that he hadn't heard in days, and it almost brought him to tears.

"Malik, is that you? Is mom here, too? Help me, please!" Nina yelled through the muffle of the bag; her voice sounded slightly different in her panic, but Malik knew it was her.

Making his decision, he looked over at Damien. "You swear that you'll let everyone go?"

Damien put a hand on his chest. "I swear it on the Nine Realms."

The air around Damien shimmered for a moment, and then it was gone. Malik nodded; that was the best he could get right now.

"Take care of them for me." Malik looked at Jaden, their eyes meeting in a silent understanding and goodbye.

He stepped toward Damien, ready to accept his fate, but a hand grabbed him. He looked in surprise to see not Bianca, but Maya, staring at him in concern.

"Are you really going to do this? We can still fight." Maya searched Malik's eyes for an answer.

He patted Maya's shoulder. "It's okay, boss, I think I have to do this. Elinam said I was going to die; maybe this is what she meant. This is the only way to find out."

He went to Damien, who stood on some sort of platform. There was a glowing sphere next to Damien, who noticed Malik looking and grinned.

"You thought this was for me?" Damien asked, laughing. "Oh no, I don't want the power, but there is someone more worthy of it than both of us."

Damien's hands glowed for a minute. A standing table came out of nowhere, and he strapped Malik down to it. Damien looked down at Malik, playing with his hair a little.

"You were like another son to me at some point, but it's time I get out of your father's shadow and make something of myself. I can't always be a servant, especially to a Prince," Damien said in a sad voice.

Rising his neck up to look at him. "Wait, what do you mean Prin-?"

That was all Malik could get out as he felt his heart be pulled out from his chest. As a hand was plunged into his chest, it felt cold and heavy. He jerked as his body was slightly pushed down, his heart left the tap of a finger and he seized once again, almost blacking out. He begged his body to blackout, he couldn't handle the torture of this experience, it was the worst thing he ever felt as though someone was violating his very soul. Playing with it as if he was nothing more than an instrument for them to amuse themselves.

Malik didn't think it'd be this painful to endure; he screamed from the top of his lungs, until his voice finally gave out. All he could do was watch as his friends stood there helplessly as they watched him be mutilated. Bianca looked away with Maya wrapping her hands around her and Jaden clutched his staff so tightly that it seemed ready to snap. All they could was watch as his heart was being torn out of his chest, bloody tears streaming down his face.

What felt like an eternity finally happened. His heart was finally coming out. Malik died for the first time.

CHAPTER 23

Is this what heaven is like? was the first thought that escaped Malik's head after he died. He had thought death would be more than this. All he saw was once again the field of flowers; this time instead of orchards, it was a field of white spider lilies. There were two beings there – Ento and, oddly enough, his demonic side tied up in a chair. Its body looked like it'd been through hell.

He walked dumbly up to them. "So, this is the afterworld?" he asked in a joking manner.

"This place is the in-between; all of our collective consciousness is keeping you from crossing to the other side," Ento explained, smiling from his joke.

He nodded. "Is that why Anomos is in the chair?"

Ento and Malik both looked over at Anomos. Ento shook her head. "No, that's the visible trauma he endured from your father, this place shows a piece of who we are."

He felt a rage unknown to him before. He hadn't felt this much rage since Damien took his sister. The funny thing was Damien had only done this because he was tired of serving his father. What kind of father abused his own children for his own personal benefit?

"Neither of us had any clue as to the extent of your abuse till today. Trust me when I say, I want to tear him to pieces," Ento said with so much venom.

"I can't really do that since I'm dead though, so why tell me?"

"You're not dead just yet, but we have a question for you first," Ento said. "The question we previously asked you, are you ready to give us your answer?"

Lost in thought, Malik stood there for a moment; he understood that power came at a price, no matter what. Would he let others give him the power or would he take it for himself?

Malik didn't want to be powerful in a small way; he knew if he accepted Anomos the way he was now, his need for destruction would be his undoing. If he chose to be the Demon King, he knew he was just a false king, not even a demon. He wanted the power to protect everyone he loved; the more power he gained, the more people he could spread his protection over.

He remembered his feeling of powerlessness when he was first attacked by the demons the first night, when Andy had saved him. Then he remembered his sister being taken and how he had felt; he had been strung along this whole journey to the tomb. If he kept begging for help and power from others, all he would be was a chained beast that relied on its master for freedom. He needed to break the chains himself, taking each step forward with his back standing straight, taking all the power he could that stood in front of him, let his shadow spread over his friends and family, eclipsing them in his protection.

"So does that mean I'm no longer the incarnation of the Demon King?" Malik asked, turning to Ento.

Ento looked at Malik. "I don't know how to answer that. It doesn't mean it's that easy to give up the Demon King's power or who he is. I think the Demon King's original plan to be reincarnated was to take all his memories and power to simply transfer it over to your body. You see, if the soul of an individual is intact, they can be reborn repeatedly. That's technically what a god is, in a roundabout way, but I think that never happened with you. Maybe it was your demonic heritage or something that happened somewhere down the line.

"My theory is that by your father splitting your soul, you could never truly become the Demon King; whether he knew what he was doing or not, it gives you more room to grow even stronger than the previous Demon King. Even though you show the signs of being that man, you can forge your own path and destiny. Perhaps someday you will show them what a true Demon King is but at this moment, you're still Malik Anomos Blackwood. Losing your heart doesn't even matter – you still have the will of the Demon King and that's enough for now."

He finally understood the king and his power. It didn't

come from some mystical place, but from the core of him; his very soul was the house of his power.

His shifted his eyes between the two of them. Anomos slowly rose, even though he was still in tatters. The look of defiance in the face of the inevitable was all Malik needed to know his answer.

"Can you guys give me five minutes?" Malik asked.

They looked at Malik in curiosity but nodded their approval to his question. Malik walked over to the seat Anomos vacated. Malik started to think long and hard about what he wanted. Malik thought about how Ento being trapped in the All-Seeing Amulet and the purpose of the Demon King. Malik then imagined the torture Anomos endured, everything he had once endured. Malik didn't think he could have withstood that torment.

Having learned much about the Demon King's history from his journey to the tomb helped him decide on his answer.

"I think I know what you need to do Malik," Ento said after waiting for his answer.

She stood there for a moment, staring into his eyes, before her wings unfurled from their resting position and she plucked out the most beautiful feather he had ever seen. It was a glowing silver feather, and it felt as if it held all the knowledge in the world.

"I've lived for centuries, and I've never found someone as brave and selfless as you, Malik. I see you one day changing the world for the better. I think you'll make the king proud in your own way. It's time that we old relics of the world leave and let the new generation of godlings rise, to soar through the skies on their own," Ento passionately told him.

Passing her feather to him, the moment he touched it, a wave of warmth splashed his body. It greeted him warmly, and he knew what he had to do. As tears rushed out of his eyes, he reached out to the essence of Ento that rested all in the feather. He then remolded her into a heart, once he was sure about it. Malik reached out and pulled his heart back in. Tears openly flowed out of his eyes as he mourned someone he had come to treasure.

Ento slowly started to disappear, to some place beautiful to finally rest. As Malik stared at her angelic glory one last time, she smiled at him.

"Thank you, Malik, for finally giving me my final rest. I've given you parting gifts as well, I hope one day you will find a use for them." Before Ento disappeared, she leaned forward and kissed Malik's forehead as if to say goodbye to a son.

It was a kiss as soft as a butterfly, warmth, and lightness he didn't think was possibly washed over him before it slowly faded away. Malik suddenly felt his heart seize and reform itself; it now sat in his chest as a swirling golden energy sphere, the side of a softball.

Now he was alone with Anomos, who was waiting for

his answer. Malik looked at him carefully. "I'm not sure if I'm ready for you just yet, Anomos, you're a part of me, but you're still too much of a raging storm and I refuse to abuse you as our father did. So, work with me for now, I'll let you have your chances of taking me over, but just know I won't give up without a fight and if I do let you out, you'll follow my commands to the letter. Does that sound reasonable?"

Staring at the hand being offered to him, Anomos glanced at it in uncertainty but shook his hand in approval of the request. "I want to live, even as your shadow."

As Malik felt Anomos accept him for being the master of their body, he now knew things that he hadn't thought possible, and couldn't wait to test his newfound power. Malik looked to Anomos as he once again went to sit on the chair. He felt somewhat alone but realized staring at Anomos there was someone who understood his pain.

"Be careful out there, you don't know who's an enemy or an ally. I'll let you do this just this once. Take complete control of your demonic power and save our sister," Malik heard behind him before leaving.

Appreciation coursed through him as he nodded to Anomos, acknowledging his warning. Taking one last look, he noticed flowers seem to either blossom, rot, or change to an unnatural purple color. They were breathtaking.

When Malik came back, he noticed the most bizarre scene before him. Law and Ash were both fighting their father. Everyone else seemed to be fighting demons and losing.

He noticed his body was still on the table. Malik quickly had his shadows unstrap him. Everyone noticed Malik and they all froze. He'd expected them to be shocked that he was alive but didn't expect this much of a response. That was until he saw the piece of glass on the floor showing his reflection. Malik saw his body was wrapped in golden light, his armor made of a thousand shadows. Malik almost gave himself a heart attack, looking like more of a monster than a man. He didn't know what was going on, but he planned to finish what he started.

Getting himself out, he quickly found Damien fighting his children. Malik went up next to Law and looked him in the eyes, and with a voice cold enough to stop a man's heart, he declared, "He's mine. Take your sister and go somewhere else before I destroy both of you."

Seeing how serious he was, Law grabbed Ash and quickly left the fight. Damien took everything in stride. He looked at Malik curiously, as if fascinated by the new development and not at all scared.

"It seems like you've found a new source for your heart," Damien said with a giddy curiosity.

He clenched his jaw and his armor tightened. He was ready to end this demon once and for all. "You want my heart? You can have it; I don't need it to beat you!"

He rushed Damien, bringing all his power into the blow. Damien brought his sword up to block it but was thrown across the room. Malik didn't let Damien stop even to crash; he came through a shadow portal next to the demon's side, putting a large sword wound through its chest. Damien cried out in pain, now fully transformed into his demon form. Standing nine feet tall, a monster with fangs and eyes that bore hatred stared at Malik.

He didn't remotely care what face the demon wore, and continued the onslaught of attacks, picking up speed and working over Damien's body until dark blood was pouring. Causing the demon to be able unable to heal fast enough to stop his attacks. Whenever the demon was too close to the ceiling, Malik would cut parts of it to make jagged edges fall on him.

He made spears made from shadows, five of them. Each pointed at a part of the demon's body, and he did everything he could to push the demon into slowing his attacks. The demon was starting to get sluggish, and Malik saw his chance, making another close stab wound straight through the demon's heart. The spears came from all sides, perching through Damien's body to the wall. The demon screamed in unbelievable agony. He made sure to throw the demon down onto the ground and pummel him with rocks repeatedly.

He still went to work at the demon, hacking off all parts of its limbs, starting with its legs then to its arms, only leaving the main body and head. Malik finally stopped and looked at his bloody work. Malik saw the demon wasn't dead just yet most likely regenerating its limbs. Malik recalled a move he absorbed from the previous Demon King. Malik made claws appear in his hands, looked at where the demon's heart should be, and thrust his hands in. Malik could feel the demon trying to regenerate its power and grinned maniacally as he stopped it's funneling of power and fed that power to himself. Malik shuddered, nearly drunk on the power of Damien. He hadn't known it would feel so good.

This would hold the demon for now. He cleared his head, pushing the power deeper inside himself. Malik looked over to see everyone still fighting. Malik, in his focus on Damien, hadn't realized that everyone was still fighting.

Everyone was evenly matched now. Malik was ready to end this now, once and for all.

Malik opened his voice, projecting it with multiple shadows across the room. "Demons, I'll give you this final warning. Leave now or not even Hell can save you from my wrath."

Everyone froze and looked up to see Malik standing next to a mutilated body hanging on the walls. The demons, seeing their leader on display like that, dropped their weapons. Malik saw that some of them were bowing to him, which he ignored.

"Malik, wait, you don't have to do this," said Jaden.

He looked to his friend; these creatures were nothing

but scum, he had to destroy them. He didn't know if that was his thoughts or Anomos but right now they agreed on something, they had threatened his family. What if they came back to finish the job?

"Yes, you don't have to. What if there was another way?" Ash asked, next to Jaden.

He clenched his jaw. He wasn't sure if Ash was an enemy or an ally, but Jaden trusted her, so he would hear them out.

"What do you guys think I should do instead?" Malik asked cautiously.

"Have them join you, make them swear loyalty to you. This would technically make you their Demon King," Ash said in a slow voice to not upset him.

Malik thought about it; it wouldn't hurt to have subordinates follow his command. But he had seen what it had done to the Demon King, the mistrust and responsibility of being the leader of others. Malik wasn't ready to take that type of responsibility on himself; he wanted to live as much as normal life as he could now.

"No, thanks. They can go home now; I promise there won't be anything done to them if they just drop their weapons and leave. The ones that do stay, just know I won't stop till you're down. You threatened and hurt my family, don't think I'll be forgiving whatsoever." Make shook his head.

He wasn't sure he could trust them all, but he knew

that sometimes even monsters needed to be reminded of their humanity again. Malik nodded at Ash, who visibly let out a breath of relief, as well as Jaden.

Clearing his mind and making a portal for the demons to leave. More than half left the minute he made one. Then the rest slowly started to trickle away until there were only five left. They were still bowing on one knee. Malik stared at them for a moment.

"I think they want to stay," Jaden told Malik.

"Hmm, I guess so. What do we do? I'm kind of tired of fighting," Malik said honestly.

"My lord, we wish to serve you, even if for just a moment," the first one spoke, its voice barely a whisper.

He stared at the five still kneeling. Malik then turned to Law, who was standing awkwardly on the side. Malik pointed at Law. "Okay, I don't have time for y'all, go with Law and I'll decide what to do with you later. Hey Law, I assume you don't want to go with your father?"

Law vigorously shook his head, and Malik grunted in acceptance; he would use Law to help him with his problem. Though, another problem came with him not trusting Law completely – Law was good at switching sides, apparently. That'd be another problem for another day.

"Okay, I need you to find a way to house these demons." Malik pointed at them.

"I think I can find something, but most of them are

from the demon realm, I don't have the power to do something like that," Law admitted.

Thinking about it, he looked to Damien, who gave him an idea. Malik brought Law next to him through a shadow portal. He peered at Law and noticed that he wasn't lying about not being powerful enough to make portals. Though he could just ask Jaden, he knew that it would probably tire him out making so many portals.

He could take another demon or being's power, but what if he could give some away? This idea excited him. Malik looked at the core of Law's power and noticed that pieces were missing. He started to create a small ball of energy in his hands till it formed to how he wanted it; Malik held it out to Law, which reminded him of how Jaden helped Ash.

"Law, if you do this, just know you'll be one of my lieutenants. You'll die for me whenever I tell you to, you'll be my eyes in this world, and your life is no longer your own. Are you ready for that?" Malik looked into Law's eyes, letting him know he was dead serious.

"All I've ever wanted was the power to help my people, with this, I can help you and my people," Law graciously accepted.

Once Malik was sure, Law grabbed the energy ball and changed. The horns he once had before disappeared, but his body become a little bigger and grew taller. Even Law's face had become more rugged as if he'd aged some years. Once the transformation was completed, Malik nodded at Law's look.

"Can you hear me, Law?"

Law's eyes widened and he nodded to Malik. Malik now knew he could create his own army and make super soldiers of his own.

"Get these demons home, we have much to talk about once you're done."

After giving the command, he ignored Law after that, already knowing he'd do what he was told. Malik was ready to leave this place for good with his sister.

Everyone that was left came to Malik once Law started barking orders at the demons. The demons had all pretty much disappeared at that point. Everyone except Nico and Elinam was there to hug Malik. Malik felt so good, glad no one was seriously injured.

"So, is Nico all right?" Malik asked, not having seen the werewolf jock yet.

"He'll be fine, he's just recovering right now," Ash said reassuringly.

"So this was your plan?" Malik asked Ash and Jaden, looking at them closely.

They both looked away guilty. "It's okay, Malik, everything turned out fine," Jaden said with a shrug.

He just snorted; he wasn't entirely mad, honestly. Jaden had been doing everything to make sure that they would survive this, he just wished he had been informed.

"I'll let y'all go for now, but you're going to tell me later how you did everything," Malik said, not letting them off the hook just yet.

Once getting a promise from Jaden to know the full story, Malik looked around to see a girl just a couple of years younger than him being led out to Malik. He frowned. This couldn't be real, she looked like the splitting image of his mom, but that wasn't possible; Nina was only eight. This girl coming to him was about twelve or thirteen.

He glanced at Ash, trying to send her a silent message about the girl.

"Malik, your sister isn't the same as she once was."

Realizing how he must look, he quickly changed his body to clean himself up before she saw him, in just a regular set of clothing. The girl finally walked up to him and hugged him tightly, and he instantly knew it was still Nina.

"Nina, how are you feeling?" Malik asked in a soft voice.

Nina, whose voice had also matured a couple of years, said, "I'm okay, they didn't do anything to me, except somehow make me age."

Feeling his anger rise again, he pushed it down. Malik looked at his sister. "It's okay. You'll be fine, we'll find a way to fix it."

"Can you take Nina with you to see Nico and get her something to eat?" he asked Ash.

Ash nodded and quickly ushered Nina with her toward a portal to take her away. Malik breathed a sigh of relief; Nina was officially gone from this nightmare of a place.

Almost everyone was gone, the last of the demons and the reinforcements had left. Malik was ready to get out of there when he heard Damien.

"Don't think there won't be more of us coming after you. I'll be back to destroy you next time for good," Damien said with venom dripping from his voice.

His feelings once again rose at the demon; it was time to end it for good. He was done being played, he moved over to kill Damien once and for all.

That was until Malik saw a portal made of fire appear from nowhere. Malik and the others geared up to take down the new threat, but all that came out was a giant arm that grabbed Damien and dragged him to who-knew-where. Malik's eyes filled with rage; the next time he saw the demon, he would destroy the demon without hesitation.

"Okay, I shouldn't tell y'all, but this place is about to disappear into nothingness," Jaden said.

Everyone looked at Jaden in surprise, but he just grinned. The whole chamber started to shake as he spoke.

"Well, get us out of here, dummy," Bianca said, annoyed.

Jaden gave a pained expression. "All my power was

concentrated on keeping the portal open for backup to come in, I can't do anything else right now."

He could only roll his eyes. So he was right about Jaden having a limit on how many portals he could open.

"Take us here, Malik," Jaden suggested, having enough power to set a destination for them. He had made a symbol for Malik to focus on.

Thankfully, he still had power coming off himself and with one push, created a portal for all of them to enter. The others all looked at Malik with a nervous expression on their faces, except Bianca, who seemed to trust him completely as she jumped through the portal. That seemed to be all they needed as Maya and Jaden jumped through the portal.

Malik was about to jump through as well when a crow with something in its talons swooped by and dropped it from the sky. He quickly grabbed it- a sphere, clear and unweathered by anything. Malik recognized this object and grinned; he tucked it into his pants and went through the portal. The portal had somehow led them to the council room. Malik hadn't known that this was their destination, but it did make things easier.

CHAPTER 24

As everyone appeared before the whole supernatural council of Portland, Malik realized just how small they were. All the petty fights and rules they had over this town was something so mundane now that he knew gods and worse monsters existed. They were simply the small monsters he knew the best, nothing more.

If he wanted to find Damien as well as his father from completing their plans, he had to move past their little issues and work with these city's resources. He knew he couldn't take on an army all by himself; maybe next time, Oscar and the others wouldn't be able to support him. As he finally came through the portal, he was once again rushed by guards that wanted to stop him.

He just turned toward them and let some of Anomos out; they obviously saw the madness in Malik's eyes and stepped back, shaking with fear. Jaden looked at him as if he couldn't believe it, face-palming in the process. Malik grinned; this was going to be easier than he'd originally thought.

"Well, what happened?" Regina asked them, having gotten over her initial shock of them all appearing.

"Wait, aren't we going to ask how they got in here in the first place? I thought you said no magic could breach this room no matter what, Regina?" one of the council members asked.

"That's easy, your magic can't stop me," Malik bragged, not because he wanted to but because he had to. He needed them to see his resourcefulness.

All the members and people present were visibly shaken by the news. More guards appeared to take down Malik. Maya and the others all seem to be ready for any confrontation. Thankfully, he was safe, so he didn't have much to worry about. He guessed they were more fearful, shrugging he had to play the villain for just a minute longer. It left a weird taste in his mouth, making him feel like his dad.

"Everyone just relax, Malik just means his power doesn't exactly collide with ours, that's all," Maya broadcasted, surprising everyone that she would be the one to reach out to stop the violence.

"I'm not going to hurt any of you," Malik said, echoing Maya's path of choice.

"How can we believe that? It's obvious that you're not human anymore, since you're a demon, we are within our rights to exile you from this city," a short mousy woman several feet up in the stands yelled down at them.

Malik mulled that over. While it didn't seem such a bad idea to leave the area, he still had his family to worry about.

"How about this – I don't bother you and you don't bother me?" Malik suggested, hoping they'd take the deal.

"We can't do that, not knowing that a demon of your level is out here in our sanctuary," a man with a big round belly said. Many people seemed to be caught up in his voice.

"We should have you submit to us and our way of life, or else your family will pay the consequences," the man continued, grinning as if he somehow won. Less than a second had passed before he felt something cold and dark next to him; the feeling of helplessness intensified as sweat dripped down the man's neck.

"Are you threatening my family?" Those words were uttered in barely a whisper, but everyone felt them in every corner of the room. As if the darkness was threatening them itself.

His voice was barely even as he had to force the demon down from taking control. Malik actually wanted to tear this man to shreds right there and then, but he needed them to fear him, not hunt him down. His previous fight still raged within him, while Anomos had agreed to work with him, their emotions were too in sync to tell who was thinking what at the moment.

"No, I'm not, but you're obviously a demon. We can't

have any in our home," the man's voice trembled in fear.

"If you believe I'm a demon, then test me," Malik countered.

The whole building was shocked, but Malik just smiled. His own body was still going through adjustments right at that moment. Malik doubted they would be able to tell what he even was. A man appeared next to Jaden carrying a device, and Malik walked next to the machine. He allowed them to hook him up and was tested. Everyone held their breath before the results came in.

"Malik Blackwood ... you're not a demon, but a celestial. There's no way that's possible," the man testing him protested.

It was all thanks to Ento that it read wrong – she was herself a celestial, having once been an angel. He silently thanked her for the parting gift she'd left him. He obviously knew that the reading was a lie, but they didn't. He just grinned at the man and removed himself from the machine, looking at all the faces that stared at him in fear. Malik didn't plan on being in this city for too long; he didn't see the point of it if he had to find the others and enact his revenge.

This city could be a great base of operations though; this place could be the first part of the puzzle.

"Okay, now we have gotten that out of the way, there are a few things we need to clear up. I won't be joining your little council; well, I mean to say *I won't*; one of my people will. As well as my family is off-limits to any of you; if one hair is harmed on their head, all of your heads will roll and don't think for a minute that I won't know you've done it," Malik stated, looking everyone in the eyes now. All of them froze from the seriousness of his voice.

Fear could only control this conversation for so long; he needed to have his own leverage or the minute his back was turned, it would get stabbed.

"I'm going to place the Underworld under my protection as well as this city. If anything comes in, and you can't handle it, I'll be willing to help. As you should know, the world most likely knows about me now. If I leave, they'll think this place is vulnerable and most likely attack it, so you'll want me around for sure." By the time Malik finished speaking, the whole room looked pale.

Seeing they finally understood the very importance of why he needed to be around, Malik looked at Jaden, who went to work talking to the council on how things would be. Malik trusted Jaden to set up everything without him even having to tell him; he did owe him for orchestrating most of these events.

After half an hour everything was just about set up, so Malik could be left alone. He badly wanted to see his mom and sister, and explain to them who Virgil really was.

One of the men looked at Malik and spat, "Are we really going to side with this thing standing in front of us? You expect us to provide aid to demons that mean nothing to us, why should we do it?"

Ash once again appeared from Jaden's chest, in full demonic form, her Guardian sword in front of her for all to see. They now knew who she was, and once again looked like they were about to have an uproar, but Ash put her hand up and spoke.

"Do you have a problem with a demon protecting your lives?" Ash asked, looking everyone in the eyes.

The room all shook their heads; they could live with a demon protecting them and would in turn provide for the demons in the Underworld City. Just then, Law appeared from a portal and bent down in one knee to Malik. The whole council room saw this and stiffened, as they knew what that meant. The demons were all loyal to Malik.

He grinned; he knew to call Law at that specific time just to demonstrate his power.

"This is Law; he'll be the liaison for the Underworld. Everything you need to know, either from about the city or for me."

They all looked at Law, who straightened. Malik approved of giving him power but hoped he wouldn't regret it one day. He didn't like the look Law had in his eyes but chose to ignore it.

Seeing that everyone was settling into the new normal for them, it was time to face his father. Malik thought back to where he would believe his father would be; he was ready to leave this stupid little meeting at that point. Ready to say his goodbyes to everyone, he saw his father standing in the corridor. Malik ran after him, leaving everyone.

His father disappeared into a portal, and Malik quickly followed him. He found himself standing in an open field; they stood in a high place and behind his dad, the ocean waves beat against each other as they loudly crashed. The sunset was high, it was peaceful, and no one was there except them. His father had still the same type of clothing he'd always worn around him.

"Was any of it real, Dad? Did you ever love me or Mom?" Malik asked his father angrily.

Virgil ignored him, staring out into the ocean, seeming to ponder something. He nodded without looking at Malik, seeming to like what he heard. "Good, you're angry, anger keeps you moving. Of course I love your mom, I wouldn't have spent so many years creating this persona that she sees today just to not love her. Trust me when I say creating a fake life and family that stretched back many years isn't easy. I worked so hard to find the right person and the right conditions to get to where we are today. I love you and Nina, you are the only children I've ever had. Raising both of you to have values of good people… I really wished you had come out normal like your sister."

His mouth hung open. All he could muster was a stare at the man he once thought loved him. Now he realized it was the idea of the man that he loved him; his own father only saw him as a tool to do whatever he wanted to.

"Why do all of this?" Malik asked in a desperate voice, trying to understand him.

Finally, pulling his face from the ocean, Virgil turned to him, shrugging. "I was tired of my time in Hell being a Prince, so I came to Earth. I heard about the so-called rebirth of a Demon King. I thought if I could do everything right, I could somehow gain the powers for myself. You don't know tired I am of demons being treated like dirt and less-than insects; I figured if I could get the Demon King's power or control it, I could set things right."

His father did this all for some misguided quest for power. At least that's what Malik thought, till he started laughing. Malik watched as his father cackled uncontrollably.

"Oh, come on, you really think I was like Damien, the one that wanted to make equality? Please, there is no such thing as equal beings on this earth. No, I have but one single purpose – to bring back the World Eaters to have them reclaim their position as the rightful rulers of this pathetic world. All the secrets to doing that are from your heart, which I now have thanks to you." Virgil grinned at Malik. "Though you should thank me, son, I'm the one that tampered with your heart, pouring some of the Ancient One's power into you. That's why you were able to endure so much. I thought it would kill you, given the Demon King is also one, but luckily it just made you more powerful."

Tired of the conversation, Malik attempted to create a sword out of his shadows, but for some reason couldn't access them. It dawned on him as he stared at his father as he came to understand that he was in danger.

"You didn't really think that I'd experiment on my son without taking precautions? You'll be fine, but you'll find it hard to attack me now," his dad smiled sadly. "This is just me saying good-bye, son. Take care of your mother and sister for me. If you come after me, next time I'll kill you instead of letting you go."

Suddenly, Malik seized up, his body jerking violently. He could feel his new heart trying to repair whatever was going on, but he couldn't seem to control it at all. His body poured black liquid rapidly; he fell to the ground, looking up at his father, who watched him in disappointment. Raising his hand out in desperation, as the black liquid started to seep from his eyes, all he could do was watch in utter shock when his dad just walked away.

That's how it was for hours; by that point, he had seen his father leave with Damien through a portal. At some point, Jaden and a few others found him laying there with a pool of black liquid all around him. They rushed him to a hospital and that's where he had been for a full week.

After they got him there, he heard Jaden's explanation that his father had somehow overloaded him with some black liquid, which was most likely the Ancient Ones' power, causing his body to have an episode as if it was fighting an invading virus. He had been pumped multiple times, causing him to drift in and out of consciousness. Once he had healed enough, his body did most of the repairing himself.

The minute he was well enough, he sent Law and a few demons to protect his family. His mom and sister had visited a couple of times, most times when he was unconscious. He could tell that his mom had forgiven him for what he had done, but Malik could always see the mark he had left on her neck subconsciously. This was an important reminder of when he'd let himself lose control, which he would never allow again. Nina, while having aged, didn't seem so different now. Jaden said he didn't believe there were any residual effects on Nina, and Malik hoped he was right.

He had many people come to visit him thought those days. While in the hospital recovering, he had found out that Nico had been changed since seeing the Great Wolf Spirit. His eyes, instead of their usual red, now glowed a pool of silver he'd never seen before. He guessed that the spirit had imparted his power onto Nico, which he approved. Oscar had decided to quit the police and contribute his time to the pack, and Nico seemed to be fully embracing being the Alpha now. Malik still had the claw from the spirit, which he had no idea what to do with now.

Both Maya and Bianca had decided to celebrate Día de Los Muertos. Somehow Elinam had gotten in contact with

Omen and asked him to bring their mother to talk to them, which had greatly mended their relationship. Maya had started to regrow her wings. She had explained that while she had cut them, she had Jaden block her from regrowing them in the past, but since talking with Bianca and their mom, she was ready to put the past behind her.

When everyone was good, Malik and the others had a chance to talk about how everything went the past couple of weeks.

"Why didn't we meet any vampires?" Elinam asked, causing everyone to look at her strangely. It was the type of thing Malik would ask not her.

"Oh, we don't talk about vampires here!" Jaden roughly shook his head, causing Maya and Bianca to snicker behind their mouths as if they knew some big secret.

Malik was starting to get curious from Jaden's behavior, "why don't you guys?"

"Don't even start Malik, I said we don't and won't talk about them," frustration evident in Jaden 's voice. It was odd to see Jaden act so flustered especially regarding an innocent topic.

"Okay, okay. My bad," Jaden sighed deeply, "now I feel guilty. Okay the reason we didn't see vampires are because they hate this part of the country. They prefer the big cities like New York or Atlanta, it's better feeding grounds for them. There's bad history between vampires and demons that I don't think you'll need to know about right now."

"it's not a big deal Jaden but yeah basically what he said. Besides my cousin is in going to be in town the next time my dad comes back anyway, she's a vampire too so you can ask her," Maya added onto Jaden's explanation.

Everyone knew there was nothing more that could be said, but now he knew that he would be seeing his first vampire soon. It only made him wonder how many more amazing things they could see.

"Wow, so much has changed, hasn't it? It really feels like decades ago we just met, and I lost my eyebrows," Malik said, recalling how everything started.

His friends nodded. Jaden also seeming to remember the past, said, "Who knew so much would happen?"

"What I still don't understand is that prophecy you told us a while ago. How did it go again?" Malik innocently asked Jaden, who raised an eyebrow in surprise.

"For death's greatest regret is to have lived, the coming of the promised land will bring about the destruction of life.

For the son of the sinner will raise his brothers and sisters to lead the greatest and loneliest wars imagined.

The brother who walks in two worlds will rise to claim his true heart and be whole once again.

The sisters that rise to the heavens shall bring the rain of death.

The brothers that howl at the moon will once again dance in harmony.

The generals of death will each claim their title before their Age of Enlightenment or die by the hands of their greatest beloved.

For the world will feel the sorrow of the King and rejoice in their coming death.

For the King shall come risen to bring his vision, at the cost of what he holds dear.

Who shall conquer who, only time will tell whose blood spills in anguish to madden Nightmare?"

"Something about that doesn't sound right to me," Malik told everyone honestly.

"What doesn't?" Maya asked.

"The first line is about the promised land that will bring the destruction of life, but we didn't go to any promised land at all, did we?" Malik asked.

"Technically we did, though there were two promised lands," Elinam answered. "The first was the Spirit Realm, which is technically the land after this one, which we enter, and maybe the destruction of life was our innocence since some of us chose to find out how we would one day die."

Bianca continued for her, "The second is the Demon King's tomb, which we were supposed to reach in the promise of saving your sister and the world. The destruction of life was obviously yours, Malik since you literally died and came back to life. You're not even human or a known supernatural anymore; who knows how much you're changing on the cellular and psychological level."

He understood that he was the most unusual human now. Some part of him was slowly starting to think less than a human and more than something darker; his new heart kept him from crossing a line, but he wondered for how long.

"The next line doesn't really matter since there's no war and I hope there never is," Maya stated.

He rounded on Jaden. "Didn't some of the people we met call you the son of the sinner?"

Jaden nodded. "But it could also be you since your father is a demon as well; it could be either of us, but since neither of us is about to start a war, it's safe to say we're good. I think we honestly have to wait till more events happen; we can't know for sure what's going on, so let's leave the prophecy for another day when we all have a clearer idea."

Everyone agreed with Jaden and decided to focus on rebuilding everything around what they now had. Malik still had his questions and decided to pull Jaden aside from the others for a moment.

"Tell me something. Why is it that you can use magic differently than most witches?" Malik asked, looking at Jaden closely.

He suspiciously looked at Malik. "No reason, it's still the same magic. Why the interest?"

"I think you've been lying about something from the

start. I don't think you could ever use a grimoire at all, even if they didn't allow you. I feel like if you wanted something, then you would have gotten it," Malik answered.

Jaden rubbed his face. "If you're accusing me of something, then just say it."

Malik built up his courage. After everything he had gone through over the past couple of weeks, he wasn't as scared of the answers he might be given, and he'd rather know just how much trouble he was in.

"You're not a wizard, and you also somehow planned this out, even without me having some solid proof," Malik accused. He watched his friend, hoping whatever he was thinking was a complete lie and Jaden would just laugh it off.

"You're right," Jaden started to answer. "You're right that I'm not a wizard, but you're wrong on other accounts. I think you remember me telling you about how magic works in this world, and you've seen how there are hybrids of other species much like half-demons. I'm not entirely sure, but somewhere down my mother's line, there's an Elder God in my bloodline. Before you ask, an Elder God is a being made of entirely magic essence; they legit create magic from within themselves. Centuries ago, another race of magic users were their descendants, and I'm sure you know what they are."

Jaden paused for a moment before continuing. "My

father wasn't just a Fallen, but a Fallen that had once allied with the Demon King, who wasn't even a demon. Do you remember how he told us that he gave away some of his spirit to me? By doing so, it's literally killing me. The more magic I use, the faster I die, but if I keep it all in, it's just as dangerous. I'm truly a walking nuclear bomb ready to go off. I did want you to come here when I heard my father mention your ancestor's story. He told me of an object that could save me from losing my very soul. While your soul is split in half, mine is tearing at the very seams. The only true reason I'm not dead is that I've been learning a new form of magic to keep myself from falling apart."

"The living writing on your body," Malik answered quietly. He was so amazed at how Jaden was able to keep it all together and not fall apart. If he was in his shoes, he wouldn't know how to handle it all. To know and possibly feel yourself dying every moment of every waking day. It must be agonizing.

Malik felt tears come down his cheek and quickly brushed them off. "Wow, why didn't you ever tell me? I would have helped."

Jaden shook his head. "It's my responsibility to bear, not yours. You've got your problems to deal with. I want to sincerely apologize again for what Law and I planned, we never meant for anything to happen. We didn't know any of this would happen. We just figured if you came back to your grandparents' home, you'd trigger the tomb and we'd be able to find the artifact, which we sadly never did. We didn't know your dad and Law's father would do this."

Malik nodded. He couldn't be mad all Jaden wanted to do was survive. "It's okay. I wish I wasn't kept in the dark for so long, but I understand, you guys care for each other. I've only heard of one character from D&D that's described like your magic type and that's a sorcerer, is that correct?"

"Yeah, you're right, I'm a sorcerer. Sorcerers are forbidden from existing, mainly because we're too powerful for our good. We *are* magic and don't need tools to make it all work; we're much like divine beings such as angels and gods. The only reason I haven't been found out is that my father's soul is overwhelming, and people just assume that I'm a wizard Nephilim."

"So you've been masquerading as a wizard all this time … how much longer do you plan on hiding it?" Malik asked.

"Until I can find a way to save myself, I need to be here, and hopefully with your help get back in the tomb to find some clues," Jaden told Malik, who was surprised. "Oh, come on now, I noticed a while ago when you were unconscious that you had the dimension sphere to get back into the tomb whenever you want to. You're its proper master, so it'll always let you back in."

"Oh okay, so what do we do now?" Malik asked.

Looking deep into his eyes, Jaden transformed into his Nephilim form and stood before Malik, before getting down on one knee. "Let me serve as your sorcerer until I've reclaimed my soul from destruction. You can use me however you wish."

A bad feeling crept into his stomach as he looked down at Jaden in alarm before grabbing him and pulling him up. "Wait a minute, you're more powerful than me, so it should be the other way around. Let's just keep being friends and possibly brothers-in-arms. I don't want servants, I want friends and family, so be the first of my new ones, please! We're both going to need each other in the coming years."

Letting himself be pulled up, Jaden smiled, quickly wiping away a tear from his eyes. "You're going to be a great leader one day, I'll make sure that happens. Okay then, partners until the end."

"Good, for now, let's get back to making sure everyone is good, okay?" Malik smiled, feeling better doing things this way.

Jaden nodded, thinking about the next step. "Yeah, sounds good, but I think we need to start looking for your so-called lost Generals of Legend."

They made plans to have that talk another time, now focusing on making sure their community and friends were all okay. Elinam, he found out later, had left in search of someone to teach her, while Nico wanted to go with her to help. But since Nico was now the official alpha and considered to be the most powerful Were in existence, he needed to stay and protect his pack.

Surprisingly, it had been Bianca who had decided to leave them to accompany Elinam on her journey. Malik and Jaden both made precautions that if they were in any real trouble to come ask for aid.

Bianca and Malik had a chance to talk about their own future together; while it hadn't turned out so well, Malik understood.

"We can't be together right now Malik, and I think you know why," Bianca had said.

"Why not? I like you, and you like me, what else matters?" Malik had asked.

"You're still figuring out who you are and your place in the world. I'm doing the same. I just found out I have suppressed memories of my mother's death and while Maya throws herself into the Paladin work, I need to find my place in the world and maybe in the process become closer to my mother."

Deep down, Malik knew she was right; he couldn't be selfish. He was grappling with what his father did to him, and she was still finding a way to put herself back together.

"I'll wait for you," he declared.

She looked at him with a sad smile. "Please don't! Don't deny yourself happiness just because of me. You don't know when or how I'll be back, even if I do get the chance to come back. Let's just end this at friends who once had feelings for each other and nothing more," Bianca whispered her final words.

She gave him a final kiss before she and Elinam left that very night into an unknown world.

Ash, which was short for Ashia, had become quite popular with everyone, given she was stunning and a great warrior. Malik didn't see how that couldn't have been possible. Malik did find it funny that Jaden had become sort of jealous, which Jaden claimed came from their connection. The demons had all settled into their new homes and all seemed happy that Malik had welcomed them.

Malik was still getting a flood of new demons entering the Demon City from the past few days as more and more demons found out that they were protected by Malik, who they had come to call the Prince of Darkness. Thankfully with Law still being the head of the town, it was now starting to grow into a city worth protecting, Malik was glad he had met Law; it made him wonder if they would have been childhood friends if things had played out differently.

At the end of the week, Malik, instead of going out of the hospital the normal way, had just sent himself to his room. Malik plopped himself on his bed and slept for hours, with no concern since Jaden had upped the security crazy high. He had time to think of a crazy plan to stop his dad and become very powerful in the process. To do the crazy, though, Malik would need his friends and team ready. He was still scheming when his mom came into the room.

"Hi, Mom, how are you?" Malik knew his mom still wasn't okay with what his dad did to him, to their family. She had taken an extended break from her writing, even telling her agent it was personal business.

"Hi, Malik. I just put Nina to bed, how you are feeling?" Imani asked. She had been asking him that repeatedly for days now.

Malik once again reassured his mom that he was fine. Malik knew she felt guilty of not knowing that his father was experimenting on her son's body for all these years. "I'm honestly good, Mom, nothing for you to worry about."

"Oh okay, just relax, I can bring some food for you."

"Mom, why aren't you calling me Anomos anymore?" Malik asked with some curiosity.

He'd wondered why his mom no longer called him by his other name. Now that he knew that Malik was from his father, he felt weird using it, but he wasn't ready to become Anomos just yet. He guessed Damien's idea of names was partly true. Malik wasn't ready to be Anomos "violator of the law" yet.

"Um, I don't know, it just feels unusual calling you that name if it's the demonic side of you that associates itself to that," Malik's mom said nervously.

He understood what she meant, but now Malik knew why Anomos endured so much. His father had threatened to harm them to get Anomos under control; Anomos only cared for his family and would do anything to protect them, even if he didn't like to admit it.

"Mom, I think you should keep calling me Anomos, he likes when you do that. It's not like I'm two different people; he's a part of me, and I'm part of him, but we're just not entirely the same," Malik explained.

Imani looked at her son and found that he needed to hear her say it. She ruffled his hair. "Just know I love you, Anomos – *both* of you."

He could feel Anomos inside him sort of sigh in relief, and Malik released a breath he'd been holding as well. He nodded, thanking her for saying that for both of them. His mom left to get food for him, leaving Malik alone once again.

He wasn't alone for long, though, seeing an Asian girl perching on the window, just watching the night sky.

"Yo, Malik, the self-proclaimed Demon King, just come to give you a warning," the girl said with a distinct Chicago accent. "The Coven is coming for you,"

He just looked at the girl. He wasn't scared of some group of magic practicers coming for him. "Okay, let them come. I'm not scared of them," Malik said, looking at the girl, who just shrugged and disappeared.

"She's kind of cute."

Hearing Anomos in his head, it pulled him out of his thoughts. So Anomos was finally feeling chatty for some reason.

"So, you're finally talking?" Malik asked.

"Well yeah, I guess I am, since you can finally listen, but get that girl's number for me when you get the chance."

Shaking his head at his other half, he stared outside his window, watching the first set of snowflakes fall lightly on the glass. Finally winter in their town, he watched half-demon kids run outside and play with the snow.

"Hey, are you going to blow out your candles or what?" Nico asked impatiently, outside his door, tapping his foot.

Malik knew he was still changing at the core level; at some point, he wouldn't be a human, demon, or anything close to that. For now, he would just be with his friends and family. He stopped thinking so much and joined them for the moment. Malik would be able to handle a crisis another day.

"Yeah, give me a minute. Don't get your fur twisted, man," he answered back with a smile, before getting away from the window and joining the party for his seventeenth birthday.

EPILOGUE

All Elinam could do was run as the indigenous people came after her and Bianca. Why did Bianca, of all people, choose to follow her in the search for her family? Why couldn't it have been Nico, Jaden, or god forbid, dark, brooding Maya? But here was she stuck in this humid, bug-ridden, sweat-inducing jungle with the crazy Bianca?

"Do something!" Elinam yelled at Bianca for the tenth time.

"What do you want me to do? You know all I'm good at is fighting, you want me to burn this place down?" Bianca yelled in between breaths, getting irritated as well. "Why don't *you* get a portal for us, then?"

"You know it doesn't work as easily as everyone else's; I need time to prepare!" Elinam was irritated mostly by her useless abilities than anything. Elinam yelled at Bianca as she panted for breath with each word. "Why did you grab that artifact?"

Bianca for her part tried to look innocent. "I just wanted to know its history, it's not my fault it was booby-trapped!"

The only good thing out of this was Bianca was having an even worse time than Elinam, as she had to continually dodge the arrows being thrown at her. Five months. Elinam couldn't believe she'd spent five months with Bianca and survived for so long.

But in those five months, Elinam had gotten to see so much of the world and its supernatural side. They had fought giant sea serpents, found hidden cities, and even met a god or two. Elinam and Bianca had grown in power as well, in so many ways. Elinam had Bianca to thank for that.

"So, what do we do?" Elinam asked as they finally lost the mad natives.

Breathing heavily, Bianca just stood there for a moment before replying, "We should be good for now, but as I was saying before, this artifact shouldn't even exist. I've read every known history, whether it's supernatural or not, and this thing is from before recorded time."

"Why does that matter? Don't we know other worlds exist? Maybe it's from one of those," Elinam replied.

Seeming to disagree, Bianca shook her head. "No, trust me, this is more important, I feel like we're missing a piece of the puzzle."

Finally, catching a good spot of shade, Elinam sat down as the sweat started to get too much for her. Bianca paced back and forth.

"We came here searching for clues about the legends of the generals from the Demon King period, but all we know is that they disappeared right after the King did, but no clue how they would ever come back," Bianca said.

It did make sense, but they had hit a dead end just days ago, only to find the artifact in the middle of a shrine as if placed there. The artifact itself was weird – it was a statue of a hydra of sorts, but instead of nine regular heads, it had nine different heads of animals. Each head was of a different animal, some normal and some were bizarre. It was symbolic in some way.

She had suggested to just taking pictures and coming back to look, but Bianca decided she needed to feel it, whatever that meant. So now here they were, lost in a jungle with a weird-looking statue.

Bianca was still playing with it when she turned it over, and she saw something. Elinam knew that look. "Wait, don't do anything yet!"

It was too late–Bianca pulled at whatever was stuck, and a small disk popped out. Elinam rushed to grab it, but when she did, it burned her. As she yelped and threw it on the ground, light poured out from it.

When the light finally dimmed, Bianca and Elinam looked at each other in terror and said simultaneously, "We need to warn them."

"Malik's in danger, we have to leave now!" Elinam added. Would they be able to reach them in time?

As Elinam and Bianca raced out of the jungle, leaving the disk on the ground, they didn't notice the person with a dark hood approached the disk, pick it up, and said in a dark voice as they melted into the shadows. "It's almost time."

Mohamed Omar is the author of debut
novel Infamy The Godling Saga, which he has
toiled over for the past few years to complete this
story. He lives in Indiana, with a large assortment
of roommates. If he's not joining in on their
shenanigans, you can find him reading a book or
trying a new hobby. He is currently in college
finishing his last year. If you'd like to keep up to
date on any new projects or next book in the series,
you can find him at mohamedomarauthor.com or
follow him on Twitter @momarauthor.